DIRTY BEASTS:

SOLOMON

NEW YORK TIMES AND USA TODAY BESTSELLING AUTHOR

JASINDA WILDER

DIRTY BEASTS:

SOLOMON

WELL, THIS IS A REAL FUCKING PICKLE, ISN'T
it?

"You're *sure* it was him?" I ask this in
Spanish because I'm in Colombia, near the Brazilian
border; the man I'm speaking to is a local native, and he
doesn't speak English or Portuguese. Just Spanish and
whatever dialect or tribal language it is he speaks natively.

"Yes, I'm sure." He points with his machete. "American.
Big man. Yellow hair."

I pull my sat-phone out and find the digital photo of
him—an old one, snapped from his official CIA security
ID. "This guy? You're *sure* it was him?"

"Yes, yes, no doubt."

I suppress a sigh, pocket the sat phone. "And was he
alone?"

"No, no. He was tie up, like this." My informant puts
his hands behind his back, wrists together. "Many bad men
are with him. They have guns."

"Which way?"

He gestures south down the trail with his machete;
we're at a crossroads, featuring a small hut with an old

red well-pump and a small, covered porch. "Camp. By the river."

I shove a wad of mixed currency at him—dollars, Brazilian Reals, and Colombian Pesos. "Here. Thanks."

"Wait, wait. Lady, you crazy. They are bad, bad, bad men."

I just grin. "And I'm the baddest bitch in all the land," I say in English because it doesn't translate properly into Spanish. "I'll be fine. He's my…friend. I have to help him." This part is in Spanish, to him.

He shakes his head. "You will die for your friend, then."

"You don't know me, or him."

Another shrug. "South. A long walk. Three days of walking, and then two kilometers from the river, up on the hill."

I thank him, and he swings his leg over the seat of his dirt bike, kicks it on, and speeds away in a cloud of dust.

Leaving me alone on a trail in the middle of the Colombian jungle, hundreds of miles from any city, let alone an embassy, much less yet a CIA satellite office.

No one knows I'm here.

I'm not on a mission.

There's no backup to call in.

And the man I loved and lost has been taken prisoner by the most dangerous group of terrorists on this side of the ocean.

How?

That's what I'd like to know. I got an encrypted email, unsigned but undoubtedly from him, with nothing but a set of coordinates and a date.

Here—today.

I assumed he was dead. I was told he was dead.

I *watched* him die.

I saw him take the bullets—six of them.

Meant for me.

I put him on the last helo out of Caracas myself. I saw his eyes. I saw him fucking *DIE*.

And then I get an email, from a dead man, with co-ordinates and a date.

Of course I went. Wouldn't you? I was pretty sure it was a trap because Sol's dead.

But this guy, my occasional informant, tells me he *saw* Sol with his own eyes, alive, a prisoner of a dissident off-shoot of the FARC, an even more extremist group that's been getting bolder and bolder.

The kind of people who take pride in extravagantly brutal torture and execution methods.

I swipe my camo hat off my head, yank my hair out of the elastic band, and scrub my hands through it—it's gritty and greasy, but what else is new?

I catch my reflection in the glass of the ramshackle little hut—distorted, wavy.

Five-seven, and slender—a naturally lean build that I keep lean through extreme fitness routines and a hard-as-fuck lifestyle. Black hair bobbed just past my chin—long enough I can tie it back or style it and look feminine if needed, yet short enough it stays mostly out of the way if it's loose. Narrow hips, a small, tight ass, and not much by way of tits, but I work with what I've got—and when it comes to men, a tit is a tit, no matter how small.

The name on my government-issued ID is Scarlett Luisa Gutierrez.

But to anyone who knows me, I'm Scarla.

And yes, with the long, wicked scar pulling down at my left lip and eyelid, some people call me Scar—or Scarface, if they like swallowing their teeth.

I tie my hair back, fit it through the hat's opening, and settle it back on. Sweat drips down my back, down my chest.

I wish I knew...well, anything. Was it Sol? Did he somehow survive? Why didn't he come back for me, or find me, if he did live?

Probably because he assumed I was dead, too—there wouldn't have been any official word, and in all the insanity that was going on, the death of what would have looked to anyone else like just another poor Colombian girl wouldn't have exactly made the news.

Is it him? It's hard not to get my hopes up.

Only one way to find out: start walking.

———— ◆ ————

Three days later, I'm exhausted, starving, and mightily an-noyed. I'm well into Brazil by now, but exactly where, I've got no clue.

I've fallen off a waterfall, nearly got bit by a snake—which I then killed and ate—lost my favorite knife, en-dured a twelve-hour monsoon...

And I still haven't found this damn camp.

I've trekked up and down this fucking river on both sides for miles in every direction—fuckin' nada.

"It better be you, Sol," I say to the river. "If I'm doing all this and it's not you? I'm gonna fuckin' *murder* someone."

Instinct sends me to my belly in the river before I have time to even blink—the water is cold and fast, pulling me downstream several feet before I manage to roll to the edge and pull myself onto the far shore, laying on my back and aiming my Glock 19 down my body as bullets snap through the air where I was and over my head where I am.

Four men stand in a line on the other side of the river, yelling at me in Spanish and Portuguese. Oh, and shooting at me with assault rifles.

"Fuck this," I snarl, and watch their shots go consistently high and wide, waiting for them to run out.

BAM-BAM-BAM...BAM.

They drop like ducks in a row, headshot, headshot, headshot... gutshot.

Gotta get one talking, after all.

I recross the river and kick the rifle out of the survivor's hands. "Where is he?" I snap in Spanish, digging my pistol barrel into his wound.

"*Puta.*"

BAM.

I send a round after the first, through the red weeping hole in his belly. "Wrong answer, jackass." English, but he gets it. I put the barrel against his dick. "American. Where?"

He starts jabbering. "Up the trail, two kilometers. On the hill. But you won't get him, not alive."

"Says you," I grumble, standing up and finishing him off. Two rounds through the stomach, out here? He was dead anyway.

I check their guns: an AK-47, an old M16, and a couple of super old WW2-era carbines. I take the AK and his mags, their cash, their canteens, and a new knife. Not as good as the one I dropped down that fucking ravine like a dumbass, but something.

Head the way they came, through the jungle away

from the river, until I stumble onto a narrow trail, barely more than a faint set of ruts. Two kilometers, up a hill—I see the elevation rise on the left, so I head in that direction.

A few minutes later, I hear voices—duck off the trail and hide.

A couple of tangos wielding AKs and bitching about some assholes going missing when there's work to be done.

Shit.

Into the jungle, following the trail. Up, up. Hot, sweaty, being eaten alive by bugs, but again, what else is new?

Finally, I smell humanity—shit, piss, sweat, smoke, and food. Hear voices: chatter, laughter, a yell.

Staccato gunshots indicate target practice.

Creep to the edge of the clearing and assess.

Which turns into hours of silent, immobile observation—sniper training has its uses, in times like this.

Night falls; a centipede crawls over my hand. Fires flicker.

"Come on, Sol," I whisper. "Where are you?"

Near dawn, I spy movement.

The camp is a ring of huts, crudely made, with cookfires in front of each, and then an inner ring of larger buildings—meeting hall, storage, who knows. On the inside, a central bonfire, a cask of some sort of alcohol, stacks of guns, roasting food, bubbling coffee.

Movement comes from a hut to my left. A soldier shoves open the door, reaches in, and jerks Solomon out. He's bound hand and foot, shirtless, jeans torn and dirty, barefoot. He's been beaten badly, but he's moving okay.

The soldier shoves Sol off the porch—he goes flying,

rolling, landing heavily, groaning. Not twenty feet away from my position prone just inside the tree line.

Not yet, Scarla. Not yet.

Sol struggles awkwardly to his feet and does nothing in retaliation.

The guard shoves him toward the edge of the clearing—right to me. I hold my breath, go even more still, willing myself to melt into the undergrowth.

The guard yanks Sol to a stop, slices his wrist bonds, and then backs up, leveling his gun at Sol.

"Get on with it, American," he says in halting Spanish.

"Yeah, yeah, I got it," Sol mumbles in English. "I'm going, I'm going," he says in fluent, perfectly accented Brazilian Portuguese.

He unzips and flops that big, lovely dick of his out. His pee stream goes barely a foot wide of my face.

I wait till he's done and shaking it off before I inch my hand out under the brush and rest it on his bare foot.

He doesn't so much as twitch. His eyes cut down, and he sees me.

His deep, dark green eyes meet mine, and his twinkle, just for a moment.

The way they only do for me.

I withdraw my hand, and he lowers one eyelid in a wink and then zips up. Turns back.

"Any food?" he asks his guard.

"Shut up."

A shrug. "Gotta feed me, my friend. I'm no good to anyone faint with hunger."

As he heads up the steps, he trips and sprawls onto the steps. Angles his body toward me, as if rolling to his back—signs to me:

MIDNIGHT.

I give no indication, of course, but he knows I saw it. He rises to his feet. Lets the guard rebind his hands and shove him back in. The lock is a freaking hook and eye. Sol could kick it down in a heartbeat.

Midnight he says. So, midnight it is.

It's Sol, that's what matters.

He's alive.

He's here.

He's *mine.*

CHAPTER 1

REINCARNATED

I FEIGN SLEEP WHEN I HEAR THE GUARD RETURN TO check on me—and give me a quick kick to the ribs, just to make sure I don't actually get any sleep. These guys are no joke—they physically put eyes on me once an hour, twenty-four hours a day. The only chance at a getaway is in that hour between checks. And even then, it's gonna get hairy.

I can't fucking believe Scarlett is here. How is she here? Seriously—how in the shitting blue *fuck* does she even know I'm still alive, much less my current predicament? How did she find me way the fuck out here in the middle of the Brazilian jungle?

I don't know, but I plan to find out. I've been tracking the hours—there's a gap between the hinge and the door that gives me a good look at the sky, and I can watch the sun arc and the moon rise. Plus, the guards come every hour. When the sun goes down, I watch the moon rise and vanish beyond the doorway—it's midsummer, and the sun goes down around nine, which leaves three hours till midnight.

The guard unlatches the door; it creaks open; a

brief silent pause follows; the door creaks closed and is re-latched.

No kick this time.

Two hours.

I doze off, starting awake when a boot hits the wooden porch slats. Another check. This time, I do get a boot to the ribs, rolling me over and driving an unfeigned groan of agony from my cracked and bleeding lips.

One hour.

Doze off again, knowing I'll need all the energy I can get for what's to come.

Last check.

I wait till his footsteps have receded before rising to my feet. I do some squats, bend and touch my toes, arch backward to crack the kinks out of my stiff spine, and swing my arms around.

I grasp the hard tip of the four-inch-long leather-working needle I hid in the seam of my jeans, work it free, and then wait, listening. Even at night, it's sweltering and humid, and sweat slides down my back and burns in my eyes. There's desultory chatter and a quiet burst of laughter, but nothing too close.

Time to go.

I use the needle to lift the hook out of the eye and then slowly ease the door open; they depend on regular checks to keep me in, and the remoteness of the unforgiving jungle to kill me if I did escape.

Joke's on these fuckers—I can survive anywhere, and that's without Scarla out there. Me and Scarla, together again? Shit, son, it's over.

My heart pounds just thinking about her. I don't know how she's here, but god*damn* am I grateful. She was raised in a concrete jungle somewhere in Central America until she was eighteen, at which point she walked, by herself, from Colombia to Texas, illegally crossed the border, and somehow managed to get herself recruited by the CIA. I still have no fucking clue how she went from illegal immigrant to CIA black ops badass. The woman's as closed off as a walnut and twice as hard to crack. I spent years working with, living with, and fucking that woman, and I still know very, very little about her other than she's tough as nails, cold as ice, hard as concrete, and deeper than the Grand Canyon.

I listen again. There's a flurry of shouts, a gunshot, and then silence. More shouting.

Now.

I pitch black out, only the light of the moon and the stars providing illumination. I can make out the jungle twenty feet away. Scarla's out there—I can feel her, sense her, a viper coiled under a leaf, waiting to strike.

Slip off the side of the porch rather than the creaky-as-shit stairs. Pause, listen, look. Nothing. Creep forward slowly and silently, scanning my surroundings.

I'm almost to the edge when a guard emerges from a path junction, pauses to light a cigarette, and glances around idly. I freeze, holding my breath.

He frowns, wedging the cigarette in the corner of his mouth and gripping his rifle as he saunters this way. He sees something, just isn't sure what.

I inch backward toward the coverage of the jungle, hoping he'll follow rather than sound the alarm. He keeps coming, barrel angled down and held with one hand, the other snagging his smoke to tap ash off the cherry.

So far, so good.

I crouch; I hear a rustle nearby—Scarla, alerting me to her proximity. "Got it," I hiss. "Hold your position."

The rustle happens again, twice—an affirmative.

He's fifteen feet away.

Ten.

Five.

He tosses his cigarette to the dirt and crushes it with his foot without breaking pace, tucking his rifle against his shoulder. Slows to a crouched shuffle, peering in my direction.

"Quem está aí?"

My muscles tense, ready. Three feet. I see the moment he realizes what he's looking at, but by then it's too late. I spring, one hand shooting toward his throat, the webbing between forefinger and thumb smashing into his Adam's Apple, silencing his cry before it leaves his lips. He gurgles, dropping his rifle to hang from the strap at his hip. I step behind him, wrap an arm around his head and choke him to unconsciousness, hopefully short of killing him. Which, by the way, is a fuck of a lot harder than it looks in the movies. Don't try this at home, folks.

He goes limp and I let him drop, strip his rifle and hang it from my shoulder, rifle through his pockets for his shit—a soft pack of Colombian smokes, a cheap plastic lighter, two spare mags, a small folding knife, and a packet of gum. His shoes are several sizes too small, so I cut his shirt off of him and take it deeper into the jungle with me, trusting Scarla to follow and find me.

Shit—I left the door to my erstwhile prison open; I'd meant to close it.

Once I'm a hundred yards into the jungle, I sit on a downed tree, cut the shirt into strips, and wrap them around my feet. Not exactly a nice new pair of Danners, but it'll have to do.

"Sol?" Her voice is barely a whisper behind me.

I go still, taken back years just by the whisper. I hear her pad toward me and stop just behind me. I feel her. Smell her—she's been out here a while.

"Scarlett." I pitch my voice to a murmur.

She's silent for a moment, and still. "I got your email. Took a chance it was really you, despite…" she trails off.

Climbs over the tree trunk and sits beside me. I have to make myself look at her. Fuck, she's more beautiful than ever. Thick, raven-black hair pulled through the back of a jungle-print camo ballcap. Torn, wet, filthy camo fatigues, the sleeves of the top long-since ripped off, as per her usual style, to reveal hard, densely muscled arms. Narrow, heart-shaped face, big deep black eyes. A long, wicked, keloid scar runs from her hairline down to her jawline, tugging down the corners of her eye and mouth, making her scary and intimidating to most. To those who know her, scary and intimidating is the nice version; you don't want to be on the wrong end of the not-nice version of her.

Neither of us speaks for a few minutes—we can go hours without speaking to each other. It's part of what makes us so good together.

"What email?" I ask, finally.

She swivels her head in that robotic way of hers to look at me. Frowns. "Encrypted to fuck and back, with a set of coordinates and the date three and a half days ago."

"What made you think it was from me? Was it signed?"

Her glare is pissed off, but then, Scarla is usually pissed off. "It came to my Scarlamon email."

"Oh."

Years and years ago, when we first started knocking boots, we created secret, private emails for just the two of us. Heavily encrypted, pinged halfway around the world a dozen times to a bunch of bogus IP addresses, they're email addresses literally only the two of us know about. We'd use them to communicate when we were on assignment away from each other. We'd send each other nudes, jokes, email versions of sexting, updates, whatever.

And then, I died.

When I was resurrected, I was far from everyone and everything I knew, and the whole world—including the US government, my team, my CIA handler, and Scarla— thought I was dead. I wasn't sure why I wasn't.

The only one I cared about was Scarlett. But Inez told me in no uncertain terms that if I contacted her in any way, it would get her killed and reveal that I wasn't dead. Which would be bad. Very, very bad.

So, I stayed silent. It was agony. I hated myself for it—still do.

I checked that email daily for years.

In the years since I received one single email from her. "I miss you, Sol." Those four words, nothing else.

I never sent her an email.

Her email address was Scarlamon, mine was Solarett. Cheesy and stupid, but it was for us and no one else.

"Who did you tell about the emails?" she asks after a minute.

"Fuck you. No one."

She glares at me. "Then how did I get it?"

I sigh. "Probably either Inez or my boss. The Boss has deep pockets and a lot of resources."

"Who's your boss?" she asks.

"That's a conversation for later. We gotta put klicks between us and these tangos." I eject the magazine from the rifle and check the load—full. "Come on."

"Where are we going? We're in the middle of the god-damn jungle, Sol." She stepped in front of me. Stares hard into my eyes.

"Fuck if I know, just not here."

She holds my gaze as only she can, speaking volumes without a word out loud. "You fucking *died*, Solomon."

"I know."

No emotion, visibly or in her voice. Only in her eyes. "I mourned you."

"I know."

"The *fuck* you do, Solomon Alexander Cabot." She steps close, so close I can smell her body odor, which doesn't bother me; we've spent more time like this, dirty, smelly, hurting, and up Shit Creek without a boat, much less a paddle, than we have showered and clean and in civilization.

I lift a hand to her face, stopping short of trailing my index fingertip down the line of her scar the way I used to. "I know, Scarlett Luisa Gutierrez. I mourned you, too."

"I didn't die."

"You may as well have."

She snorts, shakes her head, and twists her AK-47 around behind her back, pushing past me, heading south. "You owe me a story," she says. "The truth, for once in your slippery life."

"You'll get it." I catch up to her, grab her hand and pull her around to a stop.

She breaks my hold and knocks my hand away in a

swift, painful move. "Don't fucking touch me, Sol." In a flash, she has a knife out. "You don't get to fucking touch me."

"Scar, hold on a second." I don't touch her because I know better; if she has a knife out, she'll use it, no matter who you are.

She glares at me. "What?"

"Thank you for coming."

For a split second, her face softens, then goes back to hard as stone. "I didn't have a choice."

"Of course you did."

She shakes her head. "No, I did not." She closes her eyes for a moment, then opens them to look at me. "It was you."

There's too much to say and the words to say any of it don't exist in this moment. Just seeing her in the flesh is overwhelming. "Fuck, Scar. You look good."

She smirks. "You don't. You look like moldy shit."

I laugh "Well, I've spent the last few weeks being starved, dehydrated, beaten to shit, locked in hot boxes, and kicked around. I'm not exactly in peak shape."

"You gonna make it, WindWalker?"

I shake my head at the old nickname. "Now there's a name I've not heard in a long, long time."

I'm rewarded with a lip twitch. "Still with the *Star Wars* quotes, huh?" she says.

"Always."

The faint sound of shouts filters to us through the jungle.

"And that's our cue," I say.

The next few hours are grueling. Both of us are well-trained and experienced in evasion tactics, and we put every trick we have to the test. Voices echo all around us, but it's impossible to tell if they're just grid-searching or if they have an idea where we are.

Also, hiking through the jungle at night is hard.

Furthermore, despite my bravado to Scarla, I'm not in the best shape. I mean, I *have* been worse. As in, clinically dead. But this is pretty bad. My ribs scream like a motherfucker with every move I make. My feet are killing me. I haven't eaten in days. I'm damn near the edge of very problematic dehydration.

Finally, I reach a point when I know I need to rest. My feet slow against my will and eventually refuse to carry me a step further despite my usually iron and indomitable will.

I'm dizzy.

Nauseated.

Everything hurts.

"Scar." My voice is raspy and scratchy. "Need a minute."

She pauses and looks back at me, frowning. In the ten years I've known her, I have never once "needed a minute," even when shot.

"You good, Sol?"

"Uh, yeah. I just…need a minute."

She comes back toward me, where I'm leaning against a tree trunk. "You really do look like warmed-over death."

"I've felt better, if I'm honest."

This makes her blink in surprise. "Sol, you're worrying me."

My legs give out, and I land on my knees and then topple backward. Fuck. Not good. Not good at all.

"Sol!" She drops to her knees and pulls my head onto her lap. "You gotta talk to me. I can't help you if I don't know what you need. And don't say you just need a minute."

"I may have left out the torture."

"Fuck me." She shifts to her butt, putting her back to the tree I was using for support. "Talk to me, Sol."

"You know, the usual. Needles under fingernails, which they then heated up. A lot of beatings. The beatings were fine; I can take a beating. The unholy acupuncture wasn't my favorite."

"The what?"

"I called it unholy acupuncture. They tied me face down on a table, stuck a bunch of needles all over my back, and heated them up. Nice and red hot. Felt super awesome."

"What were they after?" she asks, grabbing my hand and examining my fingernails.

"No clue. They didn't ask any questions. They did video the torture sessions."

"So it was just for the hell of it?"

"Don't think so. I think I'm bait." I groan as a wave of nausea passes through me. "I need water, Scar."

Just then, thunder rolls and cold droplets sprinkle on us, and then the sprinkle turns into a torrential downpour.

She shifts my head off of her lap. "I'll be right back."

My time sense is warped, so I have no idea how long she's gone. She returns with a makeshift bucket woven out of fat, thick, glossy leaves. The rain is so heavy you can barely see ten feet in front of you. She finds a spot where the rain runs off a wide leaf in a steady stream, catching it in the bucket. Which, obviously, isn't exactly watertight, but she is able to collect enough that she can bring it to me. I lever myself on an elbow and she helps me sip. She takes a few sips for herself, and then collects more. Feeds me some, and herself.

Eventually, I feel a good bit refreshed. Enough to not be nauseated anymore, at least. It's something.

"I haven't heard anyone in a while," she says. "I think you should try to rest a minute."

"Mmm. Yeah. They kept me awake for a while, too."

"How long is a while?"

"Few days."

"Sol."

"Mmmm?"

"On a scale of one to ten, ten being the best day of your life, one being the day you died, how would you say you feel? Truthfully."

"One point five."

"Fuck."

"How about you?"

She snorts. "I'm fine. I could eat something, but I'm good." She tosses the bucket aside and finds a seat next to me, leaning against the same tree, shoulder to shoulder. "Just worried about getting you out of here in one piece."

"I'll make it, babe. You know I will. Quit ain't in my lexicon."

"Don't call me babe."

"I dunno why you're so mad at me. I fuckin' died, Scarlett."

"Yeah, but not all the way."

"Yes, all the way. I was dead. Clinically fucking dead for several minutes."

"You're alive now, though. You've been alive for *three fucking years*, Sol. You could've contacted me."

I sigh, my eyes heavy. "Scarla, I left the club one time

since I died. Once. That was three weeks ago. My mother murdered my father and then killed herself. My brothers and I went to the funeral. Six hours after the funeral, I was driving my car south on Ninety-Three and got boxed in by three semis. Bunch of dudes in elite tactical gear jumped out, surrounded my car, and hauled me out. I had no fucking chance to even pull my piece. They zip-tied my hands to my ankles behind my back, gagged me, blindfolded me, and kicked the living hell out of me. It was a planned grab by very serious and very well-trained professionals." I let my eyes close. "If I had contacted you, there was a very high probability you'd be dead. Or, at best, used as bait to get to me by whoever the fuck it is that hates me so much."

"Which is a long list."

"Very long. Most of the people I've pissed off the worst are South American, though, so this tracks for me, I just don't know who it is that had me."

"Extremist off-shoot of the F-A-R-C, as far as I could tell."

"Cool, cool."

She's processing what I've told her—I'm familiar with the flavors of her silences, and this one is a thinking silence. "What club?"

"Long story."

"I've got time."

"Scar, babe, I told you—I'll tell you everything. I promise."

"And I told you, don't call me babe."

"Okay, sweetheart."

"Sol." It's a growled warning, the kind that is usually followed by someone missing body parts.

I chuckle. "Fucking with you. Relax."

"Fuck you. You relax."

"Trying. Someone keeps asking me questions."

She lets out a sound that's equal parts sigh and snarl. "Fine. Come here, you big baby."

She grabs a handful of my hair and hauls me, not exactly gently, onto her lap. "Shut the fuck up and sleep."

Despite her rough treatment and sharp words, her fingers trail absently through my hair.

The way she used to, back in the day. We'd fuck like pornstars, and I'd always fall asleep with my head in her lap, just like this. She'd play with my hair. Nothing has ever soothed me like Scarlett's fingers in my hair.

I don't dare move, barely breathe, for fear of making her aware of what she's doing.

I know she's angry—because she's hurt.

She has reason to be angry and hurt.

Eventually, I let myself drift off to sleep, knowing Scarla will keep watch.

CHAPTER 2

THE AMAZON IS, LIKE, BIG

SEEING SOL IN SUCH BAD SHAPE IS FUCKING HARD. He was always superhuman. No matter what happened, he never slowed down. Never fell behind. Never let anyone take point.

Which means that what he's told me he's been through is probably just the tip of the iceberg.

Deep inside my chest, locked within a very hard, dense, impenetrable, unbreakable shell, there's a part of me that loves this man with wild, tender ferocity. I know it's there. It's been there for a fucking decade. What's more, I think he knows it. I think he has something very similar locked away inside himself.

But neither of us has ever been able to let it out or express it. God knows I can't start now. We're in the fucking jungle, for fuck's sake. Chased and hunted by who knows how many very bad men. Miles and miles from anyone or anything. No food. No water. He doesn't have any fucking shoes. He's been tortured, starved, beaten, and who knows what else that he hasn't bothered to mention.

Plus, I'm pissed off at him.

Yet, here he is, passed out with his head on my lap, and I can't seem to stop my fingers from playing with his hair.

What a fucking pickle.

I let myself rest a little bit, eyes closing, body loose, rifle at my side. It's not sleep—my ears and other senses are on high alert, and I can go from resting to killing faster than a snakebite. Sol always joked that he was checking his eyelids for holes.

I still can't believe he's alive.

Three, maybe four hours pass and Sol is dead asleep. Maybe "dead asleep" is the wrong turn of phrase, but the man is out for the count.

My mind is still trying to make sense of the whole situation. Somehow, Solomon survived six gunshot wounds to the torso. Liters of blood lost. Clinical death. I mean, if anyone could have survived, it doesn't surprise me that he did. There's a reason we called him WindWalker. But he disappeared, lived in some club, left for his parents' funeral, and was promptly captured by what seems to be an extremist faction of the FARC—The Revolutionary Armed Forces of Colombia—People's Army, a Marxist-Leninist guerilla group, originally. It was officially militarily disbanded in 2017, but a host of smaller breakaway groups mixing political and military agendas have cropped up in its place. The question is, why do they want Solomon Cabot? I mean, sure, he's done his fair share of bloody work all over Central and South America, so it stands to reason plenty of people hate him. But he's an operator so far off any books that he doesn't officially exist on any government record. Very few people even know his name. And why torture him but ask no questions? And why are these rebel dissidents from Colombia hiding out in the Brazilian jungle?

There are no answers from where I'm sitting. More intel is needed to even form a hypothesis. I'm not sure he knows. And honestly, right now, it doesn't even matter. Getting us out of the jungle is the first problem. Avoiding his captors is another.

He needs food. He needs medication. He needs electrolytes. He needs a week of rest.

None of which are gonna happen any time soon.

I don't even know which way to go—where the nearest thing like human civilization is.

And this is some of the most brutal and unforgiving terrain on the planet.

Quite a fucking pickle, indeed.

I hear a stick crack off to my left and come instantly alert. A murmur. Rustling.

I tap Sol on the shoulder twice, and he's awake and on a knee with his right to his shoulder in a split second. Fuck me, the man has not lost his edge, that's for damn sure.

Another crack of a stick—to my right. Sol points at me and to the left and then to himself and the right. I nod. Creep toward the sound. Put Sol out of my mind—even in his current state, I'd rather have him at my back than all of SEAL Team Six.

I tug my second favorite knife out and let my AK hang by the strap at my back as I sift silently through the jungle, ducking under low-hanging fronds and stepping over rotting trunks.

I catch a glimpse of movement out of the corner of my eye—a tango. Two. Three. Shit. They're coming toward me in a line abreast, six or so feet between them. Sunlight shifts and dapples through the canopy, shedding twisting shadows.

I lay on the jungle floor in the cold, wet, slimy mud, wedged against a fallen tree they'll have to step over. I take a moment to smear mud on my face, hands, and arms—protection against bugs as well as further camouflage.

I hear them now. One hisses something to another in Portuguese, which I neither speak nor understand—I don't have Sol's facility with languages. He can speak several fluently, and Brazilian Portuguese especially he can speak like a native. I am a native Spanish speaker, however, so I can blend in pretty much anywhere south of Oklahoma.

One steps over the log and his bootheel bumps off my knee—I chomp down hard to keep from expressing the pain verbally. He doesn't even look down, assuming he stepped on something natural.

I wait. He's over, and then his companions.

Now for the tricky part—eliminating all three without firing a shot or allowing a shout.

I ease to my feet and creep up behind the rightmost target, noticing a nice big fixed-blade hunting knife sheathed at his waist. Helpful.

I reach my hand around his face, clap it over his mouth, and cut his throat, slicing deep. Grab his knife from the sheath, flip it so I'm pinching the blade, and hurl it at the farthest left target. It buries in the side of his throat, sending him gurgling to his knees. The middle tango spins, rifle lifting, mouth opening to shout, but I've already brought my blade up under his ribcage into his heart. He gasps, blinks at me in wide-eyed confusion, and then hits the ground. The guy I threw the knife at is still thrashing around like a fish out of water, so I finish him off and then retrieve the extra blade, as well as the sheath, from its original owner. I find a few more spare mags for my AK in their pockets, as well as four protein bars and a half-full canteen. Score.

I give Sol our old signal, a whippoorwill call; a few seconds later, I hear him return it and follow the sound to him. He's laid out three of his own and now has a handgun holstered low on his left thigh, a canteen, and a battered but functional and fitting pair of combat boots on his feet.

He's panting heavily, which tells me he's still struggling physically. He, too, has covered himself in mud, including his once-blue jeans.

He grins at me, teeth white in the wet, caked mud on his face. "That worked out."

He tosses me a sheathed machete, a match to the one strapped across his back over the now-crusted mud.

I toss him a protein bar. "Eat, Sol."

He catches it, and I don't miss the relief on his face. "Thank fuck."

"Name is Scarla, not fuck," I quip.

He unwraps the bar and takes a very small bite, chewing it thoroughly—he knows from both training and experience that if you try to eat too fast after extended hunger, you can cause yourself a world of hurt.

He digs his hip pocket and produces a compass. "This'll be useful. Not that I know which direction to go."

"Me either," I say. "We can back-track the route I took to get here, which'll put us within a few days' walk of the Colombian border, but that's three days through the jungle from that camp. We gotta find the river first, though."

He shrugs. "As good a plan as any, I guess."

I jut my chin at him. "How you feel?"

Another shrug, of which he has many. "Meh, I'm decent. Rest, water, and this," he lifts the protein bar he's slowly eating, "will help a lot. Sleep deprivation, hunger, and dehydration were the worst of it. The rest is just mission-usual aches and pains."

"Sol, you were beaten and tortured for three weeks."

He stares at me, gaze hard. "And?"

I know better than to push him when he looks like that. I snatch the compass out of his hand and orient myself facing northwest. "Border should be this way. Let's go, tough guy."

He gestures with a broad sweep of his hand. "After you, m'lady."

I flip him off. "I'm no fuckin' lady." I push past him, machete in hand.

"Maybe not, but you've still got the tightest ass I've ever seen."

I stop, turn, and glare at him. "No."

He grins. "Yes."

I put the point of the machete in his face. "No. Meaning, you don't get to do that with me, Solomon. Hands off, eyes off. No jokes. No comments. Just fucking no." I turn and hack with unnecessary violence at an unoffending vine that was not in my way at all.

"Fuck that vine in particular, huh?" he says. A few moments later: "You know, we're gonna have to talk about this, Scarlett."

"I hate it when you call me that, and you fuckin' know it."

"Yeah, I know."

"So stop calling me that." I hold up my machete. "I'll cut your dick off."

He just laughs at my threat. "You will not. You love my dick. You used to call him Megatron, remember?"

My core pulses because I do, in fact, remember. All too well. I haven't had a dick even half as amazing as his since he died, and believe me, I've looked.

His jocular insouciance fills me with unreasoning rage, however. Does he not understand the agony I've endured the last three years?

I whirl, and only his lightning-fast reflexes save his life—he rears back as the blade of my machete slices through the air where his head was. "*Fuck* you, *Solomon.*" I put my nose in his space, glaring up at him, annoyed as always that he's so much fucking taller than me. Makes it hard to stare him down when I have to stare up. "*Fuck… you.*"

His eyes spark with anger of his own, and that makes even me a little nervous. "Scarla, babe, you get that one for free. Next time you swing a blade at me, you better kill me, or I'll take it from you and paddle your fine little ass with it. Hear me, sweetheart?"

I seethe at him. "I'd like to see you fucking try."

"Don't tempt me. I've dreamed about that ass of yours every single fucking night for three fucking years, woman."

Fucking hell. My anger and confusion and hurt are all tangled up with a scorching, boiling arousal. Memories of the last time he and I were together uncoil in my mind and take root in my belly, my pussy.

Caracas, three years ago. Twenty-four hours before the mission. A shitty little hotel a few blocks from Ciudad Universitaria. It was a hundred degrees and humid, a clear, cloudless day. We'd spent the whole night drinking cheap rum and smoking primo Venezuelan weed because we knew the mission was fucked from the jump. The city was a seething, violent, angry time bomb, and we were in the middle of it. It was doomed from the start, and we fucking knew it, so we decided to spend what we assumed would be the last day of our lives partying like goddamned rock stars. He fucked me so good that night. Jesus—so good. We slept till noon, and he got up and found us coffee and breakfast, and then he hauled me out of bed and bent me over the railing of the balcony and fucked me in full view of anyone who cared to look. He had such a death grip on my ass that I had bruises in the shape of his fingers for a week. I walked funny for three days.

Best sex of my life.

I think about it every goddamned day.

He gives me a hot, arrogant smirk. "You're thinking of that day in Caracas, aren't you? Yeah, you fuckin' are, sweetheart." He sidles closer, huge and hard and violent and primal and lethal. "Remember what I said before I ripped your clothes off you?"

I can't help answering. "'I'm about to give you the hottest fuck of your life, Scarlett. I'm gonna fuck you so good you'll dream of it after I'm dead and gone.'"

"Damn right." Closer, body to body, brilliant emerald eyes boring into mine. "I'm a man of my word, Scar. So *do not* tempt me. I recognize that you're pissed off, and you have every right to be. But I'll only let you punish me for so long. Hear me?"

I don't give him the verbal answer he wants—I'm not ready to let him force me into submission yet. He's gonna have to work for that. And work damn hard. I stare up into his eyes and give him a hint of the rage and the pain and the sorrow I've felt.

"Did you know?" I ask.

"Did I know what?"

"That you'd die."

He turns away, pacing two steps and stopping. Head hangs. "Sorta. I had a bad feeling. We both did. The intel was fucked. The mission directive was fucked. We had no business being there. We should've…I don't know. Gone AWOL. Refused to obey and take the consequences. Something. Anything other than go through with that FUBARed piece of shit mission. But I guess, yeah, I did. I had this…dark, heavy pit in my stomach the moment we were in-country. A sense of foreboding."

"I would have gone anywhere with you," I whisper.

"I fucking know, Scar. I know."

I shake my head and go back to hacking my way through the jungle. We leave the conversation hanging between us like an antipersonnel mine.

It's slow going, but we make progress; Sol wasn't lying, either. After a few hours of rest, some water, and some protein, he's a new man, trailing behind me with something close to his usual unflagging vigor.

Around midday, the sky clouds over and then opens up into another torrential downpour that slowly washes the mud off of us both, leaving us soaked and miserable. Again. Or still.

I don't know that I've been dry in almost a week at this point, and I'd cut off my right tit for a change of clothes, a hot meal, and a real bed.

I can't imagine how Sol must feel.

After a few hours of unrelenting rain, it tapers off and then stops, leaving the jungle ripe and thick and clean. The sun returns, now close to setting.

"Scar, stop."

I halt, glance back. He points with his machete down

the ravine on our right—several trees have fallen across the ravine in a tangled web of trunks and rotting foliage, creating a natural cave-like opening beneath it.

"We could probably have a fire down there," he says. "Dig in-ground and the leaves'll dissipate the smoke."

"Sounds good—*if* we can find dry wood," I say. "You go down there and check it out. I'll look for something that'll burn."

An hour later, I managed to find a few armloads of small sticks and deadfall that should be dry enough to ignite. Sol has cleared out the space beneath the fallen trees to make a cozy little den just big enough for the two of us to sit. He even dug a Dakota firepit—a hole in the ground about twelve inches deep, with a horizontal tunnel directing the smoke away. Motherfucker even has a lighter and cigarettes, somehow.

Within fifteen minutes, we have a small fire going, and the small space heats up quickly. We both remove our boots and socks.

He lights a cigarette and takes a puff, making a face at the taste. "Fuck, that's shitty. But a smoke's a smoke."

I take it from him and draw on it, coughing. "Jesus, no kidding."

Neither of us smokes regularly, but in situations like this, it's a coping mechanism of sorts. We share the cigarette in silence.

"Sleep," I tell him. "I'll take first watch."

"Scar—" he starts.

I put my hand against his face, the heel of my palm against his chin, fingertips on his forehead. "Nope." It's another old thing between us, and like the other old familiar habits, it just comes back on its own.

He laughs. "Fine. Have it your way. Three, four hours, yeah?"

I nod. "I know how it works."

"No shit. My point is, don't take the whole watch because you think I need it. I don't. I'm fuckin' fine. I can pull my weight."

"Sol, you not pulling your weight is never the issue. The issue is that you tend to pull your weight *and* everyone else's until you're half dead."

He lays back and shuts his eyes. "Glad it's you who rescued me, Scarlett."

I don't answer. I just watch him fall asleep—I know his tells. His left bicep and his right hand twitch sporadically when he's falling asleep.

Am I glad? Yes. And no. I'm still pissed at him for fucking abandoning me, the bitch. I don't give a fuck if contacting me puts my life at risk—I'm an operator, for fuck's sake. That's the whole job. But also, it's Sol. The only human on this godforsaken planet I've ever fully and completely trusted. The only person I've ever loved—not that we ever said it. I came close that day in Caracas. Impaled on his big fat cock, staring down at his deep green eyes, feeling seen, feeling safe in a very unsafe place, I just knew. I love this man. But I couldn't say it. Too chicken.

The moment passed, the mission started, and then went way the fuck off the rails and he died and I almost did, and I never saw him again.

Which brings me to the burning question: if it wasn't Sol who emailed me from our private email addresses, who did? His boss, or someone named Inez. Questions for him for later, I guess.

It's a quiet night, only the ambient sounds of the

jungle. I resist the urge to touch him—not like that, just…
put a hand on his shin or his arm. We did that a lot back
in the day. We'd sit in the jump seats of a C-130 on the
way downrange and hook pinky fingers between our legs.
None of our team ever said anything about us being together, but I always wondered if they knew. We did our
best to keep it platonic and professional around anyone
else—not because it was against the rules for us to be together because it wasn't, but because we didn't want any
drama. We didn't want to make it weird for the others. So
we kept it a secret. I think also it was just in our natures at
the time to be secretive.

I'm not sure I could keep him a secret anymore. When
he died, I ran out of fucks to give. I started taking the most
dangerous ops. Took risks—sometimes stupid and unnecessary ones. I didn't, and don't, have a death wish; I just
didn't give a single, solitary, flying fuck. About anyone or
anything. Not without Sol at my back. Off-base and away
from the ops and the team, I did what I wanted. Fucked
who I wanted. Drank more than ever. Put up big-ass walls,
thick, crunchy, crusty, frosty walls of don't-give-a-fuck,
don't-fuck-with-me attitude. I got harder, darker, and even
more dangerous. My temper got worse.

I nearly got court-martialed and did get busted down
a rank for nearly killing a new guy who thought he could
put the moves on me at the bar. Before, I'd just kick him
in the nuts and call it a day. Now? I had to be restrained by
Dougal and Cope before I cut his dick off. The little shit did
walk away with his dick intact, but he wasn't as handsome
as he used to be, not with a nice scar on his stupid face.

The brass called it "uncalled-for aggression against a

fellow team member" when they busted me back down to sergeant first class. Whatever.

No, the issue isn't keeping Sol a secret. It's figuring out how I feel, what I want, and how to get it, assuming we make it out of this fucking jungle.

Which isn't a given, even for us.

The Amazon, is, like, big.

CHAPTER 3

WHAT IS THIS? TOM FUCKING CLANCY?

SCARLETT WAKES ME AFTER THREE AND A HALF hours. She gives me her watch, since mine was taken, and then lays down and rolls over. She's asleep within seconds, as only an operator can fall asleep.

I stretch my muscles as best I can in the shelter, forcing myself awake.

Mostly, I think about Scar, everything we went through, and how things ended. I mean, I fucking died. Not my fault. But she seems to be harboring a hell of a grudge that I wasn't actually dead and never contacted her. What was I supposed to do, though? I'd stopped officially existing the moment I joined the CIA's off-book kill unit. So when I "died," she was the only one to miss me. The rest of the unit was dead already except her and me, and our CO wasn't the type to shed tears that I wasn't coming back. I woke up in a strange place and was told I was starting over and could have no contact with anyone from my previous life. I thought I was doing her a favor. I figured she'd get over me and move on.

I never did. I couldn't. I loved her. But she wasn't ready to hear that—I almost told her that day in Caracas, but I pussed out. It wasn't the time. Maybe it was, but I was too goddamned scared of her not loving me back. So I didn't say it, and then I took six slugs to the chest and never saw her again.

Why stir up the old hurt? Let her believe I was dead. I never thought I'd see her again, so I tried to move on. I did. I really fucking tried. But no matter how many of the girls down in Hel I slept with, none of them ever stirred more than a little affection and sexual relief in me. Not exactly shocking, I suppose, considering I was paying them for sex and didn't even try to get to know them on a personal level beyond idle pillow chat. Except Violet, but that's a different story.

Mainly, the problem was that they just weren't Scarla. They didn't know me. I wouldn't let them; they wouldn't want to. Not really. Not the real me. Even my brothers don't know the real me.

Dawn comes, and Scarla's three-and-a-half hours of sleep finds her waking up on her own.

She looks at me. "Let's move."

I nod, and we wiggle out of the crawlspace beneath the fallen tangle of trees. I fill in the Dakota pit and create a mess of branches and dirt where we'd been, so it looks like we were never there. Within ten minutes of Scarla opening her eyes, we're gone down the trail.

Such as it is, at least. We're way off the beaten path, so our trail is merely us winding and weaving steadily north-west toward what we hope is the Colombia-Brazil border and something like human civilization.

Several hours of exhausting hiking later, sweating, panting, hungry, and irritable, we crest a ridge and come out onto a road…

That's occupied by a cluster of armed men standing around a battered, muddy old SUV, sharing cigarettes and a plastic liter bottle of something that's not water. They see us, we see them, and then all hell breaks loose.

I drop to one knee, sling my rifle up, and crack off half a dozen rounds in their direction. Scar puts down a pair of three-round bursts as well, and the men scatter. We both dropped two, but there are at least four more—it was hard to get a head count before the scrum started. I scramble back down the ridge with Scar beside me as bullets whizz overhead, automatic weaponsfire rattling.

"We gotta get that jeep," Scar hisses at me. "I'm fuckin' sick of hupping my ass through this fuckin' jungle."

"On it," I say. "Cover me."

"Sol—goddammit." She crawls after me as I shimmy on my belly back up the slope to the crest of the ridge, peek over, and see that the SUV has been temporarily abandoned.

I put a round into the brush in front of the jeep— It's not an actual Jeep brand, but we tend to call any SUV found in the wild a jeep. A shout follows my exploratory shot, and a flurry of long bursts sends a hail of rounds over my head.

"You can't just run over and take it, Sol," Scarla snaps. "You'll get your ass killed…again."

"No shit, Sherlock," I snap back. "So fuckin' cover me."

"While you do what, exactly?" she asks.

"This." I lurch onto the path and sprint as hard as I can for the brush behind the jeep. As I get closer, I recognize the SUV as an old-as-fuck Nissan Patrol—like a Toyota FJ40, and almost as good. Almost. Whatever—it's wheels.

I dive into the underbrush as bullets buzz and

snap—too damn close. Shouts follow me, and bodies stomping through the brush after me. I can only hope Scarla takes the hint.

I crawl parallel to the road, away from the SUV, hearing my pursuers close behind. I come to a downed log, slink over it, and then rotate to put my barrel over the log. Wait—wait.

One, two, three, four—five. I'll take it. I open fire, putting a slug through the leg of the rear-most tango, sending him screaming to the ground. I rake my fire forward on full auto—half the rounds go high and wide, of course, because fuck full auto. But it does what I intend: injures them. For good measure, I put a few more slugs into non-lethal areas. The bullet wounds won't kill them immediately, so I'm keeping my oath if they can't get help fast enough, that's not my fuckin' problem.

God, this no-kill oath is a pain in the ass sometimes. Hard to remember when the bullets start flying. The instinct is to put down headshots.

With our pursuit bleeding onto the jungle floor, I run back for the road, finding Scar in the Nissan, engine idling, waiting for me.

"Took you fuckin' long enough," she mutters as I climb into the passenger seat.

"Oh, fuck off. That was, what, three minutes?"

She snorts. "And the Sol I used to know would've dropped 'em all in one."

"Yeah, well, things change. People change." Probably a good time to tell her about my oath. "One thing that's changed is this." I show her my tattooed-over brand—the broken arrow.

"The fuck's that supposed to mean?" she asks. "Broken arrow, like the nuclear code thing?"

"Not exactly." She's not gonna like this. "I don't know where to start, honestly."

She glances at me, eyebrow arched. "That's ominous."

I snort. "Not ominous. It's just kind of a story."

She laughs. "Well, Sol, good thing we have several thousand miles of Amazon to cross while you tell me."

"Fuck, fine." I scrub my face and then trace the raised lines of the brand. "It's not just a tattoo."

She brushes my hand away and feels the brand with her fingertips. "You tattooed over a fucking brand? Who branded you?"

"That's where the story comes in. It was a choice I made."

She shoots me a very thoughtful side-eye glance. "And I'm guessing it has something to do with why you ghosted me—literally?"

"Ghosted you," I echo. "A pretty on-the-nose way to put it."

"Just tell me the fucking story, Solomon. Quit hedging. Jesus."

I frown at her. "Is it me, or are you pricklier than ever?"

"Fuck you. Tell me the story, asshole."

Yeah, not me—she's pricklier and more pissed off than ever. Which is saying something. But I imagine it's probably my fault.

"So, Caracas. I took six rounds—four of them hit my vest, which absorbed the worst of it, but still broke most of my ribs since the fucker was right fucking there."

She scrubs her face. "I see that moment over and over again, every fucking night, Sol. You were point. The whole fucking city was on fire, it seemed like. Riots everywhere. Crowds skirmishing with police, military pouring in, separatists, cartels, fucking everyone was trying to get a piece of something that day. And there we were, eight fucking Americans on an off-book op with lousy intel."

I can tell she needs to talk it out, so I let her. "Lousy intel plus a massively unstable situation. Shit was changing by the hour."

"We fought our way across the whole damn city, door by door, block by block. We were nearly to the extract location. What, like two blocks away?"

"Barely that. I could hear the helo. But they were taking heavy fire from the street. They couldn't wait."

She nods. "So we double-timed it. You called a halt at an intersection. It looked clear. I was right behind you, and it was fucking clear. You gave the signal to move out, went around the corner, and that asshole popped out of nowhere and just fuckin'…unloaded."

"We couldn't see him where he was and where we were. He was in a doorway around the corner; I think he was trying to put a bead on a sniper or something."

"Yeah, some asshole was taking potshots at anything that moved. He wasn't very good, though." She laughs. "Whoever it was couldn't hit the broad side of a barn with a fucking shotgun."

"Exactly. So I rolled out, and he was rolling out to cross the street at the same time. He saw me and I saw him. I actually fired first—I put three right in his fucking throat." My eyes close as I remember—I see it in flashes. "He was so surprised. How the bastard kept his feet, I'll never fucking know. But he did. I thought he was done. He had three fucking NATO rounds in his goddamned trachea. I let my guard down. That was all it took. He leveled his rifle at me and blasted half his magazine before I knew what was happening. I didn't even feel it at first—I thought he missed."

"So did I," she says.

"Turns out most of 'em hit me. As I said, the vest took four, but he was so fucking close I still took a lot of damage. Broken ribs, punctured lung. Another went under the vest—a ricochet, they told me, since it went in at an upward angle. Bounced off a rib, left a shitload of shards all inside me, and tore my liver all to hell. Super fun. The other hit my hipbone and went up the other way, nicked my kidney and the already punctured lung."

She shakes her head, glancing at me. "How the fuck did you survive that, Sol?"

"I shouldn't have. You put me on that helo. That's the last thing I remember is you and Donk throwing me into the helo. Donk was hit bad, and you were hit."

She waves a hand. "Grazed my arm. It was nothing." She chews on the inside of her cheek. "Donk died about ten minutes after that helo took off. He knew he was dead, though. He was just fighting it off long enough to get you out."

I choke. "Fuckin' Donk, man. He was a beast."

"No one else like him."

"I remember seeing you. You grabbed my hand as the helo started to lift off. I...I couldn't figure out why you weren't coming with me."

"Wasn't room. Helo was already overloaded. I could pass for a local, no one else could." She shakes her head, huffing. "I wanted to go with you."

"I know, Scar."

"So. How'd you survive?"

"That helo wasn't military. Or rather, it had been hijacked, sort of. There was a medic on board, and he kept me alive. How, I don't fuckin' know. Some sort of medical miracle. Kept my heart beating and plugged the holes so my blood stayed on the inside, I guess."

"Hijacked? Who the fuck could and would hijack a CIA helo in Caracas fucking Venezuela?"

"My boss. He has some sort of contact really fucking high up in the Pentagon. Someone feeding him intel on operators. People on the edge."

"Edge of what?" she asks.

"The shit. Burnout. Psych failure."

"You were solid, Sol. Don't try and tell me you were losing it."

I shrug. "I don't know. You and me…my brothers, losing Gabe in that mess in Kandahar…I wasn't solid, babe. I was a fucking mess."

"Gabe biting it really fucked with your head, huh?"

"In a bad way. It was so unexpected and so unnecessary. Should've been a quick raid, no casualties. Take out the target, exfil, easy. Done. But that fuckin' kid, man. I hesitated. Gabe hesitated. He wasn't even fucking nine, Scar. *Nine*. With a suicide vest. Gabe and I both hesitated and then the kid grabbed the deadman's switch and Gabe tackled him. Saved all of us. Wasn't anything left of Gabe to take home."

She reaches out and squeezes my knee. "I know. I guess I didn't realize how bad it affected you."

"I didn't want you to. I lied about it to the psych eval board. Lied about it to the CO. to you. The whole team. Yeah, yeah, I'm good, I'm fine. I was *not* fucking fine. I was wrecked. I had no business being on that op in Caracas. I was out of my mind, grieving Gabe. Losing myself in you. I wasn't focused. If I'd been focused, I'd have hit that shooter in the head, but I fucking missed, Scar. I fucking missed."

"He was your best friend."

"And I'm supposed to be a goddamned professional operator. We handle that shit and move on. I didn't handle it."

She doesn't answer right away. "It's done, Sol. You gotta let it go at some point." She glances at me. "On with the story."

"I woke up in a medical facility. No windows. Patched up and hurting like a motherfucker. Hurt to breathe, hurt to move, hurt to just fuckin' exist. I was in and out of consciousness for a while, and as far as I remember, no one ever came to visit. That's how I knew I wasn't in a government facility. It sure as fuck wasn't Walter Reed."

"I'm on the edge of my seat, here," she deadpans.

"Har-har-har. I'm not the storyteller Diego was, okay?"

She snorts. "Diego could turn picking up a burrito into a riveting story."

"No shit. Remember that story he told about the hooker and the muffin?"

She splutters. "I damn near cracked a rib laughing."

"Anyway. Eventually, a doctor came in. Didn't speak a lick of English or any language I know. Checked my vitals, went over my various stitches and incisions and shit, and left. More time alone. No TV, nothing. Not a goddamn thing to do but lay there and hurt and stare at the fucking walls and ceilings and try not to crawl out of my skin. The light never turned off. No way to track time. I coulda been in there days, hours, weeks, who the fuck knows. Probably a few days, assuming the doc checked on me twice a day. Also part of the fun, if they had me on any painkillers at all, it was minimal, just enough to take the edge off."

"That doesn't sound fun at all."

"Honestly, it was worse than what those FARC fuckers did to me. I'll take a good old-fashioned beating over being bedridden, bored, and in constant all-over pain any day of the week. I nearly lost my goddamn mind. Maybe I did, I dunno. I talked to you. I talked to Gabe. I swear to fucking God, I heard Gabe tell me to get my shit together—I heard his voice as clear as I hear yours right now."

"I've heard that can happen."

"It was trippy."

"So, at some point, someone showed up, I assume."

"Eventually, yes. A woman. A lot like you, as a matter of fact. Tall end of medium height, slender, hard as fucking nails. Latin origin of some sort, who the fuck knows what—she doesn't share. Calls herself Inez and says she has an offer for me."

"An offer?"

"She told me she worked for an individual who shall remain nameless, and he's responsible for the fact that I'm still alive. He intercepted the original extract helo and replaced it with his own crew, including state-of-the-art mobile medical, which was the only reason I survived long enough to get to a hospital."

"Again, who the fuck can intercept CIA transport without the CIA knowing?"

"Right?" I shrug. "I still don't have an answer for that. He has seriously deep pockets and serious connections all over the world. And for some reason, he decided to put together a team of fucked up former operators." I growl, frustrated. "I'm not telling this well. Go back. The offer Inez presented was simple. Door number one, recuperate where I was long enough to stand on my own two feet and then take my chances out in the world. But the problem with that was I was listed as deceased, and because of my status as an off-book black ops operator, JSOC wouldn't recognize me or take me back. I'd died in Caracas, mission failure, no acknowledgment, yada yada yada. Plus, she made it clear, with very convincing evidence, that I had enemies out there. Evidence that what happened in Caracas was not an accident. It wasn't just bad intel."

This gets her attention. She jams on the brakes and stares at me. "The fuck are you saying?"

"I'm saying she showed me very convincing evidence that the op in Caracas was compromised. Someone wanted me dead, and they managed to make sure shit went sideways." I wait for the penny to drop.

"Meaning, someone on the inside." She frowns, thinking. "Someone at the CIA wanted you dead? What is this? Tom fucking Clancy?"

"Except I didn't and still don't know anything that would put me in the crosshairs of anyone powerful enough to pull that off. She didn't know who, but she had enough dots connected that I couldn't ignore the possibility that she was right. If I tried to go back in, I couldn't be sure whoever had twisted the Caracas op wouldn't finish the job."

"There are only a handful of options, Sol," she says. "Val Tomlinson, Chad McMaster, Albert Ridley...shit, what was Chad's direct superior's name? Kelly something."

"Kelly Kyle."

"Yeah, that bitch. Fuck, I hated her. Snooty ass bitch. Thought she shit roses and pissed rosé."

I laugh. "She did give off that attitude, didn't she?" I shake my head as Scarla drives onward again. "The only other option besides the ones you listed would be Admiral Harmon. Those five are the only ones who knew enough about the op to be able to fuck with it. Val told me that even the fucking White House only knew the barest outlines, so they'd have plausible deniability."

"And good luck proving anything. Those five are some of the most powerful people in Washington that no one has ever heard of. You'd have to have concrete proof to even make the accusation, and good luck surviving long enough to get that proof." She yanks the shifter down into second, shoves it up into third, then looks at me. "The other option?"

"Accept her offer. Which was, again, very simple. Remain officially dead. Cut all ties to my previous life, no exceptions. Take an oath and join the team her boss was putting together."

"A team for what?"

"She wouldn't say. I had to take the oath first."

"So, cut all ties, disappear from what little life you did have, and take an oath without knowing what you were swearing into?"

"Pretty much."

"What was the oath?"

"Once you're in, there's no going back; never take a life; loyalty to the brotherhood above all."

She accepts this in silence, staring straight ahead. "You swore an oath to never kill anyone?"

"I did."

"You're... you're fucking WindWalker, Sol." She looks at me. "By my count, you've taken out...what, seven, eight people so far, just on this little adventure of ours?"

"Didn't kill any of them. Choked out the guard back in the camp and wounded and disabled the rest. Now, that said, being wounded out here is as good as a death sentence, but that's not my problem. I didn't kill them. Not my fault if they can't get help fast enough."

"That's a pretty major handicap in this situation."

I laugh. "No shit. It's hard as hell to remember to pull back."

"Jesus, Sol. So...you took the oath."

"I did. At that point, all I knew was it looked a whole hell of a lot like someone back in Washington wanted me dead for reasons unknown. I assumed you thought I was dead. And if they wanted me dead and found out I wasn't, they'd use you to get to me. I know, you can take care of yourself. But...I was fucking *dead*. I did actually literally die—I coded twice, I was told. You watched me die. The safest bet seemed to let you think I was dead. I couldn't go back anyway. I was sick as a dog, Scar. It was gonna take fuckin' months to get back to anything like normal. So it's not like I could just go and hunt down whoever had it out for me. I couldn't even get out of bed to take a piss on my own, for fuck's sake. So yeah, I chose to let you think I was dead. And from what Inez told me, you'd never find out otherwise. That was the plan."

"We'll get back to that. For now, keep going. Tell me about this brotherhood."

"Once I was healed enough to travel, which took three months of bed rest and PT, as well as several surgeries, she brought me back Stateside in a private jet. Out into the desert somewhere outside Vegas."

"And you still don't know what the job is at this point?"

I scrub my face. "God, I'm shit at this. No, she told me some on the flight across the pond. Her boss is a reclusive entrepreneur putting together some kind of ultra-exclusive nightclub in Vegas, and he wanted dedicated security. But the catch was he wanted very specific people. Guys like me, she said. Men who didn't officially exist, operators who were broken and fucked up. Men who wanted more than a life of being a ghost, only to eventually become a ghost with no one to mourn you when you inevitably take one to the T-box."

"Sounds pretty fucked, if you ask me."

"I guess it does, doesn't it?" I laugh and then sigh. "But the way she framed it…it appealed. I mean, I got recruited into the CIA in my sophomore year of college. Straight from Harvard Law to the Farm. From the Farm to a wet ops squad doing the CIA's dirty work in the armpits of the world. It was exciting. I didn't care about the money, you know? My brothers were all I cared about, and they had their own lives. I checked on them, you know. They got pulled into organized crime and had some good gigs going. They didn't need me. So fuck it. I put everything into my career with the Company. Eventually, Chad roped me into the deep dark shit, and you know the rest. But…" I trail off with a sigh.

"After Gabe died, "she starts, knowing where I was going.

"Exactly. Gabe dying did something to me. Gabe was a top-tier operator. Stone cold, smooth as silk, fearless, and loyal as fuck. And when he died the way he did, it just broke something in me. And then Caracas? Losing you? I thought something was off about that op from the jump. I fuckin' *knew* it, Scar. I knew it. Inez's intel just confirmed what I felt. So...giving up the Company who had no qualms hanging me out to fuckin' dry? Yeah, no problem. Leaving you behind was fucking torture, but it was safest for you. You had a life. It was how I could protect you. I know, I know, you didn't ask me to. But I did. I had to."

"But...Sol. Nightclub security? For one of the best operators in the fucking world? Come on. That's like a Formula One driver taking a job driving cabs. Still driving, but not the same."

"I know. But it made sense. A quiet life, away from everything. Everyone. Stable, predictable, and safe. No more buddies dying next to me."

She sighs. "I guess I get that."

I laugh. "No, you fucking don't. Nice try. Anyway. We landed at some little airstrip in the middle of fuckin' nowhere, and she put me in a van. We made one stop—a safe house in the suburbs. The door opens, and who climbs in? My fuckin' brother, Silas. God, what a reunion. I'm the oldest, and I left home for Harvard the day I graduated. Never saw either of them again."

"Why not?"

"Chicken. It was just easier. I knew they'd leave home sooner than later."

"Your dad."

I nod. "My fucking father. The bastard. And I was right, they both ran away not long after I left. Wasn't much I could do for them anyway."

"So then..."

"So then me and Si trade stories—he was an assassin for a crime syndicate called the Cabal and got assigned a mark he refused to eliminate. An FBI agent he got a little too cozy with. That put him on the outs with his former employers, and there he was, taking the same oath as me. He lost track of Saxon at some point. So, Inez takes us out into the desert, and there he fuckin' is, my baby brother, Saxon, all grown up and running from his own shit, same as me and Si. Plus two other dudes, huge dudes. Former Spec Ops guys with tragic stories just like ours. All of us were recuperating from bad injuries. All of us should have been dead. None of us had a life to go back to. All of us had enemies who wanted us dead and would make sure we stayed dead if we showed back up in the land of the living. So we all chose the oath—the brotherhood."

"So this guy was putting together a private security team comprised of rejects from the Island of Misfit Toys?"

I laugh. "Pretty much. So, she gathered us around a little campfire in the desert and made a speech. 'You five men are the start of something,' she said. 'My employer knows your stories. He knows what it feels like to be at the bottom, staring your own death in the face. Nowhere to go, no up, just death. Well, he offers you a chance at something else. You're all warriors in your own way. I'll leave it to you to share your stories with each other, but suffice it to say that you have each faced death and stand here victorious. The question you have to ask yourselves now is whether a life of violence and death is the life you want. Step beyond the light of this fire and you know what will happen. Your enemies will hunt you down and kill you. There will be no quarter, no mercy. Choose that, and…well, best of luck to you, and may whatever god you believe in be with you.

"'Or, vow to be different. And by vow, I mean a solemn oath, here among men like yourselves. Take the iron and brand each other, if you choose this path. By doing so, you choose to join a new family. A new brotherhood. The vow is simple: once you're in, there's no going back. Never take a life. Loyalty to the brotherhood above all. You will work for my employer, you will live with each other in the home my employer will provide: a safe place, a bunker beneath the club at which you will work. That will be your life. You can't go back to your friends or whatever family you may have. Your old life is gone. If you do try to return to your old life, you will not be welcomed back, even if you do survive your enemies. You will serve each other and forsake the lives now behind you. If you so choose, step forward.'"

She's quiet for a while. "I never could understand how you can memorize shit the way you do."

I laugh quietly. "Eidetic memory. Anything I see, hear, or read, I remember."

She sighs. "I get it, Sol. There've been times I want to leave everything behind. So I get it." She navigates around a series of hairpins that take us upward. "So you branded each other?"

I nod. "Rev was first, and Inez branded him. He branded Chance, Chance branded Silas, then Silas branded Saxon, and Saxon did me. A few months later we got Kane, and then Lash. Once everyone's brands healed, we tattooed over them."

"What's the significance of the broken arrow?" She asks.

"It's what we are. Former tools of death, now broken. The cycle of violence is broken."

"What use is a broken arrow, though?"

I chuckle. "Had that same thought. I honestly wrestled with it for quite a while, trying to find an answer."

She downshifts as we round another hairpin turn. "And?"

"It's a symbol that the part of me whose only use or value is in my capacity for violence has been broken. I don't need it anymore." I roll down my window and adjust my rifle into a more comfortable position. "You can repurpose the parts of an arrow. The heads can be melted down and reforged into a tool. The shafts can become tools as well. The fletching can become bedding or pillow stuffing. Whatever. The point is that I am no longer merely a weapon to be pointed at an enemy."

She nods, glancing in the rearview mirror and then back at the road. "That makes sense, actually." A long pause. "So now you…what? Live in a basement under a nightclub in Vegas, work as a bouncer, and hang out with your other broken arrow bros?"

I snicker. "Pretty much, yeah. We work out, watch movies, play video games. We work the night shift since the club is open from eight p.m. to four a.m. And it's not just the bros anymore. It was for the first few years, which honestly was necessary. We all had to learn how to deinstitutionalize ourselves. We were all career military, except for my brothers and the Cabal functioned on a quasi-military basis."

"So, what? Chicks can be broken arrows, too?"

I frown, scrub my stubble, which is pretty much a beard now. "Hmmm, I don't know. The women who live with us are all partners. Significant others. Rev met Myka first by accident, and that started a sort of chain reaction.

Now, me and Lash are the last ones without a woman. They live with us, stay in the quarters with us, and work in the club. They haven't taken the oath, but they take the brotherhood seriously. They're all sorta fucked up in their own way, too; they're Island of Misfit Toys rejects themselves, just like us."

She eyes me. "What do you do about sex?" If I didn't know better, I'd think she was blushing, but Scarlett has never blushed once in her life.

"Well, there's always this," I lift my right hand. "But Club Sin is not just a nightclub. There's an underground fighting ring and an even more exclusive members-only section called Hel, H-E-L, that's, um...well, it's a brothel."

She stares at me. "Really? A brothel?"

Let's just say that Scarlett has rather strong feelings about brothels, forced prostitution in particular—sexual slavery. I mean, anyone with a fragment of a conscience hates that shit, but Scarla especially gets pretty worked up over it. She's never shared specifically, but I assume personal experience is the unspoken context behind it.

"It's not like that, Scar. The girls are handpicked by the boss. They're there voluntarily. They lease their room at a flat rate—which happens to be a fraction of the rates charged anywhere else. They receive free medical care. We provide security for them. They choose their clients, they set their rates, and all we do is make sure they're able to work as they see fit safely. Any hint of disrespect to our girls is treated with the utmost prejudice. Motherfuckers have left on stretchers for talking back to the girls too harshly." I see the question in her eyes, so I answer it. "Those of us who have availed ourselves of their services always pay, even if the girls would give us an employee discount."

She's quiet for a while. "You have a favorite?"

I shrug. "Sure."

"Tell me about her."

"Why?"

"Curious."

"Bullshit."

"I am. I'm curious."

"Fine. But you gotta tell me about your boy toys."

She eyes me. "Deal. You go first."

"Her name is Violet. I doubt that's her real name, obviously. She's mixed-race, Hawaiian and Black. She was raised ultra-conservative religious and got into sex work as a kind of…reaction, I guess, to the way she was raised. She's attending UNLV, studying social work. She's doing sex work partly to pay for school and partly because she wants to. She enjoys the work. She charges a lot and is very selective about her clientele."

"Sounds like you've spent a lot of time with her."

"Eh, not a lot. But we do talk. She's a great listener, and so'm I. I care about her." I sigh. "It's a weird relationship, to be honest. It's not platonic, but it's not romantic, either. Sort of like friends with benefits, but we talk about serious shit, too. I dunno. I haven't been to see her in a while, though. Or anyone."

"Why not?"

I shrug and shake my head. "Not sure, honestly. I was starting to get confused, maybe? The serious talks were happening more and the sex less. And I think it was true for her, too, so I backed off. We both knew what it was and what it wasn't, and it wouldn't be doing either of us any favors if we let things get muddy."

"She got big titties?"

I cackle. "Scar. Come on."

"I'm serious."

"Why do you want to know that?" I turn to face her more squarely. "You're not fooling anyone."

She frowns at me. "What's that mean?"

"You can act like you don't care all you want, but we both know you do." She opens her mouth, but I talk over her. "I don't expect you to admit anything, Scarlett. We're not there yet. We don't have to be. But don't play games, and don't bullshit me."

She blows out a rough, harsh breath. "It took me a fucking year after you died before I could even think about hooking up with anyone. A fucking year, Sol. A *year* of celibacy. You know what a raging bitch I was that year?"

I laugh. "Scar, babe, you're always a bitch."

She nods, points at me. "Exactly. Now multiply that by extreme sexual frustration."

"Oof. Bet your team walked on eggshells around you," I say.

"Very thin eggshells."

"I'm sorry, Scar."

She leans away from me. "Fuck you. Fuck your sorry."

"Scar—"

She shakes her head. "No. Shut the fuck up and leave me the fuck alone."

"Scarlett, we have to talk this out at some point."

Her hand blurs and the barrel of a pistol touches my forehead. "I said, shut—*the fuck*—up."

I hold up my hands. "Fine. Fine. Keep burying your head in the goddamn sand, then."

She puts the gun away and drives in silence.

It seems I have a lot of work to do before I can get her

to admit how much she missed me. Shit, before I can get her there, I have to get her to express her anger at me—without killing me, preferably.

Maybe, eventually, hopefully, we'll get to the point where I can get her naked and show her how much I missed her.

Chapter 4

Dangerous Chemistry

THE ANGER SEETHING INSIDE ME ISN'T HEALTHY. I know this. But I just don't know what to do about it. How to deal with it.

He was dead. Now he's alive. And he fucking abandoned me. And I just don't know how to have a conversation with him about it. That's not us. It's not me. It's not him. We don't talk about that shit. We shared a little bit about our pasts, but we were both pretty reticent to get too deep.

But things feel different now. He's different. So am I, but he seems like he's better as a person than he used to be, whereas I feel like I went backward. Which also pisses me off.

He knows me, though. He knows I need time and silence, so he keeps his mouth shut and lets me drive. Miles and minutes become hours. I'm no longer seething, but I feel uneasy. Confused. Bothered. Annoyed. Frustrated. Scared.

I hate being scared. I've always hated it. It makes me feel weak and pathetic, like the lost little girl who had to cross Central America by herself on foot.

I push that away—I can't go there, even in the confines of my own skull. I've never told anyone that—not all of it. I told my recruiter some of it. Sol knows some of it. No one knows all of it.

A hot knot burns in my throat, bubbles upward, and becomes a question I can't seem to hold inside. "Why do you hate your father?"

He glances at me, surprised by the question. "Um, well? He was a fucking bastard, mainly. He was a perfectionist. Nothing was ever good enough. Nothing I did, nothing my brothers ever did, nothing my mother ever did, none of it was ever good enough. And he was a drunk. A mean, vicious, abusive drunk. I took the brunt of it. Missed weeks of school because he'd broken ribs. Left me black and blue. Black eyes, broken nose. He wasn't just abusive, he was…" I shake my head. "I don't know the word. Vicious. Absolutely without mercy. A drunk, abusive perfectionist. Richer than god. Powerful. No one could do anything to stop him. And my mother…fuck, she was weak. So weak. She let him do whatever he wanted to us as long as he didn't do it to her. So I joined clubs and did sports just to stay away as long as possible. Studied in the library till they kicked me out. Anything to not go home. Si and Sax were the same. So, I guess the short answer is I hated my father because he was an evil, soulless piece of shit and a monster."

"I guess that makes sense of how you can take so much pain," I say.

He nods. "I lived in pain every moment of every day my whole life until I left for college. I was so used to being in pain that I didn't know what to do with myself at Harvard. I sought out fights. Worked out so intensely I could barely move because I didn't know what to do without pain."

"How'd you get recruited?"

He eyes me, speculative. I can see him wondering why I'm asking so many questions all of a sudden. But he's smart enough not to call me out. He just goes with it instead.

"I mean, how I landed on a recruiter's radar, I don't know. Test scores, maybe? I don't know. They didn't tell me. There was a career fair, and there was a table with a couple of suits behind it. I chatted with them for a while, but it never really went anywhere. And then one afternoon, I was in the law library studying, and the same two suits sat down and started talking to me. Pitching a career in the CIA. Told me I should show up at a specific address at a specific time if I wanted something more exciting than briefs and precedent. Something more meaningful. Make a real impact on the world and the security of the United States."

"You showed up," I say.

"Yes, I did. I picked law because it was sort of...expected, I guess. My father was a lawyer, my grandfather was a lawyer, my great-grandfather, all my male relatives going back to the Revolutionary War. Every single one of my forefathers all had their law degrees from fucking Harvard. It was expected that I would follow tradition. And I went with it because it meant getting away from my father. But when those two agents spun this pitch to me about a life of action and service, it sounded...interesting. A fuck of a lot better than doing what was expected of me because of stupid goddamn tradition. Fuck that. So I went to the Farm and became an agent. Didn't take long before Chad poached me from analytics and put me in training for wet twork. Turns out I had a hell of a talent for it, and I never looked back."

I tense, expecting the return question, but to my surprise, he just looks at me expectantly.

"What?" I ask.

A shrug. "Just waiting for the next question."

"You'll answer it?"

"I'll answer any question you ask, Scarlett."

"But?"

"But nothing. I don't expect you to answer the same questions. I admit I'd love to ask, but I know you better than that."

I frown. "Maybe you don't. Not anymore."

"So if I asked why you hate brothels so much…"

"Figured it was obvious."

"Sure, I can make some pretty safe assumptions. Doesn't mean I don't want to hear the whole truth from your lips. You don't have to tell me. I've never asked because it's obvious you won't answer. But I want to know."

Bile burns in my throat at the prospect of discussing that. "Ask something else. Something…easier."

"Is Scarlett Luisa Gutierrez your real name?"

I laugh. "No. I mean, it's not the name I was born with. It's legally my name now, though." I sigh. "I was born Maria Consuela Rodriguez in a little village on the Pacific, in Panama, on the wrong side of the Darién Gap."

"Maria, huh?" He looks at me as if trying to pin that name on me.

I shake my head. "Nope. I haven't been Maria Rodriguez for almost twenty years."

"That long? I thought the CIA picked your new name or something."

I shake my head again. "No, I did. Maria Rodriguez died a long, long time ago. She died in the Darién Gap. She died in a roach-infested whorehouse in Sonora fucking Mexico. She was sixteen when she died. She was killed by degrees, one john at a time."

"I remember you telling me you left home at eighteen," he says.

"I entered the US at eighteen. My father left for the US when I was twelve. He sent money back regularly for three years or so, and then it stopped. When it stopped, my mother couldn't feed us anymore. Not in the village." I swallow hard. This is fucking hard to talk about. "She tried to bring us to a bigger town, but..." I trail off with a growl, my eyes burning and my throat closed off.

"Scar, babe..."

"You wanna know? Then shut the fuck up and let me talk."

He looks at me expectantly, one hand trailing out the window. Ahead, the jungle opens up and thins out, promising something like civilization not too far away.

"My brother got sick the third day. I don't fuckin' know what it was. Dengue, something like that. He got a fever, and then he was just fuckin' dead. My sister got it. Mom got it. They all died within a week. I never got it, no idea why. I couldn't do shit but watch them die. I couldn't bury them. I couldn't go home. I was fifteen and alone. So I left them where they were and started walking. Hooked up with a group trying to get to the US. We crossed the Gap together."

"Jesus, Scar."

"The stories of the people I traveled with were all a lot like mine, if not worse. The fucking cartels, man. My anger started there, hearing the horror stories of what those families were running away from. I got sick halfway across the Gap, and…Luisa, she nursed me to health. I took her name as my middle name when I changed it. She was a second mother to me. Took care of me. Taught me shit. Self-defense. How to deal with assholes who think they can take what they want from me. How to stand up for myself. She was a small, quiet woman, but she didn't take any shit from anyone."

"What happened to her?" he asks.

"Died. Costa Rica. A gang caught us. They killed the men we were with and tried to take the women and children. Luisa fought them off. She killed four of them before they put her down. She…" I choke, try again. "She told me to run. She bought me time to get away."

"Sounds like a real badass." His voice is soft with understanding.

"She was. I think about her almost every day."

He lets the silence extend as we trundle down a long shallow slope—a village appears in the distance. Hopefully we can find some food and gasoline. A bed would be nice, but I won't hold my breath.

"So you were on your own again, then?" he asks.

"Yeah," I answer. "Hiked, hitched rides, whatever. Through Costa Rica, Nicaragua, Honduras, Guatemala, and most of Mexico."

"By yourself…at *fifteen* years old?"

"Yep." I shrug. "Did what I had to. Stole, begged, fought, did odd jobs. Washed clothing for a bowl of rice. Cleaned a house for a spot to sleep out of the rain. Stayed away from men. And I fucking walked. Got lost a lot."

"Jesus, Scar," he murmurs again. "And then you ended up in a brothel in Sonora."

"Hitched a ride with the wrong person. This old guy. Figured because he was, like, a hundred years old he was safe. He fucking wasn't. He delivered me right to a fucking cartel boss. They beat me senseless, raped the shit out of me, and put me to work. If I didn't work, they beat the shit out of me. They liked to fill hoses with sand and hit my stomach and thighs. I became a favorite of this one guy. Cartel money guy. He came to fuck me three, four times a week. I pretended to like it—to like him because then he was nice to me. He'd bring me food. Pain pills. Sometimes, he'd bring clothing. Pretty stuff that he wanted me to wear, but still."

"Sixteen."

I nod. "You know damn well that that isn't unusual, Sol. I was one of the older girls there, actually."

"Fucking disgusting."

"No shit. That's why I hate that shit. I got no problem if someone chooses sex work. As long as they choose it. But I know first fucking hand that most of the time, it ain't voluntary. It's drugs. It's desperation. They're forced into it. Trapped in it. I wasn't a whore, Sol. I was a sex slave."

"I understand."

"No, you fucking don't."

He shoots me a look I can't decipher. "You know what I mean, Scar."

I growl. "Yeah, I do. Sorry, I just—"

"Don't apologize. I know I can't ever know what you went through, what it was like."

"Just like I'll never know what it was like to be brutalized by my own father."

"You ever find out what happened to him?" he asks. "Your father, I mean."

I nod. "He was murdered by some white trash thugs in El Paso. I hunted them down and killed them after I was recruited by the Company."

"How'd that happen, anyway?"

I sigh. "That's a story for another time. I can only handle so much talking about the past." I point ahead of us. "'Sides, we're here."

"Wherever the hell here even is," he mutters.

"Does it matter?" I say. "I have some cash. I can probably get us food and fuel. Maybe even a shower and a bed."

It's a tiny place, a collection of huts and some old crumbling buildings. Folks come out and stare, muttering to each other.

I park in front of a general store sort of place advertising beer and cigarettes. "Stay here, gringo."

"You know someone here is an informant, right?" he says.

"No shit. I was a field agent before I got into wet work." I gesture around us. "I specialized in turning informants in places exactly like this."

He frowns at me. "There's a fucking lot I don't know about you, isn't there?"

"More than you do know about me, Sol." I point at him. "I'm serious about my old name. You never mention it again—to me, or anyone else, ever."

He holds up both hands. "I got it, Scar."

I leave my rifle in the SUV, but I still look exactly like what I am: a soldier who got lost in the jungle. I'm filthy, smelly, armed to the teeth, scarred, and immensely cranky.

I fucking hate talking about my past. But for some

stupid fucking reason, Solomon's resurrection is bringing it out of me. Along with a lot of other shit I don't know how to handle.

Like attraction and arousal—I've been so shut down lately that I haven't even wanted sex for months. I haven't so much as diddled my bean in weeks. Too exhausted, lonely, and pissed off. Just...existentially lost.

And now he's alive and close to me and all I want to do is put my hands on him, my mouth, my body. I want to ride him like I used to. I want him to eat me out for hours like he used to. Fuck, I just *want* him.

But I'm too angry to let that happen.

Confusing as hell is what it is.

I saunter into the general store, fishing my wet bag out of my cargo pants pocket—it's a waterproof bag with rolls of cash in various currencies, a passport, and a burner satphone in case of extreme emergencies. I peel a few Colombian bills out of the bag and an American $20. The shopkeeper watches me do this with beady, greedy eyes. He's middle-aged, shirtless in the sweltering, humid heat.

There's a small glass-front fridge containing bottles of water, beer, and soda. I put two bottles of water on the counter and shop for food. I find some decent options—not a hot meal, but better than old protein bars that probably spent weeks in a pocket.

When I approach the counter, the shopkeeper addresses me in Spanish.

"I know that truck," he says, not looking at me.

"Probably," I agree. "I borrowed it."

"They will not like that."

"Probably not." I meet his eyes. "Tell them we were here. Tell them anything. It doesn't matter."

He nods. "You need something else?"

"Fuel. Somewhere safe to sleep. A hot meal." I let him see the $20. "There's more. But if you try to take it, you'll die. Slowly."

He's not fazed by the threat. "I can get you gasoline. I will bring you to my wife. She will cook for you. Best food you ever eat."

"We don't want to cause trouble for you."

He shrugs. "We hate them. They're no good. They think they can do whatever they want. They can go fuck themselves."

I grin. "I like that answer. You do not need to lie if they ask you questions about us. Tell them what they want to know. It won't make a difference."

He shrugs, nods. "Let me lock up. I'll show you the way."

"My friend is American."

He nods again. "I can see. He cannot be worse than them."

"He's running from them. We killed several of them."

He grins at this. "Good. Kill more. They are evil. They are not working for us, despite what they say on the radio. The government is no better."

"This isn't political for us. We just want to get out of here."

He shrugs. "Everything is political. Especially when an American like that is involved." He juts his chin at Solomon, visible in the SUV, through the store windows.

I wish I could deny the truth of what he's saying, but I can't. So I just nod. "I will be out front. Thank you."

"Five minutes."

A couple hours later, our bellies are full of home cooked rice, beans, and pork. Best food I've had in a long time. His wife is a plump, pretty woman who bustles about her microscopic kitchen with frenetic energy, whipping up a feast like it's nothing. Solomon is fluent in Spanish, to their surprise, and they give us more context for the activities of the group that had Sol.

They're what I assumed—a breakaway faction of the now-defunct FARC. They're extremists, terrorists with designs on pulling a coup and taking over Colombia and turning it communist. Or something like that—the politics of it are complicated, and honestly, I don't give a fuck. None of that explains why they had Sol, and Jose and Anna can't answer that any more than I can. They tell us that there is suspicion that the group is getting outside funding and resources, but no one knows from who or how. They control a large swath of territory around the border, which explains why they had a camp inside Brazil—Colombian forces can't get to them there, not easily and not legally.

Once we've eaten, José, our host, and the shopkeeper, says he'll make a trip to get gas for us while we shower and get some rest. I give him a handful of Colombian Pesos and the $20 bill and tell him to get any other supplies he thinks we may need.

He agrees and trundles away in a rattling old white compact Toyota pickup spewing purple-white fumes, several red gas cans tied down in the bed.

He had us park our stolen SUV in the back behind his house, surrounded by a variety of broken-down cars in varying states of disrepair. He gave us a ripped blue tarp for us to cover it with, and then it was just another hulk in a backyard filled with ruined hulks just like it.

The shower is a makeshift thing outside, with an eight-foot-high fence around it for privacy, the water heated by a squealing old boiler run by a gas generator.

Anna shows me how to work the shower, with instructions to turn off the generator and boiler when we were both done, and with a warning that the little boiler only has enough hot water for maybe ten minutes. And then she leaves, claiming to have errands to run.

Sol gets the generator and boiler going. "You first."

"Sol, I—"

He gives me his patented don't-fuck-with-me glare. "Scarla, get in the damn shower. You crossed who knows how many kilometers of jungle for my ass. You're taking the first fucking shower."

I know when not to argue with him. "Fine. Thank you."

He leaves, heading outside to sit on a wobbly old blue plastic outdoor chair with a cigarette.

It feels weird to peel my clothes off—I've been wearing them so long they're stiff. Once I'm naked, I use the antique washboard and the bar of homemade soap to scrub my clothes under cold water, rinsing them thoroughly. Only then do I turn on the hot water and scrub myself clean. It's tempting to soak under the spray until my muscles loosen up, but I resist. Sol has been through hell and deserves a hot shower as much as I do.

There are a handful of tattered old towels in a stack just inside from the outdoor shower, and I dry off and wrap it around my torso—it's a tiny little towel not much bigger than a hand towel, so it doesn't quite cover me. Fortunately, we're alone, and our hosts live outside the little village at the top of a hill—by local standards, José and Anna are quite rich.

I exit the shower, wearing a pair of flip-flops I found. "Sol, your turn."

I'm used to co-ed showers with my male teammates, so I don't even think about the fact that the towel doesn't close in front of my yoo-hoo, or cover my boobs. Also, it's Sol. He knows every inch of me…*very* well.

Which is why I'm not prepared for the way he looks at me: like he's a man on the brink of starvation, and I'm a steak fresh off the grill.

"Goddammit, Scarlett." He takes a last drag from the cigarette, crushes it under his bootheel, and then rises to his feet.

He stomps past me and into the shower; I hear the water turn on and the sounds of him scrubbing his clothes clean.

Still reacting and not thinking, I follow him into the shower, perplexed and annoyed by his reaction.

"What the hell was that about?" I demand, coming around the corner.

Where I'm confronted by the sight of a naked Solomon. His ass is sculpted from marble, a taut round bubble of solid rock, with thick, hairy, powerful thighs, a broad back and wide shoulders rippling with muscle. If anything, I'd say he's even bigger than he was when he was an active operator.

He doesn't turn around, scrubbing his fingers over his scalp aggressively. "What was what, Scar?"

"You, just now." I drop my voice into a rough growl. "'Goddammit, Scarlett.'"

He rakes his hands over his scalp and then rubs his face. Part of me desperately wants him to turn around, and the other half that's more concerned with self-preservation is screaming at me to turn around and run away.

Too late. He turns around.

Fuck.

Yeah, he's way bigger, heavily muscled and brawny. Hard, anvil-like pecs, block-like abs chiseled from the same marble as his ass. Thick, veiny arms. Jesus, he's even hotter now than he ever was.

The only thing that hasn't changed is that big, fat, beautiful cock. It dangles heavily, swaying with his movement. Dripping shower water.

"Scarla." I wrench my eyes up to his.

"What?"

He takes half a step toward me, hands at his sides, green eyes burning. "You should leave. For your own sake."

"Don't tell me what to do," I whisper, knowing he's right, and why he's saying it.

He shakes his head with a sniff of mocking laughter. "You don't want to play this game with me, honey." His voice is low, rough. "We have a whole fucking lot to talk about before *this* happens."

"Nothing is happening," I say, my gaze drawn once again to his cock.

"Scar." He takes another step. "You remember how it was with us."

"How was it with us, Sol?" I ask in a stupid, stupid, tempting, teasing, idiotic whisper.

Another step, and now he's too close, towering over me, naked and wet and huge and fucking glorious.

"Room full of goddamn nitro, babe. One wrong move

and…" he lets his eyes rake over the parts of me that are exposed: the seam of my pussy, my abs, and a hint of inner boob. "Don't fucking tempt me."

"Sol…" I back up a step. "You don't get to be angry at me. I didn't fucking abandon you."

"But you don't get to prance around mostly naked and not expect me to react how you know fully goddamn well how I'm gonna react to seeing you like that. When have I ever been able to keep my hands to myself around you, Scar? Hmmm?"

"I'm not being a tease. I just don't wanna put on wet clothes yet."

"So go somewhere else. Stay away from me." he prowls closer, once again towering over me. This time, he lifts a hand, traces a fingertip down my scar just like he used to. And just like then, I melt under his touch. "Goddammit, Scarlett," he says again, this time in a reverent whisper.

"Don't call me Scarlett," I mutter.

"Why? You chose the name."

"You don't get to call me that." I choke on the next words, but they won't stay in my throat. "Not yet."

His eyes fix on mine, and I see a boiling inferno of emotions in his gaze. Too much. Too intense. Too messy. Most of all, I see desire. Need. His cock is responding to my proximity the way it always does: unfurling. Thickening.

No, no, no.

I could never resist him. Never.

I'm not ready for this.

"You'd better fucking run, Scar," he growls under his breath. "Don't tempt me. Last warning."

"I'm not doing anything."

"Don't fucking have to."

I also can't back down from a challenge. Run—stay. There's no winning.

He touches the tip of my chin with his thumb, tugging my lip down. Brushes that thumb over my lips.

Trails his index finger down my throat. Over my breastbone. Into the fold, keeping my towel in place. I can't breathe. I need his touch like I need my next breath—

With a guttural snarl, he whips around and stomps over under the steaming spray. Ignores me, brusquely scrubbing his body with the soap.

"Go, Scar," he murmurs. "While you still can. We both know you're not ready for that."

Trembling worse than I do with the post-gunfight shakes, I leave the outdoor shower and hide inside.

What the fuck is wrong with me? What was that?

Our physical chemistry is stronger than ever. But just as clearly, I'm seriously fucked up about Solomon Cabot.

CHAPTER 5

A BIG FIRST STEP

I THINK ABOUT STAB WOUNDS AND BLOWN-UP BODY parts until my hard-on subsides.

Fucking Scarlett. I cannot figure out where her head is at. One second, she nearly takes my head off with a machete. Then she tells me the backstory I couldn't get out of her with any amount of liquor, cunnilingus, and fucking. She makes it crystal fucking clear I'm not touching her. Don't call her Scarlett. Don't act like we're "us." Like I have any right to her body or her emotions.

Fine, I get it.

But then she flounces out of the shower in a tiny little towel that covers precisely nothing. Follows me into the shower and looks at my dick like it's her next meal. Acts sultry, confused, aroused, emotional...

What am I supposed to do with any of that?

I finish my shower and shut off the boiler and generator. Towel off and wrap it around my waist. Go back out to the chair and try not to think about Scarlett.

Or her body.

Her tight little pussy. Those lovely little tits, just barely a handful.

I resist the urge to have another smoke—that way ad-
diction lies, and I'm not about to let that happen. Instead,
I sit and breathe.

Avoid thoughts of Scarlett. Resist the urge to take a
trip down memory lane—all the many ways I've made her
scream my name.

God, she can fuck.

No, no, no.

Violet comes to mind. She's Scarla's polar opposite.
Curvy, soft, gentle, and sweet. She doesn't have a violent
bone in her body. She's been through her own personal
hell, but she never let it make her bitter. I suppose that's
why I'm drawn to her—she has a maternal, nurturing manner about her that speaks to something I needed at the
time. But the last time I visited her, she gave me a look.
A long, searching, emotional look. And I just knew—I
had to stop seeing her. I could never give Violet what she
wanted and deserved.

My heart has always belonged to another, even if I
knew I'd never see her again.

Yet here I am, in the middle of the Colombian rainforest, pursued by terrorists who didn't seem to want anything specific from me, with Scarlett.

She's lean, whipcord thin, hard, lithe, quick, violent,
closed off…a stone-cold killer and one of the most naturally talented and highly skilled operators I've ever known.
I'm one of the few, if not the only one, who knows that
she has another side. A softer side. A side that likes to be
held after sex. A side that wants long, wet kisses and whispered conversations. A side that is needy and greedy and
perpetually horny. A side that may not ever speak of love

but shows it in every action in private. I saw that in her be-fore, but *very* rarely.

Right now, all I see is Scar, the operator. That other side, Scarlett, the woman, the lover…there's no sign of her. For a brief moment, I caught a glimpse of her. But I knew that if I touched her, I'd have her naked and I'd be inside her within seconds. Sex would take over, the way it always does with us.

And I knew—I *know*—that she's not there. She's not ready. We still have deep, dark, difficult shit to discuss be-fore we can go there.

But god, that was hard. Turning away from her, not touching her? She wouldn't have stopped me. I know the look in her eyes when she wants me. She had that look. I could have done anything I wanted.

But she'd resent it later. The deep shit we've never discussed, her anger and resentment toward me, all of that would still be there. But sex would distract us from it. We'd fuck instead of sorting out the issues.

And for the first time in my life, I'm ready to face the hard emotional shit. I have a second chance with Scarlett. I'm not about to fuck it up by thinking with my dick.

Even if my dick is mad at me for it.

Irritated by the whole stupid situation, I put my wet clothes back on. Which sucks, but it's far from the first time. Plus, it's hot enough that they'll dry soon.

The property is a veritable junkyard of useful shit, so I scrounge up a few items and set about cleaning our fire-arms. I disassemble, clean, and reassemble the AKs first, and then my handgun. Without a word, I trade my cleaned pistol for Scar's and clean hers. With nothing better to do, then, I kick my feet up in the chair and doze off.

It's late evening when José and Anna return—together, despite having left at different times and in different directions.

José looks freaked out and has a conversation with Scarla in Spanish so rapid I have trouble following it.

The gist is that my enemies are on their way here. He offers to hide us, but Scarlett and I both refuse. Scar shoves a wad of pesos and dollars into his hands, and then we rip the tarp off and get the old Nissan going.

Jose gives us a ragged section of a paper map with a route traced in red marker; Anna, meanwhile, has packed a dirty old Styrofoam cooler full of food and a milk carton full of bottles of potable water. We have three five-gallon gas cans tied down in the back, as well.

So much for sleeping indoors tonight; at least I got a shower.

I drive this time, and Scarlett navigates. I drive as fast as I safely can, putting as many miles behind us as possible.

After an hour or so of switchbacks and turns, we reach a stretch of the route without any turns for several hundred miles—our route is taking us to Bogotá…more than halfway across the country.

Scar dozes, then. I drive until the gas tank is on fumes. When I pull over and refill, Scar takes the wheel, and I sleep.

Several hours later, the sun is coming up and we're on the last gas can. As the gas gauge is nudging the E, we come to a decent-sized town. This one has an actual gas station, where Scar fills up the tank and all three gas cans. She also finds us hot food—spicy as fuck, and delicious. Then it's back on the road.

We haven't spoken two words to each other since the

shower incident. She has to break the silence—she has to decide how this is gonna go.

So I wait.

We switch every time we refill the gas tank.

No sign of pursuers, but we both know they're behind us. We both know they'll catch up to us in Bogotá.

Afternoon on the second day out from Jose and Anna, Scarla finally breaks the tense, rigid, uncomfortable silence.

"Thank you for not pushing, Sol," she says, her voice barely above a whisper. "Back there. The whole…shower situation."

I'm driving. I regrip the steering wheel and upshift as we reach the bottom of a long, shallow hill and begin another ascent.

"I haven't forgotten who you are, Scar. Or who we are. If we start down that road, it'll take over."

"I know," she says.

"We have shit to talk about. But you have to be willing to go there. If you're not, okay, I'll accept that. But in that case, we're gonna have to stay former teammates and nothing else."

She was looking out the window as I spoke; when I say that, her head whips around. "Solomon, come on."

"Come on, what?"

"It's all or nothing?"

"Fuck yes, it's all or nothing, Scar. You're confusing me. Either you want to move past what happened and do what you gotta do to get past it, or you don't. You're two different people with me and I never know which version of you I'm gonna get."

She shakes her head. "I'm just me, Sol."

"Bull-fucking-shit. There's two distinct sides to you.

There's Scar, or Scarla, the operator. Stone-cold, badass, tough as nails, take no shit. Walls a million miles high and a million miles thick. Nothing gets in, nothing gets out. Scar is locked down tighter than Fort fucking Knox. There's no mercy. Not an ounce of hesitation. And that's what makes you the best motherfucking operator I've ever worked with."

A smirk touches the corner of her mouth. "The best? Ever?"

"Fuck yes. On a purely professional standard, no personal or emotional bias, I'd take you at my back in any situation in the field, anywhere in the world, at any time, over any other entire squad. Hands down."

She swallows hard. "Means a fuckin' lot, coming from you, WindWalker."

I snort. "WindWalker is dead. But I mean it."

"Well, thank you." She hesitates. "And the other side?"

"That's the human being. Scarlett. The woman. The sexual creature. The lover. The friend."

She stares out the window as the jungle slides past. A monkey screeches somewhere in the distance and a parrot of some kind answers.

"I'm not sure who that is anymore, Sol."

"I know. That's the problem."

She shakes her head slowly. "I think she died in Caracas along with you." A bark of laughter escapes, earning me a death glare from her. "Something funny about that, Solomon?"

"No. Well, yes. Not funny, it's just...fuck, I don't know. I'm not making fun of you. But Scar, babe, that version of you was barely alive before Caracas. She was on life support."

She stares at me silently for a long time. "I guess I don't know what you want me to say."

"I was no better. Honestly, I didn't find that part of myself until after Caracas. I had to have my career taken away to understand that I'd made it my entire personality. I had to figure out who the fuck I was if I wasn't an operator."

"And who is that?"

I shrug. "I'm Solomon Cabot. Former CIA operative. Combat veteran. I like good whiskey and bad action movies. I hate running for exercise. Cheesy rom-coms are a guilty pleasure, and if you tell anyone, I'll cut your fucking tongue out. I feel guilty for abandoning my brothers. I'm not sad my dad is dead, and I honestly wish my mom had shot his ass a lot sooner. I wasn't surprised she killed herself. I'm not good at being friends with people—I'm still learning how to open up and let the other guys in."

She blinks at me a few times and then looks away, thinking. After several long minutes of silence, she looks back at me. "Yeah, I don't know the fuck Scarlett is."

"I know that. You never have."

"And how the fuck am I supposed to know?"

I laugh, then. "What do you do in your downtime?"

"Go to bars and get blackout drunk. Find some dumb soft civvy to fuck. I dunno."

"When you're with a guy, what are you like? Not me, other guys."

"Sol, we're not talking about this." She drums her fingers on the outside of the door, not looking at me.

"Why not?"

"Because it's awkward and uncomfortable. We're...I dunno. Exes?"

"We're not exes. We didn't break up."

She barks a laugh. "Then what the fuck are we?"

"Complicated. And we've shit side by side, Scarla. I think I can handle the conversation."

"Shitting in the jungle because you have no choice is not the same as talking about fucking other people with someone you were romantically involved with."

"Were we, though? Romantically involved? Or we were just fucking?"

Her gaze goes shocked, and then hurt, and then angry. "Fuck you, Solomon."

"For real. What were we?"

"You meant something to me, Sol, and you fucking know it."

"You meant something to me, too."

"Then what the *fuck* is your point?"

"We never went deep, that's my point. I've learned more about you as a human being in the last three days than I did in all the years we worked together, lived to-gether, and slept together."

She huffs. "Fuck you," she says again, but this time without any real venom to it.

"Scarlett."

"Don't call me that."

"Why not?"

"I don't like it."

"Why not?"

"Because."

"Not an answer."

"Because I'm not Scarlett out here, Sol! I *can't* be. Scarlett is soft and weak and she'll get me killed. Scarlett is a fucking liability." She turns back to the window.

I grab a knife and surreptitiously palm it, lay it against my thigh where she can't see it.

"Scarlett."

She ignores me.

"Scarlett."

Ignore.

"Scarlett!"

"What?" she snarls, whirling on me.

I slice at her with the knife, driving it at her face. Her hand flashes up in a blur and catches mine before the blade comes within six inches.

"The fuck, Sol?" she snaps, wrenching the knife out of my hand.

"Proving a point."

"Maybe prove your point without trying to fucking kill me?"

"Says the woman who damn near took my head off with a goddamn machete."

"Shut up."

"My point is, your skills don't go away."

She rolls her eyes. "It's a matter of focus."

"No, it's not. That's an excuse."

"Fuck you, no it's not."

"Fuck you, yes it is."

"I don't know what you want from me here, Sol."

"I want the real you. I want honesty. I want you to be vulnerable with me. I want to talk about what happened and how we both feel about it. I want to have real, adult, meaningful conversations about shit that fucking matters without you literally trying to take my goddamn head off. I think you think you can put it off till we're not out here, like, 'I have to focus on the mission, so I have to stay frosty.'"

"Exactly! We have a whole fucking lot of very bad dudes after us. We're in the middle of the fucking Amazon. There's no backup, no extraction waiting at a nice cozy little L-Z. We have to stay fucking frosty or we fucking die, Solomon!"

"Wrong." I swing a hand behind us. "Look back there. You see anyone?"

"We have a head start. If you think that means jack shit, then you've been out of the game too long."

"You think I've forgotten how shit works?" I glare at her. "I took a vow not to kill. Doesn't mean I forgot how the game works. My point is I'm not your fucking mission, *Scarlett*. Your skills and talents and instincts don't dry up and hibernate because we have a fucking conversation."

"Sol—"

"No. Just no. You're scared of opening up to me, so you're hiding behind Scar, the operator. You've hidden behind her for a very long time. So long you don't know who Scarlett even is. I get that. You went through hell. But you survived it. You got out. You're allowed to have a life, babe."

"I'm not your babe."

"Yes, you are."

Her hand twitches, and she clenches it into a fist. "Taking a lot of self-control to not put a knife through your fucking eyeball."

"I know. But you're doing it—good job."

"Don't fucking patronize me, asshole."

"I'm not! I'm being serious."

"What the fuck do you *want*, Solomon?"

"I want to know why you're so angry at me."

"Because you abandoned me! You left me behind! You died and I didn't! I watched you fucking *die*! But then it gets worse! You *didn't* die, and you *never fucking told me*!" Her voice shakes, and her eyes haze over with tears I know she won't let herself shed; she shakes her head harshly, fighting them off tooth and nail. "I would have walked through fucking fire with you. I spent four and a half days in this goddamn jungle based on a single fucking email *hinting* that you were alive, Solomon. Just to find out if it was really you. So yeah, I'm pissed at you. You chose life without me."

"I did it to protect you!"

"*I DIDN'T ASK YOU TO PROTECT ME!*"

Silence.

"I know you didn't. I just…" I squeeze the steering wheel until my knuckles hurt. "What was I supposed to do? Ask you to give up your entire life? We weren't even…" I trail off, not ready to go there.

"We weren't even what? Say it, motherfucker."

"What we were, Scar?" I ask rather than answer.

"Together," she whispers. "We were together."

"It was a secret from *everyone* we knew, everyone we worked with. And again, we both kept each other at a distance. You never let me all the way in, and I never let you all the way in."

"I don't even know what that looks like, Sol—letting someone all the way in. How do you do that?"

"Ask me anything."

She goes silent, watching the jungle rather than face me. Finally, she looks at me. "Did you love me?"

Fuck.

"Yes."

"You never said it."

"Didn't know how."

She shakes her head. "But you're on *my* case about not opening up."

"Have you not heard a word I've said? I've said multiple times that I know I was no better. This isn't easy for me, either." I venture my hand across the space between us and rest it on her leg, just above her knee. "Ask me something else."

"Tell me about Violet."

I groan. "Why?"

"Because I'm jealous."

"How does hearing about it help?"

"I don't know. Maybe it doesn't. But you said anything. That's my question."

"What do you want to know?"

"Did you love her? Or *do* you?"

"No. I didn't and I don't. That's why I pulled away from her—she was falling in love with me and I knew I'd never be able to give her that back."

"Why not?"

"Because she's not you."

"But you cared about her."

'Yes."

"So tell me about her. Tell me everything. Why her? What was it about her?"

"You won't like the answer, Scarlett."

"Probably not." She looks at me long and hard, and then at my hand on her knee; she makes a fist with her left hand, opens it again and shakes it out, and then rests her hand on mine. "But I'm asking anyway."

"She was everything you aren't. And I don't mean that

as a dig or an insult, it's just a neutral fact. Physically, emotionally, she's your opposite. She's...soft. In every sense of the word. Curvy. Soft-spoken. Gentle. Sweet. I'd never been around anyone like that before. Even the women I hooked up with before you were...not like that. I had a type: women who could, in some capacity, understand the kind of man I am. Violet...she didn't have it easy by any stretch of the imagination, but violence wasn't part of her life."

I space out as I drive, thinking of her. Assessing what drew me to her so I can explain it.

"Being around her felt like a departure from who I was. There were other girls I could've spent my time with, girls who would get me, to some degree. But Violet... Didn't. She didn't have to."

"What was the sex like?"

"You really want to know?"

"Yes."

"Crazy woman. But okay—if you're sure."

"I am."

"It was...healing. It wasn't rough. It wasn't aggressive. It was soft and sweet. That was her whole thing, what made her in such high demand. She had a year-long waiting list to get time with her. Because she had this way of making you feel...I don't know how to put it. It didn't feel transactional. With me, at least, she made me feel...fuck, I don't have the words. It was what I needed at that moment. A total one-eighty from everything I'd been, from the kind of relationships I'd had, such as they were." I pause again, thinking. "I thought you were...behind me. I missed you. I wanted you back. I nearly emailed you a million fucking times, but I couldn't. I couldn't stomach the idea of dragging you into something that would get you killed. I couldn't ask you to give up everything and come live in a fucking basement with me. I like it. It's what *I* need and what *I* want, and I don't think I'll ever leave. But how could I ask that of you?"

I look at her, waiting for a response, but she just stares right back at me and says nothing.

"But at the end of the day, two things always kept me from letting myself think it could ever be more than what it was with Violet. One, I was paying her. She would have given me her time for free. She told me as much, and I think she was hurt that I insisted on paying her. The other problem was that she just wasn't you. She'd never know the real me."

"The real you?"

I gesture at the world around us. "This. Being downrange. That will always be the real me. To a degree, at least. WindWalker will never die. But...I don't want to be WindWalker anymore. That's what I eventually realized, being with Violet and working at the club, being around the guys. And then watching the guys find these women who...who *see* them. Who accept them for all the nasty, gnarly shit they've done and been through. I want that. But...how can I have it? Who can ever *know* me? You can't know *me* without knowing WindWalker. And He's dead."

"I thought you said he'd never die.

"What's dead can never die, right?"

She laughs. "That makes no fucking sense."

"I know."

"I'll never be Violet, Solomon. My body will never be soft. My tits will never be triple Ds. I'll never have a big juicy ass. I'll never be soft and sweet like you're saying she is. Any part of me that was soft and sweet died somewhere between Panama and that whorehouse in Mexico—it was dead long before that recruiter ever found me."

"Your body is perfect exactly the way it is, Scarlett."

"You're saying you don't like big titties bouncing in your face?"

I laugh. "Sure I do."

"And I'll never be that."

"I don't need you to be that."

"Then what do you need?"

"Scarlett—I need Scarlett. I need you to let Scar, the operator, rest beneath the surface sometimes. I need you to trust yourself. Trust your skills and your instincts. When shit hits the fan, I have no doubt you'd do what needs to be done. Even if you and I are having a deep conversation or if we're fucking. Making love. Whatever. You're not going to suddenly forget who you are because you let a softer side of yourself come out."

"I don't *have* a fucking softer side, Solomon!" she shouts.

"Yes, you do!" I shout back. "You just refuse to let her out. You keep her buried under a layer of ice."

"Because the ice is all that's keeping me alive." She drops her voice to a whisper. "After Caracas, I went looking."

"For what?"

"Someone to replace you. To fill the gap you left inside me."

"And?" I ask.

She shakes her head. "I found a lot of self-centered assholes. A lot of weak fucking pussies. A lot of macho, wannabe tough guys. And a lot of dicks that just weren't…

yours." She blinks hard. "I found a lot of men who just weren't you. They didn't see me. They didn't understand me. They couldn't handle me."

"How so? How couldn't they handle you?"

"I tend to take over. I'm way too alpha for most men. Give me an inch, and I'll take over. They like it at first. They like it when I throw them on the bed and fuck them till they can't move. But they don't like it as much when they discover I'm not about to give control to them under any fucking circumstances, and they're all too fucking pussy to take it from me. They all think they can find that part of me that you're talking about, but they can't because it's *not fucking there*—it's not there to find. I'm not soft. I'm not sweet. And I don't know how to be. They never got Scarlett. They only got Scarla."

"The in-between. Not quite Scarlett, but not Scar, either."

A nod. "Pretty much. It's as close as I could come."

"Who came closest?"

"Tom Daughtry, Sergeant First Class, USMC. A Raider. He's a lot like you, actually, but the Walmart version. Tall, blond, built, hot, and a pretty damn good operator. We worked together on an op. Had a few drinks together after the op was over. A few drinks turned into a few rounds in the sack."

"Was he good?"

She grins. "Very good." The grin fades. "He thought he could…conquer me, I guess. He couldn't let me be me. He couldn't accept that I just couldn't give parts of myself to him."

"That didn't turn out well, I bet." I eye her, watching her.

She snorts softly, shaking her head. "Not at all. He got in my face about it, got all aggressive on me. I put him on his ass and damn near cut his fucking throat. And that was the end of that."

"Because you couldn't give him what he wanted or because you bested him?"

"Both. His ego couldn't handle either one, let alone both."

I let out a sigh. "I can see that."

"And I...I guess I'm afraid that...that even if I did try with you, it'd end up the same way."

"You think I'm threatened by you? Scar, babe, you know how hot it gets me when you put me on my ass."

She laughs. "You're a twisted fuck like that, though."

"Exactly. Especially now, out of the game, my skills aren't what they once were. I know that. I have no problem with the fact that you're a better operator than me, now. I just need you to give me a chance. Give *us* a chance."

"How?"

"One step at a time, Scarlett, that's how. Don't shut me out. Let me in, one little bit at a time."

"And assuming we get out of this jungle alive, then what?"

"Fuck if I know. But that's down the line. I can't answer that right now. All I can do now is what's in front of me. We get out of the jungle. We figure out who ordered the snatch. We figure out us. We figure out what then... then."

"And you want me to soften up out here? Let you in, out here? When our lives are on the line. When I have to be on my A-game every moment?"

"You don't have to be on your A-game every moment.

When we get to Bogotá, yeah, we'll have to lock our shit down. Someone catches up to us, we'll handle them. But in the meantime, in the moments like this when it's just us, you can set Scar aside and learn how to be a little softer with me."

She looks at me. "Fucking terrified of that, Sol."

"I know."

"What if…" she swallows hard. "What if you don't *like* the softer me? What if soft me gets us killed? What if I give you soft me and I never get my edge back?"

"What if I love the softer side of you?" I shoot back. "What if I *can* handle everything you are? What if I *can* love the badass as much as I can love the woman in you?"

"I'm always a woman, Sol. Just because I'm not soft doesn't mean I'm not a woman."

"That's not what I meant."

"Sounded like it. You know how often I get that? How many people assume I'm a lesbian or act like I'm less of a woman because of who I am and what I do?"

I wince. "I'm sorry. I didn't mean it like that. I know you're a woman."

She sighs. "I know what you meant. Scar is one of the guys."

"I've never lost sight of who you are, you know." I turn my hand so our palms touch. Tangle our fingers together. "I see you. I just…I think you can be more without losing who you already are."

She looks at our hands. Then at me. "Maybe…" she swallows hard. "Maybe I can try."

I squeeze her hand. "This *is* you trying, Scarlett. This is a step—a *big* first step. I'm not asking for everything all at once."

"This is scary enough as it is." She squeezes my hand back. Rubs her thumb against the knuckle of my index finger. "But I'll try. Be a pussy if I didn't, and I'm no pussy. Just..." her voice drops to a whisper. "Just don't drop me, Sol."

"I lost you once, Scarlett. I won't ever let that happen again."

She just nods.

But she doesn't let go of my hand.

CHAPTER 6

WHAT ARE YOU AFRAID OF?

NIGHT FALLS, AND WITH IT, A SOFT WARM RAIN. We park on the road, engine off, and listen to the rain going tick-tick-tick-tick on the roof.

"The money guy was my way out," I say after an hour of silence.

Sol says nothing. Waits. He's stretched out as much as possible, hands folded on his belly, eyes closed; I know he's listening.

"He was obsessed with me," I continue. "Twice a week turned to three, and then four, and then every day. The more I pretended to like him, the more obsessed he became. Eventually, he bought me. Fifty thousand US dollars—that was the value they put on my life. Fifty grand. He paid in cash and smuggled me into the US. He had a false rear bench in his van. It opened up with a secret latch, and there was a space for a person to hide. It was hot and stuffy and loud and smelled fucking awful. He took me to Texas, to his home. He locked me in his basement and..." I choke. "It was a very nice prison. No roaches, no mice, no ants. I only had to let him fuck me. He fed me three times a day. I had a real bathroom with a real shower—something

I'd never even seen before. He never hit me. He…he liked to pretend we were a couple. He brought a TV down and made me cuddle with him and watch telenovelas."

"Fucking weird."

"Right? He was this fifty-year-old dude, not ugly or anything, but just…weird. Obsessed with me. He'd bring me dresses and lingerie and make me pretend like I was a model. He wanted me to speak like a little girl. Soft, quiet, submissive. He had all these rules. I always followed them because he…he'd get this look in his eye. Crazy eyes. Killer eyes. I didn't understand it at the time, just knew that it scared me shitless, so I did what he said. Now I know it was the eyes of a killer. Not like you and me are killers, though. Someone who gets off on murdering people. I think…I think some part of me recognized that. I think I knew that eventually he was gonna kill me."

"How'd you get away?" he asks, eyes closed.

"He was getting erratic. Making weirder and weirder demands. Dress up and play with puppets, and lick his feet and all sorts of weird shit. And he'd get pissed really fast if I so much as hesitated. He…" I let out a breath. "He tried to rape me…anally. That was my breaking point. I fought him. Kicked him off me and fought for my life. To this day, that's the hardest kill I've ever made. I got him in a leglock and choked him to fucking death. But fucking god, he wouldn't *die*. I had to choke him for fucking *minutes*. Maybe I wasn't strong enough, I don't know. I got dressed and raided the upstairs for anything I could carry. A backpack and food and as much random shit as I could fit. And I fucking ran."

"Goddamn, Scar."

"I was in that basement for a year."

He opens his eyes finally and looks at me. "A fucking *year*?"

I nod. "I remember seeing a newspaper from a distance at a gas station once he had me across the border. I noticed the date. When I got out, I saw another newspaper. I was in that monster's basement for one year, two months, one week, and six days."

"So…you were never an illegal immigrant."

"Not by choice. I was brought across the border against my will. I had no identification. I don't think I was ever even on any records in Panama. I've never existed."

"What'd you do?"

"Begged. Starved. Suffered. Walked a fucking lot." I sigh. "About six months after I escaped, I was walking around some shitty part of El Paso. It was late. Dark. A car drove past me. I was walking along a wall in the shadows, so I guess they didn't see me. Turns out, I stumbled across a secret meeting between a CIA agent and an informant from south of the border. And I saw them. Heard everything. The agent didn't notice me himself until after his informant left. I didn't know what I'd seen at the time, obviously, only that I knew it was something I wasn't supposed to see. And then I accidentally kicked something. Gave myself away. The agent had a gun to my head in seconds. But it was obvious right away that I was just some homeless girl. I guess he took pity on me. I dunno. He brought me to an all-night diner and bought me food and pumped me for information. I told him everything. My family dying. Luisa. Being a captive. Everything. I guess he saw something in me because he brought me to his boss. That's how I went from illegal homeless immigrant and former sex slave to CIA agent. They made me a whole identity. Helped me pick my name. The works. Put me through testing and training. Eventually ended up a field agent working south of the border, turning informants—making double agents out of cartel informers. Got into wet work by accident. I was meeting another agent and a senior case officer when we were ambushed. The senior case officer was impressed with how I handled myself in the gunfight and recommended me to Chad, and you know the rest."

"Fucking Chad," he says.

"Fucking Chad," I agree.

"Sol?"

He opens his eyes and looks at me. "You were the first person I had voluntary sex with."

He frowns. "What?"

I nod, shrug. "Yep. After what I'd been through, I sort of turned off my sexuality. Wanted nothing to do with it. Couldn't. It wasn't until I met you that I even knew what it felt like to be attracted to someone."

He looks at me thoughtfully. "Makes sense why it was such a fight to get you to sleep with me. I thought you were just playing hard to get."

"Wasn't playing. I was scared out of my fucking mind. I had no idea what I was doing. What I wanted. What it was supposed to feel like."

"I wish you'd fucking told me, Scarlett," he murmurs. "I'd have done things so much differently. I had no idea. You seemed so strong, so fearless, so confident."

"I'm a good actress. I didn't trust you. I didn't want anyone to know what I'd been through. I was ashamed. Fuck, I still am."

"Ashamed? Of being a victim?"

"I'm not a fucking victim," I snarl at him. "Horrible shit was done to me. But I'm not a goddamned *victim*."

"I don't understand that, Scar. What's wrong with understanding that you were victimized?"

"I *do* understand. But identifying yourself as a victim comes with a weight I *do not* want. If I think of myself as a victim, the weight of everything I went through will crush me. So therefore I'm not a victim. I'm a survivor. A fighter. I fought my way across the Darien Gap. I fought my way across Central America. I fought to stay alive in that whorehouse. I fought to stay alive in that basement. I fought Alejandro and I won. I fought to stay alive on the streets of El Paso. I fought to the top of my class at the Farm. I have had to fight for everything I am, everything I have, every moment of every day my whole life. I'm a fucking warrior, not a fucking victim."

"That I get," he whispers. "But Scarlett, you don't have to fight when you're with me. You can let your guard down. You can relax."

I bark a laugh. "Relax. Good one, Sol."

He turns to face me on the bench seat. "Close your eyes."

I look at him. "Why?"

He arches an eyebrow at me. "Call it an exercise in trust."

I let out a slow breath and then force my eyes closed. "Now what?"

"Now breathe. Just…breathe. In through your nose, out through your mouth. Eyes closed."

"I understand how breathing works, Sol."

"Then shut the fuck up and do it."

I snort. "Fine. Breathing."

I settle more comfortably into the seat, lace my fingers across my stomach, and breathe as he instructs.

"I'm going to touch you," he murmurs. "Don't react. Don't do anything. Just keep your eyes closed and breathe."

I feel myself tensing. "Sol…"

"Trust me."

I feel everything tense inside me. This is Sol, but I'm still nervous. What's he going to do? I need to know.

Instead, I focus on breathing. In for four, hold it for seven, out for eight. Eyes closed. Trust him.

A single fingertip touches the center of my forehead. Traces down my nose. It's gentle, a ghost of a touch. Pauses at the tip. Back to my third eye and down to the tip of my nose again.

I'm breathing hard—not quite panting, but long, deep breaths that I'm not in control of.

"Relax and breathe, Scarlett."

"Trying."

This time, his fingertip trails down my nose, over my philtrum, and then pauses on my lips. Traces my lips from one side to the other and back to center.

My skin tightens and tingles. My heart pitter-patters.

His palm, large and warm and rough, cradles my cheek. Slides down my neck, pauses, loosely circling my throat—it takes every ounce of self-control not to break his arm. I focus on breathing. On his touch.

He slides his hand down the outside of my arm. His fingers slide between mine.

"What are you doing, Sol?" I whisper.

He doesn't answer.

Instead, he lifts my hand, and I feel his lips touch the

center of my palm. He kisses me there, and my whole body twitches at the delicate touch of his lips.

"Easy, Scar. Just breathe. Relax."

"How can I relax when I don't know what you're going to do?" I ask.

He laughs. "Exactly. You don't." He skates his touch back up my arm to my shoulder and then cups my face again. "Do you think I'm going to hurt you?"

"No."

"Does it feel like I'm making a move? Trying to get into your pants?"

"That'd be easier to deal with."

"I know." His thumb ghosts over my lips again. How do I know it's his thumb and not a finger? I just do. "Trust me, Scarlett."

"Fucking hard."

"You trust me in a gunfight."

"Yeah, but—"

"If some tango had you in a chokehold with a gun to your head, would you trust me to take the shot?"

"Absolutely."

"If you were running through a building, and I was on the radio telling you where to turn, and I told you to jump out of a window, would you?"

"Without hesitation."

"You *do* trust me."

"Sol…"

His palm goes to my cheek again. "So trust me in this, babe."

His hand slides down. Palm over the hollow at the base of my throat. Fingers circling my throat—gentle, delicate…even affectionate. Yet, my pulse pounds frantically.

"Sol," I gasp.

"Eyes closed. Breathe."

"Sol. Stop. Let go."

"Am I hurting you?"

"No, but…"

"Would I *ever* choke you out?"

"No."

His touch tightens just a little. Holding, now. His fingers are against my pulse point, so he must feel how frantically it's pounding.

"Sol," I gasp.

"It's me, babe. Just me. You can breathe. You know you can break my wrist in a split second. So what are you afraid of?"

"I…I don't know."

"You can lie to yourself, but you can't lie to me."

"I like it," I whisper. "I don't want to like it."

"Why not?"

"Submission."

"You're not submitting. You're allowing me to touch you. You're still in control." He cups my face again, brushes his thumb over my lips. Cradles my throat in his hand again.

"You're in control, I whisper."

"Am I?"

"Yes."

"How?"

"You have your hand around my throat. One squeeze and I'm dead."

"But you know I won't."

Panic is building. A memory. Something I've blocked out is coming back. Tears burn behind my eyes.

"Let go, Sol. Please let go. It hurts. I don't like it. I don't—I don't like it."

His touch is gone. He takes my hand and guides it to his throat. "You try."

I try to pull away, but he holds onto my hand. "Sol. No."

"Tell me what you're afraid of, Scarlett."

"Maria was weak. She had no control." It's barely a whisper. I'm shaking. Trying like hell not to cry—I haven't cried in twenty years. Not since Mama, Hector, and Daniela died.

"Tell me." He guides my hand to his throat, presses on my hand with his. "Tell me what he did to Maria."

"He…his name was Alejandro. He…" Tears leak out.

"Tell me. Tell me everything he did to Maria."

"He made me feel things. At first, I only pretended. The other girls did it, too, at the whorehouse. We talked about it at night, after. How to fake what they wanted to hear. I faked it. But then when he brought me to the basement, he…it was different. He touched me. And…it…it felt….good."

"Your body felt it. Nothing wrong with that. It's normal."

"It's *not*. I was a prisoner. A slave. But he was patient. He knew when I was faking, and he'd stop. He wanted it to be real."

"So you let it be real."

"Yes."

"Tell me."

"He would touch me. He'd…he'd get me right there. And then he'd choke me. Right when I was about to pass out, he'd let go and make me come all at once. It was scary. The relief, the…the orgasm. It was too much."

I find myself squeezing his throat and force myself to let go. "I forgot about that. Till just now. I blocked it out."

"You had no control. If you hadn't forced yourself to give him what he wanted, he would've killed you. You knew that instinctively and did what you had to do to survive. That was you fighting, Scarlett."

"Didn't feel like fighting. Felt like giving up."

I take his hand and bring it to my throat. Open my eyes and meet his gaze—green eyes, soft, gentle, understanding. This is Solomon, the man. No longer WindWalker. Not the man I used to know. Someone new.

I hold his hand against my throat, my hand on his. "You're not him."

"No, because you chose your moment, and you fucking killed him."

"My first kill."

"Always the hardest."

"What was yours?" I ask.

"First op on a kill squad after transitioning from analytics. Orders were to take out a cartel assassin who'd killed a judge and fled to Belize. Shot a guard from fifty paces away. Snap. So fucking easy. He just dropped. It didn't register till much later after the op. I threw up. Didn't sleep for three days afterward, kept seeing the guy fall."

His hand on my throat feels like affection, somehow, now. Just telling him…did something. Changed something inside me.

"Sol…" I whisper, looking at him. "I've never talked about any of this. Not to anyone except the agent who recruited me, and he died in Afghanistan five years ago."

"I've got you, Scarlett."

"Scarier than any gunfight."

"I know."

"Tell me something you've never told anyone." I touch his lips with my fingertips.

His lips are soft. Damp. Touching them like this, gently, reverently, tenderly...I've never touched anyone like this.

"I killed a kid. In Iraq." His voice is a low growl. "We were hunting a warlord. Had his location narrowed down to a block in Baghdad. Rounded a corner, and this kid was in the middle of the street. Maybe six. Little boy. He had a gun. A pistol. He could barely hold it with both hands. Pointed it at me. I...I meant to wing him at best. Make him drop the stupid thing. Not like he could hit me, could barely hold it. He was so small. Why'd he have a fucking gun? Who gives a six-year-old a fucking gun?" His voice is tight and harsh. "He moved. Last second, right as I fired, he threw the gun down and ran...took the round to the fucking skull. If he'd just stayed where he was or even moved in any other fucking direction, I'd have shot the gun out of his stupid little hands or just plain missed. But he moved wrong. It was an accident. I have nightmares about that kid all the goddamned time. Never talked about it with my squad, in a psych eval, nothing. Ever. Not till now."

"Fucking hell, Sol."

"That was the hardest one. First kill was just shock. But that fucking kid, man." He flops back in his seat, head smacking the headrest. "We completed the mission. Went back the same way, and the kid's body was gone. Heard a woman crying. Sobbing. Never heard a sound like that before or since, the way that woman was crying. I'd do fucking *anything* to take that back. Let the kid shoot me. Fuck me, man. Fuck me."

"Been there. Everyone is a combatant. You don't know who has a gun. Who has a bomb vest. Who's gonna toss a grenade at you. IEDs everywhere. Every step, every room, every civilian…some kid has a gun on you, what are you supposed to do?" I touch his shoulder.

He looks at me. Green eyes are damp. Full of agony. "He was just a goddamn kid. *Why?*"

"You know there's no answer to that."

"I know. Can't help asking, though."

His shoulder is thick and dense under my hand. Flashes of memory skitter across my mind: Sol, above me, limned by the red dawn sun, moving over me, in me. My hands on his shoulders as he fucks me slowly. Hair loose and messy and sweat-wet. Grinning. Panting into the side of my neck.

"Tell me," he murmurs.

He can read me so damn easily. I shake my head. "No."

"Scarlett."

I can't help brushing his hair off his forehead. Something else I've never done. I'm a total stranger to tenderness. "Thinking of us. Remembering." I swallow hard, touch his shoulder again. "How I used to hold on to your shoulders."

His eyes light up. "I remember."

"You'd have nail marks for days."

"I always had them, Scarlett. That was your thing. Digging your nails into my shoulders while I fucked you."

I look out the window at the darkness. "One of us should sleep."

He snorts. "As if either of us could."

"I couldn't."

"Me either."

He faces me. His other hand drifts across the space between us. Rests on my knee.

I just look at him. Wait. Hold his eyes.

His hand slides up my leg to midthigh, pauses. His gaze dares me to stop him. I can't. I won't. Don't want to. Not now.

Further up, until his fingers catch against my crotch, against the seam of my pants.

Another pause. I just hold his gaze, breathing slowly.

Up. Fingers nudge my shirt up, baring a sliver of belly. Find flesh, and my skin pebbles at his touch.

I have no idea what he's going to do, what he wants, what I want. He asked me to trust him, and I do. I always have. Fuck, I came to this fucking jungle for him when I wasn't even sure it was him. I came on a thin hope.

Whatever this is, then, I'll play along.

He finds the button closure of my pants. Flips it open. Tugs the zipper down. My heart starts pounding.

"Breathe, Scarlett," he murmurs.

"Trying."

"Yes or no?" His hand is flat on my bare belly, fingers at the waistband of my utilitarian black briefs.

"Yes," I breathe.

"Then close your eyes and just breathe. Trust me."

I close my eyes and go back to slow breathing, counting each breath, fighting the panic. Why am I panicking? This is Sol.

"Why am I so scared right now?" I whisper.

"I don't know. Why are you?" He runs his fingers from hipbone to hipbone, fingertips under the elastic.

"Because it's you," I answer. "But everything is different."

"How is it different?"

"It's not just sex anymore." I put my hands over my face. "I don't know. It meant something to me before, Sol. I swear it did."

"For me too."

'But this is different." I swallow hard. "Tom was my last. And that was four months ago."

"You're in control, Scarlett." He pulls my hand from my face and guides it to his hand. I grip his wrist. "Show me what you want, Scarlett. More, or less?"

My lungs are tight, like there's a band around my chest. It's so stupid—this is Sol, he knows my body. I trust him. But…god, I'm scared. I'm scared of letting this go further and…and what? Falling in love? I was already in love with him.

"I was in love with you," I whisper.

"I know."

"That's why I'm scared. It ended. I lost you. I fell in love and I lost you. And it fucking hurt, Sol. It hurt so god-damned bad." Grip his wrist hard. Swallow. "And then I find out you were alive the whole fucking time. I get why. I understand. It makes sense. It was the only choice you could have made. But I still feel angry that you weren't dead. It makes no sense and I know it, but it's how I feel."

"So be angry at me." A pause. "Look at me, Scarlett."

I look. His eyes are shining with too many things to name.

"I'm sorry. I didn't mean to abandon you. But you got hurt anyway, and I'm sorry."

I swallow hard around a hot lump. "Fuck you, Solomon."

"I'm sorry, Scar."

"Fuck you."

"I'm sorry."

"Fuck you for dying."

"I'm sorry."

"Fuck you for leaving me alone in this stupid, cruel, violent world. Fuck you for living without me. Fuck you being able to live without me. Fuck you for finding comfort with Violet and not me. Fuck you for letting me… for…for—" It's hard to let the words out and hard to stop them at the same time. "For letting me be with Tom. For letting me feel good with someone else. Fuck you. Fuck you. Fuck you."

Stupid hot fat tears slip down my cheeks. I can't stop them. I grip Sol's wrist in both hands and push downward. His fingers slip under the elastic of my underwear and find skin, find the soft thatch of trimmed hair over my seam. I've never been a shave-it-all girl. Sol told me once he liked it this way, and I've kept it like this ever since.

"Sol, "I whisper.

His long middle finger fits against my seam. "Scarlett."

I fit my hand over his and guide his finger inside me. "Make me feel something else, Solomon."

"Something other than what, babe?"

"Afraid of loving you and losing you again."

I gasp, then, as his finger delves inside me, finding me soft and wet and ready.

"Eyes on mine, sweetheart," he whispers. "Don't look away. Look at me while I make you come."

I whimper softly as he curls his finger inside me and

withdraws it. Slides it back in. Deeper. Fuck, I forgot how good it feels when he touches me. No one knows my body like he does. How to touch me. My body doesn't respond to anyone like it does him.

"Sol," I whisper.

He just gives me that arrogant half-grin of his, the one that says he knows exactly how he's making me feel, and he likes it. "Breathe, Scarlett. Keep breathing."

I suck in a breath and realize only then that I was holding it. "Sol, fuck. Please."

"Please what, Scarlett?"

I slink down on the bench and angle sideways, my back wedged into the corner between the door and bench, head tipped back. I crush my fingers around his thick, strong wrist. Torn between yanking his hand away and begging for more, I can only hold on and hope he knows what I want, what I need, when I clearly fucking don't.

"I don't know," I admit.

His finger curls into me again, delving into my wet center. He shifts closer, torso angled to face me. He nuzzles his nose against my cheek. "When was the last time you came?"

"I don't know."

"A week ago? A month ago?"

"Weeks. Maybe a month."

"Did you make yourself come?"

"Yes."

"Was it good?"

"No. Not really."

"When was the last time someone else made you come?"

"Months. Tom. It...he..." I trail off, uncertain how much he really wants to hear.

"He what, babe? Tell me."

"It was better than on my own, but..."

"But what?"

"No one has ever been able to make me come like you, Sol."

His breath washes over my ear, hot and slow. His lips touch the sensitive skin behind my earlobe. The side of my neck. My skin pebbles, tightens, and my core pulses around his finger.

"You want me to make you come?" He plunges his finger in and out of me a few times, slow and teasing. Adds a second finger, middle and ring, diving in and curling, withdrawing, slicking back in with a soft wet squelch.

I whimper as his palm brushes over my clit. "Yes," I whisper. "I want to. I want you to."

He slides his fingers out of me and draws them over my clit, smearing my wetness over the tender, erect bundles of hypersensitive nerves. I gasp as lightning sears through me, forcing my hips to drive upward against his touch.

"So fucking wet, Scar." His words drop against my ear, and I pulse, gushing more arousal.

"Sol," I groan.

"Give me your tits, Scarlett," he orders.

I rip my shirt up, dragging my tight, plain black sports bra with it. My tits spring free, and immediately Sol's mouth covers one, teeth scraping my skin, tongue flicking greedily against my hard nipple. At the same time, his fingers press onto my clit and swirl. A soft cry escapes my lips. He sucks on my nipple, transfers to the other breast and grazes my nipple with his teeth while his fingers fly side to side against my clit. The striking lightning becomes a crescendo of intense pleasure that drags another clenched-teeth scream out of me, stars bursting behind my eyes, hips flexed up, buttocks tensed, stomach sucked in, chest thrust out, head thrown back.

"Scream for me, Scarlett," he growls, his words rough against my damp nipple, which he licks, suckles, and then nips hard enough to elicit a surprised yelp from me. "Who's making you come?"

"You," I breathe.

"Say my name. Scream my name for the whole jungle to hear, Scarlett. Tell everyone who makes you come."

He drives two fingers inside me, fucks me with them once, twice, three times, and then smears my essence over my clit and brushes his fingers in a wild, frenetic circle while his tongue flicks against my nipple.

My orgasm breaks open inside me all at once, and I feel my pussy spasming, clenching around nothing, and a scream rips out of me. "*SOL!*" I scream. "Sol, oh fuck, fuck, fuck, Sol!"

I can't breathe, can't draw a breath, can't scream—I can only ride the waves of ecstasy as they ripple through me. He bites my nipple again, thrusting his fingers deep inside me, and another spasm wracks me as my inner walls clutch his driving fingers, and I push my hips against him, sucking in a shuddering, gasping breath...only to be wracked yet again. And again. and again.

Wrecked by the orgasm, I pant and whimper as the aftershocks keep me quivering. I pull his hand up and away, forcing my eyes open.

His grin is arrogant and satisfied. He puts his fingers in his mouth and licks them clean.

A surge of exhaustion hits all at once, and my eyelids grow heavy. Sol sees it and sits up. Pats his thighs. "Lay down, honey."

"Sol…"

He tugs his pistol free and lays it on his thigh. "I'll keep watch. Put your head down and rest. I've got you."

"But what about you?" I rest my hand on his zipper, which is bulging with the strain of his trapped erection.

He pulls me around, bodily turning me and guiding my head onto his lap. "Plenty of time for that later, Scar. For now, close your eyes and rest. I've got you."

"I don't wanna leave you hanging," I protest, even as my eyes drift close, drowsiness starting to swallow me whole.

"You're not. I'm fine. This was about you. Only you."

"Sol, I…"

His fingers graze through my hair—my hat came off at some point during the last few minutes. "Hush, Scarlett. I've got you. Rest."

I let myself drift, then, choosing to trust him. His fingers trail through my hair, stroking softly and slowly, affectionately, soothing.

He's got me.

Satisfied yet aching with arousal, I slip into sleep.

CHAPTER 7

ALL THE SWEET I'VE GOT

I ALLOW MYSELF TO CATCH A FEW MINUTES OF REST here and there as Scarlett sleeps. I'm never fully asleep—I'm too well trained, even years out of full-time operator status, for that to happen.

God, I forgot how fucking gorgeous she is when she comes. She gave herself over to me so willingly, and it was fucking beautiful. A peek at the woman within the operator. A look within the walls.

I want more. A lot fucking more.

My cock hasn't fully subsided, even hours later. Not with her on my lap like this. I focus on the sounds around us—the windows are closed to keep the biting bugs out, making it a bit stifling in here, but that's better than being eaten alive. Still, I can hear the night sounds, chirring and chirping, hooting and rustling. A shadow of something slinks across the road, pausing halfway across for a moment before scurrying off into the shadows.

Drowse.

Blink awake, assess: all is still quiet.

Scarlett slumbers on my lap, and I wouldn't disturb this moment for anything.

She rolls on the bench, putting her cheek on my thighs, millimeters from my painfully constricted dick.

I do my best to ignore it.

Drowse.

The night sounds halt all at once, and I come fully awake, clicking the safety off my pistol and checking mirrors. Nothing. But the sounds have gone silent.

It's the start of dawn, darkness fading into dim gray; a slender figure appears on the road—a male from an indigenous tribe. He looks right at me. I look at him. My heart pounds as he moves silently toward me. I keep my gun out of sight as he approaches the window. Looks in. He sees the rifles, the sleeping form of Scarlett, my pistol on my thigh, finger along the barrel. He's young, but his eyes are mature and hard. Assessing. Deciding. Without a word, he vanishes into the jungle again, and a few minutes later, the song of waking birds and beasts replaces the night sounds.

I let out my pent breath.

The last thing we need is the local indigenous population pissed off at us.

Another hour passes, marking about three since Scarlett fell asleep on my lap. She stirs, making a quiet grumbling sound. Her eyes pop open and lift to mine.

"How long was I out?"

"A bit more than three hours."

"Anything?"

"Indigenous hunter checked us out and went on his way. That's it."

Her head still on my lap, she just looks up at me. Her eyes, still a bit sleepy, are as unguarded as I've ever seen them. Bright, happy, and aroused.

She moves her hand from beneath her cheek to resting on my zipper.

"Scar, we don't have to go there." I tuck a tendril of thick, glossy black hair behind her ear.

"Maybe I want to." She fiddles with the button of my jeans. "Maybe I've missed you."

I feel my cock responding, going from the state of semi-arousal I've been in for the last three hours to an excruciating hardening, blocked from unfurling by the zipper.

I ghost my fingertips over her cheekbone, tracing the shell of her ear, the delicate curve of her lips. "Do what you want, babe. I won't stop you. But do it for you. I want you to be comfortable with how things happen between us."

"I'm not comfortable with anything, Sol. All I know is you're here. You're alive. I have you back. I'm scared to fucking death of how different and intense my feelings are this time around, but I'm no pussy. As long as you can promise me you won't die on me or abandon me again, no matter fucking what, I'm game. I'm all in."

"Can't promise I won't die, but I will promise you I will fight as hard as I can to stay alive, and I can promise you I won't abandon you again, no matter what."

"I'm still scared as hell. I don't know how to do this— what this is, what I'm doing. What we are. I'm scared."

"Me too. But I've got you, Scar. No matter what, I've fuckin' got you."

She licks her lips. Turns her gaze from mine to my zipper. "This doesn't look comfortable." Her finger traces the line of the zipper, bulging with the strain of my cock.

"It's not," I growl.

"I might have a solution."

"Oh yeah?"

She smirks, still lying on my lap. Twists the button of my fly open, draws the zipper down. A breath of relief escapes as my cock pushes through the opening—I'm commando under the jeans. I close my eyes and let out a long sigh as Scarlett teases her fingernail down the curved outline of my cock.

"Get it out for me, Sol," she whispers. "Let me see that big, beautiful cock of yours."

I lift my butt off the bench and shove my jeans down past my ass.

"I've really, *really* missed *this*," she murmurs, clasping my aching cock in her hand.

I groan at the feel of her soft small strong fingers wrapping around my hot, hard flesh.

"When was the last time you came, Sol?" she asks, holding me near the top, rubbing he thumb over the very tip.

"Few days before they grabbed me."

"Was it Violet?"

I shake my head. "No. I jerked off."

"What were you thinking about?" She glides her hand down my shaft. "Tell me the truth."

"You," I answer.

Her eyes meet mine, surprised. "Me? For real?"

I nod. "Yeah, for real."

"Tell me."

I groan as she pumps my length slowly a few times. "I was thinking of that day in Santiago, a couple months before Caracas. We were waiting for the final orders to come down. Holed up in that hotel, remember?"

She smiles, caressing my length a few more times before pausing at the top again, twisting her fist around me and then rubbing the precum-weeping tip with her thumb. "I remember. We did a lot in that hotel. What specifically were you thinking about?"

"I went out to get coffee and breakfast. Second day we were there. You were asleep when I left. Came back, and you were just waking up. Naked from fucking the night before. The covers were off. So fuckin' beautiful, Scarlett— long legs rubbing together. Tight little tits begging for me to grab 'em. I could tell you wanted me from the way you looked at me."

"What'd I do, Sol?"

"I set the coffee and the bag with our breakfast on the side table and kissed you. I was gonna fuck you, but you had other ideas. You unzipped me and pulled my jeans down. Slipped off the bed and got on your knees."

She gazes at me with a sultry, aroused grin on her face. "What'd I do then?"

She pumps me again, watching her hand slide up and down my length. Pulls my shaft away from my torso and runs the fat flat of her tongue against my tip in a long, slow lick.

I groan, shuddering all over. "Fuck, Scar. Feels so fucking good."

"What did I do next, Sol?"

"Took me in your hot little mouth."

"Like this?" She fits her lips to my head and swirls her tongue around me, ripping a growl from me as a climax builds in my balls.

"Fuck," I growl. "Yeah, babe. Just like that."

She pulls away with a wet popping sound. "Was that all I did?"

"No."

"Then tell me, Sol. Tell me what I did." She strokes my length a few times, eyes on mine. "Did I lick it like this?"

She runs her tongue up the underside from the base to the tip.

"Ahhh fuck, honey. No. You…fuck, fuck." I throw my head back as she takes my shaft sideways in her mouth, sliding her lips and tongue all over me. "You…you—"

"What, Sol?" she whispers. "I wanna know. Tell me what I did so I can do it again. Need you to refresh my memory."

"You took me deep, sweetheart. You fucked me with your mouth."

She grins at me, shifting upright. "Then I'm gonna need a better angle. Lay down for me, Sol."

I stretch out on the bench as far as I can, and Scarlett yanks my jeans down around my ankles as she kneels astride me on the bench. She hovers over me, hands on my chest and trailing down to my belly. Her lips follow, starting at my chest, kissing the muscle before flicking my nipples with her tongue. Kisses a line down my torso to my navel, hands resting on my hipbones. Shifts lower. Her hands drift to my thighs, and her mouth stutters against my cock, lips bumping the tip. She spends a few moments like that, hands rubbing up my thighs and over my belly while her mouth presses soft wet kisses to my cock, dotting them down the shaft to my balls and then back up. Climax boils in my balls, but I hold it back, not wanting this to end too soon.

And then, without build-up, she slides me into her mouth and down her throat, gasping and whimpering and then gulping noisily.

"Fuck, Scar, fuck—just like that. So fucking hot, watching you take my cock like that."

She backs away and I pop free of her mouth, a string of saliva connecting us. She grasps me in both hands and strokes my length, twisting her hands in opposing directions on the way down and then taking me in her mouth and sliding down on me once more.

"Fuck," I snarl, gathering her hair in my hands. "Nothing has ever felt the way you make me feel, babe. Nothing. No one. *Ever.*"

She strokes me faster, then, looking up at me. "Gonna come for me, Sol?"

"You want it?" I ask.

"Yeah," she whispers. "I do. I fucking want it."

"Where?" I ask. "You gonna swallow it all, honey?"

She hums as she fits my throbbing head in her mouth again, rolling fast shallow bobs until my hips give me away, flexing and bucking.

"You taste so fucking good, Sol," she whispers. "Love your cock. Fucking love it. Missed it so damn bad. Missed the way you feel. The way you taste. Missed having your big, perfect cock ramming down my throat."

"Show me, Scar. Let me see you take my cock down your throat."

"Watch," she whispers, and takes me in her mouth, teases a few shallow strokes, and then goes down until I feel her throat rippling around me.

I grip her hair and hold her there until she pulls away with a gasp, panting.

"So fucking big," she mutters, caressing my length with both hands. "I can barely take it all."

I'm right at the edge, and I know she knows. Her eyes

light up as I hiss and growl, hips pushing my pulsing, aching cock into her hands.

Something squeals outside, and a car door opens and thunks closed.

"Fuck," she mutters. Pops up to peek over the back of the bench. "Company." She winks at me, kissing the tip of my cock. "Got it. Stay here—don't move."

"Scar," I start, but she's already twisting to shove open the passenger door, palming her pistol.

I stare down my body, cock out and throbbing and glistening with her saliva as she exits the car. Her pants are still undone.

"Hey boys," she says in Spanish. "Look."

She has her pistol hidden behind her thigh as she uses her other hand to lift her shirt, flashing whoever it is.

And then her pistol flashes up, free hand slapping into a Weaver stance—BANGBANG!—BANGBANG!—BANGBANG!

"Ha," she snorts, dropping the stance to stand normally, righting her shirt. "Dumbasses."

She turns to look at me, grinning. "Now. Where was I?"

She crawls onto the bench, leaving the door open. Sets the pistol on the floor near to hand and gathers my cock in her hands, tilting me toward her.

I'm harder than ever, and she knows it. "That turn you on, Sol?"

"Fuck yeah it did," I answer, and then groan as she bends over me and wraps those lips around me again.

"Told you your edge won't go anywhere," I say. "You can be sexy and badass at the same time."

She bobs on me a few times and then lets me slip out

of her mouth, grinning at me as she strokes my length, slowly at first and then faster and faster. "You were right."

I'm seconds from the edge, but something keeps me from letting go.

It takes a second to identify what it is: I don't want the first time I've come since our reunion to be like this, in a car, down her throat. As hot as it is, I want more. I'm all about letting her suck me off—fuck, it feels incredible. Obviously. But I need her to know that this isn't just sex. It's not just physical.

I groan in agony as I pull her hands away and lever upright, ignoring her surprised resistance.

"Sol, what—" She starts.

I slash my mouth over hers, devouring her protest, capturing her tongue. I shift forward toward the open door, taking her with me.

"Sol, what are you doing?" she asks, instinctively wrapping her arms around my neck and her legs around my waist.

"Not coming down your throat right now, that's what," I growl. "Been more than three fucking years since I've had you, and our first time together won't be like that, I can guarantee you that shit, babe."

"But I wanted to," she whispers, reaching down to plunge her fist onto my raging erection. "I wanted to taste you. I wanted it."

"You'll get it. This time, sweetheart, I need *you*."

I spin and pin her against the side of the battered old SUV, ignoring the three bodies in the road not twenty yards away. I shove her shirt and bra up, baring her tight, firm little tits, palming one while supporting her with the other under her ass.

"Sol," she gasps as I bury my face in her breasts. "God."

I set her on her feet. Shove her pants down, then her black briefs. Lean into her, taking her mouth with another hungry kiss—I'm desperate, suddenly. Ravenous for her. I scour her mouth with my tongue, taste her, take her tongue. Touch her sweet hard little clit and get her gasping, dipping at the knees.

"Boots," she gasps, "can't … can't get my pants off."

"Fuck," I growl. Her combat boots will take a goddamned eternity to get off and back on. "I fucking need you, Scarlett. Right the fuck now."

"Sol," she starts, gasping as I relentlessly work her clit until she's whimpering and dancing on my finger, dipping and thrusting into my touch. "Fuck. I need you inside me, Sol."

"You covered?" I ask, my voice rough.

"IUD," she says through ragged panting breaths. "New one a month ago. We're covered."

I yank her off-balance so she falls against me. "I'm gonna show you romance, Scarlett. Show you how I feel about you."

Her eyes go soft at this. "Sol…"

"But not right now." I twist her in place and bend her forward over the bench seat.

She twists her head to look back at me over her shoulder. "Yes, Sol. Fuck me. I want it. I need you. I fucking need you, Sol."

I grip my cock and let her watch me stroke it. "This? You want it?"

She whimpers, pushing her ass up in the air. "Need it, Sol. Need that big hard cock inside me. Right the fuck now."

I reach up between her soft strong thighs and find her slit, find it wet and weeping for me. Fit me against her. Slide in a few inches, receiving a shrill, breathless gasp of shocked arousal.

"Can you take me, sweetheart?" I demand.

Her mouth hangs open, working silently as she tenses around me. "Fuck, Sol. Forgot how huge you are."

"Keep talking, beautiful. Tell me how it feels."

"Too fucking big," she breathes. "I…I can't. Can't take it."

I pull back just a little. "Should I stop?"

Her eyes go wide again with panic. "*No!* No. No. I want it. Just…ohhhh fuck, oh god, so big. Just…give me a second."

"Touch yourself, Scar. Touch your pussy."

I feel her shift, reaching one hand down to her clit. Her fingers swirl, nudging and bumping against my cock, and I feel her pussy ripple and pulse around me as she touches herself. "Just like that, darlin'. Keep touching yourself."

"Oh god, Sol. Give me more. I need more."

I grip her hips and then squeeze the taut bubble of her ass as I push in a little more.

She whines in her throat as I fill her, inch by inch. "Jesus, Sol. You get bigger since the last time?"

"Dunno, did I?"

"Feels like it," she breathes.

"Does it hurt?"

She groans as I give her more, going very carefully, watching her like a hawk. "No," she murmurs. "Feels perfect. Hurts so fucking good, Sol. So fucking good."

"Come for me, Scarlett. I need to feel you come around my cock."

Her fingers are flying now, and her pussy is spasming and pulsing around me, squeezing me as wave after wave surges through her, and then she's coming, crying out, pushing back into me and shaking, trembling, screaming.

"SOL!" She screams, her voice cracking as she comes. "Fuck me, baby. Fuck me. Fuck me, please please please, Sol, please fuck me."

Baby? She's never once used a term of endearment like that with me. Jokey nicknames like "hotshot," sure. "Baby?" Never.

My heart cracks and swells, but I know better than to call it out right now.

Later.

For now, I focus on her. On our connection. Her body wrapped around mine, pulsing as she came, so tight around me that I can barely move.

I drive in, and she cries out as I bottom out inside her, my hips slapping gently against her ass.

"Oh....*fuck*," she says in a guttural growl. "Yes, yes, *yes*, Sol. Fuck yes."

I pull back and then thrust in, *hard*. "Like that, honey?"

She cries out in a shrill, wordless wail as my aching, throbbing cock slides between the taut lips of her pussy. "Sol, fuck, fuck—yes, yes! Just like that. Don't stop. Don't you dare stop."

"Never," I answer, feeling her wet heat squeeze around me, feeling like heaven, like home.

"Come for me, Sol," she gasps. "Come inside me."

"Now?" I growl. "You gonna come with me?"

I feel the answer before she says it—I feel it in the mad pulsing of her pussy around me, in the way her flying fingers falter as they circle.

"Come, Sol! Come with me!" She screams. "Ohhhhh fuck, I'm coming, I'm coming—"

I grip a rough handful of her taut, tight, muscular ass, planting the other on the small of her back, and I unleash inside her with a guttural roar.

She screams in unison with me, and my head spins, vision blurring and doubling as an orgasm rips through me, making me shudder from head to toe and fuck into her as hard as I can, again and again, and her pussy rippling around me as she joins me in mutual climax only makes me come all the harder.

The sound of an engine breaks the moment; I glance dizzily toward it—a black pickup is barreling toward us, a man standing in the bed with an assault rifle aimed at us.

"Pistol," I growl.

She fumbles for it, finds it, and hands it back to me. Still buried fully inside Scarlett, I put four rounds into the engine and two more into the tires. One tire pops loudly, and the truck jerks as the driver overcorrects, and then the truck rolls. The bed gunner goes flying into the jungle, and the truck rolls to a stop, hissing white smoke from the engine.

"Fuck," I groan, smoothing my hand over her ass. " Interrupted again. Assholes."

She pushes back into me. "Sol, god, you feel so fucking good."

I bend over her, kissing up her back. "Better than I remember, and I remember every single moment with you, sweetheart."

"Let me up, now," she mutters. "I gotta go finish them off."

We both groan as I pull out, and she straightens to her feet, whimpering as her legs wobble. I catch her, hold her as she finds her balance.

She leans into me, nuzzling her nose against my chest. "Fucked me till I can't stand up straight," she says, laughing. "I forgot how that feels."

I like this new Scarlett—before, she was never affectionate. Rough affection, sure; playful, sure. Play fighting. Wrestling that turned to sex. Even sparring turned to sex. But after, she'd always pull off me, and that was that. No cuddling. No leaning into me. No hand resting on my chest as she catches her breath like she is now.

"Sol?" she murmurs, voice quiet and hesitant.

"Yeah, honey?"

"I called you baby."

"I know."

"I don't know where it came from."

"Me either. But I fucking love it, Scar. You calling me baby…it felt…" I trail off with a sigh, looking for the right way to put it. "I don't fuckin' know. Couldn't breathe for a second. Felt so fuckin' amazing, hearing that from you."

She looks up at me. "Really?"

I nod. Slide my hands down her bare spine, cup her ass. We're both standing beside the SUV with our pants around our ankles, three men dead in the road, a smoking truck half in the jungle, the occupants moaning in pain. Yet all I can think of is how much I love her body.

"This?" I cradle her head against my chest. "This is fucking *everything*, Scarlett. Holding you like this? It's… it's sweet. It's soft. It's fucking *everything*."

"Scary as fuck, is what it is," she whispers.

"What are you scared of?"

"That you'll forget about Scar. That you'll only see me as this, that you'll lose sight of the fact that I'm your partner, not just your…your girlfriend, or lover, or whatever."

I cup her chin and turn her face up to mine. "The first interruption, honey. Who handled it?"

"Me," she whispers.

"I trusted you to handle it." I point at the bodies. "And you did. Three tangos dropped in as many seconds, all six rounds right to the fuckin' T-box, like the goddamn pro you are."

"Are we fucked up?" she asks, giggling—a sound I've never heard out of her before. "I mean, who else has a gunfight while fucking?"

I laugh. "Not much of a gunfight if they don't get a round off," I answer. "But maybe we are fucked up. I don't much care."

"Me either." She bends and tugs her pants up with a grimace. "Not a fan of being squishy, though."

"Sorry, not sorry."

She laughs with me. "Hard to feel like a badass when I've got your come leaking out of me." She takes the pistol from me and goes up on her toes to kiss me. "When we finally get a bed, though, you're getting the wet spot."

"Deal," I say, letting her go.

I tug my jeans up and fasten them as Scarlett stalks across the road toward the upturned truck, stuffing her tits back into her bra and yanking her shirt down. She crouches near the shattered passenger window, pistol held sideways close to her chest. BAM!…BAM!…BAM!. Rising from her crouch, she strides to the jungle, peeking at the gunner—she holsters her gun, and I assume he's dead already.

The other vehicle is a Range Rover at least thirty years newer than the Nissan Patrol we've been driving; the engine is still idling with a smooth, well-tuned hum.

"We're trading up, Scar," I call. "I'll move our shit."

She's rummaging in the cab of the truck, pulling magazines, water bottles, a pack of smokes, a baggie of what's probably weed, and several handguns, as well as a long, heavy sniper rifle with a professional-grade scope.

She rises to her feet with the rifle. "Well now, here we fucking go," she murmurs. "Come to Mama."

I just laugh. "Happy, now? I know how you feel about a nice big gun."

She rolls her eyes at me. "Ha-ha. If you're fishing for another compliment on the size of your dick…" she slings the rifle from her shoulder and swaggers over to me, hips swaying, eyes sparking fire. "Then you're barking up the right tree." She smooshes herself against me, cupping me over my jeans. "You'd better get us to Bogotá on the fuckin' double, Solomon Cabot. Because I'm gonna need a whole hell of a lot more of your nice big gun."

"Have I unlocked a hitherto unexplored version of Scarlett Gutierrez?" I ask. "Because I like."

She kisses me and steps away. "You very well may have."

I scan our surroundings one more time. "We'd better get scarce."

"I'll grab the rifles and shit from the front, you get the stuff from the back," she orders.

"Yes ma'am," I say, grinning. "You should order me around more. It's kinda hot."

She straightens out of the driver's door of the Nissan, giving me a long blank stare as I lift the tailgate. "Sol, do not tempt me right now. We have to get moving, and we do *not* have time for any more funny business."

I give her a nice, crisp, snappy salute. "Ma'am, yes ma'am."

She flips me the bird. "You can call me ma'am when I'm riding your face. Otherwise, stuff it, bub."

"Who's tempting who, now?"

I transfer the gas cans to the back of the Range Rover and then the cooler and the water. A few minutes later, Scarlett is behind the wheel.

"Got the map?" I ask.

She hands it to me as she shoves the shifter into first, and we're off.

I feel her thinking, feel her considering her words.

"Why didn't you let me finish sucking you off?" she asks.

"As much as I love your mouth, I love being inside you a fuckuva lot more. I needed to connect with you." I wipe my face with a hand. "Honestly, I...I wanted our first time to be...not that."

"What'd you want it to be?" she asks, looking at me.

"In a bed, in a room. Private. Quiet. All the time in the world. I wanted to make love to you. Nice and slow. For hours."

"I liked what we did back there, Sol."

"Me too."

She twists her fist on the steering wheel. "I think...I don't think I'm ready for soft and sweet yet, Sol. You gotta take what you can get from me, and right now, I'm giving you all the sweet I've got."

"Didn't say soft and sweet, I said nice and slow."

"I know what you said, but I also know what you meant." She looks at me. "Give me time, okay? I'm trying, but…I can only handle so much change at once. It's really, really fuckin' scary being soft with you, Sol. It's hard and it's scary and part of me doesn't like it. Another part of me does, though, so it's…it's confusing, I guess."

I take her hand and tangle our fingers. "I hear you. And honestly, I didn't intend for things to turn sexual. I kinda meant to wait a while longer."

"Why?"

"Because with us, sex tends to take over. We have seriously combustible chemistry. And I want us to figure things out properly. I don't want to let sex take over and have all the shit we never really talked about fester."

She sighs. "Oh. I guess that makes sense. But I don't know that I can resist you, Sol. I was pushing you away because I was angry. I'm not angry anymore. I don't want to push you away. I want to figure this out with you."

"Then we'll just take it one step at a time, okay?"

She smiles at me. "Sounds good."

We lapse into a comfortable silence that lasts for a very long time, then, and the miles and the hours pass easily.

We're not far from Bogotá now. And I have a feeling this is where things are going to start getting very, very interesting because I have no clue why these dissidents snatched me or what they wanted. Who sent them?

I have a shitload of questions, and at some point, I'm going to get answers, one way or another.

CHAPTER 8

BOGOTÁ

BOGOTÁ IS A MASSIVE, SPRAWLING CITY ON THE roof of the world, eight and a half thousand feet above sea level; that's more than a mile and a half, for those bad at math. Like a lot of South American metropolises, it's an extraordinarily complex place. Home to ten million residents. For reference, New York City is home to twenty million; Bogotá has an area of about six hundred some square miles; NYC? 4600 square miles.

There's no metro. The streets and sidewalks are…not great. It's a dangerous place. Even getting in a cab can get you robbed. But there's a thriving nightlife. Spectacular museums. Amazing food, from hole-in-the-wall dives and greasy spoons to Michelin-starred establishments. Art. Music. Theater. Wonderful people. Horrible people. One minute, the sun is unfiltered and seems a few mere feet away, blazing mercilessly down on your roasting skull, and then you come out from the restaurant and it's fifteen degrees colder and raining. Or it's foggy for days and days, only to have the sun burn away the fog and beat down on you like a hammer on an anvil once more.

Driving through Bogotá is not for the faint of heart.

It's a great place to disappear, especially for me. For a massive white guy missing a shirt and covered in scars? Not so much.

I'm driving. Our rifles are on the floor of the second row, not exactly out of sight but within easy reach when shit hits the fan, as it inevitably will. We both are operating under the assumption that Solomon's enemies have eyes and ears all over this city, and it's only a matter of time before they catch up with us. Staying ahead of them in the jungle was one thing—the rugged terrain and lack of established roads worked both in our favor and against us: few people to worry about as collateral damage, easy to lose your pursuers if you're crafty and skillful. But on the other hand, there are only so many roads, and if you want to get anywhere other than to more hot, wet, unforgiving, brutal jungle, you are limited to those roads, and therefore, with a little logistical machination, you can easily set up choke points. We encountered three of them between our little...moment and the city. Fortunately, Sol and I are old pros, and a four-man choke point is child's play: stop, I jump out, Sol drives toward the choke point while I circle through the forest and hit them from the flank. They're focused on him, and I light 'em up—*pop-pop-pop*; done.

But here in the city, anyone can be a spotter or an informant. That little old granny shopping for plantains? Follow her around the corner, and you'll see her sending a text to someone she's never met, letting them know she just saw a gringo and a Latina woman in military gear. That message gets passed along to someone higher up, and that higher-up makes a call, and then suddenly, there's a pair of cars behind you full of men with Uzis, hosing you down with .22 rounds as they zip past you.

No one even calls the cops when that happens. The homeless guy taking a shit on the curb won't even look up.

This is what we're anticipating. Which means we have to play it smart if we want to get out of this alive. The other problem is that neither of us, Sol especially, is going to be content with merely getting out alive. Sol wants answers.

They've woken up and pissed off WindWalker. Not smart.

We wind slowly through the narrow, choked streets. Sol is hunched low in the seat, my hat on his head, brim tugged down.

"We gotta change cars and clothes," Sol says. "You need to look like a local, and I need to at least try to stand out a little less."

I nod, scanning the mirrors for any sign of a tail. We've only been in-city for thirty minutes, but lax situational awareness gets you killed every single time, so my head is on a swivel. "Clothes first," I say. "You're gonna stand out, but you at least need a shirt. Body like that is gonna draw eyes."

He just snorts. "I'm a six-foot blond, white guy."

"Who's built like fucking Adonis and covered in burns, bullet holes, and knife scars. Plus, you move like a soldier. People around here are attuned to that in a way most Americans aren't."

Sol shoots me a wry look. "Not my first day down-range, babe."

"Yeah, but how many times have you been the prey?"

He frowns. "Hmm. Good point."

"You gotta stop thinking like this is an op and start prioritizing some semblance of anonymity. We can't just get into gunfights, and you need to stay low and keep your mouth shut. Act like you don't know a lick of Spanish."

He smirks at me. "Yes, boss."

I roll my eyes at him. "Oh, shut up."

"Told you—turns me on when you order me around."

"Not the time or place for you to think with Mr. Willy, Solomon."

He taps my bicep with the back of his hand and points. "There. Clothes."

It's a bodega-style storefront opening directly onto the road, racks of brightly colored clothing of all sizes and styles jammed into every available square of wall space, from handmade indigenous-style garb to tourist trash with poorly translated English sayings and bad brand-name knockoffs.

He grabs my hand before I can exit. "If you buy me something stupid and make me look like some kind of gringo tourist, I'm gonna be pissed the fuck off, Scar."

I grin. "Would I do that?"

He stares, blank and droll. "Remember Quetzaltenango?"

I roll my eyes and blow an annoyed raspberry. "I fuckin told you, it was all they had, asshole. It was either the Hawaiian shirt in a double XL or a white T-shirt with a quetzal on it in extra small."

"I find that hard to believe."

"Whose fault is it your luggage got blown up?" I ask. "Certainly not mine. I didn't get made, you did. I didn't get in a high-speed car chase, you did."

"The car chase wasn't the fucking problem," he grumbles. "It was the motherfucking RPG that ended it."

"Oh, you mean the RPG that almost caused an international incident? That RPG?"

"Fuck off. I didn't shoot the damn thing at myself, you know."

"You splashed a mark in the middle of our hotel foyer in broad daylight. With an unsuppressed weapon."

"I wasn't issued a fucking suppressor, Scarlett."

"Oh, I'm sorry, I must have mistaken you for a professional." I grin at him.

He doesn't seem to think it's funny, though. "I still don't know how that fuckstick ID'd me. And what was I supposed to do? He shot first!"

"Okay, Han Solo."

"Fuck you. Han shot first. Everyone knows that. I *did not* shoot first in that situation."

I just laugh. "Sit tight, babe. I'll see what I can find for us. Try not to get in trouble, yeah?"

He holds up his hands and then crosses his arms over his chest. "Sitting here. Minding my own fucking business. Just hurry up. The bullet holes in this thing ain't exactly my idea of incognito."

"Yeah, yeah," I say. "Just sit tight and don't start any shit."

I leave the engine running and jog across the street. The little shop is empty except for the proprietor, an elderly woman with a lot of wrinkles and not enough teeth. She ignores me completely as I flip through the racks, looking for suitable options for both of us. Sol is easy enough—a baggy pair of gray sweatpants and an oversized black T-shirt with FBI in big white block iron-on letters. He's gonna hate it, and it'll be funny. But it is the best option in terms of size. It's just not going to be his idea of incognito.

It's also just a temporary solution to get him out of his filthy, blood-stained blue jeans that could probably walk away on their own at this point. We can hit a mall later and get him real clothing. For myself, the options are more limited. Bikinis, scoop neck T-shirts, sundresses, khaki booty shorts, tank tops…goddammit.

I opt for the least awful option for myself, pay in Colombian Pesos, and get back to Sol.

I toss the bag on his lap as I slide behind the wheel. "Slim pickin's again," I say. "But it'll do for now."

Sol holds up the shirt I got him, eyebrow arched at me. "Really?"

"I mean, it's not CIA?" I say, snickering. "And trust me, my options were even worse."

He starts pawing through to see, but I snatch the bag from him and toss it in the back. "Nope. You're gonna have to be surprised."

His arched eyebrow communicates wry amusement. "Well, now I'm curious."

I roll my eyes. "You'll see soon enough. We need to ditch this ride and find a room somewhere."

I pull away from the curb, and we spend another half an hour wandering the city at random—I'm looking for something, and I'll know it when I see it. We get into a gnarly barrio on the far northern outskirts, the kind of place even I would hesitate to enter even in broad daylight. If you don't live here, you don't belong here. And we definitely don't belong here. But I have a plan.

There.

A handful of young men are clustered around their parked cars, the hoods and trunks open, rap music bumping. Smoke billows, bottles are passed. I park a good twenty feet away and turn to Sol.

"Stay here, stay low, and trust me."

He eyes me. "I don't like the sound of that."

I grin. "I've got this, babe."

He shakes his head, returning my grin. "Fine. But if shit goes sideways, I'm jumping in."

"You won't need to."

"This isn't another flash-and-shoot plan, is it?" he asks.

I roll my eyes. "No, Solomon, it's not. It's a 'go over there and make a deal' situation. No flashing or shooting required. Hopefully."

I make sure my pistol is loose in the holster at my thigh, though, and peel off a roll of high-value pesos and American hundreds.

I exit the Range Rover and saunter toward them. The idle chatter, playful shoving, and raucous laughter silences as I approach, and several hands go to grips at waistbands. I keep my hands out and visible, away from my gun.

"Hey, guys," I say in Spanish. "Got a minute?"

No one answers, but no one shoots, either.

I stop some six feet away, hands visible, posture loose and relaxed. I gesture at the SUV. "Need a different car. Trade plus cash."

One of the young men steps forward, assessing me both as a female and as a threat. "Is it hot?"

"Yeah, but I promise, no cops are looking for it."

"Then who?"

"Not the cops."

He peers past me at Solomon in the passenger seat. "Who's he?"

"My boyfriend."

He smirks. "You got an American boyfriend?"

I just shrug.

"I can be your boyfriend." He gives me a leering wink.

Careful to keep my hand away from my gun, I reach into my pocket and pull out the roll of American currency. "I need a car. Something that won't take a shit and that no one is looking for."

He eyes my gun and then me again, this time with a long, raking scan of my body. "What if I don't want money?"

I keep my gaze cool, expressionless. "I'm not part of the deal, kid. You wouldn't last ten minutes with me anyway."

His friends all laugh, and even he grins at me. "Maybe I would. But I don't mean you."

"Do you have a car?"

He shrugs. "I might."

"Get it. When I see it, we can make a deal."

"I want a gun."

I just laugh. "I'm not giving you my gun."

Another shrug. "Then no car."

I sigh. "I might have something else for you, though." I jerk my head for him to follow me.

I make a point of not looking back, even though my neck prickles. This could turn on us at any moment. Guys like this are predators; they can smell fear.

He follows me, and Sol watches us approach, eyebrows knotted. The windows are open, so I murmur in English: "Stay cool. It's under control."

"What are you doing?" Sol demands.

"Making a deal. Shut the fuck up."

I go to the rear driver's side door, yank it open, and

indicate for the guy to take a look: there are two AKs, the Dragunov rifle, several handguns, and a very battered Vietnam-era M16.

"I keep the rifle and one AK and our supplies. You keep the rest of the guns and the car."

"Scar—" Sol cuts in.

"Shut—the fuck—up," I snap.

The guy glances at me, and then Sol. "American no like give me the guns, hey?" he says in surprisingly passable English.

"Ignore him. You're making the deal with me." I hold his eyes. "That's a lot of hardware, my friend." I stick to Spanish.

He nods slowly. "I think I don't want to know where you got these."

"No, you don't. Good news for you is the previous owners won't be coming looking for them any time soon."

He eyes the mud on the tires and rocker panels. "Some bad men out there." He eyes me. "Some people even we don't fuck with."

I shrug. "They won't be interested in you. Anyone comes asking about an American and a lady like me, you tell them the truth. You tell them where we came from, where we went, anything they want to know. They want us, not you."

"I don't like answering questions." His eyes are hard, cold.

I shrug. "Then don't. I don't give a fuck, kid. I need a car, that's it. You want my advice, take the deal. But get rid of the car and the guns fast."

He nods. "Okay. Deal. Wait here." He goes back to his

friends and they circle up, confer quietly for a moment, and then our dealmaker jogs away.

Sol sighs at me. "We're giving guns to thugs, now?"

I laugh. "That's rich, coming from you. We supported an operation that brought fucking cases full of hardware to people who make these kids look like angels, Sol. Don't go developing a conscience, now."

"I was following orders."

"So was I. But you and I both knew some of the shit we did was shady as fuck, Sol. Don't bullshit me with the whole 'I was just following orders.' We destabilized a whole fucking regime. Innocent people fucking died because we were '*just following orders.*'"

He looks away. "And I got out."

"And I've *got* no out, Solomon," I snap. "Unless your boss wants to take me on and brand me, too."

"You don't need a brand, Scarlett." His eyes search me. "No?"

A shake of his head. "Nope. Just need me."

"You?"

"Me. Or, us, to be specific." A shrug. "And the willingness to forsake everything you have, everyone you know, and everything you once were."

"So I can join the club…but only as your little woman, is that it?" I growl.

He laughs. "If you wanna look at it like that."

"Fuck that. I'll take the brand, Sol. That's my way in."

"Not up to me, but I'll talk to Inez."

"You can't talk to the boss directly?" I ask.

"Nope. Don't know the first thing about him. I don't know his name, where he comes from, what his end goal is, where he got his money, nothing. Never laid eyes on him.

Never heard his voice. For all I know, he doesn't exist. All I've got is Inez's word for it, and that's always been good enough for me. I'm loyal to him because he's kept his side of the deal. Gave me a new lease on life, and for that, I'm loyal."

I sigh, frowning. "Weird. It's a weird situation, Sol."

A shrug. "Yeah, I guess. But we take orders from mystery men in DC all the time, right? Some suit in the Pentagon or wherever decides some drug lord needs to be taken out, and they send us. How do we know he's a drug lord? We don't. We follow orders and take the word of our superiors. This is no different. Only the orders are 'keep your head down and be cool,' not put bullets in people's fucking skulls."

I laugh. "Well, when you put it that way..." I roll my shoulder and sigh. "If I'm giving everything up for you, I want the fucking brand. I'll do it for you, but I'll do it *with* you. As your equal."

"And like I said, that's not my decision. But I get you, and I'll make that clear to Inez." He smiles at me. "It'll be good, babe. Promise."

A few minutes later, a small red Toyota pickup appears, and our guy slides out, tucking a handgun in the waistband at the small of his back. We make short work of transferring our supplies to the bed, and we shoulder our rifles.

"Anyone looking for the truck?" I ask.

The young man shakes his head. "No, it's clean."

I shake his hand. "Remember, the people after us are bad-bad. Don't fuck with them. It's not worth it."

He just grins savagely. "They don't wanna fuck with us, either." He gestures around.

I follow his gesture—in every window and doorway and shadow around us, there's a face watching, and I assume each of them is armed and just waiting for us to pose a threat. We'd be lit up in a split second.

I nod. "Just be careful. We appreciate the business."

He jerks his chin up at me and turns away—we're dismissed. Sol climbs into the passenger seat, and I take the wheel.

"Now we need to get off the street and find somewhere to get some rest," Sol says. "And maybe some hot food."

I smirk at him. "Anything else you need, princess? A massage and a latte?"

"Well, since you're offering, I'll take a six-pack of Corona, a porterhouse steak, and a blowjob." He grins at me, winking.

I roll my eyes. "Yeah, I'll get right on that. I can maybe figure out one of the three."

For the next hour, we weave slowly around the outskirts of the city, watching for signs of a shadow or pursuit.

Sol glances at me. "You have any contacts here?"

I shrug. "Nope. Used to, but he was the unfortunate recipient of a Colombian Necktie."

"Eventually, I'll need a phone so I can contact Inez." He's been keeping his head down, slunk low in the seat, brim tugged as far down as possible. Even so, people on the street notice him and whisper. "We gotta get off the streets, Scar," he repeats. "I'm getting noticed."

"Working on it," I mumble.

He frowns. "So far, all we've done is cruise through increasingly shitty barrios."

I glare at him. "You wanna drive?"

"Just saying."

"Well, *just say* less. This ain't fuckin' amateur hour, Sol. I know what the fuck I'm doing."

In truth, I have a bad feeling. A pit in my stomach. Rising hackles.

I glance at Sol. "Tell me you feel it, too."

Instead of answering, he checks the load of his rifle mag, pulls the charging handle, and then checks and racks his pistol.

"Hold the wheel," I say.

He keeps us going straight while I check my firearms and get them ready for action. We both set spare mags for long and short guns near to hand.

We're crawling down a rutted dirt road between old, crumbling brick buildings that open directly on the road, which is muddy from the recent splat of rain that just ended. A couple of younger women, wet and bedraggled and annoyed, barely glance at us as we pass them. On our left, an elderly face appears in a second-story window, cell phone held to his ear, his eyes following us. A moment later, he slams the shutters closed.

A beige sedan crosses the street a hundred yards ahead—the driver's eyes pin us as he crosses, and he whips a cell phone up, hits a speed dial contact, and puts it to his ear.

"Shit, shit, shit," I mumble. "They're onto us."

"No shit." Sol leans forward, rifle held tight to his torso, the butt up near his right ear, barrel between his knees. "Turn here." He indicates an intersection coming up.

I hang a sharp right and gun the motor; mud sprays and we lurch forward, the back end slewing and fishtailing before I let off the accelerator long enough for the tires to catch. I turn left at the next intersection, left again, and a third time, coming back to the road we'd been on originally, where I stop.

A truck much like ours rolls past, the bed stuffed with armed men. One of them spots us, whacking the roof of the cab and shouting.

"Switch with me," I snap.

I shove the door open as Sol does the same, and we sprint around the car in what has been called, for reasons I've never understood, a Chinese fire drill; it just sounds racist in ways I can't quite pinpoint. Sol shoves his rifle between the door and his seat, jerks the shifter into gear, and takes off in reverse.

I sit in the open window, ass on the sill, rifle aimed over the cab. I crack off a trio of quick shots, putting one through the engine blocks, dropping one of the shooters in the bed with a headshot, and missing totally with the third, the round cracking into the side of a building.

"Pulling around," Sol says. "Hang on."

I slip back down to the seat and grab the oh-shit handle as he slams on the brakes, whips the steering wheel around, shoves the shifter into first, and then nails the accelerator again, pulling off a clean J-turn.

Once more, I lean out the window, now aiming behind us as rounds whizz overhead, missing wildly. I don't bother trying to aim at anyone, instead pouring a layer of suppressing fire at them. I manage to wing one and hole the engine block again, which is now spewing smoke and steam.

"Nice shooting," Sol says, grinning at me. "Saw that headshot."

I grin back. "That one was lucky."

Sol turns at random, driving as fast as possible, jamming on the brakes at the last second and gunning it halfway through the turn, putting as much distance between us and the erstwhile pursuit as possible.

"Head south," I tell Sol. "Toward city center. We need to disappear, and we can't out here."

"Then why have we spent the last hour trolling the outskirts?" he asks.

I roll my eyes. "You've been gone too long. We had to pull them out of hiding. See what their reaction time is between spotting us and putting men on our six."

I can tell he's pissed at himself for missing that. "Fuck," he snarls. "Should've thought of that myself."

I reach out and pat his thigh. "You're a bouncer, now, Sol. Those instincts need to stay honed or you lose them. You're with me, babe. We're good."

Sol meanders indirectly south into the center of Bogotá; the buildings get nicer and newer, the roads are paved, and traffic is thicker, with nicer cars and more pedestrians on the sidewalks.

"There," I say after a good twenty minutes of random turns. "A hostel."

He spots what I've seen—a sign advertising rooms for rent with private, off-street parking. Sol circles the block twice before pulling into the lot and parking the truck in a spot not easily visible from the road.

There's a tattered gray wool blanket shoved behind the passenger seat and the rear wall of the cab, which we use to hide the rifles, keeping our pistols in our waistbands hidden behind our shirts. Sol carries the cooler with our food and the carton of water, following me to the clerk's desk.

I get us a room; Sol waits behind me, head down while

I negotiate. Our room is a third-floor corner, with a single twin bed. The windows are filmy with grime, and the floors are somewhat less than clean, but an examination of the bedding assures me we won't get bedbugs, at least.

I point at the bed. "You rest. You're still healing. I'm gonna change and find us food."

He rolls his eyes at me but sits on the edge of the bed and removes his boots and socks with a relieved sigh. "A real fucking bed."

I strip down to my skivvies and pull on the outfit I got myself.

"Not a fucking word," I snap at Sol, whose eyes are wide.

Khaki booty shorts at least a size too small, leaving the lower third of my ass cheeks hanging out, with a tight scoop neck T-shirt.

"It was this or a fucking dress." I wiggle my hips and tug at the hem of the shorts, vainly trying to cover more of my ass.

He shrugs. "You picked the place, babe."

"I fucking know," I growl. "Who the hell dresses like this, anyway? Jesus."

He grins. "Hey, I'm not hating the view."

I sigh, pushing and pulling at my boobs. "I almost have cleavage in this stupid shirt."

"If you had a better bra, you would have cleavage," he points out.

"Helpful, Sol, thanks," I deadpan. "I had no idea how boobs work. What would I do without you?"

"I mean, even out of uniform, you don't typically go for this kind of look," he says, which is as tactfully as he could have phrased that particular sentiment.

"Slutty, you mean?"

He snorts. "This is several degrees away from slutty, babe. Just sayin'."

I turn my ass to him and give the undersides of my butt a tap with both hands. "Oh, really? Do tell."

He rolls his eyes. "Okay, it's a little slutty."

"I'm a fucking top-tier operator, not some two-bit trollop trolling for rich dick at a nightclub."

Sol cackles at this. "Hate to break it to you, babe, but if you were a two-bit trollop trolling for rich dick at a night-club, you wouldn't be wearing that."

I frown. "Oh? Then what would I be wearing?"

"A little black or red dress. Lots of cleavage, more ass hanging out, and the highest heels possible."

"You're an expert in this, are you?"

He grins. "I work at a nightclub frequented by rich dicks and two-bit trollops, Scarlett. So yeah, I kinda am."

"Think I'd snag a rich dick?" I ask, unable to help my curiosity.

Sol blinks at me. "How'm I supposed to answer that, babe?"

"Truthfully. If I was a honey trap..."

"Scar, c'mon."

I grin at him. "Too pussy to answer?"

He rolls his eyes. "No. But you're shit-stirring. That's not the kind of agent you are."

"No shit, Sherlock."

"Then don't ask dumb fuckin' questions. You're not that girl, babe. You wanted to, sure, you could flirt your way into pretty much anyone's bed. You'd hate every second of it, though."

I tug at the shorts again. "Fuck, this is so uncomfortable. I've never understood dressing like this."

Sol just laughs. "Well, you look hot."

I toss the bag at him. "Your turn."

He peels out of his jeans, and we both laugh when he can, in fact, stand them up on end.

Now stark naked, he steps into the baggy gray sweatpants, which I'd assumed would be too big for him. I seem to have underestimated his size, though, because while they hang to his heels, they cling to his massive thighs.

And his cock. Each step makes it sway and bounce behind the gray cotton.

I grin at him. "I approve."

"I bet you do," he mumbles.

"Hot men in gray sweatpants is a whole thing, and you could be the poster boy for it," I say. "Not that your ego needs any help."

He pulls the shirt on, which doesn't do much for my raging libido—it stretches around his chest and arms, only serving to highlight the sculpted perfection of his body.

He swaggers over to me, putting his body against mine. His hands cup my ass and pull me to him, his lips grazing mine. "Keep looking at me like that, Scar. See what happens."

"Threaten me with a good time, why don't you," I murmur back.

"Food, Scarlett. Hot food."

"Then let go of my ass."

He does, and I back out of his hold, shoving my gun into my waistband. Sol barks a laugh. "Not exactly hiding it with that shirt, honey."

I shrug. "I'm not going out there unarmed, so unless

you have a smaller one somewhere that I don't know about, this is what it is."

I head for the door, pausing with my hand on the knob, glancing back at him. "I feel you staring at my ass, Sol."

"What can I say? Hate to see you go, love to watch you leave."

I cackle at this. "That old line? Really?"

"Old but good, babe."

"Yeah, like you."

He splutters indignantly. "Old? The fuck you say."

I wink at him. "Teasing, Sol. Just teasing."

"Get out of here," he says, waving me onward with a flip of both hands. "Before I tie you to the bed and have my wicked away with you."

"One, I'd like to see you try to tie me up. Two, a threat is supposed to be a deterrent, not a temptation."

On that note, I head out and down to street level in search of a hot meal.

CHAPTER 9

SLOW AND SWEET

INTEND TO STAY AWAKE WHILE SHE'S GONE, BUT exhaustion wins—Scarlett wasn't wrong when she said I'm still healing. I've been toughing it out, but I'm still sore and under full strength from the weeks of starvation, dehydration, and abuse.

Which is how I find myself asleep, kicked out on the bed, pistol at hand, hat over my eyes.

Feels like I've barely closed my eyes when a noise brings me awake—a footstep on a stair tread. I remain in place, as if asleep—the way the hand carefully tries the knob tells me it's not Scar.

Fuck. I don't love the idea of an unsuppressed gunfight in a place with walls as thin as this. Stray rounds will carry and hurt innocent people, not to mention the noise will bring a lot of attention.

I roll off the bed and creep quickly across the room to stand against the wall, disgusted with myself for leaving my knife across the damn room.

The door creaks open slowly, and a suppressor enters the room, followed by the rest of the gun and a long, burly arm.

Not a pro, though—he fails to sweep the room properly; you always check the inside corner and then behind the door. This guy just barges in, firing at the bed blindly. Unlike in the movies, the suppressor doesn't quiet the report to a weird little puff of air—it's still fairly loud, a clack that echoes in the room.

I lunge, wrap an arm around his gun arm, bend it the wrong way and smash it inward with my fist, breaking the elbow. Strip the gun from him while putting his body in front of mine—he jerks as several silenced rounds smash into his chest, and I shove him forward at the second shooter, dropping to a knee and firing between the first shooter's legs, catching the second mark in the knee. He drops, shouting, and I sweep up to my feet and lash out with a front kick, catching him under the chin. His head snaps back, teeth cracking together. I smash the butt of my pistol against his forehead, dazing him, and then again, rendering him unconscious and likely giving him a pretty severe TBI. The first mark is gurgling on the floor, bloody froth at his lips, the holes in his chest whistling.

"Fuck, fuck, fuck," I growl. "Stupid amateurs."

I go to the window and look out: our room facing an alley on one side, and the street on the other. Directly below the window is an open dumpster overflowing with trash.

Perfect.

I shove the window open, toss my pistol onto the bed, and then drag poor Mr. Sucking Chest Wound by the heels to the window. Pin his feet to the floor with my feet, pull him by his hands onto my shoulder, and stand up with him. Dump him onto the windowsill and then shove him unceremoniously out. He lands in the trash, wriggling weakly. Shooter number two is already coming to—motherfucker must have a hell of a hard head. I haul him over and dump him out, as well; unfortunately for him, he falls wrong and cracks his head on the side of the dumpster, leaving a red smear.

He moans weakly, writhes a few times, and goes still.

"Fuck." I wipe my face. "He's fine."

"What the fuck, Sol?" I hear behind me.

I whirl to see Scar in the doorway, carrying a plastic bag loaded with carryout containers.

I shrug. "Had a situation. Handled it."

She sets the stuff down on the bed, grabs the silenced pistol from the floor on the way to the window, and peers out.

"Well, they're still alive…mostly," she mutters: POP—POP. "Not anymore." She grins at me. "You didn't kill 'em, I did."

I sigh. "I mean, yeah. But they'd have died anyway."

"Still, it doesn't count in my book. Right? I pulled the trigger that ended them." She checks the gun in her hand. "Suppressed Glock 19. Fuckin' beautiful."

"Make that two," I say, grabbing the other one.

She shakes her head. "Can't even get food without trouble finding you."

"Any sign of anyone out there?" I ask.

"Nah. That's what took so long—I took the long way back and made sure I wasn't followed."

"So, do we stay or go?" I ask.

She shrugs. "Stay for now. I'm eating while this food is even remotely warm. Plus, I need a nap."

We shut the window and sit on the bed—it's close quarters, being a twin, and me being the size I am.

"This is fucking fantastic," I say. "What is it?"

"It's called Bandeja paisa," She answers. "Beef, beans, rice, plantains, and avocado, and some other shit. Close, cheap, and filling."

Once we're both finished eating, we set the empty containers aside.

"I got some rest," I tell her. "I'll keep watch."

She shrugs. "We'll both hear if anyone comes."

I slide down and pull her onto my chest—before, she always resisted this kind of close contact unless it was directly preceded or followed by sex, and even then, she'd only allow it for a short time before putting distance between us.

This time, she just sighs, her hand on my shoulder. "Why did I fight this so hard?" she murmurs sleepily.

I shrug. "Dunno. You tell me."

"Too tired for self-reflection," she mumbles.

"Doesn't matter. I've got you. Rest."

"Mmmmm."

A moment or two later, she's sound asleep. I doze again, too, but don't let myself fall asleep all the way, not with these assholes finding us fast as they have been.

Daylight fades to evening as an hour passes, and then two, and then three. A cell phone rings just outside the window—one of the shooters. Which gives me an idea.

Later, though. Scar is still asleep on my chest, and I'm not about to disturb her.

She feels too damn good like this, her head on my chest, hand on my belly. Close. Warm. Mine.

I doze again.

Movement brings me awake—Scarlett stirring.

"Slept awhile, huh?" she mutters.

"Few hours," I answer. "Feel better?"

She nods against my chest. "A lot, actually. I think there's something about your chest—I dunno."

I rub her back. "It's called feeling safe, babe. You can actually relax a little because you know I've got you."

She sighs deeply. "Maybe you're right." She snuggles closer. "I guess I could get used to falling asleep and waking up like this."

"Me too, honey."

A long pause. "I didn't like feeling safe," she says, answering my question from earlier. "I didn't trust it. It's still hard for me."

"I see you trying, Scarlett. Means more than I can say."

I slip my hand under her shirt and find the soft warm skin of her back. She hums quietly as I caress her back between the waist of her shorts and the band of her bra.

"That's nice," she whispers.

So, I keep doing it. Rub her back, scratch in wide lazy circles, smooth with my palm where I scratched.

After a few minutes, she lifts up on an elbow, looking down at me. Her hair is tied back in a stubby ponytail. "Keep doing that and I'm liable to fall back asleep."

"Wouldn't be the worst thing."

"We need to move. Been here too long as it is. I'm honestly surprised they haven't gotten another hit team here already."

"Probably won't be too long. One of their cell phones rang outside earlier," I say. "We should grab it on our way. I can use it to call Inez. Maybe even get her to do some magic and figure out who these fuckers are being sent by. Because they wouldn't still be after me if it wasn't a high-dollar payout."

"And you have no idea who or why?"

I shrug and shake my head. "Nope. Like you said, I'm sure I have a lot of enemies out there, but it's hard to say who actually knows who I am and has the skills and resources for an operation like this. Lotta cash being spread around, looking for us."

She lets out a breath. "I think we take one alive and do some enhanced interrogation."

"Works for me."

For a moment or two, neither of us speaks. She looks down at me with a million questions in her eyes and a million feelings.

"What, Scar?" I whisper.

She buries her face in my chest, covering the subtle flush of her cheeks. "Nothing."

"Bullshit. Don't *nothing* me. Tell me."

"I just…" she whispers against my chest, words muffled. "I might be willing to see what soft and sweet feels like."

I touch her chin, tilting her face up to mine. "In that case," I whisper, my words a breath on her lips, "let's dance."

"Dance?" She says, brow furrowing. "I don't—"

I silence her with my mouth, capturing her lips with mine, but this is not a ravenous, aggressive kiss. I start it off slow and gentle, sliding my fingers into her hair, feeling the contours of her skull with my fingertips, tasting her mouth, her tongue, her breath. She whimpers softly as I claim her tongue, the kiss wet and deep, and slow.

For several long, luxurious minutes, I just kiss her. Making her hungry and eager and then backing off to slow and soft, and then ratcheting up the intensity again. Until she's half on top of me, fingers digging into my chest over my shirt, panting into the kiss.

"Sol," she gasps, pulling away an inch or so. "Jesus."

"You like that?"

She presses her forehead against my cheek, nodding. "Yeah," she breathes in answer. "I do." She palms my jaw. "Kiss me like that again. Please."

So, I do.

Long, slow, not moving past kissing. The deeper we kiss, the more she writhes against me, and yet I keep my hands away from her curves, caressing her face, her hair, her back.

She grinds her core against my thigh. "Sol," she whispers. "I need you."

I put her on her back and lean over her, pulling her hair out of the ponytail. "Tell me what you want, Scarlett."

"Everything," she pants. "You. Just you."

I dip closer and consume her in another kiss, this one hotter and hungrier, finally allowing my need for her to break free of the iron control I've kept it under.

She arches her back and whimpers as I turn the kiss wild and needy, letting my hand skate up over her belly to cup her breast over her shirt. Her nipple is a hard pebble even through the layers of bra and shirt.

She lifts into me, and I help her sit up. She raises her arms over her head, and I peel her top off, taking the bra with it, letting her soft small taut breasts bounce free. I cup the back of her head and capture one of her nipples in my mouth, suckling it until she gasps. "Fucking love your tits, Scar."

"You don't—you don't wish they were bigger?" she pants.

"No. Never." I lay her down and worship her breasts. "I love them. They're perfect."

"They're tiny."

"They're you. That's all that matters. I wouldn't change a single thing about you, Scarlett."

I kiss down her belly, dip my tongue into her navel. Open her shorts. She lifts her ass and shoves shorts and underwear down, kicking them off together inside out.

Her fingers dive into my hair, tangling and tracing. "Sol, please."

I laugh, kissing her hipbone. "Please what?"

She pushes my head toward her center. "Eat me out, baby. Please."

"Love it when you call me baby," I answer, and then fuse my mouth over her clit.

"Feels weird, to be honest," she answers, and then gasps. "Oh *fuck*—it feels weird, sounds weird."

"It's not weird. I love it."

She cradles my head as I lap at her. "Love hearing it, too."

"I know."

I take my time, then, devouring her slowly, building her to a climax and backing away before she can come, again and again, until she's writhing under me.

After the fourth or fifth time I deny her the orgasm, she growls like a feral cat. "Sol! Quit fuckin' teasing me."

"When I'm ready, sweetheart, when I'm ready." I slip a finger inside her and resume my slow circling of her clit with my tongue.

This time, when I bring her to the edge, I let her fall over it into climax. She clutches my head and shoves me against her core, grinding her hips and wailing through gritted teeth.

"Sol, Sol, Sol," She chants as wave after wave slams through her.

She slumps back against the mattress, panting raggedly, sweating, flushed. Still shaky and out of breath, she starts tugging at my shirt. "Off. Off, dammit."

I chuckle at her impatience, peeling out of it. "I'm not going anywhere, honey," I tell her.

She ignores this, dragging my sweatpants off and grasping my cock the moment it springs free. "We don't have a lot of time and I need you."

I kick the sweatpants off and fill my hands with her curves, carving my hands over her body as she caresses my cock and kisses my jaw, my throat, my mouth.

I roll into her, and put her on her back. She's never liked this position, so I don't give her all my weight, which would make her feel trapped. Brace my weight on a forearm and cup her cheek. "Okay?"

She nods. "Yeah."

"I know in the past you said you don't like—"

She cuts me off with a kiss. "Things are different. I'm good for now. I'll tell you if I'm not." She reaches between us and finds my erection, guiding it to her entrance. "Just... just make I—" she exhales sharply, cutting herself off. "Just make me feel good, Sol."

"Coulda said it," I whisper. "We both know what you were gonna say."

She closes her eyes, shakes her head. "Not ready for that yet."

"We know what it was between us before, Scar," I murmur. "Even if we never said it."

"Sol," she says, wrapping her thighs around my waist. "Talk later. Fuck now."

I chuckle. "Ohhhh, Scarlett." I touch my forehead to hers. "So impatient."

"Yeah, I am impatient," she snaps. "I don't want to get halfway to an orgasm and then have to stop to shoot people."

"The way things have been going," I say, "that's exactly what would happen."

I touch my forehead to hers and ease into her. She gasps, and then her breath catches, and she claws her fingernails into the backs of my shoulders as I enter her in a long, slow, grinding thrust.

"Holy fuck, Scar, you're so goddamn tight," I growl.

She hooks her heels together at the small of my back and grinds eagerly against me, impatient and wild. "Sol, please."

I know what she's doing—now that she's here beneath me, she's having second thoughts about soft and sweet.

I trap her hands in one of mine and pin them over her head. "Hey, now. Ease up, wildcat."

She struggles. "Let go, Sol."

I loosen my grip but don't let go. "Scar, trust me."

"Sol—"

I stay buried deep, rolling my hips against her gently, slowly. "Scar, honey. Look at me."

Her eyes are squeezed shut—she's fighting panic. "Get off."

"Open your eyes, sweetheart. Look at me."

She shakes her head, but her lids part a tiny bit, enough to see a hint of her brown eyes, hazed with unshed tears. "Sol, I—"

I grab her hands and put them on my face. "It's me, baby. Look at me. Feel me. Be here with me."

"I keep feeling…him," she whispers. "Aleja—"

I cut her off with a kiss. "He's dead, babe. You killed him. You're here with me."

"I see him. I see him."

"Eyes on mine, beautiful," I say, cupping her face. "Touch me. Tell me what you feel."

She fixes her eyes on mine, panting heavily, heels wedged against the back of her thighs. She touches my jaw. "Your stubble."

"What's it feel like?"

"Rough, but kinda soft, too."

"What else?"

Her hand moves to my shoulder, my arm. "Your skin. Your muscles."

"Keep talking, honey. Touch me. Talk to me."

She runs her hand down my back. "Your back." To my butt. "Your ass." Both hands grasp my buttocks. "I *love* your ass, Solomon."

I ease another slow, gentle thrust. "Feel that, sweetheart?"

She gasps, nods. "I feel it."

"Who is it?"

"You."

"Who?"

"You. Solomon."

I roll another thrust, just as slow and gentle. "Who's inside you right now, Scarlett?"

Her eyes are wide, now, still scared and filled with panic, but locked on mine, fighting, trusting. "You, Solomon. You are. You're inside me."

"You're here. You're safe. You're with me." I brace both hands beside her face and set a slow, easy rhythm. "Move with me, honey. Show me whatcha got."

Breathing heavily, still, she clutches my shoulders with biting, bruising force, whimpering in her throat with each thrust; faltering at first, she starts to meet my thrusts with her own. Then, she loosens her death grip on my shoulders.

She finally lets go and moves her hands down my back to clutch at my ass, pulling at me. "More, Sol. Harder."

"No way, honey." I shake my head, nuzzling her cheek, her nose, her jawline. "Just...like...this."

Slow, soft, gentle—I roll each thrust into her tight wet pussy, groaning as she clutches around me, rippling tighter as she moans. She pulls at my butt with each thrust, now, Heels tucked tight against her ass cheeks, knees flung wide.

"Oh god, Sol. Sol...Sol."

"That's right, baby. Keep saying my name. I'm the one fucking you, baby. It's you and me. You gonna come for me, Scar? I wanna feel you come for me. Need you to scream my name."

"Not—not yet. I'm not there yet."

"Good, me either."

"It feels good, Sol," she whispers, cupping my ass and pulling with each of my thrusts into her sweet hot depths. "Feels good like this. You feel good."

"Just good isn't anywhere near enough," I say.

"Incredible. Fucking amazing."

"That's better."

"I wanna come, Sol."

"What do you need, honey? Tell me what you need."

"Just... just you, baby. Don't stop—I'm close."

"You want to touch yourself?"

She shakes her head. "No. Just—just you, Sol. All I want is you. Just…just don't stop."

I hold the pace, stay at the same angle. Move into her slowly, pacing myself. I'm not holding back yet, but I'm not far off either. I stare down at her, locking eyes with her. "Look at me, Scar. Stay with me. It's just you and me."

She nods, mouth falling open, expression going soft and full of wonder as a climax builds inside her. I feel it in the way her thighs shake, in the way her thrusts falter against mine, in the way she gasps, whimpers, and groans. "I'm with you, Sol."

"Come for me, beautiful. I feel you. You're right there. Give it to me. Come on my cock, Scarlett."

She grabs at the back of my neck and pulls me closer, panting raggedly in my ear. "Sol—oh god, *Sol*. I'm gonna come."

"Whose cock is this?" I demand, thrusting hard now. "Who's fucking you, Scar? Who's making you come?"

"You are. Solomon, oh god, oh god, Sol. You are— you're making me come. Oh fuck, don't stop. Give me that cock, Sol. Feels so fucking good when you fuck me like this."

I groan as she ripples around me, squeezing so tight I can barely move through her clamping, spasming walls. "Fuck, Scar, that's right, that's it, honey. Come for me."

"*SOL!*" She screams. "Oh god, oh fuck, oh godohfuckohgodohfuck!"

I hold back, then, focusing on her, thrusting slowly as she comes around my cock. God, I could come, but I'm not ready yet. I want more. I need more.

I slide my hands under her, lift her as I sit up and shift cross-legged. Her legs wrap instinctively around my waist, and she sinks onto me, groaning low in her chest as I sink so deep inside her that it aches down into my balls.

"Scarlett, god, you feel amazing. Love feeling you come around me." I cup her ass with one hand and the back of her neck with the other and bury my face in her breasts. "Say my name again, sweetheart."

"Solomon—my Sol, my sweet, strong, beautiful Solomon," she whispers, and my heart swells fit to burst hearing her speak like that.

"Yes. Yes. Yes. Yours. I'm yours, Scarlett. Your Solomon."

"Mine," she gasps, rising, lifting so I'm nearly out of her, and then crushing slowly down onto me. "My Sol."

"Are you mine, Scarlett?" I demand.

"Yes!" she cries. "Yes, Sol. I'm yours."

"Gonna make me come, Scar? I'm right there."

She nods, chin moving against the top of my head. "Yes, Solomon. I want it. I want you to come."

"Gotta make me, sweetheart. Make me come."

She sets the pace, then—hard thrusts, bodies meeting, her tits bouncing, ass slapping against my thighs. "Need it, Sol. Need you."

"Then take it. Take me, honey. Take all of me. Take me how you need me."

"Oh god, Sol. I need—-I need to fuck you."

"Then fuck me, honey. Fuck me as hard as you want."

Her arms wrap around my neck and she clutches my face to her chest, and she fucks me—hard. I meet her, match her, driving up into her with a steady chorus of groans and growls.

I feel it, then, a hot, heady, dizzying wave of ecstasy

boiling in my balls, and then in my gut, and then in my chest, expanding, swelling.

"Scar, oh god, baby. I'm—I'm gonna come."

"Yes!" She cries. "Come with me, Sol. Come with me, baby—right now!"

She wails, then, a loud shrill breathless cry of release as her pussy spasms around me and rips my orgasm from me. I grunt, and then the grunt turns into a roar as the orgasm tears through me like wildfire. I can't see straight, can't breathe, can only drive up into her and let loose. She's wild with her own climax, snarling in my ear and slamming down onto me.

White heat batters at my skull and washes down my spine, and then bursts out of me through my cock and into Scarlett, and I press my mouth to her breasts and groan, my throat raw and raspy as I pour into her in wave after wave of release.

The door is kicked open at that moment; my back is to the doorway.

Scarlett slaps a hand out and finds the stolen, silenced Glock; she doesn't slow in her thrusting down onto me or quiet her loud cries as she comes around me. She squeezes off three rounds—*POP-POP-POP*; adjusts her aim and fires again—*POP-POP!—POP-POP!—POP-POP!*

I hear the thud of bodies hitting the floor; I turn to look, but she grabs my face and turns it back to her. "Don't—stay with me, Sol. Don't stop fucking me."

Aching and pulsing with the aftershocks of my orgasm, I keep moving with her, and I feel her shuddering again. She fits her ring and middle finger to clit, hanging onto my neck with her other hand, leaning way back and riding me hard.

"Oh fuck, *SOL!*" She screams, shattering all over again. "Oh god, oh god, Sol!"

After a few more minutes of slowly, lazily riding me, she finally goes still. She hangs from my neck with both hands, staring into my eyes.

"Solomon—Jesus." She searches me with her eyes. "That was—"

I topple us forward, pinning her to the bed—I lose her in the process, and she whimpers, but the whimper turns into a moan as I kiss her. "That was us making love, Scarlett," I whisper.

She touches her cheek to mine, nodding. "I know," she breathes. "I'm not ready to say it, though. Or hear it."

"I know."

For a while, we just stay like that, wrapped up in each other.

Eventually, she pats my back. "We need to go."

I pull back to look down at her. "I know you're not ready to say it or hear it, but you need to know it. So, when I say 'I've got you,' just know that's what I mean. Okay?"

"As you wish," she replies, grinning up at me.

I laugh. "Best possible answer."

"I'll never admit it to anyone else, but that's my favorite movie," she says. "When I missed you really bad, I'd put that on. Made me feel connected to you."

I choke. "You did? No bullshit?"

She nods. "I did. Couple times a month, at least."

"Me too," I whisper. "I watched it all the fucking time. My brothers thought I was fucking nuts."

"Blood brothers or teammate brothers?"

"Both."

She smacks my ass. "Come on, hot stuff. Get off me

so we can get out of here. We don't have time or resources to deal with all these bodies."

Within five minutes, we're both dressed and hauling our shit to the truck. We take everything, including the shell casings and all the spare mags the dead dudes were carrying. Once the truck is loaded, I jog around the side of the building and fish the cell phone out of the dead guy's pocket.

Sixty seconds after that, we're gone.

Scarlett drives with one hand on my thigh and a not-so-secret smile on her face.

I put my hand over hers. "Got you, Scar."

She smiles brighter than ever, so bright the sun seems almost dim. "Got you too, Sol."

Bring it on, assholes. With this woman at my side, I can do fucking anything.

And she loves me.

CHAPTER 10

THE ICE QUEEN COMETH

MIDNIGHT. WE'RE PARKED IN A GRAVEL quarry high above the city, spread out below us like a tangled net of string lights. We're stretched out in the truck bed, staring up at the sky.

It's been a hell of a day since we left the hostel this morning. Afternoon? I don't even know. We took down no fewer than four different kill squads. We even captured a guy. We brought him way the fuck up here to talk to him because up here, no one can hear him scream. Turns out, he didn't know shit. He was a street-level thug who took orders from a slightly higher-up thug, who took his orders from someone else…the chain was so fucked up that there was no feasible way of untangling it. Not without CIA resources, at least, and since I'm here alone, that's not an option. In the movies, the plucky hero/heroine would have a handful of key favors to call in. I have no favors owed me. If I were to call my CO or friends in various departments and ask for a lookup, shit would get messy. Questions would be asked. Sol's existence would be outed. So, no. Not an option.

Therefore, the thug's body is a couple hundred yards away under a small avalanche of gravel.

Sol scrubs his face, staring at the burner phone he liberated from the dead guy back at the hostel. "Was hoping it wouldn't come to this."

"Just call her, Sol," I grumble. "Quit putting it off." I glance at him. "What's the hang-up, anyway?"

A shrug. "Never been the one who needed to be bailed out. It's embarrassing. I should be able to handle this."

"You can't, Sol. *I* can't. *We* can't. It's too big. We've kicked ass so far, but it's only a matter of time before one of them gets lucky or they stop sending these stupid little squads and start sending real numbers. You need to call your boss and get some real solutions."

He growls. "I fuckin' know. I just don't want to." I hear the keys beeping as he dials a long string of numbers. "But, here we go."

It rings a few times. He's close enough that even with the phone to his ear, I can hear the ringing and then a smooth, cool, dry female voice that comes on the other end.

"Solomon," she says. "You're alive."

"I am," he says.

"Where are you?"

"Bogota."

A pause. "Are you alone?"

He hesitates. "No."

"Brief me."

"I think maybe you know."

A soft, dry chuckle. "I suppose I do, at that. Tell Ms. Gutierrez I said hello."

"You coulda just called me," I say. "Subterfuge wasn't necessary."

"This was the most effective method," she says. "You would have had a lot of questions before you even got to the questions of how, why, and where to rescue our dear friend, Mr. Cabot. This way cut all that out."

"What do you know, Inez? About the people who snatched me?" Sol asks.

"Very little. Did they ask you any questions?"

"No. They just beat the shit out of me. Never asked me question one. Not my name, nothing."

"And you're being actively pursued?"

"Very much so. So far, squads, trios, and pairs of amateurs. No real triggermen, thus far."

"Your oath?"

"Kept it. Scar's done all the killing. I've made some messes, but I haven't killed anyone. Old habits die hard, but they can die."

A long pause. "I haven't been entirely truthful with you, Solomon."

He goes very still. "Meaning?"

"I do not know anything for certain, but I…I think this may not be about you."

"Inez, you're gonna have to elaborate, here."

"It goes against my nature and my training and everything I am and everything I do, personally and professionally, to divulge more than absolutely necessary. But I think at this point, it is becoming necessary." She pauses again.

Sol sighs. "This is about you, isn't it?"

"Possibly," she answers.

"Inez."

"Like you all, I left a lot of enemies behind me when

I went to work for our mutual employer. In the interven-
ing years, I have…worked to eliminate the greatest threats.
But there is one enemy that is beyond my capabilities of
eliminating."

"You're being vague, Inez." Sol frowns at the stars.
"Wait, did you take the same oath as us?"

"I have not."

Sol sits up. "So whoever it is, is either too well insu-
lated for you to get close enough to eliminate them, or
they're too big and too powerful to eliminate."

"Or both." A sigh. "This enemy is the type that can
hire an entire terrorist organization to do its dirty work.
Namely, putting out bait for me."

"Meaning…" Sol trails off, thinking. "You're saying I
was snatched off the streets of Boston, transported to fucking Brazil, beaten, tortured, starved, and dehydrated in an
attempt to get you out of hiding?"

"Correct."

"Who the *fuck* is your enemy, Inez? Fucking hell."

"Not someone I'm willing to discuss over the phone."

"Well, we need options," Sol says. "So far, we've
come out ahead. But if this person or group or whatever
is this powerful, it's not gonna stop. We need a way out
of Colombia, at least. Or, we need a plan to put an end to
this. Something."

She sighs. "I know. I'm working on it. Can you hold
out a little longer?"

"Probably. But I'm gonna need some real motherfucking explanations, Inez. I think you owe me that much if I'm
going through all this for you." He laughs. "Funny thing
is, I've been racking my brain trying to figure out who the
fuck could and would go through all this to get at me. And

I've been coming up empty because the people who may have a grudge against me would just put a slug through my brain from half a mile away the first time I left the fucking Club. I can't think of anyone who would take me alive and kick the shit out of me just for fuckin' shits and giggles."

"Correct."

"But what I'm not following is why me? You're my boss, not my friend, not my partner, not a lover or an ex. You give me orders, and that's it. What makes them think you'd come after me?"

"Solomon, if you think that you mean that little to me, I'm insulted."

"I don't know the first fucking thing about you. Not even your last name. You don't hang with us. You don't talk to us. So forgive me if I assume our relationship is business casual at best."

Inez sighs. "I am not someone who is given to shows of emotion, Solomon, any more than you are. But I care about you. I care about all of you. Who do you think followed you and watched you and assessed you before bringing you into the Broken Arrows, Solomon? Who do you think made sure there was a medic on that helo in Caracas? Who made sure your brothers were brought in as well? Each and every one of you Broken Arrows is here, alive, and part of the brotherhood because I chose you. I brought you in."

"I thought we were chosen by the boss?"

"You were. I was given a selection of portfolios, but he left the final selection to me, and then he approved them. He gave me seven slots to fill and twenty-one options. I chose the seven of you, and together, we arranged each operation to retrieve you and bring you in. I am invested in each of you. I am invested in seeing you succeed. In seeing you move beyond the traumas that brought you all to me in the first place." A tense pause. "I *care*, Solomon." Her voice shakes on the last three words. "I care *very* much."

He seems stunned. "O-okay, Inez. I hear you."

"Good." Back to cool, calm, and collected. "I am going to clean this up. You have my word."

"You gonna get the guys on this?"

A pause. "I do not believe so. I think between the three of us, we can resolve the situation."

"Meaning, you're going cowboy on this."

"Indeed."

Sol growls. "Inez…"

"I am already en route. Our employer is aware of the situation."

"So what's the plan?" Sol asks.

"I cannot be certain that this is a secure line, Solomon. Retain this phone. Stay alive at all costs. When I land, I will make contact."

"Wait, hold on. You're coming out to play? You, personally?"

"Correct."

Sol cackles delightedly. "Fuck yeah. This oughta be good."

"My presence is only going to exacerbate the situation. You got free, but you're still the bait. They hoped I'd come to get you myself. Well, they succeeded in luring me out." She lets out a long, slow sigh. "It's going to get messy, Solomon."

Sol laughs. "*Get* messy? Inez, babe, it's *been* messy."

"Please do not refer to me as *babe*, Solomon."

"Sorry."

"Indeed. My point is that when my presence there is known, the mess you've encountered thus far will seem like a walk in the park." She pauses yet again. "My plane lands in a few hours. I'll be in touch. Stay alive till then."

"Inez, wait."

"What is it, Solomon?"

"This isn't just business for you, is it? The people doing this. It's personal, not professional."

She doesn't answer for a moment. "Yes. It is personal."

"I hope you understand that you owe me some very clear and thorough explanations, Inez."

"I understand."

"One last thing."

"Yes?"

"Scarlett wants the brand."

"You wish to take the oath and join the brotherhood?" This is, obviously, addressed to Scarlett.

"Yes, I do," I answer.

"That can be arranged once this has been settled." She clears her throat. "I assume Solomon has explained what that means. What it entails?"

"He has. And I'm ready. I've been ready, I think."

"Why do you think I chose you to retrieve Solomon, Ms. Gutierrez?"

"Because I have the skills?"

"As well as the motivation. I'll let you in on a little secret, Scarlett. Your file was one of the twenty-one. But in my assessment, you were not ready, then. You are, now."

"Ready for what?"

"To start a new life. To take the oath and keep it."

I go silent at this revelation.

Inez clears her throat again. "I have other calls to make. I'll contact you when I've landed."

"See you soon, Inez," Sol says.

"Yes. Until then."

Click.

Sol pockets the phone.

I look at him. "Well, that was interesting."

He barks a laugh. "You could say that."

"Meaning?"

"Meaning, until this, I always sort of half-suspected she was, like, a robot or something. There's never been so much as a hint of who Inez is as a human being. She's the literal textbook definition of an ice queen." He shakes his head and laughs again. "And then I get snatched as bait for her? What the fuck. You mean to tell me none of this is even *about* me?"

"Are you pissed off about that?" I ask.

He frowns, rolls a shoulder. "I dunno. Sort of? Part of me thinks that if I'm gonna go through all this bullshit, it should damn well be my own fuckin' enemies."

"But?" I prompt.

"But, the only organization that could make someone like me disappear is the federal fucking government. And you and I both know that when *they* want you gone, you're gone and you *stay* fucking gone."

"Right," I say. "So with that being the case, it's probably a good thing this isn't about you because this doesn't smell like The Company to me. Too clumsy."

"Way too clumsy," he agrees. "No, this feels like a cartel, maybe. Or something like The Syndicate that my brothers worked for. That kind of thing."

"Which means these squads aren't trying to kill us," I

say, the realization hitting me all at once. "They're keeping us moving while we draw the real target out."

"Fuck," Sol groans. "You're right. You're goddamned right. So whoever it is has no problem throwing people away like they're expendable. Because how many have we dropped so far, you think? Thirty?"

"Oh, yeah, at least."

"That's a lot of manpower. And even the chump change you pay street thugs like this adds up when you're talking the kind of numbers they're sending against us." Sol scrubs his face with his hand. "Begs the question, then, who *the fuck* is Inez?"

We both doze, then. We're isolated, and there's no way to sneak up on us, so we feel comfortable allowing ourselves to relax our guard a little bit.

Night fades to dawn.

The burner rings. Sol answers sleepily. "Inez. You touch down?"

"I have," she answers. "But I'm certain that the airport is being watched. The moment I step foot off this jet, I'm dead. I'll need you and Scarlett to provide a distraction."

"Send me your coordinates," Sol says.

"Sending now. When you're in position, let me know."

"Will do. Be there ASAP."

"I look forward to it."

He ends the call, and a second later, the device beeps with an incoming message: a set of coordinates. Fortunately, the burner phone he liberated is a smartphone with a native GPS map app that turns the coordinates into a physical location and directions to get there.

We set out, both of us silent.

"You feel it, too?" Sol asks, after a while.

"The feeling that we're walking into a trap?" I ask. "Yeah, I feel it."

"We just walk into it then?"

I laugh. "We make 'em think we are, at least. I'm not sure they realize who they're fucking with, though. You know anything about Inez's capabilities?"

He shrugs, shakes his head. "No. I get the feeling that she can hold her own, though."

———— ◆ ————

An hour later, we're parked on the roof of a parking garage. Half a mile away, a private jet idles on the tarmac, on its own far from the rest of the passenger jets and private prop planes coming and going. We've been watching.

The situation is...not good.

We've ID'd a sniper on the roof of a Quonset hut on the far edge of the airport's grounds, with a direct line of sight to the private jet. We've also watched several squads of armed and armored soldiers move into position, cutting off all egress points from the jet. They're clearly expecting heavy resistance. What's less clear is whether they're expecting us.

"Plan?" Sol asks me.

I shrug. "I've got a pretty good spot right here. I can provide overwatch while you light 'em up."

He nods. "Works for me." He calls Inez, who answers

on the first ring. "We're in position. Lots of marks, Inez. A whole fucking lot."

"I am aware."

"Well then, all that's left is go time. You'll know the distraction when it happens." Sol chuckles. "It won't be subtle."

Inez snorts. "I don't imagine so. I'm ready."

"See you soon, boss."

"Yes. Quite. Do be careful, Solomon. Scarlett, you as well."

"Locked and loaded," I say. "Just be ready to fuckin' run."

"I am ready. But there will be no running. I have done enough of that, I think."

Sol hums thoughtfully. "Gotta say, Inez, my curiosity is at an all-time high."

She laughs, then. "And it shall be assuaged as long as you two can provide enough of a distraction to get me off this jet. On that note, my friends, the time for talk is done. Let the violence begin."

"Let the violence begin," Sol echoes. "See you soon."

Click.

I look at him. "She's an odd duck, you know that?"

He shakes his head. "She's a fuckin' mystery, that's what she is."

I set about stripping and cleaning the Dragunov. "You'd better get going. Once you start, I'll pick off around the edges. Get close and pull them away from the jet. I'll provide covering fire for her to make her break for it. Once you have her, swing by this way and grab me."

"Got it," he says.

We spend the next couple minutes silently cleaning

our weapons and checking our mags, a pre-op ritual we've done side by side countless times.

It feels different, this time.

He finishes first and tosses his AK into the cab. "Hey."

I look up at him from reassembling the rifle. "Yeah?"

"Got you, Scar."

"Got you too, Sol."

He cups my jaw and tilts my face to his, claiming a quick, hot kiss. "Stay frosty, sweetheart."

"You too, hot shot."

Sol drives away in the truck, the engine rattling noisily as it fades down the garage ramp. With my rifle cleaned and reassembled, I set up on the rim of the rooftop. Check the windage. Distance from my location to the jet, and then dial in on the sniper. The forces on the ground have all taken up spots out of sight, inside Quonset huts and hangars, behind luggage carts and stacks of luggage.

Now, I wait.

It's not a long wait, though. I watch Sol park the truck and jog on foot toward the tarmac.

"What's your plan, Sol?" I murmur to myself.

Something still doesn't feel right.

Maybe it's just the fact that it's Sol, Inez, and myself against at least two dozen. I don't know. But something isn't sitting right in my gut.

It's been wrong before, but not often.

Nothing to do about it now, though—things are in motion that cannot be stopped.

Sol vanishes from sight between a pair of buildings.

Silence.

And then...all hell breaks loose.

CHAPTER 11

LORENZO

I USUALLY HAVE A BETTER PLAN GOING INTO situations like this. But alas, I don't. The best I've got right now is "fuck shit up; don't die; try not to outright kill anyone."

This shit was a hell of a lot easier when I didn't have to worry about killing people. I mean, my whole job was to eliminate problematic motherfuckers, violently and messily.

I'm pressed up against the side of a hangar. Inez's jet is about two hundred yards away, maybe closer to three hundred. Around the corner to my left, a lot of dudes with guns; around the corner to my right? A lot more dudes with guns.

Another dude with a gun is on a rooftop, but I trust Scar to have that under control. There are more dudes with more guns hiding in the area as well; I'm not sure where, but I have to assume they're there somewhere.

The plan, then, is to cause a ruckus, draw out all the dudes with guns, and do violent shit to them until Inez can get clear.

Pretty thin, as far as plans go.

I check my mag for the third time in thirty seconds, pat my pockets for the spares, and make sure my sidearm is secure at my back.

Ready…

Go.

I roll out around the corner and drop to one knee. They don't see me because they're focused on the jet. Check left, check right. A quick headcount shows eleven targets, which I can see from here.

Pull back, hit the charging handle, draw in a deep breath.

Let's dance, motherfuckers.

Roll out right, pop off single rounds, putting them through kneecaps—one, two, three, four.

Pull back.

CRACK! The Dragunov speaks.

I cross to the other side and inch forward, lean out and aim down the iron sights. *BAMBAMBAM!* Best I can do is high torso shots, putting the rounds through shoulders and hopefully not any major organs. This time, gunfire follows me, and rounds whizz, snap, buzz, and ping off the wall near my face. I jerk back with a muttered string of curses—one of those was so close I felt it buzz past the tip of my nose.

I fall back to my previously prepared position: a stolen tractor-trailer full of luggage that I parked across the space between the buildings. I take cover behind the tractor itself and wait for a slow thirty count.

Pop up and check my sight lines: here they come.

CRACK! The Dragunov barks again, and I hear a shout. *CRACK! CRACK! CRACK!* Gunfire follows the cracking of the big rifle, and I glance up at where I know she's positioned: the shots are going in her general direction but are nowhere near her exact location.

I wish we had comms.

I pop up again after ten seconds and lay down a long burst of suppressive fire. Most of it goes over their heads or wide by design—they drop and fall back, which is when I hit the deck and fire beneath the luggage tractor, hitting ankles, calves, and thighs.

One of them spies me as he's hauled back by a friend, pointing at my location and shouting in Spanish.

Weaponsfire fills the air with chattering, rattling, and barking, and sparks fly as the rounds hit the tractor, whining as they ricochet off the ground.

The Dragunov cracks again, a slow series of probing shots. I pop up and drop a mark with a round to the gut—lethal if untreated, but fuck me, this is a full-on gunfight and we're hideously outnumbered; what the fuck am I supposed to do? Tickle them?

I hear a truck engine—an ex-military Humvee rolls to a stop in the opening between hangars, a fifty cal gunner drawing a bead on my location.

"Fuck, fuck, fuck, fuck," I grumble. "Not good."

A fifty cal at this distance will rip through this little tractor like it's made of fucking paper. Hoping Scar can get a shot on him before he can tear me to shreds, I suck in a sharp breath, figuratively cross my fingers, and pop up, spraying several bursts in the direction of the Humvee.

CRACKCRACKCRACCRACKCRACK! The big fifty-cal opens up, and the luggage explodes in a cloud of shredded clothing and pieces of suitcase; the rounds go high, but they begin walking down toward me.

Time to fucking go.

CRACK!

Right as I'm about to make my exit and regroup, Scar takes out the gunner. Switching plans, I decide to pursue a reckless and probably idiotic idea: take the Humvee.

I sprint for it. The driver's door swings open and a tango hits his knee and brings an M4 carbine to his shoulder, firing at me; his rounds slice high and wide. I bring my rifle to my shoulder and put a round through his left shoulder and another through his right hand. He drops, yelling and cursing in Spanish. Two more targets emerge from the vehicle, but the Dragunov sprays their brains across the tarmac before they can even get their guns to bear.

I skid to a stop, yank the yowling driver out of the way, and throw myself behind the wheel. I slam the door closed, catching the driver with the corner of the door. It's still idling, which is good news. These Humvees don't start with a simple turn of a key—it's more complicated than that. I gun the engine, and the gunner thuds to the ground as the huge, heavy vehicle lurches forward. I pull it around and head for Inez's jet; the door opens downward as I approach, becoming stairs.

Immediately, gunfire rattles, and rounds plink off the side of the jet; a muzzle burst from inside returns fire. I hear Scarlett's rifle cracking steadily. They've realized the Humvee is no longer theirs—this deduction is made courtesy of the deafening barrage of rounds dinging and smacking off the doors and bulletproof glass.

I whip around to a stop at the stairs, pull the trans out of gear, shove open my door, and put down suppressive fire. It sort of works—more so because of Scarlett, though. Her rounds drop targets every time. Not a single bullet misses. Headshot, headshot, headshot. The wicked accuracy puts the targets under cover long enough for Inez to make it off the jet and into the Humvee.

"GO!" She shouts at me. "*LET'S GO, LET'S GO!*"

I slide behind the wheel and gun it, the Humvee echoing with the metallic thunder of ricocheting bullets.

I swing between buildings, and the clink and rattle of bullets hitting us stop all at once. The Humvee blasts out from between hangars, coming face to face with two pickups parked nose-to-nose across the road, blocking our way forward.

"Got it," Inez says, scrambling over the seats into the rear and taking the fifty cal.

It's deafening, shaking thunder rolls, and I don't bother even slowing down. "HOLD ON!" I shout.

The fifty cal erases the soldiers from existence in a pink spray, and we smash through the trucks, knocking them aside easily while we barely slow.

Inez stays on the fifty as we barrel down the roadway running behind the row of hangars; I make the turn that takes us toward the parking garage where Scarlett is positioned. The fifty belches and the whole Humvee shakes with the recoil; Inez knows what she's doing, that's for damn sure. She fires in steady bursts, taking her time and aiming. I both hear and feel rounds plinking and zinging off the vehicle.

Inez snarls in pain at one point, a pissed-off cry.

"You good?"

"Good," she calls back. "Creased my arm."

Fucking weird—I'm in a gunfight with *Inez*. Who had that on their bingo card for this year? Not me.

One more turn, and we screech to a halt behind the

garage. I'd originally intended to pile us all into the little pickup, but plans changed.

A minute later, the front passenger door opens and Scarlett hops in, red-faced, sweaty, panting. Her face is peppered with red dots: a round hit a little too close, spraying her face with shards of concrete.

"Okay, baby?" I ask, glancing at her.

She grins. "Five by five, hotshot. You?"

"Dandy." I glance back. "Inez? How you holdin' up?"

"I'll be better when we put distance between us and this entire situation."

"I meant physically."

"Fine. Just drive."

"Not exactly incognito in this big bitch, boss," I say.

"I'm well aware. Plans have been laid. For now, just get out of here. I'll stay up here and make sure we are not pursued."

Scarlett glances at me, eyebrow arched. "Plans have been laid?"

I just laugh. "It's how she is. But that said, this is a side of her I've never seen. I heard her tell my brother Saxon that her background is wetwork, but this is the first I've seen it."

"Well, she's a deadeye with that fifty, I'll tell you that for free," Scarlett says. "Never seen anything like it."

I smash through a chain-link fence and we jounce over a curb and onto a service road.

"Slow down, Solomon," Inez calls, sliding down from the gunner position. I slow to an inconspicuous thirty miles per hour. "Turn right here."

We're in the maintenance crew staging area—luggage tractors and jet tugs in need of service are parked everywhere, and a row of parked landscaping trucks line the far end of the lot. Crew members mill around doing various jobs and few of them pay attention to us even when we brake to a screeching halt in the middle of the repair yard.

Inez hops out first, beelining to a middle-aged man wearing khakis, a white button down, a tie, and a bright yellow hi-vis vest with a hard hat; he's on the phone, gesticulating angrily. Inez walks right up to him, snatches the phone from his hand, ends the calls, and speaks to him. The man tries to argue, but only once. Something Inez says stops him cold—he nods, backing away. Maybe it was just that icy look she gets—that'll stop anyone in their tracks.

He points at a newer pickup, a model not available in the US—it has a magnetic decal on the side announcing it as a telecom company truck. Inez climbs behind the wheel and brings the truck beside the Humvee.

Scar and I scramble out; Scarlett takes the back seat, leaving me to take the front.

A few seconds later, we're gone. Five minutes after that, we're off the airport grounds, passing a long line of police cars flashing lights and sirens on the way to the airport.

Glancing behind us, I see no sign of pursuit.

"Looks like we're clear for now," I say.

"Well done," Inez says, not looking at me.

Her jaw is tight, the corners of her eyes crinkled with tension. I scan her—the so-called "scratch" is actually a deep gouge along the outside of her right bicep, and it's bleeding profusely.

"Inez, dammit," I mutter. "That needs attention."

"So attend it," she says, her voice back to her usual cold, dry, rattlesnake rasp.

I rummage through the glove box and center console and find a small med kit and a wad of carryout napkins. I dab the worst of the blood away with the napkin, apply a liberal glop of AAA cream, and then tape bandages over the wound.

That done, I give my boss another once over.

She's about my age, maybe a little older—mid-thirties or so. Latin American origin, with long black hair in a thick braid down her back, wearing a black cap. Short-sleeve black shirt, black BDU pants, combat boots, tactical gloves.

I've never really *looked* at Inez, not really. I've only ever seen her as my boss, a figure of authority. She tends to come, give orders, and leave. But now, I see her in a new light.

She's beautiful. Sharp, angular, symmetrical facial features, and bright black eyes radiating lethal energy. A puckered round hole divots the side of her neck near her collar.

Not thinking, I touch the bullet scar. "That one had your name on it."

A pistol appears by magic, the barrel touching my jaw. "Do...*not*...touch me. Ever. Got it?"

I hold my hands up. "My bad. Sorry—I'm sorry. Won't happen again, boss."

The pistol vanishes. Her jaw ticks, and she glances at me. "We all have our hangups. Being touched is one of mine. Do not do it, please." As close to an explanation and apology as I'm gonna get, I realize.

"All good. Shoulda known better, boss. Sorry."

She lets out a soft breath. "It is fine."

We drive in silence for a while—she's heading in-city, taking a direct route as if she knows exactly where she's going and how to get there.

"So, we have a plan?" I ask.

She nods. "We do."

"Care to enlighten us?"

"Not at this time." She glances in the rearview mirror. "Scarlett Gutierrez, I am Inez. I am glad to meet you."

Scarlett leans forward between the seats. "Nice to meet you too, Inez."

"We have an additional problem," Inez says.

"And that is?" I prompt.

"Lash volunteered to come find you." She sighs. "I was not entirely truthful with the others about your situation. I told them it was CIA-related. Lash left to find you, and we have not heard from him since."

I groan. "Well, shit. Last known location?"

"On a jet somewhere between Las Vegas and Rio de Janeiro," she answers. "Jean-Paul reports that his jet, which Lash was riding in, vanished from radar somewhere over Mexico. There have been no reports of crashes, and it has not reappeared."

"Who the fuck is Jean-Paul?" I ask.

Inez rubs her face. "Someone connected to Silas. All three of you Cabots encountered…difficulties at the same time. Silas and Saxon both had to face the ghosts of their pasts via The Syndicate."

"Shit. They good?"

She nods. "All is well, now. Things were interesting for a while, with all three of you gone at the same time."

"They turn up with women?"

"Indeed. Seems to be a running theme," she says, glancing at Scarlett over her shoulder.

"So, Jean-Paul is…"

"Someone at the top of the Syndicate. Silas and

his...paramour, I suppose we can call her...created some changes at the top of the pyramid within the Syndicate. Jean-Paul was impressed, and he's a hard man to impress." Inez flips her braid back over her shoulder with a flick of her head.

"So we gotta find Lash, too?" I ask.

"Jean-Paul claims he can find a location for the jet; it will just take some time—he has to get the original designer, Valentine Roth, to authorize a trace of the black box."

"They can trace black boxes, now?"

"This one they can. The jet was...experimental, with a lot of very advanced technology."

Scarlett chimes in. "I've heard of him—that Roth guy. Billionaire, owns, like, half the world. He and that robotics guru, Xavier Badd, are working on some kind of new device for exploring hostile environments like Venus and places like that."

"Valentine Roth has fingers a lot of pies," Inez answers. "He is a close associate of our employer."

I frown. "He is? He knows him? Like personally?"

She nods. "Indeed."

"Interesting." I hesitate. "So...Inez."

She shakes her head. "Not now, Solomon. That little scrum at the airport was just a shot across the bow. They want me alive, so they let us go."

"Didn't feel like they let us go."

"They have military-grade hardware, Solomon. They could have put a Stinger up our tailpipe."

"Smacks of cartel," I surmise.

She sighs. "I promised you answers. I will keep that promise. For now, we need to get to my contact."

"Your contact?"

"A ghost from a former life. One of the few humans outside of you seven and our employer whom I legitimately trust. His name is Lorenzo." I notice the way her shoulders go tense, the way her jaw tightens and her eyes harden, go distant; she's got history with this Lorenzo.

I feel Scarlett's hand on my arm, and I twist to look at her; she gives me a minute headshake—don't bring it up.

Inez, however, doesn't miss a trick. Her lips twitch in something very nearly like a smirk. "Yes, I have…a personal connection to Lorenzo. Things might be somewhat awkward, but that is my worry, not yours."

"It's almost like you're a real person," I say, chuckling. "Smiling, sharing info, having personal connections and shit. Welcome to Earth."

Her head twists slowly to level a blank stare at me. "And what, may I ask, does that mean?"

I sigh. "Inez, it's not exactly classified intel that you're…aloof."

Her brow furrows. "Aloof?"

"Yeah, aloof at best. You've been our only point of contact with the outside world since the day we all took the brand and swore the oath, yet you've consistently been… inaccessible at best, as a person." I hold up my hands. "I know, I know—you're a superior officer, for all intents and purposes, not our friend. But you've given us precisely zero insight into who you are. As a group, we accept that. You're reliable, loyal, dedicated, and highly skilled. But as a human, you're a total void to us."

Her fist twists on the steering wheel, and her jaw works. Her eyes scan restlessly, checking mirrors and blind spots, rooftops, intersections, doorways—constantly assessing threats.

"I have had my reasons, Solomon."

I look at her. "We know. Trust me, we, of all people, understand that. But…" I sigh. "Never mind. Not my place."

Inez glances at me. "Speak freely, Solomon."

I look back at Scar, but she just shrugs—this one is all me. "Well, first, call me Sol. Second, what I was gonna say is that we understand the separation between us—between you and us guys. You're the big boss's second in command. We're all soldiers—we all understand the chain of command. But at the end of the day, we're not military anymore. We trust you because you've proven yourself to us. You show up when we need you. You provide what we need, which is a big fuckin' deal for us, Inez—we have no contact with the world outside the club. You're it. But it's hard to fully trust you when we don't fuckin' *know* you. Not a goddamn thing. You have our files. You know every last fuckin' thing about us, personally, professionally, and medically. You know our deepest, darkest secrets. You've seen each of us at our worst. We don't even know your last goddamned name. We can live without knowing the first thing about the guy who employs us, the guy who saved our lives and gave us a new lease on life. But you're our handler, Inez. Our liaison. We've all felt like we need a little more from you, personally. You don't need to be our best friend. You don't need to get trashed with us if that's not your thing. But you need to come down from your mountain once in a while and show us you're an actual fucking person."

She lets out a short, sharp breath. "I shall require time

to consider what you've told me…Sol. That's all I can give you at this time—I hear you, and I'll consider what you've said." She glances at the cheap Timex on her left wrist. "We're late. Lorenzo will be waiting."

We're downtown, passing by a stadium of some kind. She pulls into a parking garage and heads down to a far back corner. A battered, dirty, mud-caked, dented, rusty FJ40 is backed into a parking spot; as we approach, the driver's door opens, and a tall, broad-shouldered man rises from the vehicle. He leans back in and retrieves an HK MP5SD and a khaki military rucksack—which is heavy, judging by the way he swings it onto his right shoulder.

I assess him as he approaches our vehicle. Six-three or six-four, he's in his late thirties, with messy, longish jet-black hair under a battered red-and-white ballcap bearing some obscure Brazilian logo. He's densely muscled, and he moves with the confident, predatory grace of an operator. He's wearing faded, dirty blue jeans and a plain gray crewneck T-shirt with dusty, battered black combat boots. he has a sidearm strapped low on his right thigh. He wears a short, neat beard framing a hard jawline, and his eyes are deep and dark and restless. Objectively speaking, he's a helluva good-looking dude, oozing lethal capability.

He jerks open the rear passenger door, and Scarlett scoots to sit behind Inez; Lorenzo tosses his gear in and goes to the hatch of the old Toyota. He pulls out four black tac vests, tosses them into the bed of the truck, and then a huge, heavy black duffel bag that also goes into the bed. Then he slides behind my seat and shuts the door.

He lets out a sigh and then leans forward onto the console and touches Inez's shoulder, murmuring to her in

Portuguese: "It has been a long time, Sophia. You look…
quite well."

Inez's eyes flick to me, and she sighs, jaw ticking. "My
name is Inez." She says this in English.

Lorenzo nods and then shrugs, his head tipping
to one side. "As you wish. But to me, you will always be
Sophia. Sophia Bruna Santos de Silva."

Inez rests her forehead on the steering wheel, shoulders slumping. She speaks without picking her head up.
"You are a terrible listener, Ren. I'm already regretting the
decision to contact you." This is in Portuguese.

Lorenzo just chuckles. "You mean your friends don't
know Sophia?"

"They barely know Inez."

"Inez doesn't exist."

"Neither does fucking *Sophia*," she snaps in English,
whirling to glare at him.

I've never heard Inez curse, raise her voice, or show
any kind of emotion. To say I'm stunned would be a massive understatement.

Lorenzo sits back, shifting his HK into a more comfortable position. "I'll call you whatever you wish to be
called, Inez, but I will not pretend our history doesn't exist.
You asked for my help. Well, here I am. I told you many,
many years ago that I would always answer if you called, no
matter what. I keep my promises. But you cannot ask me
to pretend twenty years of history doesn't fucking exist."
This, too, is in Portuguese.

Inez picks her head up and squares her shoulders.
"I'm not asking you to pretend anything."

I turn in the seat and extend a hand to Lorenzo. "I'm

Solomon Cabot. This is Scarla Gutierrez. Thanks for join-
ing us." I say this in Portuguese.

His eyes widen in surprise—my Portuguese is nearly
as good as his and Inez's, and I assume it's their native
tongue, judging by the way they both lapse in and out of it.

He shakes my hand. "Glad to meet you, Solomon."
He shakes Scarlett's hand, then. "And you, Scarla. That's
an interesting, and accurate, nickname, I must admit." This
is all in English. He addresses Inez, then. "We need to get
out of Bogotá. This place is fucked."

Inez nods and starts back up toward street level.
"Where?"

"Anywhere that's not fucking Colombia. Quito, Lima,
Santiago, shit, Sao Paulo."

Inez snorts. "We need real options, Ren. I have a man
missing. Mercado has half his fucking organization after
me, and they used him—" a head jerk in my direction "as
bait. I can't just board a plane, and neither can they."

Ren toys with the fire selector switch of his rifle. "I
have a place in San José."

Inez pulls out into traffic and heads north. "And how
do we get there from here?"

He clicks his tongue against his teeth. "Won't be easy.
My guy has a line into Mercado's comms, says he's pulling
out all the stops for you. Mercado wants you alive, and
he'll stop at nothing to get you."

"You are not telling me anything I don't know," Inez
says; they've both switched to English. "Options, Lorenzo.
It's why I called you."

"I can get us to Costa Rica if we can get out of Bogotá.
Medellin would work. Quito would be better."

"They had military-grade hardware waiting for me at the airport," she says. "It got pretty spicy."

"Told you, darling—Mercado will stop at nothing to get you back."

Inez sighs deeply. "I'll die first. I'll put a bullet in my own brain before I let him so much as lay eyes on me."

"Figured you would want to get him alone," Lorenzo says. "You…him…a knife."

"I spent many years harboring a desire for revenge. I've moved on." She glances at me and then at Scarlett in the mirror. "Things are not going to get any easier, I'm afraid. I hope you're ready."

I put a fresh mag into my AK. "We've got your back, Inez."

She smiles at me, an almost soft look of gratitude. "I appreciate that. And I'm sorry, Solomon. I'm sorry my problems have caused you so much suffering. You too, Scarlett."

Scarlett just shrugs. "It got me Sol back. Worth it."

"Inez, can Lorenzo help us find Lash?" I ask.

Lorenzo frowns. "Find who?"

"My missing man, " Inez answers. "He was aboard a private jet from Las Vegas that went missing. A very unique, very expensive private jet belonging to a very, very dangerous individual."

"Anyone I've heard of?" he asks.

"Are you familiar with The Syndicate?"

"Yes."

"It belongs to one of the heads of that organization."

Lorenzo whistles. "Takes balls to fuck with them." He pulls a cell phone from his hip pocket. "I'll make some calls, put out some feelers."

"I would appreciate it," Inez says.

Lorenzo spends the next twenty minutes on the phone, switching from Portuguese to Spanish to English so rapidly and randomly that I can barely follow him. When he slides his phone away, he addresses Inez.

"I have my people looking into it."

"Thank you, Lorenzo." She hesitates, glances at him in the mirror, and then lets out a breath. "We have not discussed your payment."

Lorenzo snorts. "I will not accept your money. I am here for *you*."

Inez doesn't answer for a moment. "My employer will insist."

Lorenzo shrugs. "His money I will take. But I do it for you, not for money."

Inez doesn't answer again. Her eyes are troubled— seeing ghosts.

Several minutes later, Lorenzo's phone rings. He answers it with a terse English "Yes?" Listens for a moment. "I see. Thank you." This is in Spanish. He leans forward to address Inez. "The Fifty and the Fifty-six are blocked off entirely. Our only option is to take the Forty south and try to swing north at Armenia."

"That's days out of the way," Inez says.

"Well, unless you have a Stinger hidden somewhere, it's the only option."

I frown at Inez. "When he says 'blocked off,' he means…"

Lorenzo answers. "I mean, Mercado can block off entire freeways. He knows we want out of Bogotá, and he's not making it easy."

"Then won't going south be playing right into his hands?" I ask.

Lorenzo shrugs. "Yes. But we are not equipped for the kind of fight that waits for us if we try any northward routes. We can go south or east."

"I guess I'm not following," I say.

Inez lets out a sigh that's more of a growl than anything. "Mercado knows Lorenzo is with me. He knows you two are with me. He knows my contacts and Lorenzo's are mostly in Brazil, Colombia, and parts of Central America—he owns Venezuela, which is not an option, and he controls much of Brazil and Colombia, rendering those contacts of ours useless—they won't operate against Mercado, even for me."

"I think we need to know who this Mercado is," I say.

Inez runs her braid through her hand, pulling it forward over her shoulder to trail down her chest. "He's my husband."

Chapter 12

History Revealed; Checkpoint

S OLOMON STARES AT INEZ FOR SO LONG IT BECOMES awkward. "Your...*husband*?"

Inez huffs. "It's complicated."

Lorenzo laughs. "It's really not, though, is it?" He pats Inez on the shoulder. "I can explain if you'd like."

I don't miss the fact that *he* can touch her, but Solomon can't—I know Sol hasn't missed it, either.

Inez flips a hand. "Be my guest."

Lorenzo thinks for a moment or two. "Head for Quito." Inez nods, and Lorenzo sits back. "So, this woman, whom it seems you know as Inez, was born Sophia Bruna Santos de Silva. She is true cartel royalty. Her father, Bruno de Silva, was a warlord who took control over several of the largest militias back in the early eighties. Sophia was bred and raised to be his successor. As a child, she went everywhere with him—attended every meeting, watched him execute rivals, watched him deal with insubordination. By the time she was sixteen, he'd put her through elite combat training, everything from hand-to-hand to C-Q-B to room clearing. At eighteen, she led his bodyguards and occasionally acted as his personal executioner."

I look at Inez, shocked down to my fucking bones, but she refuses to look at me or Sol, gazing steadfastly out the windshield.

Lorenzo continues. "I was one of the bodyguards. I came from the poorest favelas of Rio, and I was…besotted. Obsessed with her. She was out of reach, though. She may as well have been a star in the heavens for a nobody like me."

"Just stick to the facts, Ren," Inez murmurs. "They don't need the storytelling."

"Oh, I dunno," I say, grinning at her. "I could use a little narrative drama."

Lorenzo chuckles. "This is part of the facts, darling. It's relevant."

"Quit with the endearments," she snaps. "You know how I feel about it."

He just rolls his eyes. "You can imagine my shock when she noticed me after two years of working under her. It was stupid and foolish, but we began a romance. Her father would never have approved, so we kept it secret from everyone. It was very exciting. The best years of my life."

Inez shakes her head. "Foolish. We both knew how it would end."

"True, we did," he says, without a trace of bitterness. "And it ended exactly as we both knew it would—her father discovered our secret. He intended to have me killed, but I got wind of it and fled. Joined the Brazilian army and ended up in the special forces, where even he couldn't touch me."

Inez says nothing.

"To punish her for sullying the de Silva name by dallying with the likes of me, he betrothed her to his little protégé, Rafael, who later began calling himself Mercado.

Rafael is the son of one of Bruno's closest friends, who served with him in the Brazilian Army back in the sixties and seventies. They were like brothers. Rafael's father was killed in the fight to take over the favelas, and Bruno took in Rafael and treated him like a son. Even though Sophia was the apple of his eye and the natural successor, Rafael was the true inheritor of Bruno's business dealings."

"I was to marry him and be the dutiful wife. An advisor at best. Too bad the old bastard raised me to have a mind of my own. He came to regret that," Inez says.

"Why raise you as a successor, only to put a man in charge?" Scarlett asks.

"Because my mother was killed by a rival. It scarred him. So he raised me like a boy. Taught me to fight so I couldn't be killed like Mama was." She says it *ma-MAH*. "Eventually, it became clear I was not suited for the business. I had no problem killing rivals and executing those who crossed lines or disobeyed orders. But the drugs, the prostitutes, the slaves? I didn't like it. I had no taste for it. Rafael had no such reservations, so Papa put the mantle of succession on Rafael. I was happy enough not to have that burden, which I never wanted in the first place."

Lorenzo shrugs, waves a hand. "Old Bruno thought he could control everyone. He assumed Rafael would be content to take the wheel when Bruno retired. But Rafael had other plans."

"A coup?" Solomon suggests.

"Pretty much. But he bided his time. He's no fool. Sophia was given no choice regarding the betrothal. She hated Rafael, mainly because he's a vile pig with poor hygiene and disgusting sexual habits. She told her father she had no intention of marrying Rafael, which is when the trouble began."

"He locked me up. My father, I mean. Told me either I married Rafael, or he'd let his men run a train on me."

"Your own father let his men rape you?" I ask.

Inez nods. "Repeatedly, for three days."

"Holy shit."

Inez doesn't answer. The hard, cold, ice-queen expression says everything.

"Fuck me," Solomon mutters. "This guy must be bad news if *that* was the better choice."

"When Bruno realized that she wasn't joking, he pulled her out of the hole he had her chained up in, got her cleaned up, drugged her, and married her to him anyway. She was catatonic through the whole thing." His voice is dark and angry. "I watched through a sniper scope. I nearly put a slug through her skull out of mercy."

"You should have," Inez snarls. "Would have saved me a lot of pain."

"Jesus *fuck*," Sol growls. "I hope you killed his ass."

"Oh no, Rafael did that," Lorenzo answers. "Within twelve hours of marrying Sophia, he murdered Bruno with his own two hands and took control of Bruno's empire, establishing himself as one of the major players in South America. Since then, he's only expanded his influence. Very few outside a few intelligence communities know this, but he quietly controls most of the cartels across South and Central America, especially after El Chapo's capture. He lets them run things their way, but the bulk of the proceeds go to him, and they answer to him. He owns politicians, police forces, generals…he's all but untouchable."

I frown, noting that Solomon is just as lost. "We've

both worked down here extensively, and we've never heard of him."

"By design," Inez says. "Even US Intelligence only knows the vaguest outlines about him. He's deeply paranoid, intensely secretive, and absolutely impossible to get to. The CIA doesn't even know his name, only that he exists."

"How the hell is that *possible*?" Sol asks.

"Layers and layers of secrecy and security," Inez says. "Every decision is filtered through dozens of people, none of whom know anything more than they're told. All they know is that they receive orders, and they follow them to the letter. If you don't, you end up dead. And not just you—everyone you know, everyone you love. Everyone you've ever even spoken to—friends, exes, old roommates. Anyone who knows you ever existed is wiped off the map. You are erased completely. And because he controls everything and everyone, there's no investigation."

I groan. "So the fact that we got away from that camp…"

Inez shrugs. "A good bit of luck, a lot of skill, and a lot of them underestimating the both of you. He's arrogant—no one has bothered even trying to stand up to him in a long time."

"So what does he want with you?" Sol asks.

She twists to look at Lorenzo, who only shrugs.

"Yours to tell, not mine," he murmurs.

She sighs. "His son—*my* son."

Solomon rears back. "*What*?"

"He won't kill me. He can't. I'm the only one who knows where his son is." She rubs her face with one hand. "He impregnated me after our wedding. I…I played the scared, submissive little wife. Let him…" She trails off, swallowing hard. "He forgot who I am. Forgot my training. Saw what he wanted to see—the dutiful little wife cowering in the corner every time he came into the room, spread legs and a closed mouth. After I bore the child, I made my move."

Lorenzo picks up the thread from there. "She slaughtered everyone in that house. Guards, maids, cooks, everyone. *Everyone*. Took the child and fled. Disappeared. No one ever saw her or the child again."

"Except you," Solomon guesses.

He nods. "She came to me. Asked for help. She was…" he frowns, sighs. "In bad shape. It was a brutal birth, she'd lost a lot of blood and then slaughtered twenty-six people, fled on foot, bleeding, with a newborn, from her father's estate. She won't speak of it, but she somehow made her way to my barracks in Goiânia. She should have died. I've always thought she survived out of sheer stubbornness."

"The child was innocent. He deserved a chance to live," Inez murmurs. "I did it for him."

"Where is the child, now?" Solomon asks.

"I'll never say. I am the only one who knows who he is and where he is. He does not know who his father is. He has never met me. He will never meet me. I put him with a good family. He is happy. That is the only thing that matters."

"Do they know?" I ask. "His parents."

A shake of her head. "No. They do not."

"So, he wants you and plans to torture the whereabouts of his child out of you?" Sol asks.

"Torture, coerce, bribe, threaten...whatever it takes."

"Why does he care?" I ask. "From what you've told me, he doesn't exactly seem like the type to care about doing the right thing by his child."

"He was involved in a helicopter crash a few years ago. Some believe it was not an accident, not that it matters. He survived, but his new wife and son died as well. He was grievously injured and will never sire another child. So his son—*my* son—is his only legacy. He wants to pass it on, create a dynasty." Inez shrugs, flips a hand. "He knows who I work for, about all of you, everything. But our employer is protected even from him. When you left for the funeral, he saw a chance to lure me out—he knows who I am, he knows I care about you seven. He knows I would come if he took one of you. So, he did. He didn't know about Scarlett, however."

"Do you think Lash's disappearance was engineered by him?" Sol asks.

Inez nods. "It is possible, yes. It is also possible that Lash's own past caught up to him—his enemies are quite powerful and well-placed enough to pull off making Lash vanish. It is ill-advised, not only because Jean-Paul is a very bad enemy to have and that jet cost a fantastic amount of money, but Lash himself is...well, he isn't easily angered, but I truly pity the one who does manage to do so, and Lash takes his loyalty to you men very seriously."

"Short answer, you don't know," Sol says.

"No, not for certain," Inez agrees.

"So, what's our plan, then?" Sol asks. "Get to Quito,

and from there to San José—I assume you mean Costa Rica, not California. Then what?"

Inez shrugs. "Avoid Mercado. He has influence and reach, but there are forces in Central America who resent Mercado. They don't like his constant expansion. He's taking slices of pie that don't belong to him, and he's making enemies who can be dangerous even to him, especially if they combine forces. Lorenzo knows some of these people. If we can get to Costa Rica, we can get in touch with some of them, and they can protect us until our employer can get to us."

"He can't get to us down here?" Sol asks. "He can't just put a jet or a helo down somewhere?"

"We're within Mercado's sphere of influence right now. Costa Rica is outside that sphere."

"And killing him isn't an option?" I ask.

Inez shakes her head. "As much as I'd like to, no. It's really not. Getting to him, even with a sniper, is not feasible. I told you, he's deeply paranoid about assassination, rightfully so. He never appears in public. He has a massive estate with all possible sightlines controlled. Patrols range as far as two and three miles around the borders of the estate, on top of the patrols within it. State-of-the-art security on the house and ground. He has a fortified underground bunker where he can hide out indefinitely, with tunnels to an underground garage and armored cars that the President of the United States would be safe in. His private helicopter is a former Russian gunship. So no. Assassinating him is not a possibility."

Sol blows out a breath. "So, letting him get his hands on you is not an option either."

"Most assuredly not," she says, her tone dry.

———— ◆ ————

We circle back south and head out of the city without issue—almost too easily, it feels. For several hours, Inez drives us south and west, and there's no sign of pursuit.

"I don't like this," Lorenzo says, eventually. "Too easy."

Inez nods. "Indeed. He has a nasty surprise waiting for us somewhere, I imagine."

After a couple more hours, we stop to refuel; Lorenzo brings carryout, and I take the wheel for the next leg. Despite all of us keeping watchful eyes on our six, there's still no sign of anyone. It's too easy by half. It only makes me nervous for what's to come.

I still have that bad feeling in the pit of my stomach—I'd hoped it would go away after we got away with Inez, but no such luck. It still bubbles away in my gut, an oily, acidic uneasiness. A foreknowledge that something is going to go terribly wrong at some point.

Sol is still in the front passenger seat, dozing. In the backseat, Inez and Lorenzo have been whispering to each other in Portuguese for quite a while. I tune them out since I don't know the language; it's a private conversation anyway.

At one point, some four hours into my leg of the drive, Inez dozes off, her head tipping to the side, resting on Lorenzo's shoulder. Lorenzo's eyes are closed, and his breathing is slow, but he's definitely not asleep. Sol notices, shaking his head in bemusement.

We stop in a tiny place called Garzón. More refueling, more carryout food, another switch. Lorenzo drives, now. I'm in back with Sol, and Inez is in front with Lorenzo.

We're all uneasy, on edge, and unable to relax.

More boring, uneventful hours. We're in the mountains, still, the air thin, clouds wafting past us in shreds and clumps as we navigate along knife-edge precipices.

"Fuck, fuck," Lorenzo says. "Get ready."

All of us were dozing when says this—we go from nodding off to combat-ready in an eye-blink. Ahead, traffic has slowed to a stop. Brake lights burn red, smeared into blurry streaks of dull crimson as a steady rain drizzles down. The wipers *thunk-thunk-thunk-thunk* and the defroster struggles to keep the windshield clear.

"Checkpoint?" Sol asks.

"Yeah, but not government. This is for us." Lorenzo draws his sidearm, checks the load, taps it back in place.

"Plan?" I ask.

Lorenzo shrugs. "Depends on what it looks like ahead." He speaks English almost without accent, only a faint hint of one here and there. "Just be ready for anything."

The cars creep forward, passing through the checkpoint one by one. After nearly thirty minutes, we're finally close enough to see what's going on: a pair of technicals—light trucks with machine guns mounted in the beds—are parked across the road, leaving just enough room for cars to pass through single file. The chokepoint is manned by a dozen armed men, and traffic is backed up in both directions for miles as they let a single car through at a time from each direction in turn, after a thorough search.

Inez, in the front passenger seat, sighs. "Well, this is going to be difficult."

Lorenzo nods. "Yes. We have no choice but to shoot it out."

"With this many civilians?" Sol asks. "I don't like that."

"Me either," Lorenzo answers. "But there's no way out

of it. We can't turn around, we're several hours past the last place we could have taken an alternative route, and I guarantee you he has that monitored, too."

We're still a hundred yards or so back. Lorenzo taps the steering wheel in a random drumming pattern with his thumb and forefinger—he's thinking. Finally, he snaps his fingers. "Sol, Inez, get in the bed and lay down flat. Wait till I shoot, and then take out the gunners. After that, take 'em all out and try not to kill any civilians."

Sol eases the rear passenger door open and climbs directly into the bed from the cab; Inez climbs into the rear and out the same door and into the bed. They both lay down flat, rifles on their chests.

I climb up front, seatbelt off, handgun ready.

The rear passenger door opens, and a pair of vests are tossed in, and the door closes again. Lorenzo and I both don a bullet-resistant vest.

We inch forward.

My heart pounds—it always does in the minutes before the shit hits the fan.

All too soon, after what feels like a million years, we're only two cars back.

The men working the checkpoint are not military—no uniforms and everyone is carrying a different weapon. Their checks are thorough, though. Lorenzo has his window down, as do I; he has his hand hanging out the window, and he taps three times on the side of the door—a signal. A triple tap on the floor of the truck bed tells us that Inez and Sol got the message—be ready, it's about to get spicy.

I have my silenced Glock along the outside of my

thigh, another handgun shoved between the seat and the console, with plenty of spare mags in the footwell.

Closer.

A car from the opposing direction squeezes through the chokepoint. The car ahead of us pulls forward; the driver gestures with his hand out the window, communicating annoyance as he argues with the soldier, terrorist, whatever the fuck he is. Meanwhile, more men are working in tandem, checking under the cars with long-handled mirrors, peeking in the trunk and backseat. Another car from the other direction is checked and waved through.

Lorenzo taps once—Inez returns it.

I pull back the hammer, swallowing around my pounding pulse.

"Wait for me," Lorenzo murmurs.

"Copy," I mutter back.

We're waved forward as the car ahead of us vanishes into the drizzle. Lorenzo has his handgun in his right hand, held across his belly, the gun hidden by his left arm, steering with his knee while keeping his left hand hanging casually out the window.

The men in the truck seem bored, and the others milling around with their assault rifles dangling from the straps, barely paying attention. They've probably been here for hours in the soggy, cold night, dreaming of warm barracks, a smoke, and a hot meal.

"Hello," the lead guard says in Spanish as he approaches, rifle held loosely, finger nowhere near the trigger. "Security check. We will have you on your way shortly. We apologize for the delay." He says this in a rote voice, having repeated it who knows how many times.

"No problem," Lorenzo says, grinning. "Great weather, eh?"

The guard doesn't reply as his compatriots approach to check the bed and undercarriage. They're mere feet away, now.

One of the gunners in the technical lights a smoke, takes a drag and hands it down to a friend, takes it back.

Lorenzo waits until the other two are about to peer into the truck bed before he makes his move. It happens so fast I almost miss it. With a tilt of his wrist, Lorenzo squeezes off a single suppressed round—I never even saw him put the suppressor on.

POP!

The guard's head jerks backward, blood spraying. For a moment, nothing happens.

And then everything happens all at once.

I crack off a quick pair of shots, dropping the two soldiers nearest the truck; at the same time, Sol and Inez jump to their feet and fire over the roof of the cab.

Inez takes her gunner down with a headshot, Sol with a gutshot—Inez finishes Sol's off before he can topple backward.

Lorenzo puts the truck in park and kicks his door open, dropping to one knee in the opening between door and body, pistol tossed to the seat and his MP5 at his shoulder. I follow suit, sticking with my Glock, dropping mark after mark.

Inez is a one-woman killing machine—she hops out of the truck bed and jogs forward into the open, takes a knee, and cracks off rounds in efficient three-round bursts, each one dropping a mark; switch mags—keep firing.

Approximately fifteen seconds have elapsed since

Lorenzo's first shot, and the guards have gotten off maybe half a dozen wild shots.

Silence.

Thirty seconds have elapsed, and every single guard at the checkpoint is dead.

None of us says anything for a long moment.

Inez jogs over to one of the trucks, sits half inside behind the wheel, and moves it onto the narrow shoulder, out of the way. Sol hops out of the truck bed, and he and Inez haul the bodies out of the way. I move the other truck while Lorenzo helps stack the corpses on the shoulder.

All of this takes place in the rain-dappled wash of headlights from the waiting pileup of cars; no one gets out, and no one seems shocked or panicked by the sudden violence.

Once the road is clear, we hop into our truck and move on.

About a mile or so later, Sol clears his throat. "I can't believe that worked."

No one answers him because none of us thought it would work, I don't think.

Too bad I still have the uneasy pit in my stomach: that wasn't it, either.

Fuck.

CHAPTER 13

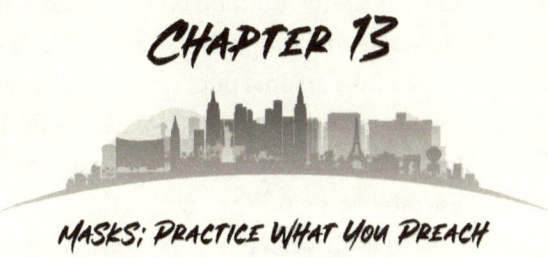

MASKS: PRACTICE WHAT YOU PREACH

LORENZO'S PHONE RINGS A FEW HOURS AFTER THE checkpoint excitement. He listens, gives a few grunts of affirmation, thanks the person on the other end, and then hangs up.

"I don't have confirmation yet," he says, "But my sources have received several reports of a strange-looking jet landing at an airport in the Bahamas."

"The Bahamas?" Inez asks, toying with her braid. "Odd." She flips the braid behind her back and shakes her head. "That jet left Las Vegas with only the pilot, copilot, and Lash on board. I watched it take off myself. It never deviated from its course until it disappeared, so it never took on another passenger, ruling out a hijacking. So then, why did it alter its course? Why did it stop transponding? Why did it go to the Bahamas?"

Lorenzo shrugs. "Excellent questions. Unfortunately, there are no answers from here."

Inez huffs. "I don't like it. Accompanying us to the airport to pick up Saxon and Terra was the first time he'd left Club Sin since taking the brand, and it was a last-minute decision on his part. No one knew we were leaving. There was no registered flight plan. I do not see how anyone could have known Lash would be on the plane—it belongs to Jean-Paul, and I simply must believe Jean-Paul would have vetted his personal pilot quite extensively."

"That's an understatement," I say. "When I looked into the Syndicate after discovering my brothers were part of it, I learned a few interesting tidbits, such as the fact that all support staff, such as drivers, pilots, personal attendants, and assistants, are hired from within. They do not out-source anything—everything is internal. So when they recruit, they are actually quite selective. And in fact, they even have their own version of an ASVAB that is pirated from the actual armed forces test and adapted to their uses. So, when someone in the upper echelons, like Jean-Paul, needs a chef or a driver or a pilot, they simply request one from within The Syndicate, ensuring that they will receive a loyal and thoroughly vetted individual."

Inez nods. "I heard something similar."

Scarlett shakes her head. "So you can technically work for and be a part of an international crime organization and be a fucking personal chef?"

I laugh. "Right? Here's the kicker—it's a good career path if you can get around the moral and ethical issues of working for a criminal organization specializing in trafficking drugs and humans. They pay damned well, offer great benefits, and a lot of room for advancement."

Scarlett stares at me in disbelief. "Benefits?"

I nod. "Not just perks like access to drugs, booze, and women, but actual employment benefits, like retirement funds, healthcare, even fractional ownership stakes, sort of like a stock option. It's wild."

"Sounds great, except for the whole human suffering

component," Scarlett mutters. She glances at me. "And we just allow them to proliferate?"

I shrug. "I mean, yeah. They're not headquartered in the States, they just do a lot of their business there. I'm not sure they even have a central headquarters. Part of why we haven't taken them down—they're fuckin' smart."

"As interesting as The Syndicate is," Inez says, "we have more pressing issues to discuss. Namely, the double-headed dragon of Mercado and Lash's disappearance."

"How worried are we about Lash?" I ask.

She rolls a shoulder. "Like all of you, he is more than capable of handling most anything. But also like all of you, his enemies are not to be trifled with."

"Are you at liberty to share any information?" I ask.

She muses. "I should not like to divulge information that is not mine to share. Lash is, more than perhaps any of you, an intensely private man. Even our employer and I only know some of his story. What I do know that I feel comfortable sharing is that his primary enemy, the one who sent him into hiding along with the rest of you, is an individual placed quite high in a governmental role. Not the US government, but a European one. This enemy is even more dangerous because of their position, which allows them access to resources even an organization like The Syndicate cannot bring to bear."

"So, do we go after him?" I ask. "Lash, I mean. Find him and support him, somehow?"

She spends a few minutes considering. "We must, I believe. But in order to do so, we have to escape from Mercado's sphere of influence."

"Okay, "I say. "So, what's the plan?"

"Same plan," Inez answers. "Get to Quito, and then to Costa Rica."

"But you think somewhere between here and San Jose, Mercado is going to make some sort of big move?"

"Most certainly," she answers. "We've eluded him thus far, which will displease him. He suffers from a god complex. His ego is enormous, while at the same time being quite fragile."

"Like most oversized male egos," Scarlett says, snickering. "The bigger the ego, the more delicate it is."

"Big ego, little peepee," Lorenzo says. "Such is my experience."

Inez arches an eyebrow at him, an amused look. "Oh? You have a lot of experience with penises, do you?"

"I've known a lot of men who overcompensate for their tic-tac dick with an overinflated sense of self. But really, he knows he has a teenie weenie, which is why his puffed-up ego is so fragile." Lorenzo grins at her. "It's like truth wealth. A newly rich man will flash his money with status symbols. A truly wealthy man will not—he doesn't need to. He knows his worth and feels no need to prove it to anyone."

Inez sniffs. "Rafael has much to compensate for. A small penis, which he rarely cleans. His wealth and position were obtained through deceit and murder and require a life of extreme isolation to preserve. At the end of the day, when he is alone with himself, he is a small, smelly, pathetic little boy with a tiny dick whom no one loves or even likes. His only respect is garnered through fear and bribery. He is an insect." She lets out a long, frustrated sigh. "But, he is a well-protected and very important insect."

"So there's nothing we can do for Lash right now,"

I say, feeling uneasy with the idea that he's just out there somewhere, circumstances unknown.

"At this moment, no," Inez says. "But I have a feeling that at some point, we are going to have to split up. I'm going to have to deal with Rafael myself."

"Not by yourself," Lorenzo says. "Never again."

Inez sighs. "Ren—"

"No." He says this gently but firmly—implacable, immovable. "You knew damn well what I would want when you called me. You cannot renege now, Sophia."

"*Inez*," she hisses. "I am *not* Sophia anymore."

"You are *always* my Sophia."

"And I promised you nothing."

"Yes, you did. By contacting me, by pulling me into your orbit again, you knew damned well that I would not and will not simply vanish again." Driving, Lorenzo glances at her, his gaze hard and angry. "I let you go *twice*, Sophia. *Twice*. For love, I let you go. For love, I went against everything within me. I would have run away with you, but you told me to join the army. So I did. I would have taken care of you, protected you and your son, even if it meant betraying my oath to my country and my men. But instead, I helped you place your son in a safe, loving home, and I watched you walk away from me a second time."

Inez's shoulders lift around her ears more with every word from his mouth. "Lorenzo, enough. This is not the time for this."

"It is. I could not care less what Solomon and Scarlett do or do not know about you. Nor should you. Let them know." He grabs her hand and kisses the back of it. "I will not let you go again, Sophia. I have lived too long without. I have spent too many lonely nights dreaming of you. No more. You are here, and I am with you. And so it will be. If Rafael is going to be dealt with, we will do it together."

Inez doesn't answer, nor does she withdraw her hand from his.

God, the guys aren't going to believe a word of this.

———— ◆ ————

Quito is one of the most fascinating places I've ever been. It's *old*. And like many very old cities, it's been built up layer by layer over the centuries; but unlike many other old cities, in Quito, you can see those layers due to the mountainous nature of the geography. In the oldest sections, you can see where the oldest builders began and watch the stonework age in reverse. Modern homes and businesses are built on foundations centuries and possibly even millennia old. Other areas away from the colonial center are much like any other city in South and Central America.

Lorenzo seems to know where he's going, moving us through the city at an easy, unhurried pace, as if we didn't have a care in the world.

All of us are scanning in three hundred and sixty degrees, fingers itchy along the trigger guard, ready for Mercado's forces to descend upon us at any moment.

Yet, nothing happens, even when Lorenzo pulls under the portico of a hotel—not a luxurious place, but not a roach-infested no-tell motel, either.

"Inez," he says, putting the manual gear shift in neutral, "get us two adjoining rooms and leave a key at the front desk for me under the name Luiz."

She nods, tucking her handgun into her waistband. "And you?"

"We need a new vehicle, and I need to make contact with my sources and see if I can find out anything about Mercado's plans." He grabs her hand before she can get out. "Leave the rifles and everything else. Just yourselves and your pistols."

Inez yanks her hand away. "It's not my first day, Ren. I know what I'm doing. See to yourself and do not worry about me." She's out of the truck and stalking toward the hotel entrance without a backward look.

Lorenzo watches her go. "She is much changed since I last saw her."

"I wouldn't know," I say. "But you do bring out a side of her I've never seen before."

He nods. "She was always a very deep and very complicated woman. Now, however, she keeps everything that makes her the woman I once knew buried very deep."

"So deep I didn't even know it existed till you showed up," I answer. "Good luck with that one."

Lorenzo chuckles. "Luck has very little to do with it."

"Oh?" I say, laughing. "Then what is it?"

"Patience." He glances at me over his shoulder. "Have you ever broken a wild horse?"

I snort. "Hardly."

"Well, a wild horse is very difficult to break, naturally. A young horse, one you have known since it was a foal, you must merely show consistency and patience. A wild horse is a whole other thing. They are smart, wary, and stubborn. Sophia, or Inez, as she insists upon these days, is a horse that was once domesticated and has now found the joy of freedom. She will not easily take a bridle again."

I laugh. "I would not make that comparison to her, Lorenzo."

"God, no. She would shoot me."

"I think shooting would be the kindest reaction to being compared to a stubborn animal," Scarlett says. "And on that note, c'mon, Sol. There's a shower and a real god-damned bed waiting."

Twenty minutes later, we have a room paid for with cash under a fake name. Out of long habit, we don't just barge in and lounge on the bed like normal people—we clear the room first, sweeping corners, checking behind the shower curtain and under the bed. Inez went into her room without a word to either of us, and we heard the door connecting the rooms lock.

"I guess she needs to be alone," I mutter quietly to Scarlett.

Scarlett laughs. "I'd say so. She was forced to call on someone I doubt she intended to see again. She's probably going through some serious shit right now."

"I suppose if anyone understands how that feels, it's us." I toss my pistol on the single-king bed and then sit and gratefully peel my boots off. God, I would kill some-one for my fucking Danners. These boots are like having my feet encased in soggy bread on the sides, with wood planks for insoles. Total shit. Better than being barefoot, but only marginally. And don't even get me started on the goddamn socks.

Scarlett is sitting beside me, doing the same. For a while, then, we just sit side by side, wiggling our bare toes and enjoying a moment of quiet.

"I almost forgot how grueling this shit can be," I say after a while. "On the road, covert, seeing people who want to kill you behind every shadow."

Scarlett just nods. Glances at me. "Sol?"

I meet her eyes. "Yeah, babe."

Her voice is quiet, pitched so I can hear without it carrying to the other room. "Am I like her?" she asks. "Inez."

I let out a breath, thinking about it. "Honestly, yeah, now that you mention it. In some ways, at least. But just to be clear, the Inez you're meeting is not the Inez I've known. She's way more open and personable."

"She's cold, prickly, and standoffish," Scarlett says.

I look at her. "I mean, yeah, and that's the personable, improved version. The Inez I've known is an isolationist ice queen. She shows up, gives orders, and that's it. She never talks about herself, gives away nothing about who she is, and doesn't spend any more time than necessary around any of us."

"And that's how I am?"

I take her hand and twine my fingers with hers. "It's how you used to be, yes."

She nods again, staring at our joined hands. "Watching her feels like looking in a mirror, sometimes. Especially when she interacts with Lorenzo. She clearly has deep feelings for him but refuses to acknowledge them at all."

"Scar, you've grown in that respect a tremendous amount in the last few days."

She looks at me, then. "It's hard to find the balance. I…" pink touches her cheeks. "When it's just you and me, I like being…" she trails off, shrugging uncomfortably.

"Being what, babe?" I ask. "Don't get shy now."

"I dunno the word," she says. "Soft? Girly? Feminine? I like…I like feeling…" she laughs, shaking her head. "I really don't know how to put it."

"I know what you're getting at," I say. "And I like seeing that side of you."

"I just…I can't be that person when it's go-time." She looks away, lifting a hand palm up. "But that feels…fake, or something."

I shrug. "Hell, I'm not the same Sol when it's go-time as I am when it's just you and me. We've all got…masks, I guess." I consider it for a second. "Not masks—that's not the right word. Facets. Who we are in different situations—the face we show. Right now, this is the part of me that's your man, your lover, your partner. When we gear up and go do violent shit, that's another part of me. When I'm hangin' out with the guys, that's another part of me, too. It's not fake, and it's not being two-faced or not genuine. It's just adapting to the circumstances. It would be weird if we were in a gunfight and I was all like, 'Hey baby, come sit on my lap, let's kiss.'"

Scarlett bursts out in laughter. "Yeah, Sol, that would be a little fucking odd." She tugs her hair out of the ponytail and shakes it loose. "Mainly because I don't know that I've ever sat on your lap."

"Then we should fix that." I grab her and haul her onto my lap.

Predictably, she's stiff at first. She sits bolt upright, hands on her thighs, shoulders square, not leaning against me at all. "This is…it feels weird."

I chuckle. "Because you're stiff as a board, babe. Relax. Get comfy."

"It just feels unnatural. I kill people for a living. I don't sit on laps." She clenches her fists and unclenches them in synch with her intentionally slow breathing.

"Right, but you're not Scar the operator right now, are you? You're Scarlett, my…girlfriend? My woman? I don't fuckin' know what word to use, but this is just us right now."

She blinks at me. "*You're* not relaxed. We're on the edge of the bed. If I put my weight on you, you'll have to brace to support me. Which means you're not relaxed, and I'll feel it, and then I won't be able to relax."

I frown. "Hmmm. Can't argue with that logic." I stand up, taking her with me—she flat-out yelps in protest, her arms going around my neck.

"Jesus, Sol, warn a bitch, next time," she snaps.

I just laugh. "More fun this way."

"Where are you taking me?" she demands.

"God, relax, Scar, shit." I circle to the far side of the bed and sit, stuffing the pillow behind my back and stretching my legs out. "There. I'm comfy as fuck. Your turn."

She sighs, still sitting stiff as a fence post on my thighs, knees half-bent, shoulders back, head high, almost in a sort of seated version of parade rest. "Can't I just relax, you know, *next* to you?"

"Nope. Cuddle time."

"*Cuddle*?" She says the word as if it's been dipped in lemon juice.

I can't help but laugh, snickering as I try to contain it, only to lose it entirely, pressing my face against the back of her neck. "Yes, Scarlett. *Cuddle*."

"That's not in my skillset, Solomon."

I laugh all the harder. "It's not a skill, you silly goose."

She twists in place. "Silly goose?"

"Yes. You're being a silly goose." I wrap my arms around her, pull her flush against my chest, and then sit back, taking her with me. "It's the easiest thing in the world. All you do is…nothing."

"Exactly. I'm not good at doing nothing." She's laying against me, but still stiffly. "Can't we just fuck?"

Instead of answering, I wrap one arm around her shoulders above her breasts, the other low across her hips, and just…hold her.

"Solomon, why are we doing this?"

I put my hand over her mouth. "Hush, baby. Just relax."

"I don't…know…*how*."

"This is you learning."

"I'm not a baby."

"You called me baby the other day."

"Heat of the moment. I was out of my mind."

"Still counts." I nuzzle my nose behind her ear. Whisper against the tender shell. "I've got you, Scar. Close your eyes, breathe, and just *be*. Just be here with me. You're safe for now. You can turn it off, just for a bit."

Her head shakes, but I feel her pull in a deep breath and hold it. When she lets it out, her body softens a little bit.

"There you go," I murmur. "Good. Do it again."

Another long, slow, deep inhalation. She holds it. And…lets it out in a pursed-lip ten count. And now softer yet, starting to melt against my chest.

"Can I move?" she whispers.

I chuckle. "You can do whatever you want, as long it's not getting up. This isn't a training technique, babe, it's just fuckin' cuddling."

"I'd rather fuck than cuddle."

"Believe me, I know the feeling."

She twists to lay on her stomach—I scootch down so I'm nearly laying, and she rests her head on my chest, hands on my shoulders. For a long time, she just breathes and lays on me.

"I like this," she murmurs, eventually.

"Me too. See?"

"She teach you to cuddle? Violet?"

"Jealous?" I ask.

She nods. "Yes."

"Good."

She lifts her chin to look at me. "Wait…really?" A perplexed blink. "Why's that good?"

"Because it means you want me all to yourself."

"I do." She settles back down. "I'm mad she got to experience parts of you first."

I roam her body with my hands over her clothes, sensually but not sexually. "When we were together the first time, neither of us knew what the fuck we were doing. We didn't know what we wanted. We didn't know…anything. The only way either of us knew how to express anything was through sex."

"I still don't."

"And what I had with Violet was….transactional. She wanted more, but I couldn't give her something that didn't belong to her—it belongs to you. Always has, always will."

Scarlett heaves a deep breath. "Sol…"

"Yeah, babe?"

"I just…" her voice drops till I can barely hear her. "I do want to learn. I'm trying."

"This is it, honey. We're cuddling."

"Are there…like, other positions?"

I laugh. "It's not martial arts, Scar, Jesus. It's anything we want it to be. You don't have to figure it out. It's non-sexual physical intimacy, if you want a definition of some sort. When you fall asleep on my chest, that's cuddling. Let's say we're on the couch at home in the Club, watching a movie. Instead of sitting next to me, you get close. Whatever's comfortable. It's just closeness, honey. Being close to each other because it feels good. It's comforting. Makes you feel…" I trail off, looking for the right word.

"Safe," she whispers. "I've never been safe. Never felt safe. Alone or with someone, in the middle of a fucking army base on US soil, anywhere—I've *never* felt safe. In my own home—not that I've ever really had an actual *home*. I have *never* felt safe at any point in my life." A long pause. "Except here and now, with you. Like this."

This admission makes my chest ache and my eyes burn. A hot lump forms in my throat. "Fuck, honey."

She lifts up to look at me, frowning. "Jesus, Sol, are you…" She runs a fingertip from the tear duct beneath my lower eyelid to the outer corner. "Are you…*crying*?"

"No," I lie.

Her brow furrows deeper, blinking hard. "What? What did I say?"

I swallow hard. "That you feel safe with me like this."

She rolls a shoulder. "Nothing to cry about." She looks away but then right back at me, searching me, dabbing at my leaky tear ducts, and examining the moisture on her fingertip as if it were a mysterious substance.

"Is to me," I whisper. "You're the strongest, toughest person I know, Scar. After everything you've been through, everything you've done…for you to feel safe with me, in my arms…it's…" I swallow hard. "Fuck, I dunno. Chokes me up. Means a fucking lot, Scar. Best gift I could ever get."

She shakes her head and rests on my chest again. "Shut up." Her breathing comes shallow and fast, now. "Dammit, Sol."

"Got you going, too, did I?"

"No."

"Then look at me."

A petulant shake of her head. "No. Fuck off. Asshole."

I roll to put her beneath me, pinning her with all my weight, cupping the side of her face. Wetness pools in the corners of her eyes. "Share it with me, sweetheart. Lemme have it."

"I don't even...I don't know. I don't fucking know." She squeezes her eyes shut and tries to wiggle a hand free to cover her face.

I grab her wrist and prevent her from covering her face. "No hiding. Not from me. Not this."

She closes her eyes and shakes her head again. "No. Shut up. Go away."

"Talk to me, honey."

"Stop calling me stupid names."

"I know what you're doing, Scar."

"What am I doing?"

"Acting like a hardass because you're embarrassed. Pushing me away because the emotional vulnerability is terrifying the shit out of you."

She parts her eyelids, teardrops glinting on her thick black eyelashes. "What the fuck do you *want* from me, Sol?"

I brush my thumb oh-so-gently over one and then the other. "You're giving it to me right now."

"I don't even know why I'm crying."

"Yeah, you do."

"I don't."

"Want me to guess?"

"Sure?"

I kiss one eyelid. "You're finally getting in touch with all the soft emotional shit you've been stuffing down your whole life. It's coming out."

"Scares the fuck outta me," she whispers.

"I know," I whisper back. "But you're doing it. Because you trust me. You know I've fuckin' *got* you, Scar. Your secrets are safe with me. This part of you, the soft, emotional, vulnerable side? It's *mine*. Only for me. And I swear to fucking Christ, Scar, I will guard it with every fucking thing I've got. You can give it all to me. All that soft sappy shit. You can be that with me. I want it. I need it. And you can also trust that when the shit hits the fan, I will never, ever treat you as anything less than the hardcore, badass queen of the fucking night that you are."

"Sol—" she whispers, the words wet with unshed tears.

"I fucking love you, Scarlett."

She chokes. "Solomon—"

"You know who else I love?"

She frowns. "No?"

"Maria Consuela Rodriguez."

Her shoulders shake, and her eyes squeeze shut as tears finally burst free and run down her cheeks. "Shut up—shut up—shutthefuck*up*, Sol."

"Nope." I kiss the sharp angle of her cheekbone and taste tears. The other side. "I love you."

"Fucking shut up!"

"Nope." I cradle her face. "I love every part of you. I love Scarlett Luisa Gutierrez, the whole person you've become. I love Scar. I love Scarla. I love Scarlett. I love the badass. I love the lover you're becoming. I love the woman. I love the killer. I love the cold prickly bitch you can be."

She's shaking all over with silent sobs. "Sol, please. Stop."

"No." I kiss her other cheekbone. Each closed, wet eyelid. I kiss her cheeks. Her chin. Her lips. "I love Maria Consuela Rodriguez."

"She's fucking dead. I'm not her anymore."

"You buried her, but she's not dead. I see her coming out. And it's beautiful, Scar. *You're* beautiful."

"I'm not beautiful. I'm a lot of things. Beautiful ain't one of 'em."

"Wrong. You're beautiful. Inside and out. And I love you." I cup her face. "Look at me, beautiful."

She squeezes her eyes shut and shakes her head. "No."

"Come on, honey. Look at me."

Her eyes crack open. "What, goddammit?"

I laugh, kissing her lips now. "I love you."

"I heard you, Sol. You only said it, like a billion times." She wipes at her eyes.

"Scar, honey. You don't have to say it. Not till you're ready, whenever that is."

"What if that's never?"

"Nah, you'll get there."

Her hands steal beneath my shirt to find skin. "You're sure?"

"Absolutely. If you can give me *this*," I wipe at her tears, "then someday, you'll be able to tell me you love me. I know you do."

She nods, a tiny, fractional dip of her chin. "Yeah."

"Then that's all I need, honey—to know that you do."

"I'm trying so goddamned hard, Solomon," she whispers. "This shit is so far away from...from everything I've ever been that...I don't even know how to...." she trails off with a frustrated sigh. "It's so hard and so scary. Walking around Kandahar naked would be less terrifying."

"Why is being with me so scary?" I ask. "You trust me with your life, why not your heart?"

"Because..." she pauses for a moment. "Because I don't know who I am on the inside."

"Why'd you join the CIA?" I ask.

She frowns at the abrupt change in topic. "Um? Honestly, because it was the only option other than being homeless and starving. When I accidentally happened across that meeting, I hadn't eaten in days, hadn't slept properly in who knows how long. My shoes were coming apart. I was walking around considering either killing myself or voluntarily going back to selling myself... and suicide was the more appealing option. So when that agent suggested I join the CIA and explained that it would mean I'd get paid, and that I'd have somewhere to sleep at night and something to eat, and I wouldn't have to let some greasy, smelly, fat old white man fuck me, yeah, it seemed like an easy choice."

"What kept you doing it?"

"Why are you asking me this now?" she demands. "Why does it matter?"

"Humor me."

A roll of her eyes. "Fine, whatever. Because I swore an oath, I was given citizenship despite having entered illegally. I was given a new identity. I was given train-ing—a skillset. I was given a purpose…a country to serve. I've never identified as Panamanian. Hispanic, sure. Latina, sure. But the country I was born in? No. Nothing wrong with it, I suppose, it was just…not home—I was so young when I left, you know? Inasmuch as I *have* a home, it's the US. I'm American. America gave me a life and a reason to live, and so I chose to spend that life protecting her against all enemies, foreign and domestic."

"So when you say you don't know who you are on the inside, what you really mean is you don't know who you are without a mission? Without the action."

A sigh. "Yeah, I suppose so."

"What you're *really* saying, then, is that you're not afraid of letting yourself fall in love with me—that hap-pened a long time ago. You already love me, and you know it. So do I. What you're afraid of is the idea that committing to loving me and living with me—doing life with me—means you have to give up being an operator, and you don't know who you are without that."

"Yes," she whispers. "That's exactly what I'm afraid of. I'm scared loving you isn't enough."

I smile. "I'll give you a little shortcut, Scarlett: It's not. Loving me isn't enough. If the only reason you're willing to give up everything you know and be a part of the Broken Arrows with me is because you love me, it's doomed to fail. You can't take the brand for me."

"Sol…"

"I love the shit outta you, Scarlett. But I won't let you take the brand if you're only doing it to be with me. You have to do it for you."

"I don't know what that looks like." She covers her face with her hand. "That's what I mean when I say I don't know who I am on the inside. I've lived my whole adult life with the one singular purpose of completing my assignments. Finish the mission. Survive. Get the bad guys. Do the job. That's it. Being at home, on base, alone, with no mission to prep for or debrief from, no training exercises…just free time? I have no fucking clue what to do."

"Scar—"

She cuts over me. "Ask me things about myself."

I frown. "Like what?"

"Pretend I'm some chick you just met at a bar, and you're trying to get to know her."

"Okay….last movie you watched?"

She shrugs. "No clue. Haven't watched a movie in years. I don't even have a TV."

"Favorite movie?"

Another shrug. "Princess Bride, I guess. That's the last movie I remember seeing, actually. You and me on that flight from…shit, where was it? Germany to… Kuwait?"

I smile at the memory. "I think so, yeah. We watched it on my phone in the back of a C130, each of us with one earbud."

She shakes her head, smiling. "You quoted just about every single line throughout the whole movie. Drove me fucking nuts, but it was funny as hell. Especially the 'wuv…twoo wuv' part."

"I don't think you've ever laughed as hard."

"I haven't. That's why it's my favorite movie. And honestly, one of my best memories."

I flop to my back and pull her onto my chest. "Favorite color."

"Black."

"Favorite color that's not black, white, or gray.

She pauses. "I…um. Blue, I guess. I dunno."

"Favorite genre of music?"

"I don't listen to music."

I frown at her. "Wait, what?"

She shrugs. "I don't."

"How is that possible?"

"I mean, guys on my squad will put on rap or metal when we're lifting or sparring or whatever, but I don't think I have ever, once, just put music on simply to listen to music. I'm either training, traveling, or working. Music simply doesn't have a place in my life."

I shake my head. "No wonder you're so cranky all the time, Jesus, woman."

She glares at me. "Well fuck you very much."

I dissolve into laughter. "Scar, honey, that says *everything*. Music is one of life's great joys."

She stares at me. "Okay, hotshot, then what's *your* favorite genre of music?"

"That's impossible to answer," I say. "I like metal when I'm working out. If we're all just hanging out in the common room, it's usually nineties rap—you know, the good stuff: Nas, Tupac, Biggie, DMX, Jay-Z, shit like that. If I'm just chillin' alone in my room, like reading or whatever, I might turn on coffeehouse kinda shit."

"I don't know what 'coffee-house kinda shit' even is," she says.

I laugh. "Hell, woman. Singer-songwriter. One person with a guitar and a microphone, mainly. It's quiet, soft, soothing, and thoughtful. The lyrics are usually poetry and not just nonsense and bullshit. It's chill music."

She props her chin on my chest. "Hold up, though. Question."

"Okay."

"You really just sit down and…do nothing?"

I laugh. "No. I don't just sit in a chair in the dark and stare at nothing, Jesus. I read a book. Watch a movie. So sometimes I will turn off the lights and put in my earbuds and listen to an album. I do that with piano music, usually. It's kinda like meditation."

"You meditate?"

I nod. "Abso-fucking-lutely. Meditation and breathing are a huge part of how I learned to transition away from being an operator. Because Scar, honey, I know exactly how you feel."

"You do?" She whispers.

"Fuck yes. When I woke up in that hospital room, I questioned everything. How totally fucking wrong that mission went, and how ready they were to just let us fucking die. They burned us the second the mission went sideways. Hung us out to dry. After all we fucking did. Mission after mission, shedding blood—others' and our own. Facing death time and again. Suffering from PTSD that we don't have the time or wherewithal to cope with, so we pretend we're fucking fine and go do another fucking mission. One op goes wrong, and they just fucking abandon us?"

She swallows. "I still struggle with that."

"I fucking hope so. I couldn't do it anymore. I knew that if I showed up at Langley, they'd put me back out in the field. There would be no apology, no culpability. Just

'thanks for your service, go kill this terrorist, thanks-bye.'"
I shake my head. "And that would be after I faced months
of rehab. I'd have to go to Walter Reed and answer questions and...yeah, no. They fucking abandoned me.
You. Everyone. Our *whole fucking team* got killed, and
it was fucking preventable. If just *one* goddamn person
had taken a second look at the intel and gone, 'y'know,
something about this don't smell right,' it'd have been
scrapped, as it should have been. But we were expendable. Without value. So yeah, I was bitter. Angry. Jaded.
And the choice Inez gave me was a no-brainer. I wanted
out. But once I got out, like you, I had no clue who I was.
Without a mission, who was I? What kind of a man was
I? What did I like? What did I want? I'm still figuring it
out, but the first, biggest step was admitting to myself
that I had no clue who I was and then committing to figuring that out."

"And who are you?" she asks.

"I'm Solomon Cabot. I love all kinds of music. I like
watching action flicks with the guys and picking apart all
the shit that makes no sense. I like working out. I hate
country music. I hate the color orange." I sigh, shrug. "I'm
not sure I have the same sense of purpose anymore, and
that's taken some adjustment. But there's a certain peace
and enjoyment in every day being the same after so many
years of never knowing where I'd be or what I'd be doing
from one day to the next. I miss the rush, the adrenaline,
the danger. But one thing I've learned since those assholes snatched me is that I don't miss it *that* much—as
weirdly almost nostalgic as all this is, it also kinda sucks.
When all this is over, I will happily go back to bouncing at Club Sin. It's not exciting. It's kinda boring and

repetitive. One day is pretty much like the next and the last. It's not some great purpose, like serving my country or whatever. But that's okay. My purpose is not in my work. It's in the guys and girls I live with. My brothers, Sax and Si. My other brothers—Rev, Kane, Chance, and Lash. Inez. Myka, Annika, and Angalee. They're…my family, I guess, and that's my purpose."

She rolls off me and flops to her back. "You just… live? Hang out with people, eat, sleep, lift, work, and that's it?"

I nod. "That's it. That's life."

"And it fulfills you?"

I shrug. "It's enough, for now."

"For now?"

"I think maybe someday I'd…." I find it hard to admit this. "I, um. I'd like a family."

She goes to her side, facing me, eyes wide. "Like…a wife and kids sort of thing?"

I nod. "Yeah."

She blinks, tears in her eyes. "Sol."

"I'm not putting anything on you. I'm not asking you to say anything or commit or decide—nothing. I'm just practicing what I preach—giving you honesty even though it's scary. And it's scary because I know damn well you may not ever be in a place where you can give me that. I know that, and I'm okay with it. And I still choose you."

"Sol."

"Yeah, babe?"

"You talk a lot."

I grin at her. "Yeah?"

She nods. "A fucking lot."

"So?"

She gives me a long, scorching look that communicates everything she wants. "We have a bed. We have privacy. I want to take advantage of it while we have it. You can psychoanalyze me later."

"So what you're saying is—" I start.

She throws a leg over my hips and straddles me, sits upright, and peels off her shirt and bra. "I'm saying, Solomon Cabot, that I want you to shut the fuck up and make love to me."

I slide my hands up the long, sensuous expanse of her bare back. "Well, when you put it that way..."

CHAPTER 14

THREE LITTLE WORDS

H E TUGS MY ERECT NIPPLE INTO HIS MOUTH, eliciting a sharp gasp from me. I dig my fingers into the soft cool hair on the back of his head, holding him to my chest, my head thrown back.

It doesn't last long, though. A second or two later, I find myself on my back and Sol is dragging my pants and underwear off, and then he's hauling me upright again, sitting on his chest, facing the headboard as he gazes up at me.

"Better grab onto something, beautiful," he says, a lascivious grin curving across his face.

"Sol, what are you—"

My question is answered when he cups my ass and pulls my hips forward, guiding my sex toward his mouth. Before I can so much as gasp, his tongue slashes through my lips and curls against my clit, and a sudden bolt of heat shears through me, and I fall forward, grabbing at the headboard as I keen through gritted teeth.

Sol cradles my ass in his hands with the utmost reverence, gazing up at me from below, mouth fused to my pussy, tongue slowly driving, rolling, circling. My tits bounce and sway as he laps and suckles, and my eyes close, and my heart pounds. Sol groans with pure, unabashed, male delight as I find the edge rising within me and begin to grind on his mouth, riding his hungry, eager tongue.

My eyes rip open at his groan, and I watch him lose himself in my rapture, devouring me more and more ravenously as I climb up to climax, whimpering and gasping. When I reach the cusp, he slows, to my great frustration— only to slide two thick fingers inside my empty, aching sex and bring me right back to the edge.

This time, he pushes me over it, and light bursts behind my eyes with sparkles and flashes of color; my whole body spasms, and a shuddering cry escapes my lips, and I balance above him, reaching down to clutch at his head, grinding furiously against him as I come and come and come.

I know him well enough at this point to know that if I don't stop him now, he'll keep me coming just like this, and as incredible as that feels, I have other plans.

I swing off of him and off the bed. Dance backward as he reaches for me.

"Where you goin', darlin'?" he asks.

I grin at him, crooking my finger at him.

He rolls off the bed and to his feet, stalking and swaggering toward me, and I let my desire for him flood through me—and not just physical desire, not just sexual attraction. Perhaps for the first time ever, I allow my feelings to well up inside me, to flow through me.

Need.

Attraction.

Appreciation.

Arousal.

Gratitude.

Fear.

Worry.

Nerves.

A desire to please him.

A desire to simply be held.

A need to hold him.

A need to lose myself in him.

A sure knowledge in my gut that there is no other human on this earth who will ever, ever know me and understand me as he does.

A willingness to give myself over to him, fully and completely, no matter what that looks like.

A belief in the core of who I am that he's my person, and I'm his.

A realization that I love him.

I dance out of his reach, laughing as he grabs for me and misses. His hand grazes my hip as he grabs for me again, and I wriggle the other way, laughing and giggling in a very un-Scarlett-like way as he lunges for me. It becomes a game of cat-and-mouse, and soon we're both laughing and breathless.

Until he catches me.

His arm slings around my middle, arresting my momentum and swinging me around and off the floor. My back slams against the wall beside the doorway to the bathroom, and he pins me there with his body, mouth capturing mine.

I groan as I dissolve into the kiss, giving him my tongue.

His hard cold zipper presses against the tender flesh of my sex, the hardness behind it begging for relief.

I push him away and spin us, putting his back to the wall. "My turn," I whisper.

"I need you, Scar," he murmurs.

"I know, honey," I say. "Trust me."

"I do."

I lift his shirt up and off, letting my hands roam his perfect, delicious body. "You're bigger than you used to be," I whisper. "I like it."

"Yeah?"

I kiss his shoulder, the base of his throat, the hard line of bone at the top of his chest. "Mmm-hmmm."

He slides his hand into my hair above my left ear. "So fucking beautiful, Scar."

"I think maybe you'll like this view even better," I whisper, dropping to my knees.

I've used my mouth on him any number of times in the past, of course—it's a normal, natural, enjoyable part of sex. He usually stops me before he comes, preferring to be inside me. And I have never, with him or anyone else, gone down on my knees like this. It always reeked of sub-servience. Submission. A lack of control.

But with Sol, it's different. It's a different kind of in-timacy. It's not about subservience, it's about a different kind of connection. An intimacy based on trust and the desire to pleasure the other person. I know Solomon re-spects me. I know he values me. Every time we connect physically, he puts me first. Gives me pleasure until I can literally take no more.

Being on my knees like this is for me. I could blow him just as easily lying down and it'll feel the same for him. No, giving him oral like this is for me. It's a surrender. Allowing myself to trust him. Allowing myself to give him a different aspect of myself—one that, until now, I always saw as weak. But it's not. It's not weak. It's strong. I know myself, and I know my worth, and more importantly, I know my worth and my value to Sol, and I know it won't be diminished by doing something in a posture that I always saw as weak, submissive, and degrading.

I push him up against the wall, grinning at him while running my tongue over my upper lip. Flick open his fly, lower his zipper. His cock springs into the opening, thick and rigid, veins begging for my tongue.

I tug the jeans so they fall around his ankles and he steps out of them, kicking them aside. His eyes are locked on me, heavy-lidded, brow furrowed, breath coming slow and deep—-his anticipation is delicious. He wants this. Bad. But I also know that in the seconds before he lets himself come, he'll try to stop me. Usually, I like that he stops me and turns it into an us-thing rather than a him-thing. This time, though, I intend to follow through—all the way.

But I intend to play, first.

I slide my hands up his thighs, over his sharp hard hipbones, and carve my hands over the hard blocks of his abs. Reach up and toy with his nipples while kissing his diaphragm. Run my tongue up the groove between his abdominal blocks. Caress down his hips again and kiss and lick lower and lower until the hard warm length of his shaft rests against my cheek as I kiss the tender, delicate skin behind the thick root. I circle my hands around the backs of his powerful thighs and slide my lips over his skin to the other side, his cock now nuzzling the right side of my face as I touch my lips to his skin around the root and up to his belly.

Slide my hands upward, teasing them up to his taint

and along the crack of his hard, taut ass. Cup the firm bubbles of his buttocks, scratching my nails down and smoothing my palms in circles.

"Fuck, Scar," he growls. "Killin' me, babe."

I palm his thighs and then cup his heavy, hot, taut ballsack, lifting, kissing the side of it, underneath it, the other side. "Haven't even done anything yet," I whisper.

"What you're doing right now, honey..." he rumbles, voice taut, low, breathless. "Fuckin' amazing."

"Not even touching your cock," I murmur, delicately petting his balls with my fingertips.

"Gonna make it all the better when you do," he answers.

I nuzzle my cheek against his shaft, running my tongue up his soft skin. With one hand, I roam the hard plane of his chest and rippling wonderland of his abs, and with the other I tease his taint with my middle finger, toying, tickling, tracing with my fingertip and fingernail, ever so softly and gently.

"Fuck, babe. You tryin' to make me beg?" he growls.

I grin up at him. "Maybe."

His fingers trail over the crown of my head, run behind my ears, trace my jawline. "Please, love. Let me feel that sweet mouth on my cock, Scarlett."

"Mmmmm," I hum, pressing a soft kiss to his belly just beneath his navel, the tip of him glistening millimeters away from my chin.

Look up at him, kiss again, lower. Open my mouth, eyes locked on his. Take him into my open mouth but don't close my lips around him, pulling away, only to lick up beside his shaft once more.

"Fuck, Scarlett. Fuck. Please, baby."

"You want it?" I ask.

"Fuck yeah. So bad."

Kiss the underside of his shaft, closed-mouth kisses upward from the root to the tip. Take the plump round head in my mouth and lick the tip before letting him go.

"Like that?"

He groans, head thunking back against the wall. "Fuckin god, Scar, yes. Like that. Please, honey."

"Please what?" I whisper, closed-mouth kissing the tip again. "Tell me what you need, Sol."

"Your mouth, babe."

"Like this?" I roll a few shallow bobbing thrusts onto his head, tongue flicking and swirling.

His hands rest on the top of my head, fingers pressing into my scalp. "Fuck, fuck—yeah, babe. Just like that."

"That's it?" I ask, reaching around to cradle his ass again. "That's all you want? Just this?" I repeat the short, shallow movement, taking only the head of him down to his glans between my lips, mostly using my tongue on him.

"Want more," he whispers.

"More?"

"Please, Scarlett. Got no problem begging."

I knead and claw at his ass. "Then show me, Solomon. Show me what you need."

He gathers my hair in his fist at the back of my head, holding it there with both hands and pulls me onto him. I keep my eyes on his as I let him guide me, open-mouthed, onto his cock. Deeper. Deeper. He touches the back of my throat, but before he can trigger my gag reflex, he releases the pressure and I back away.

Again, just as slowly and intentionally, he guides me onto him and stops just before it's too much for me. God, he knows me so well. I close my eyes and sigh as I lick my lips, tasting his precum, and then meet his eyes as I take him into my mouth once more. This time, I don't back away all the way, keeping him inside my mouth, lips locked around his glans, tongue swirling against the leaking tip. I pull at his butt as I go down on him, this time pushing him against my throat a little more.

He groans, and his knees dip. He locks his knees, but they nearly give out again as I plunge my mouth down his shaft again, back up, and then immediately go back down, swallowing around the head.

I moan around him as he starts letting his hips push, and I encourage him by pulling at his ass.

"Want it like that, do you?" he growls.

"Mmm-hmmm," I murmur wordlessly, pulling at him as I go lower, taking more of him.

"Ahhh fuck, babe." He gasps, and his knees buckle. "God, feels so fucking good."

Now, I start taking him in a rhythm, moaning with unfeigned eagerness as his hips push and his knees buckle.

"Baby, oh fuck. Scar, god, yes."

"Mmm-hmm?"

He pulls at my head, and I let him pull me deeper until I push against his hold—he lets go instantly, and I back away, gasping, looking up at him with a grin as I catch my breath.

"Jesus, babe."

I run my hands up his abs and back down his hips, taking his hard ass in my hands again as I slick my lips around him, tongue licking and flicking, swirling and sliding against his shaft.

This time, there's no stopping. I feel him reaching the

edge as I set a rhythm, taking as much of him in thrust after thrust as I comfortably can. His hands dig into my hair and pull me closer, encouraging each downward slide of my mouth around him, and his knees buckle and dip as he nudges the back of my throat, moaning raggedly as he takes my mouth, his need taking over as he starts thrusting helplessly.

"Fuck, Scar, fuck—fuck." He dips at the knees and then straightens, locking out, and groans long and low in his throat as he reaches the cups. "Fuck, baby. Gotta come."

"Mmmm!" I hum, backing away in preparation for tasting his release.

"Need you, baby. Want to be inside you when I come."

"Mmmm-mmm," I answer, reaching up to find his hands.

He tangles his fingers with mine, knees buckling, hips thrust forward as I take him in long, slow slides of my mouth, unhurried and wet, tongue working. Faster, then.

"Scar...holy shit—fuck, ohmygod, Scarlett—I'm... oh fuck. I can't stop. Can't—oh fuck, Scarlett. I'm coming, baby. I'm—ohhhhhhhhhhhhhfucking god..."

He groans through gritted teeth as he tries in vain to hold back, but he's got no chance of that. I crush grip his hands in mine as I give him my mouth, fast and deep.

He comes with a guttural bellow that he cuts off with clenched teeth, head thrown back, pouring himself into my mouth. I swallow his first release, let go of his hands and cup his balls, driving my middle finger along his taint and pressing as he detonates a second time, the hot salty wash of his come flooding my mouth.

He grunts helplessly, then, hands burying in my hair and pulling me onto his cock—I let him, swallowing frantically around a third pulse before letting him pop free of my mouth with a greedy gasp of air. I wrap my hand around him and pump him hard and fast, squeezing his balls as his knees nearly give out—I give his tip a closed-mouth kiss, swirling my tongue around the head as he smears a last few drops, quickly licked away.

That's when his knees give out totally, and he hits his ass. He looks almost dizzy, stunned.

"Scar—holy fucking shit, babe." He pulls me to him, hauling me onto him, straddling his thighs as he slumps against the wall, legs stretched out.

I wipe my lips with the back of my wrist and grin at him. "Hi."

"Holy shit."

"So you said."

"No, but…holy SHIT."

He palms my ass, pulling me against him—I lift onto my knees and press my belly against his lips, gazing down at him with my hands in his hair; he caresses me from shoulders to thighs, up and down and up and down again.

"What was that for?" he murmurs, kissing my belly, my ribs.

"Because I wanted to." I toy with his cool, silky hair. "Wanted to make you feel good."

"*Good* isn't even with a million lightyears of how you made me feel, my love."

I sink onto his lap and palm his cheeks, kiss him until we're breathless. "My love?"

"That okay?"

I nod, kissing him again. "Hell yes, it's okay. More than okay."

"I thought you didn't like doing it that way," he asks, searching me with his eyes. "On your knees like that."

"Discovered that with you, now, I do." I shrug. "Once in a while, at least." I wink at him. "Don't get too used to it, though."

"What changed?"

"Me."

He traces the line of my cheek down to my jaw, and tucks a tendril of hair behind my ear. "How so?"

"Trust, I guess," I answer. "Trusting you, trusting myself."

"You told me to make love to you," he says.

I smile. "You did. And you will."

He stands up, taking me with him as if I weigh nothing, and carries me to the bed, setting me down tenderly. Lays beside me and rolls me into his chest. I press the length of my body against him, cradling his thigh with mine, sex pressed against his quad, hips and belly against his, breasts against his chest. Instead of resting my cheek on his shoulder, though, he pulls me higher and claims my mouth with his.

And so begins the longest, deepest, hottest kiss of my life.

Slow at first, just lips meeting, tilting, he cups the back of my head in one hand and my ass in the other, and kisses me and kisses me. Breathless, I pull away to gasp for air, but he takes my mouth again, ravenously, and gives me his tongue and demands mine, and now the kiss builds into something else, something more. I whimper as he scours my mouth with his tongue.

Builds, and builds. He growls into my mouth,

squeezes my ass. I writhe against him, gasping as he breaks to breathe, forehead against mine.

"Sol," I whisper.

I feel him, and I need him. His cock is a thick hard ridge between us, a hot length begging for my pussy. I grind against his thigh, and he shifts me higher. I tilt my hips and catch his head with my lips, and I gasp a whimper against his mouth as I work him inside me. I'm wet and slick with need, and he slips into me easily, and we groan in unison as he fills me to the brim, burying himself inside my pussy to the hilt. On our sides, legs hooked around each other, we pull at each other with hands and with feet, and our mouths meet, touch, drift, and then lock.

I've never felt so close to Solomon as I do at this moment, physically wrapped up in him in a way I've never experienced, emotionally tuned to him, open to him, filled by him. I feel his spirit meeting mine, his soul braiding around mine. We move in perfect synch, the kiss breaking as we gasp, mouth stuttering against mouth.

There's no rush, no greed, no pounding deep or teasing shallow, just an endless, infinite wonder of togetherness, our bodies matched perfectly, his pleasure building mine, my ecstasy mounting with his. I don't need to touch my clit—only Sol.

My man.

Mine.

My everything.

I feel my climax emerging from the depth of my very soul, and it is wild and titanic and freighted with a delicate spiderweb of emotion. My love for him, so far unspoken, swells with each meeting of our bodies, welling higher and burning hotter each time he slides inside me, slicks slowly through the lips of my sex, burying inside me until I ache with him, pulse around him, squeeze his thickness as my orgasm shivers toward a maddening crescendo rapturous bliss.

Inside my quaking, drenched depths, Solomon begins to find his release as well—I feel it in the pulse of his cock, in the desperation of his kisses, in the way he cradles my ass and hauls me hard against him with each thrust.

Mine reaches its zenith all at once, and I shake all over, helplessly shrieking far too loudly as Sol releases his control, driving into me as hard as he can.

I come on a scream that fades into a breathless whine, and he buries his face in the side of my neck and roars, his hot breath damp on my skin and I claw both hands into his ass and pull, hard, as I feel his orgasm unleash inside me.

My shrill whimper becomes a chant, his name a prayer on my lips. "Sol, Sol, Sol, Sol, Sol—" I gasp, as he pounds into me, coming inside me in rush after rush, and my pussy spasms and clutches at him as mine rips me into a new dimension. "Oh god, Solomon."

"Scarlett," he gasps. "Mine—my Scarlett."

I nip his earlobe and then press my lips to his ear and finally whisper the three words I've kept hoarded in the deepest, darkest corner of my soul, now flooded with the light of this man, my best friend, my soulmate, my partner, my love: "I love you."

Sol flinches physically as if struck. "Scarlett, oh god, oh god, Scarlett. I love you. I fucking love you."

He pulls away and I cradle his face, our bodies gone still. "I love you, Solomon. God, I love you. I love you so goddamn much, and I always have."

We stay like that, locked together, until he finally slips out of me. No pillow talk, no quiet murmurs. Just physical intimacy, a closeness that I suddenly crave more than anything. We doze.

Rouse with evening light streaming through the windows. There's a slight, nagging feeling of guilt, though—like we should be doing something else, something more than this, as if we're stealing time that isn't ours.

I push that aside. I need him. Need this.

He puts me beneath him and enters me, and I take him slowly, gazing up at him and letting my love and vulnerability shine through my eyes. Hold nothing back. I tell him I love him as a whispered prayer as he fucks us to a mutual orgasm.

Again and again throughout that evening and night we sleep, rouse to make love, and fall back asleep until finally even Solomon's seemingly endless capability runs dry and my poor pounded pussy is sore and achy.

When we finally sleep, it's tangled up in each other, dreamless and deep.

CHAPTER 15

SHIT HAS OFFICIALLY HIT THE FAN

A FIST POUNDING ON THE DOOR BETWEEN THE rooms wakes us—a thin gray dawn light streams through the open windows, a cool breeze fluttering the translucent curtains.

I roll out of bed and dress swiftly, Scarlett doing the same. The moment we're dressed, I open the door. Inez is on the other side, dressed in fresh clothes, this time with a body armor vest over her shirt. Her hair is wet and braided, the braid twisted into a tight bun at the back of her head. Behind her, Lorenzo is sitting on the bed, lacing up his boots; he's shirtless, tanned, and scarred.

Inez pushes past me, going to our balcony and peering out. "They've got eyes on the building."

"Not surprising," I say, accepting a vest from Lorenzo as he saunters into the room. "Plan?"

She doesn't answer, gaze raking the street and then the rooftops of the buildings opposite. "Need your suppressed Glock," she snaps.

I slap it into her waiting hand, and she drops to a knee, bracing her support wrist on her knee and aiming carefully.

Draws in a breath and then fires once. A black shape on the rooftop directly opposite winks red and slumps out of view.

She hands it back. "That ought to buy us a few minutes. Let's go."

Understanding that she has a plan she's just not sharing with me at this exact moment, I opt to simply trust her, following her out of the room.

Scar is behind me, and Lorenzo brings up the rear, the big bag of goods on his shoulder. We exit the side of the hotel, slipping out a side door. Gone is the truck, in its place, a small van. We pile in and Lorenzo takes the wheel.

We get out of Quito without a problem. About fifteen or twenty miles later, however, we pick up a tail. They stay a few cars back, seeming content to just follow us for now. Lorenzo keeps an eye on them, accelerating and changing lanes, gunning around slower-moving vehicles. The tail makes no effort to be inconspicuous but does keep its distance, staying at least two cars behind us at all times.

A few miles turns into a few hours, and the tail stays on us. When we stop for gas and food, the tail mysteriously vanishes; we make quick time refueling and grabbing food to go, hoping to put some distance between us and the tail. Lorenzo even pulls off the highway and takes a squirrelly route along twisting, winding surface streets before getting back on the highway for the northward journey, but an hour later, the small gray sedan is back, sedately tailing us two cars back.

"Observe and report only, I guess," Lorenzo says. "May as well play along. They'll make their move at some point. We just have to be ready."

"So far, Mercado seems to be playing softball," Inez says, sounding annoyed.

"Softball?" Scarlett echoes, disbelieving.

Inez nods. "He doesn't want a shootout in a big city. He has consistently underestimated us, but he has also been playing to take us alive. Me, mainly. Now that he knows I'm down here, your lives are no longer valuable to him, so expect enemy fire to concentrate on the rest of you. Me, he needs alive. If he didn't, he'd just set up a roadblock and hose us down or light us up with a rocket."

"So we just ignore the tail?" I ask.

Inez nods. "They will move to interdict before we get to Costa Rica. Expect it to be the stiffest resistance we've faced."

"We talked about going to San José, but we never discussed The Darién Gap," Scarlett says.

"I have a contact in a place called Esmeraldas," Lorenzo says. "It's where we are going."

"I'd noticed we weren't going north," I say. "But you know this area, I don't."

Inez glances at me. "Lorenzo knows many people in many places across Latin America."

"So I've noticed. You're not still working for Brazil, are you?" I ask.

He shakes his head. "No, not for a long time. I am something of a private contractor in the intelligence community."

"So, Esmeraldas," Scarlett says. "What's there?"

"A flight to Puerto Arayas in the Galapagos and then a very long boat ride to Costa Rica," Lorenzo answers. "Assuming all goes well, which I do not assume it will."

"I've had a bad feeling for a while now," Scarlett says. "This has all been too easy so far."

I snort. "As much as I hate to admit it, it has been. For

a cartel boss with billions of dollars to blow, we've gotten away with a lot."

Inez sighs. "That is Mercado. He is notorious for his clever cruelty. He likes to let his prey think they've gotten away, only to make his move at the last second, usually when freedom is in sight. He has an uncanny ability to predict the actions of his prey. I expect him to make his real move either before we get to Esmeraldas or in Puerto Arayas." She turns to look at me. "Solomon, I need you to promise me something."

I frown. "I do *not* like the sound of that."

She retains a blank expression. "You won't like the promise I am about to extract from you, either."

I sigh. "You know I'm a man of my word, Inez. I promised to be loyal to the brotherhood, and while you may not have the brand, you're part of the brotherhood. So I'm loyal to you. I'll give you your promise, and I'll keep it."

Inez stares hard at me for a long time. Slowly, reluctantly, she peels off the bulletproof vest, sets it aside, and then turns in the seat to face me. She lifted her T-shirt up, revealing a black binding garment—like a sports bra, but more compressive. She pulls it down at her left breast, revealing the upper swell of a much larger breast than I'd expected…

And a Broken Arrow brand-tattoo—identical to the one on the inside of my left bicep—midway between the flat of her upper chest and the hint of areola. After baring the brand to me for a few moments, she lets go of the chest binder, lets down her shirt, and puts the vest back on.

"I have the brand. I swore a similar oath as yours, but an oath of leadership. My oath does not contain the prohibition against taking a life. That element came later, after we began the process of choosing a slate of prospects." She lets out a sigh. "So I *am* part of the brotherhood. Part of the team. I am your leader. The only thing you have sworn to that I have not is the prohibition against killing."

Another long pause.

"You must promise me that when I tell you to, you will let me go. You won't want to, but you must. This is the promise you must give me, Solomon."

I wipe my face with both hands. "I promise." A sigh. "But—"

"Later, Solomon," Inez murmurs. "Later, please."

I nod and say nothing. I glance at Scarlett, and it's clear she shares my overload of questions, but she just shakes her head and shrugs.

A million questions swirl in my head, but it doesn't seem like the right place or time to ask them. I stare at Inez's profile, trying to put any of the thoughts and questions into words.

◆

We reach Esmeraldas without issue, and the gray sedan never wavers, remaining constantly two cars back. My unease is growing. Surely, if Mercado is going to make a move, it's going to be before we leave the Ecuadorian mainland. Letting us get airborne seems like too big a risk.

Sprawling on the banks of the wide, muddy Rio Esmeraldas, the city is a provincial capital and boasts a small international airport, the northern subcommand station of the Ecuadorian Coast Guard, as well as a naval station. Newer buildings squat against smaller shacks, shops, and restaurants, with cracked but paved roads and bustle of people, none of whom pay us any attention beyond an uninterested glance.

I expect that Lorenzo will take us to the airport, where we'll board a private puddle-jumper. Instead, he drives right up to the main gates of the naval station. Scarlett and I trade nervous glances, but Inez seems perfectly at ease, bored even. Although, that could be an act. Lorenzo chats easily with the guard, discussing someone they both know—the Spanish is too rapid for me to translate on the fly, but I get the gist of it: Lorenzo called ahead and made arrangements with a friend, who seems to be someone fairly high up in the Ecuadorian navy. We're granted access, and Lorenzo drives us toward a remote section of the base. We get more than a few puzzled looks from sailors and guards, but no one stops us.

A small official-looking vehicle is waiting for us at the end of a pier, a gray sedan much like the one that tailed us all the way to the gates of the naval base—it did a three-point turn and drove away; I caught a glimpse of the driver on the phone.

As we approach the vehicle, a short, stocky man emerges, hat under his arm, which he places on his head the moment he's on his feet. Lorenzo parks, shuts off the engine, and gets out. Inez follows suit, and so Scarlett and I do as well.

Lorenzo approaches the officer—he bears the usual military rank insignias, but I'm unfamiliar with the Ecuadorian versions, so I couldn't say what his rank is. Lorenzo salutes him, receives one in return, and then the two men converse in rapid-fire Spanish—something to do with a delay, pursuit…fuck, my Spanish is so rusty, and the

Portuguese-Spanish carryover isn't enough to let me follow men speaking as rapidly as these two are.

"What are they saying?" I ask Scarlett.

"Logistics," she murmurs back. "The plane that was supposed to bring us to the Galapagos got delayed or something. Lorenzo isn't happy, and the officer is promising him that he's working on another solution."

"Great," I mutter.

"I trust Lorenzo," Inez whispers. "You must trust me. All will be well."

"Too bad we can't get them to take us all the way to Costa Rica," I say.

"Indeed," Inez answers. "But not possible. We aren't supposed to be here at all. The officer is an old friend of his, someone he worked closely with many years ago. He's doing a favor for Lorenzo that carries great risk to his career were he to be discovered. Ecuador has enough trouble with Los Chaneros and does not want the attention of someone like Mercado."

"But this guy is helping us," I ask.

Inez nods. "He owes Lorenzo. I do not know for what. If his superiors knew he was aiding us, fugitives from Mercado, he would face court-martial at best. Most likely, they would just throw him to Mercado and wash their hands of him."

"Jesus. Quite an ex you've got, Inez," I mutter.

She eyes me. "I never divorced him. He is still legally my husband."

"That's gotta burn," I say.

She sighs, nods. "Indeed. I wish to be free of him more than just about anything else."

"Just about?"

She shrugs. "I will not discuss that with you, not here, not now."

"Fair enough."

"So, if you had to put money on where hubby-dearest is gonna make his move…" I prompt.

Inez frowns at me. "I do not feel levity regarding that man is appropriate, Solomon."

I hold up both hands in a gesture of surrender. "My bad, sorry."

Inez lets out a breath, shoulders lifting, pausing, and falling. "Out there. On the water." She flips a hand in the direction of the sea. "It is the most logical. Consider it. There is nowhere to go. No alleys or buildings or such things to hide in and run down. They can easily surround us and force us to surrender or die. Rafael needs me alive so he can attempt to torture the location of my son out of me, but he knows I will die first. So yes. The attack will come at sea."

"Are we prepared for that?" Scarlett asks.

"To a degree," Inez answers. "It will depend on the scale, location, and manner of the assault and also upon the nature of our transportation. If Lorenzo can obtain a vessel with more robust defensive systems, our chances of survival and escape rise significantly. If we're stuck on a glorified ferry, they plummet in equal proportion."

"So it all comes down to what this guy can pull off," I say. "Sweet. Love being at the mercy of others."

"Indeed," Inez mutters.

After a few more minutes of discussion, Lorenzo saunters over to us, looking less than thrilled. "Bad news and worse news," he says. "Our flight to Galapagos is now a boat ride—that's the bad news. The worse news is that the only ship headed there in the next seventy-two hours that he can put us on is a supply ship."

"What's the likelihood of Mercado attacking an Ecuadorian naval vessel?" Scarlett asks.

"Not high," Lorenzo admits. "My feeling is he'll wait for us to board the fishing trawler we're taking to Costa Rica. I've kept that as quiet as possible, but we have to assume everyone and everything is compromised. Once we get to the islands, I'll try to pull a switch one way or another, but our options are going to be limited."

"Well," Inez says. "With no good options, we do what we must and work for the best outcome. When does the ship leave?"

The naval officer gestures at Lorenzo.

"Shortly," Lorenzo says. "Let's go."

Less than fifteen minutes later, we're on board a supply vessel headed for Puerto Baquerizo Moreno on San Cristobal Island, a journey of anywhere from two to four hours, depending on weather and sea conditions. As we depart, it's a gray, gloomy, damp sort of day, still and oppressively humid. All that changes when we reach the open seas, however.

The wind picks up, and the sullen, leaden skies darken with alarming rapidity, and then the rain begins to patter, slowly and intermittently at first and then with increasing violence.

At the end of an hour, it's obvious we're in for a storm. Upon boarding, the captain of the vessel offered us the use of the crew lounge, but none of us felt it prudent to hide in a safe, warm lounge with an enemy like Mercado after us, so we all opted to stay on deck, scanning the horizon. Lorenzo is in the cockpit, attempting to make contact with someone on San Cristobal, hoping to procure us an alternative means of transportation to San José that Mercado won't know about.

Judging by Lorenzo's increasingly foul mood, however, he's not having much luck.

As the island approaches—little more than a smudge of darkness emerging from the gloom and rain—we are all soaked, grouchy, and miserable. We haven't seen anything, and our vigilance is feeling wasted, which is a damned dangerous feeling. The second you think it's safe to let your guard down, shit hits the fan.

The port is on the north side of the island's extreme southwestern tip, and we're making the long, slow arc around the end of the island when we feel the ship's engine cut and our forward momentum slacken.

Out of the blowing curtains of rain, another ship is visible, this one a fishing trawler—long and low, with a sharp high prow and trailing boom arms; it's a dirty vessel, old and battered and small.

Lorenzo approaches, hair plastered to his forehead, rain dripping from the tip of his nose. He leans close to us, yelling as the wind howls. "Radar has spotted several vessels approaching from the northeast. The captain wants us off his ship A-S-A-P. This is our ride." He gestures at the trawler. "We transfer now."

I stare at him. "In *this* shit?"

Lorenzo tips his head toward the door leading to the interior of the ship—armed personnel stand waiting, glaring in our direction with blank, stony expressions. "Yes, in this shit. At gunpoint."

Waves roll the supply ship, pitching us through several degrees. Rain splatters and is driven in sideways sheets

by the relentless wind. Transferring from one vessel to another in conditions like this is a fucking suicide mission—I
should know, I've done it more than once with SEALs,
both in training and during live missions. It's dangerous
in the extreme, the kind of thing you only attempt when
there's no other choice. And judging by the armed naval
personnel watching us, we do not have a choice.

"Fuck." I scrape my hand down my face. "Well, we
might as well get it over with."

A rope ladder trails over the side of the ship, dangling
several feet above the choppy, white-capped waves. With
each roll of the ship, the surface rises and falls at least six
feet at a time. A tiny rubber Zodiac boat waits for us, bobbing like a cork; the pilot is skilled, using the outboard
motor to adjust position constantly in an attempt to stay
near the supply ship so we can make the jump from the
ladder to the Zodiac.

Making sure my pistol is secured, I swing a leg over
the side and cling to the rope ladder. Immediately, my
stomach lurches up into my throat as a massive swell sends
the ship bucking upward—at the same time, a ragged blast
of harsh wind spews parallel to the ship, sending me swaying sideways, clinging precariously to the rope ladder.

The ship slides down into the trough between waves,
which is deep enough that the wind fades. The timing is
the trickiest part—I miss the first opportunity and have to
ride the ladder up the crest and back down again, watching the tiny target of the Zodiac bobbing as the pilot frantically adjusts, trying to stay close enough to the bucking,
storm-tossed ship for me to make the jump.

At some point, you have to just jump and hope, and
that's what I do—at the bottom of the trough, the Zodiac

is a couple of feet away, rising as the ship falls; I leap, and the rubber slams into me, knocking the air of me. Frigid seawater sloshes over me as I roll further into the little boat; a strong hand grabs my collar and helps haul me upright, choking, coughing, and spluttering, trying to get my breath while clearing brine from my mouth and throat.

From here, the supply ship is a massive wall of metal, and I have renewed respect for the Zodiac pilot, who is so skillfully keeping the rubber craft mere feet from hundreds of tons of metal. The supply ship skates down the side of a wave while we perch on the crest of another, and I see Scarlett clinging to the rope ladder midway down the side of the ship, watching over her shoulder. Like me, she rides through the first dip, tracking the differential between the movement of the two crafts, and then, at the bottom, as the ship passes the Zodiac, she leaps. Landing heavily on the side of the boat, she clings desperately to the handhold, shaking her head as seawater sluices over her. I haul her in and drag her over to me.

Inez is next, and of course, she makes it look easy, landing catlike directly in the belly of the Zodiac. Lorenzo is last, and he almost misses, managing a single handhold, the rest of him in the ocean. All three of us drag him in, spluttering and hacking.

No more bag of goodies—there was no way to bring it with us on the switch.

That's just the first part.

Now we have to cross several hundred feet of open ocean in the middle of a storm in a dinky little rubber boat, and then transition again to the trawler, which is in some ways even harder, as you have to get close enough to grab the ladder.

Fortunately, the trawler is smaller, with a low lip, and the jump isn't terribly difficult—we all make it without issue, and then we help the pilot get the Zodiac hooked up to one of the boom arms and winched out of the sea and on board.

Soaked, exhausted, and miserable, we gratefully allow the trawler crew to guide us down into the ship's belly, where it's warm and dry. We're given towels and steaming mugs of thick black coffee as the trawler's engines rumble and rattle to life.

As we huddle together around a small table in the mess area, I lean close to Lorenzo. "What kind of fishing trawler has a Zodiac and a pilot of that caliber?"

He sips coffee. "The kind that's not trawling for fish."

Smugglers, then, likely, or pirates...or some of both. Maybe they even do some real fishing for appearances, but fish aren't their primary source of income, that's for damn sure.

"When Mercado makes his move, will they help us or throw us to the wolves?" I ask.

Lorenzo shrugs. "Who knows? Fifty-fifty chance, even with hefty compensation."

For several hours, then, it's quiet. We slowly dry off and warm up, and the crew leaves us mostly alone, except to offer us more coffee, hearty stew, and cigarettes.

We all take the opportunity to doze.

I notice that when Inez nods off, her head rests on Lorenzo's shoulder.

Inez has a son.

What a fucking world.

Scarlett rouses from a catnap, blinking and stretching. "Remember that bad feeling I said I've had for a long time?"

I nod. "Yeah."

"It's going apeshit right now. I've got a feeling shit's about to hit the fan." She pulls her Glock out and sets about stripping and cleaning it.

I do the same, and soon, both Inez and Lorenzo are awake and doing the same thing.

One of the crew members tromps down the stairs. He's older, with salt and pepper hair buzzed close to his scalp, a thick bushy beard splayed on his chest, wearing a yellow rubber slicker. "Vessels come. Bad men. We fight. You come."

Without a word, we follow him topside—the storm has abated some in the last couple hours, the waves now merely rollers, the wind slackening, the once-brutal rain more of an all-pervading wetness in the air. A grizzled bear of a man is at a storage locker, handing out AK-47s—we all accept one and a couple of spare mags. Besides the four of us, there are six men on the crew, not counting the captain, who stays in the cockpit. He has no intention of stopping, regardless of what happens.

By unspoken agreement, we all take up positions at the stern together while the rest of the crew ranges around the sides and bow.

For a few minutes, it's just us and the waves and the wind. And then a shape cuts out of the misty gloom, a long, low, sleek black speedboat skipping across the surface. The moment they're in range, one of the crew opens fire.

Shit has officially hit the fan.

CHAPTER 16

GOLEM

THE WELL-MEANING CREWMEMBER'S SHOTS GO wild, shocking precisely no one except maybe him. The speedboat approaches from the port side, well to stern, at an oblique angle. We all wait until they're closer.

As it closes within firing range, the speedboat cuts parallel, and muzzle flashes burst bright, sending rounds whizzing past us. I return fire, hearing the others now doing the same. I catch sight of a face behind a rifle as the speedboat cruises parallel past us, rounds dinging and cracking and ricocheting.

More gunfire rattles from the starboard side, and I whirl to see a second, identical speedboat cutting past, pouring fire at us. A crewmember takes a round to the chest and topples into the sea. Lorenzo moves to fill his place, and he drops an enemy right before the speedboat carves away to come about.

On our side, they've already come around and are cutting toward us for a second raking pass. Solomon is concentrating his fire on the stern near the waterline, hoping to disable the craft while Inez and I put down suppressive fire.

Another crewmember goes down.

Lorenzo takes a round to the arm, a graze that leaves him bloody but mostly okay. Another round nicks my earlobe, and Solomon takes a round at an angle from a distance—it hits his vest, knocking him to the deck, gasping as rain beads on his eyelashes. Only Inez seems to be immune, most rounds going nowhere near her even as she displays uncanny marksmanship, dropping several targets—an incredible show of skill since she's shooting at a moving target from a moving position.

A third boat appears.

The odds aren't looking super great. I lock eyes with Sol, and we share a silent moment of acknowledgment that this could be it.

And then Sol finally punches through the skin of the boat raking our port side, a hole belching fire and smoke as the sleek craft shudders and slows to a halt. Immediately, we concentrate our fire on that vessel as its occupants swarm toward the bow, away from the fire in the engine compartment. The hole takes on water as the craft bobs in the rolling swells and begins angling down.

It's not a time for mercy—Inez and I pick off targets as they jump into the water. A few moments later, the vessel is out of sight; bodies bob, staining the churning sea red.

Too bad another boat takes its place, and another behind it, swinging wide to come at us from the front, and now we're being circled by speedboats like sharks circling a chum dump.

Small arms fire rattles from every direction, chattering and barking. Rounds whizz and snap, buzz and sizzle, thunking into the deck and walls and ricocheting off the sides.

We're giving them hell, enemy after enemy dropping—the four of us are all combat-hardened and well-trained, whereas the crew tends to blast long bursts, most of which go high and wide and accomplish very little but wasting ammunition.

Now, three boats approach our starboard side, working in unison to distract the bulk of our attention. It works—we have to put the bulk of our people on that side just to keep their fire down; meanwhile, the fourth speedboat approaches our port side from the stern.

Fuck, fuck, fuck.

The port side boat slinks closer; I'm the only one on that side, and they have me pinned down behind the doorway to the cockpit. The moment I roll out, a barrage of bullets sends me right back under cover.

I hear a metal-on-metal sound: they're getting ready to board. On the other side of the boat, I hear a shout of pain and a splash. Something explodes, and I can only hope it's an enemy boat.

I risk a brief peek—they've caught our side with grappling hooks on winches and haul themselves closer and closer until they're within range of a solid leap.

I swing out and lay down fire, drop one as he prepares to leap. "They're boarding!" I scream. "Starboard side!"

I hear boots thump down and I roll out—and almost catch a round to the face. It slices my cheekbone with a hot line of pain, which I ignore. Drop to my knee and angle out, put bursts down.

The cockpit door opens and the captain tosses a machete at me. "Cut rope."

Oh, just like that, huh?

No choice, though. I sling my AK around behind me,

draw my pistol, and pick up the machete. Sol skids around the rear of the trawler and scrambles over to me, rounds walking along the deck at his heels.

"Some fun, huh?" he says, grinning. Leans out, pops off a couple of rounds, buying a moment of respite.

I sprint-lurch toward the ropes connecting the boats, hacking at them left-handed as I fire at the would-be boarders. Sol puts down covering fire, buying me enough time to hack through two out of the three ropes before I have to dive back behind the door.

"Reminds me of that op in the Indian Ocean," I tell Sol, panting. "Those pirates? Remember?"

Sol laughs. "That was a good one. That RPG round that went clear through the cockpit without exploding?"

Speaking of explosions, another one rocks the trawler, and the noise of gunfire is reduced.

"Get that last rope," Sol tells me. "I'll see if I can punch through the engine."

"Copy," I say, switching mags.

"On three," Sol says. "One…two…*THREE!*"

We roll out in unison, Sol raking rounds across the speedboat from bow to stern, keeping heads down while I hack at the last rope. It snaps, and the enemy craft bobs away.

Sol drops to a knee as it guns its engine, pushing rounds at the rear of the boat, ignoring the return fire zinging over his head. There's no explosion, but the enemy craft halts, rocking with the swells; it's quickly left behind as the running gunfight carries us forward.

We both move to the starboard side to assist there—they've taken out two of the three boats, but the trawler's crew is almost entirely wiped out, leaving only one, plus the captain, and us four.

Lorenzo is bleeding from the arm and thigh, having taken a ricochet across the quad—it's shallow, but he's losing blood from two places, and we don't have time or resources for triage.

Inez is bleeding too, shrapnel from one of the explosions ripping across her throat, narrowly sparing her life; her whole front is painted crimson.

Working in unison now, we lay down a withering barrage of suppressive fire, depleting our ammunition at an alarming rate, especially since we have no clue how many extra magazines they have.

One of the boats falls behind, spewing black smoke. The other peels away and circles back for the survivors desperately swimming in the churning sea; we leave them behind.

Abruptly, all is silent.

Lorenzo slumps to the deck, panting raggedly. "Fuck." He groans, twisting to look at Inez, who leans against the side of the cockpit. "You good?"

Inez nods. "Looks worse than it is."

She looks pale, though, making me wonder if she's not being entirely truthful.

We help each other down into the mess area and patch up ourselves and each other with the surprisingly comprehensive med kit we find down there.

Lorenzo's thigh wound turns out to be the worst, a deep, gaping gash across the front of his thigh. He's lost a good bit of blood, and he's pale and dizzy. Inez's throat wound is shallow but bleeds profusely and resists efforts to staunch the bleeding. Sol and I are mostly fine, nothing either of us is too worried about.

A while later—could be ten minutes, could be an hour; my sense of time wobbles a bit from exhaustion and adrenaline—the captain comes down and pours himself a cup of coffee, accompanied by his last surviving crew-member, the Zodiac pilot.

Lorenzo addresses him in Spanish, which I translate for Sol. "I'm sorry about your crew, Captain Perez."

A laconic shrug. "I hired them for this and paid cash up front. I told them it was dangerous and not everyone would go home. Most sent their pay to their families." He indicates the Zodiac pilot. "He is my first mate. The rest were hired just for today." A sip of coffee, followed by a flash of a lighter as he sparks up a cigarette. "Will they return to finish the job?"

Inez shakes her head. "No. Not out here. He'll try again on the mainland, though. Not your worry."

"Then I suggest you rest while you can. Gonzales will keep watch." The captain takes his coffee and cigarette topside, leaving us with Gonzales, a short, stocky man with the dark, leathery, weathered skin of a man who has spent his life at sea out in the elements.

Gonzales says nothing, only smokes and sips, staring into space. When he finishes both, he goes topside without a word.

"Captain Perez is right," Inez says. "We need to rest while we can. This was a pretty big victory for us, and Rafael will not take it well. He won't care about the men he lost, but the boats will anger him."

"Charming," Sol says.

We all find places to stretch out, and within minutes,
all of us are asleep.

---- ◆ ----

The journey to Costa Rica from Galapagos is one of days
rather than hours. The trawler we're on is a bit of a sleeper,
though, with a more powerful engine than one would
think, giving us a top speed of nearly eighteen knots, almost double the average speed of such a vessel. Which
means we'll cover the eight-hundred-some miles in more
like three or four days rather than a full week.

We hit more weather the second day after the assault,
which blows us off course and adds time. It's smooth sailing
after that, however, and we're left mostly to our devices—
all of us being who we are, we're well acquainted with long
hours of boredom during travel, and we pass it playing
poker for bullets, resting, cooking, eating, and chatting.

On the third day, I find myself restless and unable to
sleep. I pour coffee from the never-empty pot in the mess
area and take it topside. Inez is at the bow, hands curled
around a mug of coffee, her gaze distant and thoughtful.

"Hey," I say.

She gives me a chin lift as she swallows a sip.

"So, you and Lorenzo," I say.

She shakes her head. "No."

I laugh. "No?"

"No."

I laugh again. "Hey, I'm just trying to get a peek under
that armor. We've been in gunfights together. I'd hope you
know by now that you can trust me, at least a little."

She sighs, putting her back to the railing so she's facing me more directly. "What do you want to know?"

I shrug. "I dunno. Sol says he sees a different side of you than he's used to. Obviously, I don't know you from Adam. But I plan to take the brand and join you guys at whatever this club thing is." I watch an albatross coasting far overhead, its massive wings arched to catch the air currents. "You and I are a lot alike, I think."

Inez nods. "We are. You were on the list of prospects when we chose Solomon, but we determined you were not ready to leave everything behind yet. I think I told you this."

I nod. "You did."

Inez eyes me. "And you are ready now?"

I nod again. "I am."

"Why?"

I shrug. "There wasn't so much as a question in my mind that I'd go after Sol when I got that email. I didn't ask for leave, and I didn't tell my superior or any of my team. I just left. I could go back and face the consequences of going AWOL, but I guess I just don't know if I even want to go back. Not now. Not anymore. Sol and I have talked a lot since I sprung him from that camp. And I...I'm tired, Inez. I'm fuckin' *tired*. I've been fighting my whole goddamn life. I...I'm alone. I'm not close to anyone on my team—not really. They're good dudes, solid operators, but...they're not family."

Inez turns back to the railing. "That's not a good enough reason, Scarlett."

"So what is? Sol says I can't do it for him."

"You can't."

"So...what the fuck, then? I don't want that life

anymore. I've fought and killed my way through life since I was twelve. I just…I want peace, I guess. The way Sol talks about you guys and life at the Club…it honestly sounds pretty great. I've never had a home, never had a family, never had anything constant. I want the life that Sol talks about. I know it'll take some time to adjust—Sol says he still is. I get it. But I want it."

Inez doesn't answer for a while. She looks at me, thoughtful and pensive. "May I ask you something?"

I nod. "Sure."

"Have you reconciled your past self with who you want to be?"

I frown. "I'm not sure what that means."

"Maria Rodriguez."

I blow out a breath. "Ahhh. No, not really. Sol…he says he sees some of Maria coming out, now that he… we…um…"

Inez gives me a wry look. "You spoke of trust when you opened this conversation."

I sigh. "I'm learning to trust Sol. Learning that I don't have to be tough and strong all the time with him. He…I can be myself with him. I can relax my guard."

Inez furrows her brow as if puzzled. "Yourself?"

I snicker. "Right? Like, what the fuck does that even mean?"

She shakes her head. "My sense of self is not something I've considered in a long, long time. I just…am."

"What I'm discovering is that I've lost who I really am," I tell her. "I've lost sight of my self. Not myself, one word, but my *self*, two words. I don't have a self."

Inez frowns at this. "Everyone has a self."

"I bet you don't."

She blinks at me. "I do not follow."

"What do you do when you're not working?"

"Sleep."

"Right, because like me, all you do is work. Or get ready to work. What do you do for *you*?"

She shifts, visibly uncomfortable. That is immaterial. My work is who I am. The Arrows. Club Sin. My employer."

"Okay, but take that away. What's left?"

Inez turns away from me, sips coffee and stares out at the water sliding past us. "A hole, I suppose. One that you would have me fill with Lorenzo."

I can't help a snicker of laughter from escaping. "Yeah, you need to let Lorenzo fill your hole."

She narrows her eyes at me. "You know what I meant."

I roll my eyes. "Obviously. That was a joke."

She sighs. "I've never been good at humor."

"What about Sophia?" I ask, earning a whip-around-and-glare from her. "Does Sophia have a sense of humor?"

She blinks at me a few times and then turns back to staring at the ocean. "I...do not know."

"Exactly. Sol has helped me see that I can sort of partition different parts of myself. When I'm on an op, I'm Scar, or Scarla. Scarlett is...someone else. I'm still figuring that out. But Maria? I have no clue who she is. I always felt like that part of who I used to be is dead and gone. But lately, with Sol...I'm starting to think maybe he was right when he said she's not dead, she's just been...dormant."

Inez nods but doesn't look at me. "Ren insists on calling me Sophia. I don't know how to explain to him that it hurts. It physically hurts—I'm not her anymore. I haven't been her in a long time. I don't know how to *be* her."

"I get it, Inez. I really do."

She nods again. "I think if anyone could, it's you."

I try to find the right words—a tough task when I'm still actively trying to sort all this out myself. "Trust is a choice. I think it's also a journey. And you know that saying about the first step being the hardest? I think that's true here, too. I have to choose to trust Solomon. Not just once, but consistently. For people like you and me, who've been through what we have, that's a tall fuckin' order. And it's hard as hell, Inez. Hard as hell and scary as fuck. He *knows* me. He could easily use the things he knows about me to hurt me. He could change his mind. He could betray me. And honestly, he probably will hurt me at some point."

Inez's gaze remains fixed on a point in the middle distance. "I do not know if I'm capable of that."

"If I can, you can."

She looks at me, finally. "Have you?"

I nod. "I have. Or at least, I'm starting to. I have no clue what that looks like for you, and it's not any of my business. For me, it means putting the warrior away when I'm alone with him. Part of the trust issue is trusting myself, though—that was a big realization."

"Trusting yourself?" She tosses the dregs into the sea, and the wind carries it away.

I nod. "I'm not weak if I let Solomon see how I'm feeling. It's not weak to be vulnerable with him. To soften."

"Soft things die in our world, Scarlett."

"I know. But Inez, I'm not soft all the time. That's the trust I'm talking about. I trust myself to be strong and hard when I need to be. I'm still me. I don't lose anything by giving that part of myself to Solomon. I trust him with it. I trust him to take care of it and still see all of me, not just that part. Sol respects me. He knows what I can do, and he trusts me to do it."

Inez nods absently. "I see." A long pause. "I suppose I trust Lorenzo. But trusting him like that? I have never been soft, Scarlett. My father didn't raise me that way. I was never a little girl. I was his protégé. His experiment. I didn't have dolls; I had practice throwing knives. I didn't play tea party; I played Assassin. The first time I saw my father kill someone, I was six. The first time I killed someone, I was eleven. No part of my life has *ever* been *soft*. I do not know how to be that. I do not know what it looks like. I do not know how to trust. I do not have a...a soft side or a feminine side."

"You loved Lorenzo at one point, right?"

She shrugs. "I suppose. I cared about him. I...craved him, I think. I sent him away because the thought of him dying was intolerable. And then I walked away because..." she trails off. "After what my father did to me, I was... empty. Broken. Dead inside. I couldn't let him see that."

"And you never really recovered from that. You never healed. Never rebuilt yourself. You built a life and a persona—Inez. But that's not you. That's..."

"A golem," she whispers. "An artificial representation of a human."

I nod. "Yeah, pretty much." I blow out a breath that turns into a laugh. "God, that's a really damn good metaphor, Inez. A golem—a sort of...human-looking thing made out of clay, given life but isn't...a person. Not really."

"Not a person, not really," Inez echoes, her voice faint and thoughtful. "I suppose there may be an element of truth to that." She lets out a long, slow breath. "So then the task becomes figuring out how to become a person. A full human being, not just…"

"A task-completing automaton?" I suggested.

She nods. "Right."

I laugh. "I hope I'm not giving you the impression that I have any of this figured out, Inez. I don't. At fucking all. I'm just starting to understand this about myself. And I see a lot of similarities between you and me."

Another nod, this one absent and thoughtful. "I suppose allowing Ren to think of me and refer to me as Sophia is a good first step. Perhaps eventually, it will stop feeling like he's talking to or about someone else."

"I guess we'll see, huh?" I say. "It's been hard enough even talking about Maria, let alone trying to think of myself as that person again."

Inez frowns, running a hand down her braid. "Maybe…maybe the key is not thinking of that name as the person we used to be, but rather a representation of who we *want* to be."

"Hmmm," I say. "Like, when I take the brand, Scarlett Gutierrez is…set aside, or laid to rest, so to speak. And I become Maria again—but a Maria who is also all of the parts of me that will always be Scarlett. I mean, I've been Scarlett for longer than I was Maria at this point. So I can't just shuck that person. She's me. I'm just more than that. Does that make any sense?"

Inez shrugs. "I wouldn't be the person to ask, Scarlett. But it sounds right to me."

The men emerge with mugs of coffee, and the conversation turns to plans for getting to San José from the coast—a distance of thirty-some miles, depending on where the trawler drops us.

Twenty-four hours later, we're roused at first light by First Mate Gonzalez, who informs us we are approaching the coast. The plan is for the trawler to drop anchor a mile or two from shore, and Gonzalez will run us ashore in the Zodiac. We'll be on our own from there.

This is as far as Lorenzo's arrangements have gotten us—there's no one waiting for us in Costa Rica.

I still have a gnawing sense of disquiet in my gut, acidic as heartburn and heavy as a too-rich meal.

CHAPTER 17

A PROMISE IS GIVEN

IT'S A STILL, WARM, BEAUTIFUL DAY. THE SEA IS tranquil and glassy, a gentle wind fluttering the palm leaves. Sunrise is a glorious display of vivid, brilliant oranges and reds and pinks washing across the sky.

A lone figure wanders the beach, a good half mile away from where Gonzales skids the Zodiac ashore. The figure pauses, watching us for a moment, and then resumes their perambulation away from us.

There's a thin screen of palm trees and a dirt road running parallel to the beach. Each of us is armed with nothing more than a pistol and a single spare magazine. Lorenzo has a cell phone, and Scarlett has an emergency satellite phone, but using Scarlett's sat phone will alert her people at the CIA that she's back on the grid.

With no other real options available, we simply start walking inland. Lorenzo, once we're a few miles inland, gets enough of a signal to pull up a map of the area, giving us a rough idea of where to go and what kind of a journey awaits us should we have to walk the whole thing. Lorenzo tells us he does have contacts he could call, but he worries that contacting anyone at this point is a risk—Mercado has the resources to have phones tapped, and at this point, we can't rule out the possibility that Lorenzo is a known quantity. Safer just to walk, even though none of us particularly relishes the thought of a thirty-some-mile hike.

I mean, at least it's not the Amazon.

It begins well enough. Not exactly flat, but not horrible. As the day unfolds, however, the early morning warmth turns to stifling heat, and the geography becomes downright brutal—wicked, knife-edge ridges, the road cutting and curving and switching back on itself. Captain Perez was kind enough to provide us with water bottles and some food, but only enough to last the four of us a day, at most, if we ration. The positive news is that we're in an area that's civilized rather than stranded in the middle of the fucking Amazon rainforest. So, by midday, we've only covered five miles, but we do come across a supermarket. Lorenzo goes in and returns with a box of protein bars and bottles of water. Despite having lost his big bag of goodies, Lorenzo has managed to hold onto his rucksack, which he and I take turns carrying.

More hours of walking along a narrow dirt road that winds through a dense tropical forest, climbing steep hills and descending them, weaving and jogging.

In the late afternoon, we're deep in the hills north of the beach, sweating buckets in the heat and humidity, the four of us strung out with almost a thousand feet between Lorenzo at the front and me in the rear, with the women between us. Cars rush past now and then, and more frequently, cube vans and box trucks, with an occasional motorcycle or bus.

The rattle and clatter of an old diesel engine howling its way up the hill greets our ears—another delivery truck of some sort, I assume. But as it passes me, it's an ancient Greyhound bus that's been painted a garish profusion of eye-watering colors in Jackson Pollock-esque splatter and randomness. A spare tire has been mounted to the rear, and a luggage rack affixed to the roof, piled high with strapped-down luggage and at least four spare fuel cans. "Mike and Mer's Troubadour Tour" is painted on the side in white block stencils, the O's turned into 60s-style peace signs. Music notes—don't ask me which ones—surround the lettering, along with bumblebees complete with dotted line flight paths, butterflies, dragonflies, and more than a few not-so-discreet cannabis leaves.

The windows are all open, emitting the wafting scent of burning cannabis, as well as the strains of music—a guitar, played with some skill as far as I can tell, a mandolin, an accordion, and several voices, male and female.

The bus squeals to a halt and all four of us stop walking—it stops nearest me, and the others turn and come back toward me. The narrow folding door rattles and protests as it opens.

"Hey there, fellow American," the young man behind the wheel says, grinning at me. "You are American, right? You look American."

"I am," I answer. "Name's Solomon."

"Greetings, Solomon," the young man says. "I'm Mike, and this is my bus, Betty White. You like?"

I grin. "I do. She's…certainly colorful."

"Indeed she is! Where are you are your esteemed colleagues heading?" Mike asks.

"Who are they, Mikey?" A female voice says, coming to the front.

Mike is twenty-five or so, rail thin with long blond

dreadlocks bound back by a gauzy, tie-dyed scarf, a thin, wispy beard hiding a weak chin, and bright blue eyes; he's dressed in baggy patchwork pants, barefoot and shirtless, covered in colorful tattoos depicting landscapes and animals.

The young woman who joins him is pretty, carrying a few extra pounds around her butt and thighs, with dreadlocked brown hair and brown eyes, wearing a bright, flowy yellow dress, barefoot and braless, a red bandana over her hair. I deduce before she speaks that this is Mer.

"I'm not sure yet, honey-bunches, we're still working on introductions," Mike says. "Solomon, this is my celestial partner in light and love. Her name is Mer. Mer, this is Solomon."

Celestial partner in light and love, huh? Okay then.

The others have joined me at the door of the bus. We never really cleaned up much after the battle, so we're dirty, sweaty, and coated in stiff, old blood, and we are clearly not tourists who got separated from their group.

Despite being visibly stoned, Mike's gaze is perceptive. "You fellow itinerants have been through some interesting shit. I hereby officially invite you to enter the transportational sanctuary that is our dearly beloved Betty White. Come in peace and come in love, just don't come on the seats."

Scarlett turns a bark of laughter into a cough, and a quick glance over my shoulder shows that even Inez is fighting a smirk. Lorenzo has an eyebrow raised, looking less than amused.

"Where are you headed?" I ask.

"Wherever the wind takes us, my scary new friend. Where would you like to go?"

"San José?" I say, turning it into a question.

"We're goin' to San Jose!" Mike yells.

From the back comes a chorus of hooting and hollering, as if that's the best news any of them have ever heard.

The chorus of shouts becomes a chant of "San José, San José, San José!"

"Wait, Mikey—why?" A voice asks from the back of the bus. "Didn't we just come from there?"

"Yeah, but our new friends are going to San José, so back we go!"

"Cooooool," says the other voice, a very stoned male. "I forgot my ukelele at the hostel anyway."

"See?" Mikey says, throwing his hands to the sky as if he's proved a point. "The universe provides!" He does a seated bow, sweeping an arm toward the back of the bus. "Speak friend and enter."

I put a foot on the bottom step. "Am I supposed to say 'friend?'"

He just laughs. "No, man, it's from *Lord of the Rings*. Duh."

"I see," I say and step up into the bus.

The front half has been converted into a kitchenette with a tiny electric stove, a dorm-sized fridge, a sink, and a handful of cabinets. Beyond that, the back half is further subdivided into two sections. The middle section is an eating and lounging area, with a long, narrow table facing a booth-style bench. Opposite the long book, on the passenger side, is another long bench without a table. The rearmost section is a single large bed set into a platform, with storage in the platform; the king-sized bed is a nest of brightly colored pillows, blankets, oversized stuffed animals doubling as pillows, and rolled-up sleeping bags.

Four more people occupy the rear of the bus—a large young man with coppery hair and a huge beard that's been braided and adorned with ribbons and flowers and beads, hanging to his mid-chest; a woman with the largest breasts I've ever seen in real life, which are only barely contained by a thin and far-too-small camisole, concealing precisely nothing, her hair white-blond and braided into a crown around her head, also liberally decorated with flowers, beads, and ribbons; another young man, this one Hispanic, with a wild shock of thick black unwashed hair sticking out in every conceivable direction and a scraggly goatee, who is currently painting his toenails a garish Kermit green, a joint hanging out the corner of his mouth; last is a Black woman of the same age as the rest—mid- to late-twenties—with a gorgeously bouffant and perfectly round afro and a large gold hoop through her septum, wearing an eye-wateringly bright paisley romper, playing a scratched and battered guitar.

The big ginger is playing the accordion, and a mandolin is lying on the couch, hand-painted with pastel chalk paint in 60s-style flowers and peace signs. The air in the bus is hazy with cannabis smoke.

"Jesus fuck," Scarlett murmurs in my ear. "Did we go through a portal into the 60s? Holy shit."

"Better than walking all the way to San José," I murmur back. "So be nice."

"Yeah yeah," she mutters.

We take seats on the couch opposite the booth. The Hispanic kid painting his nails smiles at us, plucking the joint from his lips and handing it to us. "Hola, new amigos," he says in unaccented English. "Welcome aboard the SS Betty White."

Lorenzo accepts the joint and takes a hit, passes it to Inez, who does the same—neither one fully inhales, I notice, so Scarlett and I do the same, handing it back.

"I'm Hector," he says. "This is Yolanda, we call her Yolo," he indicates the Black woman, who gives us a smile and a wink. "Big guy with the accordion is Brian, and that's his lady wife Ella."

"Nice to meet you all," I say, pointing to each person in turn as I name them. "I'm Solomon, and this is Scarlett, Inez, and Lorenzo."

Brian and Ella greet us, a wave from Ella and a chin-lift from Brian.

Despite having not inhaled, there's so much second-hand smoke in the air from the constant train of joints floating around the bus that all of us get a little stoned, which makes the slow, winding drive somewhat enjoyable.

"So," I say after Yolo and Brian put away their instruments. "What's a troubadour tour?"

"Oh, that's us. We're troubadours."

"I don't know what a troubadour is," I admit.

"Oh, well, like, historically speaking, they were court poets," Brian answers. "It's a pretty narrow and specific thing, historically. But in modern parlance, it just means a wandering singer of folk songs."

"So you guys are just, what, driving around playing music?" Scarlett asks.

"Pretty much, Scary Lady Number One," Hector says. "Our fearless leaders, Mike and Mer, are big-time hashtag-van-life influencers. They have, like, big money sponsors and everything. So we are on an epic quest to drive the whole of North and South America. We began in Barrow, Alaska—"

"They changed the name to Utqiagvik," Mike says from the front. "We have to honor the switch to the native name, my most excellent companion."

"Right, I forgot—my bad." Brian flips a hand. "Anyway, that was over a year ago. We drove south through Canada, Washington, Oregon, and California, down through Mexico, and all the way here."

"What's the plan from here?" I ask.

"Well, South America, obviously. Down through Argentina to Tierra Del Fuego, and up the east side of the continent, back to the good old U-S-of-A and along the Caribbean and then up the east coast, back into Canada, and end up in Ut-Whatever again."

I stare at them. "That's…a hell of an ambitious trip," I say, shaking my head. "It took you a year to get this far?"

Yolo laughs. "We're in no hurry. We stop wherever we feel like stopping and hang out until it's time to go. We spent, like, a month in a little village on the coast in Baja because the vibes there were just so ferociously chill."

"What are your plans for the Gap?" Lorenzo asks.

They all stare at us, uncomprehending.

"The what?" Brian asks.

Lorenzo looks at Hector as if for help. "The Gap? The Darién Gap?"

Hector shrugs. "Don't look at me, man, I'm from Connecticut."

Inez looks like she's bitten into a lemon. "You set out on a multi-year quest to drive all of North, Central, and South America, and you haven't even *heard* of the Darién Gap?"

Ella looks at us. "You're making it sound like something we are supposed to know."

"I mean, it's a pretty big deal," Scarlett says.

"Care to fill us in?" Brian says.

"Maybe Mikey and Mer ought to hear this," Yolo says.

"A fair point, m'lady," Brian says and then turns to yell toward the front. "Yo, Mikey! Pull over and come back here. Our friends have important information to impart unto us."

The bus's brakes squeal, and a moment later, Mike and Mer glide to the lounge area. Mer reaches beneath the bench, opens a drawer, and pulls out a massive glass bong, which she fills with water from a plastic gallon jug from the fridge and then hands it to Mike, who produces a Ziploc bag of ground-up cannabis from another drawer and packs the bong.

The bong makes its way around the group, but we all wave it off, earning us shrugs but nothing else.

"So," Brian says as he exhales a billowing cloud of pungent smoke. "What's the Darren Gap?"

"The Darién Gap," Inez says, accentuating the proper pronunciation. "Obviously, you know that South America is connected to North America by the isthmus of Panama. The Pan-American highway links the continents, going from Alaska to Argentina."

"Yeah, Scary Lady Number Two," Hector says. "That's what we're taking, mostly."

"Well, you clearly didn't research enough. The Pan-American highway doesn't fully connect. There's a seventy-kilometer section between Panama and Colombia where there are no roads of any kind. It's some of the most dense, remote, and inhospitable terrain on the planet, with steep mountains, swamps, hostile jungle, and huge, fast-flowing, turbulent rivers. There are bandits, robbers, and gangs hiding out there, as well as Indigenous tribes who violently oppose anyone entering their territory. The wildlife is dangerous, the people are dangerous, and the weather is dangerous. There's no medical support." She leans forward. "What I'm saying is that it is categorically *impossible* to drive from Panama to Colombia."

Silence greets this pronouncement.

"So, like, there's got to be a ferry or something, right?" Hector asks.

"No," Inez answers. "There is no official or commercial transit around the Gap."

"So…what? It's just impossible?" Mikey says. "There's got to be a way."

"There is, but it's complicated and expensive. You need to book a RORO—" she pronounces the acronym as a word, *rho-rho,* "and you need special insurance, and there are narcotics checks, and you need separate transit for you guys and your vehicle. Also important to know is that you can't bring cannabis or any paraphernalia. Just getting the vehicle prepped and inspected takes days, and you should book the RORO weeks in advance. A travel agent can make this process easier."

"What's a RORO?" Brian asks.

"Roll-on Roll-Off," Inez answers. "A specialized vehicle transport."

"That sounds, like, hard," Mer says, frowning. "How did we not know this?"

Mikey just shrugs. "Beats me, ladylove. But at least we found out before we got to Panama, right? We still have time. Maybe we can hire someone in San José to set things up for us."

Yolo eyes us. "So, what's y'all's story?"

We exchange glances.

Inez answers. "It's best if you don't know anything about us but our names."

Mikey nods seriously. " It has not escaped my notice that you don't seem like tourists."

"We aren't," Lorenzo says.

"You're not terrorists, are you?" Mer asks. "Or, like, a roving band of serial killers?"

Brian chortles. "Mer, babe, serial killers work alone. Duh. They're not serial killers."

"Nah," Hector puts in, not looking at us as he takes a huge hit from the bong. "They're feds or something. My dad works at the Pentagon. I know the type."

"We're not terrorists, serial killers, or feds," Inez answers. "We're just some people trying to get to San José."

"But you're all, like, bloody," Ella says.

"Ella, my love, don't be rude," Brian says. "I'm sure they know."

I can't help but laugh. "Just get us to San José and then forget you met us."

"Are you *spies*?" Ella says, leaning forward, excited—the act of leaning forward makes her goddamned enormous tits spill out of her top and onto the table, which she doesn't seem to notice at all.

"Not exactly," Scarlett says. "But close enough."

"Are we in danger just from associating with you?" Mer asks.

We all hesitate. Lorenzo finally answers. "Honestly, maybe. If anyone asks you about people matching our description, just tell the truth. Tell them everything they want to know."

Brian glances at Mikey. "We did talk about being more careful about picking up strangers after that one guy."

"That was *one* dude," Mikey says. He looks at us. "My brother from another mother is still salty about the fact that I stopped for a hitchhiker who stole our weed back in California."

"That was primo flower, man," Brian says. "I spent a fortune on it."

"He was in a bad place, Bri-Bri. He clearly needed it more than us. The universe provides, right? Two days later, we picked up that old couple who gave us their whole stash of, like, even better flower. That guy stole a few ounces and they gave us a few pounds. It all works out in the end, man, you just have to, like, believe."

"I would listen to your esteemed colleague," Lorenzo says to Mikey. "Especially once you get to South America. I wouldn't go picking up strangers. It's dangerous down there, my friend."

A few more minutes of chitchat, and then Mikey wafts back to the driver's seat and we continue toward San José.

Once we're rattling and bouncing down the road again, Scarlett leans close and whispers into my ear. "I think walking may have been better," she says, giggling. "I'm high as fuck just from second-hand smoke. If we get hit, I dunno what'll happen."

I sputter a laugh. "I know, right? But it's fine. We're professionals. We'll have them drop us off outside the city. A bit of a walk in the fresh air will sober us up and hopefully make sure they stay well clear of any trouble. They're nice people, and I don't want our shit getting them hurt."

"Nice but delusional," she says. "Driving from Alaska to Baja is one thing; driving from Columbia to Argentina is a whole other thing, let alone all the way around the entire continent. Especially in this old bucket of bolts."

"I know," I say. "But you gotta give 'em credit for trying."

She shrugs. "They're gonna end up a statistic, Sol."

"Don't be negative."

She just rolls her eyes.

The closer we get to San José, the more grateful I am that we scored a ride—the terrain is brutally hilly, with knife-like ridges and endless switchbacks.

About an hour after picking us up, Mikey slows. "So, my intrepid new friends. Is there any chance that the super fun-looking dudes ahead have something to do with you guys?"

I scramble forward, kneeling to peer out the windshield. Mike has stopped at the top of a hill—at the bottom, where the road narrows around a sharp curve, a black two-ton troop transport has been parked across the road, and soldiers in black tactical gear wait in ranks, armed with assault rifles, balaclavas hiding their faces.

"Fuck," I mutter. "Yes, there's an excellent chance."

I glance over my shoulder. "This is our cue," I say to the others. "Time to go." To Mikey, then. "You, Brian, and Hector need to get out of the bus and argue loudly with each other. You're creating a screen so we can sneak off the bus and into the jungle."

Mike frowns. "I have a better idea." He parks the bus and stands up. "Impromptu concert, y'all. C'mon!"

A few minutes later, the six of them have set up at the top of the hill in a line abreast, each with an instrument— Mikey has a pair of drums that hang from his neck, Mer has her mandolin, Yolo the guitar, Brian the accordion, and Ella a flute. When they start playing, I'm honestly shocked—they're very, very talented, playing an old folk song from the sixties with an easy fluency that speaks of having played together for a long time.

I duck and shuttle behind them and into the jungle, Scarlett follows, and then Lorenzo and then Inez last. We creep out of sight of the bus and make our way roughly parallel to the road, skirting around the roadblock.

The music carries through the jungle, an incongruously joyful melody running counterpoint to the tension of sneaking past a truckload of killers.

We make our way parallel to the road, swinging wide around the checkpoint in case they have scouts watching for an end-run exactly like this.

Which they do—Inez spots him first, a black-clad figure leaning against a tree trunk, looking bored, smoking a cigarette with his balaclava pulled down. Scarlett drops him with a single silenced round to the forehead before he has a chance to even see us.

Over the next two hours, we creep, sneak, trudge, slip, and climb our way through the jungle until we've put several miles between us and the roadblock, at which point we rejoin the road, keeping a wary eye and ear out for approaching vehicles.

With San José finally within sight, we hear a familiar diesel rattle, and we scurry out of sight—a moment later, Betty White rumbles past, trailing pungent pot smoke and the strains of an accordion, a mandolin, a guitar, and singing voices—they're covering "Bad Romance" by Lady Gaga, in rousing folk style.

"God, they were weird," Scarlett says as we watch the van disappear around a bend.

"But cool," I say.

"No. Just strange," Inez says. "They should stay on this side of the Gap."

Lorenzo chuckles. "I like them. They're braver than they are smart, though. Once we have a signal in the city, I'll make some arrangements for them. Put a word out for my friends in various places to keep an eye on them."

I can't help but laugh at that. "You think they'll notice that things seem to just sort of magically happen for them?"

Lorenzo chuckles with me. "Hopefully not. That would ruin the fun."

———— ◆ ————

San José is a bustling, modern place with McDonalds, KFC, and Jeep dealerships. We manage to snag a taxi once we've hupped our way past the outskirts, and Lorenzo has the driver take a long, circuitous route through the city as we watch our backtrail for signs of pursuit; so far, nothing.

The cab driver eventually brings us to a neighborhood on the far north edge of the city and drops us off at a street corner, taking off in a blue-gray cloud of exhaust. Lorenzo leads us down a narrow alley littered with trash and across another street, dodging cars and box trucks and cyclists. He brings us to a low, red brick condominium building with bars on the windows and a broken buzzer; either the door isn't locked or the lock is broken because he waltzes right in and up the stairs to the second floor. He halts outside a door, knocks in a precise, complicated pattern, and waits. There's the sound of locks being opened, and then the door opens; a bottom-heavy woman on the far end of middle age greets Lorenzo by name, embraces him, kisses him on both cheeks, and then bustles past us without so much as looking at the rest of us.

Within, the condo is low-ceilinged, with black-out curtains across the windows keeping the interior dark and cool; a window AC unit rattles noisily, blasting frigid air. The narrow galley kitchen is lit by a single naked fluorescent bulb, and food simmers on the stove—a big pot of what smells like beans, rice, and chicken.

"She cooked?" Lorenzo mutters. "God bless that woman."

"What is this place?" Inez asks. "And who was she?"

"Sort of an aunt," Lorenzo says. "She was a mother figure to my whole squad when I was with the Brazilian army. When I retired, so did most of my unit, and she moved up here to be closer to her grandson, who lives in San José. All of us have used this place as a safe house over the years. I called her and told her I'd need to hide out here for a minute."

"And she took that to mean feed us?" Inez says, stirring the food with the long-handled wooden spoon resting across the open top of the pot.

"Apparently. It's how she is," Lorenzo answers.

"How is she connected to Brazilian Special Forces?" I ask.

"Not sure. Clerical assistant to a senior office, maybe? She was just always around, taking care of us, cooking for us, and treating us all like her favorite grandkids. To this day, I don't know who she is or what her connection is, but I love the woman like a mother."

"You can't find out?" Scarlett asks.

"Sure I could," Lorenzo answers. "But if she wanted me to know, she'd tell me. I choose not to know. It doesn't matter. Not anymore, anyway. Now, she's just an old friend with a condo I occasionally use as a safe house. She knows how to lose a tail and has her own network of spies and protection. *No one* fucks with Nina."

"Well, like you said, God bless Nina," I say. "Because that smells amazing, and I'm fucking ravenous."

We spend the next half an hour devouring the food, washing it down with a nice pale cerveza from the stocked fridge.

For a while, it's easy to pretend we are just tourists hanging out in an Airbnb.

Then, a little past sundown, Lorenzo's phone rings.

He answers it, listens, thanks the person in Spanish, and hangs up. "Break time is over, kids. That was Nina. She just got word that Mercado is making his move on our location. We're surrounded, apparently. She has people waiting for us about a mile from here, but we have to get to them. And to get to them, we're gonna have to fight through Mercado's forces."

I pull my pistol, check the load, check my spare, and glance at him. "I don't suppose this safe house has any hidden goodies, does it?"

Lorenzo grins. "I'm glad you asked, Solomon. Because yes, it does."

He goes into one of the bedrooms and lifts the bare mattress—a hidden hydraulic system raises the bed, revealing a hidden tray disguised as a platform bed. Within, a tidy array of submachine guns, magazines, boxes of ammo, and handguns, all using the same ammo size. We all load out in silence.

"Some grandma," Scarlett says. "I like her. I wanna be her when I grow up."

Lorenzo laughs at this, but the levity is short-lived.

Outside, there's a short burst of automatic weapons-fire, a moment of silence, another burst. A single sharp crack of a heavy rifle. More automatic chatter.

It's close.

As we head for the exit, Inez grabs my arms. "Sol."

I pause, meet her eyes. "Yeah?"

"If I tell you to go, you go." Her eyes are deep and dark and serious. "You promised. Remember?"

"Inez, I'm not gonna agree to leave you behind."

She tightens her grip on my arm until it hurts, nails digging in. "Solomon. You *have* to trust me. This is my fight, not yours. Not Scarlett's. Lorenzo I can't give orders to; you, I can. If I tell you to go, you go. You gather the boys, and you get me out. I'm not saying abandon me to my fate; I'm saying trust me. If I say go, you fucking go. Got it?"

I blow out a frustrated breath. "Goddammit, Inez. You know better than I do what'll happen if you get taken by this dude."

"Yes, I do." She loosens her grip, moves her hand to my shoulder in a gesture of familiarity and affection that freezes my breath in my lungs. "You are my responsibility, Solomon. And what's more, you're only here because of me. Once Rafael's men have me in custody, they'll leave you alone. I cannot and will not allow you to be killed on my account. Which is what will happen if we try to fight them."

"I'd break my oath before I let them take you, Inez. Fuck that."

"Solomon." Her eyes soften, forcing my frown to deepen. "You have to trust me. I know what I'm doing. As long as my son's location is kept secret, Rafael will not

294JASINDA WILDER

risk my death, and I can handle anything short of that for my son. You promised."

I wipe my face with my hand. "This goes against everything I am, Inez."

"I know."

I sigh. "I promise. When you say go, I'll go."

She nods, hand dropping away. "Very good. Thank you." She precedes me out the door.

Scarlett follows me out. "Allowing a monster like that to take her alive? Big brass fuckin' balls on that one. Especially knowing what she went through just to get away the first time."

I shake my head, my promise sitting in my throat like a hot, acidic knot. "Yeah."

"She'll be okay, Sol." Scarlett's voice is quiet and reassuring.

"I know." I shake my head again as we follow Lorenzo and Inez down the stairwell. "I just…I almost wish I hadn't gotten to know her like I have. It'd make leaving her behind easier."

Scarlett doesn't have an answer for that.

Outside, gunfire is loud and close, echoing and dopplering, making it hard to tell where it's coming from.

We come out in an alley, empty but for an overflowing dumpster. There's a shout, an answer—too close.

A rifle cracks.

Lorenzo is on the phone, crouched against the wall at the end of the alley. He ends the call and puts the phone in his back pocket. Shoulders his MP5.

Inez does the same. Glances back at me, nods once. I don't nod back—I'm pissed at her for forcing that promise out of me.

Lorenzo rolls out around the corner, crouched, MP5 to his shoulder, firing in short bursts. Inez goes next, and then Scarlett.

I hesitate, and then follow suit.

The veritable army facing us is a stark display of the fact that everything we've faced up until now has been little more than a feint, drawing us out, exhausting us, making us think we had a chance of getting away.

Cat and mouse, indeed.

I push thoughts out of my mind, dropping to a knee behind the bullet-riddled hulk of an old car, and start picking off targets. I'm not aiming for heads, but I can't honestly say I'm trying not to kill anyone.

Because promise or no, I don't know if I can just let Inez get taken.

I just can't.

CHAPTER 18

FROM THE FRYING PAN INTO THE FIRE

THEY'RE DRAWING US OUT. WE ADVANCE TOWARD them, and they fall back. If we try to find a route around them, we inevitably find the way blocked by Mercado's men in technicals and ex-military troop transports. The whole thing is happening on the streets of San José, and I can't help but wonder if this is going to hit the news—it's not a minor skirmish. Nina clearly knows some heavy hitters because Mercado's forces are being engaged on our flanks, the only thing preventing us from being surrounded and cut off.

It's only a matter of time, though.

We move from doorway to doorway, firing at black-armored figures. Yet, for every one we drop, another takes his place. Technicals block off side streets, firing fifty cals at us, redirecting us.

Sol is getting increasingly frantic, knowing it's only a matter of time before Inez pulls some sort of stunt that gets her taken by these assholes. And I'm with Sol—I hate the idea of her being tortured, raped, who knows what. But I understand her. I may not have a kid I'm protecting, but I'd let myself get taken to protect Solomon. I'd fight like a tiger to prevent it, but I'd let it happen if his life was in the balance. And in this case, an innocent child's life is at stake—a child who hopefully knows none of this.

Lorenzo leads us street by street away from the safe house. I'm not sure where he's leading us, but at this point, I'm not sure it matters much. We're just buying time. Delaying.

A sudden mad barrage of gunfire is exchanged behind us.

A roiling in my gut tells me that we're about to be cut off.

Huddling behind a cube van with a smoking engine bay, we cluster close, watching two and then three and then four and then six technicals sweep across the road, tires squealing as they brake to a halt in staggered formation across the road. A young woman with a toddler clutched to her chest scurries across the road and vanishes into a shopfront.

"Fuck, fuck, fuck," Lorenzo snaps. "Not good."

Inez sits with her back to the tire, swaps mags, and looks at Solomon. "It's time. I'll lead them away."

Sol glares at her. "I'm not leaving you, Inez. Not fucking happening."

Inez glares at him. "Yes, you are. I can handle Mercado. You have to find Lash."

"Inez, c'mon," Sol says, his voice low. "You've made a point of how nasty this asshole is, the kinds of shit he'll do to get what he wants from you."

Her face blazes with fury. "Doesn't matter what he fucking does to me, Solomon Cabot, I *will not* give up my son. *I will not.* And I'm not telling you to leave me, I'm telling you to get out of here and find Lash, and then come fucking get me."

"Inez—" Sol starts.

She lifts the assault rifle and puts the barrel to his chin. "I won't tell you again, Solomon. Trust me. This is the only way."

"Fuck," Sol says, the word bitten off, furious. "He's going to torture you."

"I know. Torture and worse. But I'll kill him." Her voice is soft, quiet, yet somehow that's worse than yelling and cursing; the soft is razor sharp and colder than the vacuum of space. "I will kill him, and it will be the last person I ever kill. I'll rip his intestines out and strangle him with them before I die."

Sol grabs the back of her neck and taps his forehead to hers, a rough man-to-man gesture. "I'll get Lash. I'll call everyone in on this. You stay the fuck alive, Inez. No matter what it takes, you stay alive. Promise me, or I'll die here with you, orders be damned."

With one harsh exhalation through her nose, she nods. "Agreed. I promise. I will stay alive, no matter what."

"All right. You've always known what you're doing, and I trust you to know now, even if I don't like it."

She nods once and then bolts out from behind the burning hulk and sprints away from us.

A shout echoes in Spanish: *"Get her! Get her or the chief will have our heads!"*

A pickup squeals and fishtails around the corner, braking to a stop, several shooters popping up in the bed. Lorenzo drops them all with absent-minded brutality, cratering the engine and painting brain matter across the street.

"This Lash of yours had better be worth it," he snarls, turning back to face Solomon.

Sol shrugs. "He's my brother. Do what you want, but I will follow Inez's orders. It's what she asked of me, and I trust her, and it's Lash. He came for me on his own. Now it's my turn to return the favor."

A bullet buzzes past my ear like an angry wasp, and I drop to a knee while spinning and put two rounds into the shooter's skull; three more enemies topple out of the alley we just emerged from, and Solomon bursts into action, breaking a thigh with a nasty kick, blasting around through another's stomach, and then pistol-whipping the third in the throat.

Lorenzo, from twenty feet away, puts a single round through each brainpan before I can so much as blink.

Inez's departure drew the rest of Mercado's men away from us to chase after her, and once we've taken out the last few tangos, the thunder of gunfire subsides.

Silence reigns for a moment.

"Fine," Lorenzo growls. "I have a lead on your friend's whereabouts. I do this for Sophia, however. If anyone can survive what that monster Rafael has planned, it's her. And I know her—she will give him a long, slow, agonizing death."

"From what you've told us," I say, "Even that will be too good for him."

Lorenzo's grin is wicked. "Then you don't know her. She can be very creative."

Sol glances at him. "So, your lead. Where is Lash?"

"My sources tell me he was redirected to the Bahamas and from there taken to Croatia."

Sol frowns. "Croatia? Why the fuck? Do you know anything else?"

He tips his head to one side. "Only a little. Apparently, he was taken on the orders of a man named Stjepan Juric." *St-YEHP-ahn YOO-rick.*

"Never heard of him," Sol says.

Lorenzo shrugs. "Me either. That is all I know for now. I have my people working on finding out more."

"So we need to get to Croatia," Sol says.

Lorenzo nods. "We do, and I have a plan."

"And that is?" Sol presses.

"Rafael wants Sophia. Now that he has her, or will soon, you should be in the clear. I have a contact here who can get you a passport. We fly there commercial." Lorenzo shrugs. "I think between the three of us, we can find what we need once we're over there."

Sol sighs. "I suppose so. I probably have a few people I can get in touch with."

"Me too," I say.

"But first, I need to call the guys. They need to know what's going on," Sol says.

Lorenzo hands him a phone, and Solomon dials a long string of numbers from memory.

It rings a few times. "Si, hey. Yeah, It's me—nah, I'm good. But look, we have a situation. Get the guys so I only have to say this once." A long pause. "Everyone is there? Alright, good. Listen up, fellas. We have two problems: Lash is missing, and Inez has been taken hostage by a cartel warlord down here in Quito. He's gonna bring her to his compound in Colombia. No, I'm not alone. I have two others with me. The three of us have a lead on Lash's location. We're gonna go get him. You guys need to gear up and get down here and start putting an op together. You don't do anything till we rejoin you. Just do recon and put the op together. Questions?"

For the next few minutes, Solomon talks strategy and logistics, shares coordinates, and all the other pertinent intel we have, with occasional input from Lorenzo and me—mostly Lorenzo.

Finally, they have a basic plan set up, and Sol signs off, returning the phone to Lorenzo.

A few hours later, Sol has a passport under the name James Williams, and we're crammed together in the back of coach on a flight from San José to Zagreb.

Solomon sits against the window, morosely watching the Atlantic slide away far beneath us. "I wonder what he's doing to her," he mutters.

"You can't go there, Sol," I murmur. "Won't help."

"Can't not."

"Tell me about Lash," I suggest.

He snorts. "Don't know much. He's Romani."

I frown. "Like a gypsy?"

He snickers. "Call him a gypsy to his face when you meet him. That'll be funny." I stare at him until he explains. "They consider the word 'gypsy' a slur. Sort of like calling a Black person the N-word."

"What's he like?"

"Most mysterious motherfucker I've ever known. No one knows shit about him. Even Inez says she doesn't know much of his story. All I know is, he's funny as fuck, and he can charm the panties off a nun."

I fake a gag. "Panties." I retch again. "Hate that word."

Sol snorts. "Why?"

I shrug. "I don't know. It's just gross. Almost as gross as 'moist.'"

Sol laughs. "So if I said moist panties…"

I gag, shoving at him. "Don't make me barf in your lap."

Sol sobers. "It just feels wrong flying away from Inez. Just…leaving her."

"She can handle it."

"She shouldn't have to."

"There's nothing you could have done. Either they took her, or we all died."

He shakes his head. "I fucking know. I get it. It just feels wrong. I was just starting to get a bead on who she really is under all that ice queen armor."

"I had an interesting conversation with her on the ride to Costa Rica."

He looks at me. "Oh?"

"She and I are a lot alike." I roll a shoulder. "Like, we're almost the same person in a lot of ways. If anything, she's me but…more extreme."

Sol snorts. "*More* extreme? Than *you*?"

"She was assassinating her father's enemies as a pre-teen. Ever see *Leon the Professional*?"

Sol eyes me. "I thought you didn't watch movies?"

"My crew put it on in the rec room after a training op one day. I watched it while I cleaned my gear. Sick shit, in a lot of ways. But Inez was a killer as a child. She has literally never known anything but violence. It's her whole life."

Sol nods, staring out the window. "And here's me and the rest of the guys taking vows to not kill. Makes you wonder where the connection is. Like, who is our boss? Why us? Why the club? How'd Inez become his right-hand woman?"

"I think she wants to leave everything behind—I think she wants to be part of the Arrows."

"She could be. She's always held herself aloof from the rest of us, though."

"She doesn't know how to relate to people. Think of me, Scar, the operator—shut off, closed off, doesn't trust anyone. Now multiply that by someone literally raised to be a killer. Someone who endured a nightmare you cannot even begin to imagine, Solomon." My voice shakes. "I can imagine it—I don't have to imagine it, so trust me when I say you should be glad you can't."

"Scar…"

I grab his hand and squeeze. "We talked about our old names. Inez and I."

He squeezes back. "You did?"

"I…" A long slow sigh hisses between my clenched teeth as I struggle to put it into words. "Maria. She…"

"You said she's dead."

"And you said you don't think she is, just…dormant."

He nods. "Right. And what'd you and Inez come up with?"

"That maybe we start thinking about that old name as the future. As the person I want to be."

"Meaning?"

I shrug. "Meaning, maybe someday Scarlett will retire. I don't know what I'd do, but…if I'm not an operator, just a regular old civilian living a boring civilian life, Scarlett can retire and I can become someone else. Someone new."

"Maria Rodriguez."

I shake my head. "Not Rodriguez. Maria Rodriguez *is* dead, that much is true. I'll never be her again. She was a child who crossed the Gap on foot and got trafficked into sexual slavery. I can't be that person and wouldn't want to. But maybe there can be a new Maria."

He turns our hands palm-to-palm and intertwines our fingers. "Tell me about this new Maria."

"I don't know."

"In a perfect world, who is she? What life does she have?"

I close my eyes and rest my head back, thinking. After a minute or two, I finally find something like an answer. "In a perfect world, Maria lives in a little house with a big backyard."

Saying this is like speaking your deepest, darkest secret out loud, admitting your most shameful, forbidden fantasy. It's terrifying. It's what I've secretly fantasized about in the most hidden recesses of my mind.

"A little white house. One story. A ranch, maybe. It would have pretty shutters. Maybe green or blue. It would have a big open kitchen, because in this perfect world, Maria knows how to cook. She makes a big breakfast for her husband."

"Just her husband?" Sol asks, his voice quiet and careful.

"No," I whisper. "For her daughter. A little girl named after Maria's mother. Kora—K-O-R-A." I try not to think of my mother because I'll start crying, and fuck that. "Maria, in this perfect world, doesn't own a gun. Maybe she has a dumb, boring, civilian job somewhere answering phones or…I don't know. She has friends. She watches TV at night, after work. She reads books. She goes for long runs at dawn. Her favorite color is different from one day to the next because her life never had color other than black, white, and red."

Sol frowns at me. "White?"

"Paperwork," I snicker. "After action reports."

He cackles. "Good call. Fuck that shit. I do *not* miss A-A-Rs at-fucking-all." He squeezes my hand, looking at me softly, lovingly. "What else?"

"Lazy Sunday mornings spent fucking and sleeping in. Barbecues in the backyard with our friends. Kids running around." My throat is tight and hot. "Maybe a swimming pool with a slide."

"That sounds fun as hell."

I feel a smile on my lips. "Maria has painted fingernails." I lift my fingers, showing short, dirty nails. "In a perfect world, Maria could go out for drinks with the girls and no one would ever know who she used to be." I laugh. "I don't know who the girls are, so don't ask."

Sol grins. "Oh, well, that's simple. The girls are Myka, Anjalee, and Annika…and whoever my brothers brought home."

I frown at that. "What's that mean?"

He sighs, laughs. "Well, it's been kinda weird. First, Rev got pulled into this whole thing with this chick who somehow ended up at the Club by accident. She had no business being at a club like that—she was super innocent. And he just…he was hooked. That led to him leaving the club for her, which led to a bunch of drama from Rev's past, and then Myka moved down into the Club with us. Then Kane took off, triggered by something—who the fuck knows what—and he came back with this Indian princess type. Rich girl, billionaire's daughter who ran away.

Kane helped her, and she helped him face his own shit, and then she moved in with us. And then Chance met Annika, and she had her shit and he had his shit, and then there were three women living with us. So then when my brothers and I all left for the funeral, everyone assumed we'd all come back with women. Inez confirmed that both Silas and Saxon did, in fact, come back with women while I was…away."

"And so are you," I say.

"Exactly. So you'll have a built-in posse of girls who know exactly what it's like being part of this group. Nik, Myka, and Ang are all super cool chicks. You'll like them."

I snort. "I don't like most women."

"Well, you'll have that in common with them."

I laugh. "Tell me about them."

Sol thinks for a while. "Admittedly, I was kinda… aloof, myself. So I don't know them very well. But they don't take no for an answer. Myka is a reformed good girl. Grew up super conservative religious, only had one boy-friend, that whole business. Turns out that one boyfriend was a piece of shit, and she left to see more of the world, I guess. She's sorta the human equivalent of sugar and sun-shine, which is funny because Rev is…not. He's a guy version of Inez, or at least he was before Myka. He was a Marine Recon."

"And by *reformed* good girl, you mean…?"

"We've thoroughly corrupted her in all the best ways."

"Good because I don't have it in me to pretend to be all good and cutesy."

Sol laughs. "They'd see through that shit in a second, babe. Just be you."

"So, Angalee and Annika."

"Angalee is…I guess you'd probably think she's this innocent little mouse without a backbone at first meeting. She comes across that way. Super quiet, super soft-spoken. But she's got a core of steel. She was raised in a literal tower, shut away from the real world, with all the money and luxury you can ask for but no freedom. She was betrothed against her will to an associate of her father's, one of those arranged marriages that was about her father's business. So she stole her dad's car and drove away, ran out of gas in the desert outside Vegas. That's where Kane found her."

"What's Kane like?"

"Big burly bear of a guy. A cowboy, like a real-deal cowboy. He got bucked off a horse and broke his back or some shit, got hooked on pills and booze. Got in a car accident that killed his fiancé, who happened to be the daughter of the man who unofficially adopted him."

"Oof," I put in. "That's a rough one."

"Yeah. He took it to heart, and not in a good way. Ran off and joined the army, and ended up in the Rangers…shit went sideways and he wound up with the Arrows. Anj got him to go back home and face his fiancé's father."

"That can't have been easy."

"Fuck no, but the guilt was eating him alive. The man forgave him, and Kane's a new man. Anj had to basically force him, though. Called his bluff. You know the balls it takes to call the bluff of a man like Kane? Big fuckin' brass ones."

"She sounds fascinating," I say.

"She is. Way more to her than you'd think when you first meet her."

"Next?"

"Chance and Annika. Chance is Rev's best

friend—they went into the military together, managed to get through training together and were assigned to the same squads their whole military career. Attached at the hip, those two. Chance got hooked on meth and almost died—it's how he ended up an Arrow. Annika was an Olympic volleyball athlete who had her career ended when a car took her knee out. Got hooked on drugs and spun out. Met Chance, and they sorta saved each other. She was off drugs at the time, but her life was in the shitter. She's a tough bitch, man. Doesn't take shit from anyone. She's six-three, which works because Chance is six-eight."

I arch an eyebrow at him. "A six-foot-eight Recon?"

"He was six-six at eighteen when he joined and grew another two inches vertically and put on like a hundred pounds."

I shake my head. "Jesus."

"Yeah, Chance is a big fuckin' boy."

"And your brothers?"

"Well, Sax and Si are younger than me—I'm the oldest, and Sax is the baby. Silas is the smooth one. He could sell snow to an Eskimo. He sold product for The Syndicate—drugs and guns, drew the line at people. Sax is…a little rough around the edges."

I cackle at that. "Hello pot, this is kettle."

"You'd think, but wait till you meet him. Rough, tough, aggressive, and not prone to being overly talkative." He shrugs. "He was a triggerman for the Syndicate. I guess they called him the Bloody Viking."

I snort, and the snort turns into a snicker. "Holy shit. Ordinarily, that'd be kinda cringey, but in that world, they don't give out nicknames easily."

Sol shakes his head. "No. I guess he earned that one the hard way. He won't tell us the story."

"No?"

"I caught wind of it through some back-channel sources when I was looking into them. I kept tabs on them both over the years."

"Well, now I'm gonna be on a mission to get the story out of him." I glance at him. "So, what kind of women do you think they each found?"

Sol shakes his head, shrugging. "Fuck, man, I don't even know. To catch the attention of guys like my brothers, they'll have to be pretty damn special. I don't even know how to guess, honestly."

A long silence.

Sol levels a penetrating, searching gaze at me. "What happens with us in a less-than-perfect world?"

I smile. "We take it one day at a time. I give you what I can, and you understand that I'm doing my best." I shrug. "I just…I can't retire Scarlett until I'm sure I don't need her anymore."

"I get it, babe. The only thing I ask is that you're honest with me about where you're at."

"I can do that. And right now, where I'm at is ready to get some rest."

———— ◆ ————

James Williams, April Hernandez, and Carlos Torino land in Zagreb, Croatia, in the small hours of the morning. We are unarmed and have a single, tenuous lead on Lash's last known location. We have a name and Inez's statement that Lash's enemy is someone high up in a government position—chances are good that this Stjepan Juric is an official with the Croatian government, which will make taking him on that much more difficult.

Franjo Tudman International Airport in Zagreb is a massive, airy space dominated by white ceiling trusses so intricate it looks like lace. Voices echo, and the squeak, click, and tromp of shoes bang off the curved, tunnel-like walls taking us from the arrivals concourse to the center of the airport.

That niggling worm of worry in my gut is back.

I nudge Sol as we head for the taxi line. "Something feels off."

He nods. "I know." He glances at Lorenzo. "You feel it?"

Lorenzo nods, looking grim. "Yes."

The exit is a few hundred yards away. A shoe squeaks behind us; a walkie-talkie squawks.

"Shit." Sol's voice is a bitter hiss.

I scan around us and see the reason: six tall, stony-faced men in black suits with earpieces range behind us. Ahead, a line of airport security officers block the exit.

We're unarmed in an airport. There's nowhere to run, and to fight, even if we stand a pretty good chance of winning, will mean innocent bystanders getting hurt.

"Ideas?" Sol mutters, fists clenching.

Lorenzo sighs, bitter and furious. "I should not be here. I should be in Colombia, working on rescuing Sophia."

"But you're not," I tell him. "Sol's friends and brothers are on it. Sophia can take care of herself. Right now, we need to deal with them."

The suited men approach us, fanning out to surround

us while airport security forms a protective perimeter, keeping curious onlookers away.

"They're not from Mercado," Lorenzo says. "We'd be dead if they were. This is something to do with your friend."

"Yeah, I agree," Solomon says. "They look government to me. Stay calm and go along for now. See what they want."

One of the men in the black suits steps forward—he's the oldest, with a military high-and-tight gone to salt-and-pepper, with cold brown eyes. "Solomon Cabot, Scarlett Gutierrez, and Lorenzo Oliveira Araujo. Come with us, please."

We exchange surprised glances—our real names, not the names on our passports?

"What is this regarding?" Solomon asks.

"Come with us, please," the man repeats.

"Are we being officially detained?" Solomon asks.

"I am not at liberty to disclose any information. You are not under arrest, but your cooperation is required." His voice is rough and hard and authoritative, giving nothing away; his Croatian accent is pronounced, but his English is flawless.

"I am a Brazilian citizen," Lorenzo says, "and my friends are American citizens. You can't just detain us without reason."

The man reaches into the inside pocket of his suit jacket and produces a glossy 8x10 photograph, creased horizontally from being folded in half. The photo is grainy, probably from a security camera of some sort. The figure at the center of it is a man of medium height, powerfully built, with impossibly broad shoulders, a tapered waist, and massive arms and chest. Black hair in a long, low po-nytail with a long beard trimmed to a point at mid-chest, the mustache is long and thick and curved upward across his cheeks. He's dressed in a plain black T-shirt and black pants, with what looks like a belt or sash of some sort tied around his waist, the end trailing at his right knee. The image is black and white, but I get the impression that the sash around his waist is brightly colored. He has a compact automatic pistol in his hands, and the image catches him in the act of tapping the magazine home with the butt of his palm. There's not much to see in the background other than the glass and metal of a high-rise of some sort and a bit of sidewalk.

"Do you know this man?" the agent asks.

I shake my head. "Nope. Never seen him in my life," I answer truthfully.

"Neither have I," Lorenzo answers.

"He's a friend of mine," Solomon says. "Why?"

"Your friend is a wanted criminal. He is in a lot of trouble."

Sol snorts. "Okay, buddy, tell me another one. Try the truth this time."

The agent frowns. "He is wanted by Interpol, as well as by my government."

"For?"

"Arms dealing, murder, corruption, and espionage, to begin with."

Solomon shakes his head. "Bullshit. I can personally attest to his whereabouts every minute of every day for the last three years—Las fucking Vegas, US of A." Solomon arches an eyebrow. "Let me guess, you work for Stejpan Juric."

The agent's expression gives away nothing. His

silence, however, says everything. "I have orders. You will come with us—voluntarily or in handcuffs. Your choice."

"Frying pan into the fire," I mutter. "Not much choice, eh boys?"

Solomon's jaw clicks as he grinds his teeth. "Fuck. This is bullshit."

Lorenzo looks fit to be tied. "I hope your friend is worth it. Because if Sophia dies, I cannot be held accountable for my actions. Be warned."

Solomon claps him on the shoulder. "My guys are on it. They're the best in the world."

"Who cannot take lives. Somewhat of a handicap when dealing with someone like Rafael and his many, many hired killers." Lorenzo shakes off Solomon's hand. "Let's go. Might as well get this over with." He glares at the agent. "You are making a mistake."

The agent shrugs. "Orders are orders. Take it up with Mr. Juric."

"I plan to." Lorenzo marches forward, shoulders tense, gait liquid—he's a man on the edge of snapping.

I look at Sol as we fall in after Lorenzo. "What's going on?"

Sol shakes his head. "Fuck if I know. I guess Lash is gonna have to rescue us now." He laughs. "What a clusterfuck."

"How can you laugh?"

He shrugs, still chuckling. "Because it's funny. None of this has anything to do with me. I have a list of enemies a mile long, but none of them are involved in this shit. I dunno. It just strikes me as funny."

"We don't have a lot of time to cool our heels in some

Croatian government lockup, Sol. If Mercado can't get what he wants from Inez, which we both know he won't…"

Sol nods. "I fucking know. But we can't duke it out with government agents and airport security. Not here, not now. We'll make a move. Also, don't count Lash out. I may not know much about his past, but he's my brother. He'll stop at nothing to get us out."

"I sure as hell hope you're right," I mutter.

A line of black SUVs with blacked-out windows waits at the curb, idling. We're all loaded into one, and the agents pile into two more, and then the line of SUVs takes off.

Half an hour later, the caravan pulls into an underground parking garage beneath a nondescript building in Zagreb's Low Town. We're herded through a series of low hallways with doors protected by biometric locks at regular intervals. An elevator with facial recognition takes us down further. More hallways—narrow, white-washed cinderblock walls, drop-tile ceilings, fluorescent lighting, and polished concrete floors.

At the end of a particularly long hallway, a single door. The agent opens it with a thumbprint—it buzzes and a lock disengages with a loud thunk.

On the other side, an interrogation room—dim lighting, a two-way mirror, a metal table. All six agents file in after us. We're seated in three identical chairs at the table, and then…

Nothing.

Silence.

Perhaps another thirty minutes later—although time is hard to track without any indicators—the door opens again, and another man in a suit enters.

This man, however, is not an agent. His suit is

expensive, bespoke, charcoal with pinstripes, a red pocket square, and a matching tie. His shoes are expensive, glossy leather. His watch is an Omega. Expensive haircut—dark brown hair, brown eyes.

He exudes authority, wealth, and power.

He sits opposite us. Leans back in the chair and crosses one leg over the other. Plucks a silver case from a suit pocket, flips it open and withdraws a cigarette. One of the agents produces an ashtray and a lighter and lights the cigarette.

The man inhales, holds it, and snorts the smoke from his nostrils. "Hello, friends." His voice is soft, high, quiet, fluent English, and gently accented. "Do you know me?"

Sol shrugs. "No. Should I?"

"Perhaps, perhaps not. We have someone in common." He smiles pleasantly—the smile, however, does not reach his eyes, which remain glittering, brown, icy chips of dead, flat nothingness.

"And that would be whom?" Solomon asks.

"Nicolae Dragos." A heavy pause. "At least, that's the last known alias he used. You may know him under another alias, however."

Another long pause.

"I believe you call him Lash."

"And what do you want with him?" Sol asks. "And what does it have to do with us?" He gestures at me and Lorenzo. "Them in particular. They've never even met him."

Stjepan, for this is surely him, pushes the smoke out of his mouth and inhales it through his nose. "He kidnapped my daughter."

"I find that hard to believe," Sol says. "My intel says you had him kidnapped."

"Kidnapped is such a strong word," Stjepan says, smiling that serpentine smile. "I had his flight redirected. He and I have…unfinished business to attend to. He was avoiding me, so I took some liberties."

"And incurred the wrath of the Syndicate," Sol says.

Stjepan shrugs. "I returned their fancy jet to them when I was done with it."

"I don't know where he is," Sol says. "I came to—"

"Save him from me," Stjepan cuts in. "Yes, I know. Unfortunately for you, that will not be happening. There will be an exchange. Nicolae, or Lash, if you prefer, will turn himself and my daughter, unharmed, over to our custody. You will go free. Very simple."

"Or?"

A shrug. "Or nothing. You will waste away here, forgotten."

Lorenzo laughs. "If you think you can hold me, you have not received correct information regarding my identity."

Sol just sighs. "Stjepan, listen. If something happened between your daughter and my friend, I can assure you, it's not kidnapping. And please trust me when I say we are not people you want to fuck with. Neither is Lash."

Stjepan just snorts a laugh, smoke bubbling out of his nose with each breath. "Oh, I think I know much more about Nicolae than you do, Mr. Cabot."

"How's that?"

"I trained him. I made him who he is."

EPILOGUE

PART 1

Inez

MY STOMACH ROILS.

I've been treated fine so far—after I surrendered, they zip-tied my hands behind my back and blindfolded me. I spent an untold number of hours in the backseat of a vehicle, jouncing, sliding, and toppling this way and that as the vehicle navigated the treacherous roads. Unable to use my hands and unable to see to brace and shift my weight through turns, I slam from one side of the bench to the other, cracking my head and bruising my shoulders.

I can tolerate this.

The man driving chatters idly to his friend in a dialect I do not know. I ignore them, and they ignore me.

We make another wide turn, and then the engine strains as we ascend a long, steep hill. We even out and then continue straight, going across what feels and sounds like grass rather than dirt or tarmac.

After a minute or two, I hear the roar of a propeller-driven aircraft—double prop, it sounds like. My next ride.

The vehicle lurches to a halt, doors open and thud closed. A door opens on my right, and the noise of the propellers is abruptly louder. Hands grab me and help me out of the vehicle and to my feet. I could snap these zip-ties easily, but to what point? Might as well let this play out, for now. I can't put off dealing with Rafael any longer, anyway.

"A step," a male voice says behind me in Spanish.

I step up, and hands steady me as I ascend; the hands push my head down under a door frame, I assume, and then turn me left. I walk a few feet, and then I'm stopped. The zip-ties are cut, and a gun barrel is pressed to my temple.

"Not move." More Spanish from someone for whom Spanish is not a first language. "Sit."

I'm guided to a seat, and then my hands are zip-tied to the armrests.

Hands buckle me in and miraculously do not take any liberties with my body in the process.

A few minutes later, the airplane door closes, and the propellors increase in volume; the aircraft lurches gently, and then I'm pressed back in my seat as our velocity ramps up, and then my stomach drops away as we go airborne.

I allow myself to rest. I can't see and can't move, so I may as well sleep.

I tune out the drone of the airplane, drowsing at first and then eventually falling asleep.

I'm shaken awake by the stomach churn of descent and the lurch and bark of tires as we touch down. There's waiting and taxiing, and then the aircraft halts, and the propellor noise reduces to a fading whine as they're powered down.

The zip-ties are cut once more. "Up. Hands behind back."

I comply, and my hands are bound once more. I'm assisted off the airplane and into stifling heat and humidity. Hands guide me across the tarmac; a jet screams overhead.

I hear a car engine idling, and I'm helped in, still bound. These seats smell like leather, and the interior is cool and quiet. I'm buckled in, the belt tugged taut to prevent me from shifting too much.

"Any trouble with her?" A male voice asks, this time by someone who does speak Spanish natively.

"No, chief. No trouble."

"Good. Mercado is waiting for her."

The vehicle slides into motion; this ride is smooth and easy, sparing me the jouncing and crashing. Music plays from the front seats, and I recognize a radio station local to the area near Rafael's compound.

The sound of the airport fades, and the road gets a little rougher.

"Apologies for the rough ride, Señora Sousa. We will be there very soon."

Señora Sousa? I almost laugh out loud—I was married to him against my will, raped, hunted, and now kidnapped, and yet they address me as if I'm his *wife*?

I say nothing.

"Very soon" must mean something different to him than it does to me because we bounce along for another fifteen or twenty minutes before we slow; a window hums open and tires crunch on gravel. Low mutters in Spanish, which I only catch some of—*she's here, the boss is in the* something.

My blood boils, and my stomach curdles. My pulse

pounds in my ears. It's hard to keep my breathing slow and even.

I'm here.

I'm back.

In a matter of minutes, I'll be face-to-face with Rafael again.

There's no way to mentally prepare—he's capable of anything. I think he'll try to convince me to simply tell him, first. He'll likely be genial, acting as if it's so good to see me, playing up the charm that he can turn off and on at will. When that doesn't work, he'll try coercion. Eventually, violence of one sort or another.

No matter—I will endure what I must for my boy.

I never gave him a name. I remember him as a tiny, nearly weightless bundle cradled against my chest as I dragged myself through the jungle, mile after mile. I hitched rides with locals, slept where I could, begged and stole to keep myself alive. I still have scars on my feet from the barefoot trek to Goiâna.

I do not know how I survived—toward the end, I was so starved and dehydrated I could summon no milk for my son, and he began to weaken. A native woman found me, and they helped me. Nursed me to something like health and took care of my boy. The moment I could stay on my feet, I thanked them and left. Years later, I went back and found them bringing gifts.

I often wonder what his life is like. What he looks like. How he is doing. I am tempted, nearly every day, to use my resources to find him. I could, easily. But if I don't know, I can't give him up, no matter what Rafael does to me. That's my secret, one not even Lorenzo is aware of: not even I know where my son is now. See, I lied to Lorenzo.

He found a good family, and I told him I left my son with them. But I didn't. I watched that family for several days, and I didn't like them. I couldn't say why, just a feeling—a mother's intuition, perhaps. So I found someone else.

A young woman. Sad and lonely, a widow with a good government job and retired parents she saw every day after work.

I may have barely escaped with my life, but I did not escape broke—I had quite a bit of money hidden in various accounts. I gave the woman the Colombian equivalent of a million US dollars to take my son and adopt him. I used a contact of Lorenzo's to create an identity for my son, complete with false adoption papers in his new mother's name—which I carefully avoided learning.

Then, I disappeared. I never looked back. Perhaps the woman is still living where she was when I found her, but I advised her to take her parents and the boy and move— far away. Out of Colombia, even. Perhaps she listened to me, perhaps she did not.

Rafael Sousa will never know his son. The boy will never know his true parentage.

My heart breaks anew each day—I miss him. But it was the only choice—the only way to give him a real life.

My thoughts turn to Lorenzo—as they always do.

God, that man.

I had no right to drag him back into my life. I did it because I am selfish and because I could not stand the thought of Solomon and Scarlett suffering for my sake. When I found out it was Rafael's men who took Solomon, I felt a rage so potent it nearly consumed me. Even my employer did not dare get too close to me until I'd regained control—perhaps because he, of all people, knows me best.

Better than Lorenzo, even, in some ways. Not physically—our relationship is not like that. It is a business relationship and sort of a mentor-mentee one. I respect him, but I do not love him, and I am not attracted to him like that, although he is, objectively, an extraordinarily attractive human being.

My heart belongs to Lorenzo. Always has, and always will.

I assume they're on their way to find Lash by now.

Lorenzo.

We nearly slept together in that hotel in Quito...I wanted to, dearly. But I knew this was coming. I knew I had to face Rafael before I could allow myself to have Lorenzo. Stopping before we got too carried away was one of the hardest things I've ever done in my life—truly. All I wanted was to feel his arms around me again. To feel his stubble on my cheeks, on my thighs. To kiss him. To taste him. To feel him slide inside me.

I know the men think I'm an ice queen—I am. I've had to be. The icy walls surrounding my shattered little heart are all that have kept me sane in these last years. They gird me. Keep me from losing my mind, from going mad with grief, with sorrow, with rage.

But deep inside, in the part of me only Lorenzo has ever seen, I'm a much different person. Sophia does exist. She's shackled inside the tower of ice, bound and gagged, chained to the agony of my past—the betrayal of my father, those three days of hell I spent chained in a basement room, raped by countless men, the forced marriage to Rafael, my father's subsequent murder at Rafael's hands; being held down as a doctor paid by Rafael forcibly removed my IUD so I could bear Rafael's child; the nightmarish birth, alone, in agony, terrified; the seventeen minutes I spent in a red haze, slaughtering everyone in that estate—every cook, every maid, every guard, every stable hand, every groundskeeper, all while bloody and naked, trailing placenta and umbilical cord while the midwife cared for my child. When I was done, I took my son and killed the midwife as well.

My nightmares are not of being raped in that cell or days alone in the jungle. My nightmares are of what I did that day.

Sophia exists, yes. But who is she? A feral animal? A cowering simpleton, too traumatized to even speak? A creature of psychopathic rage?

I am all of those things.

But who is Sophia? If I allow Lorenzo to melt my walls, as I know he could if I were to let him, who would I be? Inez is my armor. I have always understood that. Inez is a persona, like an armored mech suit from science fiction films.

I saw Scarlett come alive under the constancy and warmth of Solomon's love. I envy her that. I had hoped it would happen when I sent her on that wild goose chase—all I had was a possible location, a rumor of a whisper. She pulled it off, as I knew she would. And my god, Solomon exceeded my expectations. He opened himself to her immediately and willingly. He let her be herself. Let her push him, but not too far.

And I envy them that.

Again, my thoughts return to Lorenzo. No matter how I try to avoid it, he fills my mind, as he has for so long. For always. I knew I would love him the moment I saw him. He was so young, then. A boy, barely old enough to shave and drive but hard-faced and wise beyond his years. There was only the hint of the man he would become back then. Tall, still a little gangly. But his smile, my god. He was standing guard at the end of the hallway where my bedroom was, dressed in a black T-shirt and camo pants, holding an Uzi as if he knew how to use it. I, just a girl myself, albeit one who at sixteen was already a seasoned killer and my father's anointed executioner, took one look at Papa's new bodyguard and knew he would be mine.

It was against the rules—for him. I didn't care. I should have, but I didn't. I was foolish. Arrogant. I didn't want the keys to Papa's kingdom—I saw the suffering of the women he trafficked, and I hated it. When one of his men went rogue with money or drugs, I had to hunt him down. I had to kill him. I had to kill his family and his friends—I hold a secret I've never told anyone: I didn't always kill the women and children. I became somewhat of an expert in helping them disappear while making it look like I killed them. I just…I suppose perhaps I had a tiny sliver of conscience.

I hated it. I hated all of it.

I hated my father for what he made me do. I hated him for what he stood for. I would walk the streets as I hunted my prey, and I saw the victims of our drugs strung out and listless in alleys. I saw people sobbing as their daughter or sister disappeared into my father's brothels. I saw it all, and I hated it all.

I was relieved when Papa chose Rafael to take over. The relief was short-lived, though.

Lorenzo.

See? Always back to him.

He saw me. He knew who I was. And yet, he also saw

something else. He saw *me*. He saw something in me that I never have.

I wasn't a virgin when I took him to my bed. Neither was he. But still, it was like the first time for both of us because our connection was something not of this world.

The months that followed, sneaking around to meet Lorenzo? Bliss. I thought I could get away with it. I thought I was hiding it. I should have known better. I overheard two of Papa's men discussing their orders to garrote Lorenzo and dump him in a swamp for touching the boss's daughter.

I tipped him off and told him to run. Join the military—one of the few places Papa couldn't reach him. So, Lorenzo went back to Brazil and joined the army and became an operator, then a spy, and then a junior case agent before finally retiring to work freelance, as he does now, often in close coordination with the Brazilian government.

When I saw him again in that parking garage, my heart nearly burst through the ice. I wanted to leap into his arms and beg him to kiss me.

But I couldn't. I dared not.

I can't let my walls down. I can't let him melt the ice. I need it to survive what's to come.

Inez has one more mission.

Her last one.

Kill Rafael Sousa, the drug lord known as Mercado.

———————— ◆ ————————

The SUV—I assume a top-end Range Rover—glides to a halt. The engine shuts off. Doors open and close. Mine opens, and I'm unbuckled. Hands help me out.

"I am going to remove your blindfold now, Señora

Sousa. It will be bright on your eyes." The voice from earlier—solicitous, respectful.

I do not answer. Simply stand and wait, eyes closed.
The blindfold is removed and light lashes my eyes. I squint
one eye open, blinded by brilliant sunlight. And then the
other, slowly letting my pupils adjust.

"Are you ready, Señora Sousa?" The speaker is a short,
slender man in his late forties, balding, with a terrible mustache. He's wearing a custom navy blue suit, bulging at the
left chest with a shoulder holster.

I stare at him, giving him my coldest, most venom-
ous gaze.

Like everyone else before him, he quails away, paling.
"Th-this way, please," he stammers.

I very nearly smile to myself at his reaction. But that
would spoil the effect, so I don't.

I take stock of my surroundings. We stand on a gravel
driveway, the stones white and neatly raked. Behind us is a
wide grassy circle, at the center of which is an ornate marble fountain. The driveway circles the fountain and runs
ruler-straight to the south between a tunnel of arched trees,
their manicured branches and leaves providing cool shade.
Before me, the house, although such a word barely covers
the ornate monstrosity.

It's a mansion of epic proportions, a veritable
Versailles. White marble blocks polished to ashine, a roof
of scalloped slate tiles, multiple chimneys, three stories. A
balcony with an elaborate wrought iron railing overlooks
the fountain—beneath which is the porch, held up by ionic
columns, stone lions guarding the stairs. A verdant, manicured lawn stretches away in every direction, rolling across
dozens of acres. Half a mile or so from the main structure

is a horse barn, as massive and overly ornate as the house, with white three-row fencing extending away to encompass even more acreage of prime grazing land. Glossy-backed horses amble in pairs and singles. In one of the turnouts, a stable hand scoops manure into a wheelbarrow.

A helicopter, a former Soviet gunship, perches insect-like on the lawn a few hundred yards from the house, bristling with rocket launchers and machine guns.

Everywhere you look, armed men roam the grounds in pairs, wearing mirrored sunglasses and earpieces.

My skin crawls, and I turn my gaze up to the balcony.

A tall figure stands at the railing. Trim waist, narrow shoulders, black hair slicked back, wearing white slacks and a white linen shirt open to mid-chest, sleeves rolled up.

Rafael.

I swallow hard, my stomach turning and churning, blood running cold. I hold his dark gaze, however, expressionless and even.

I'm not afraid of you.

"This way, please, Señora Sousa." Rafael's sniveling toady gestures solicitously toward the fifteen-foot-high polished mahogany front doors with the antique bronze lion-head knockers.

I ignore him, not even looking at him as I ascend the steps with an attitude and posture that says, hopefully, that I'm doing it of my own volition and not because he told me to.

As I approach, the doors swing inward on oiled hinges, each one held by an armed guard. Within, black-and-white checkered tiles spread away from the foyer; a crystal chandelier hangs fifty feet overhead, sunlight refracting through it to send rainbows glittering and dancing on the walls, floor, and ceiling. A suit of armor, likely actually of medieval vintage, stands on a pedestal in the center of the foyer, wielding a halberd. More suits of armor line the walls to either side. Twin staircases arc in graceful half-spirals up to a second-story landing.

Straight ahead, a glimpse of a kitchen, glass doors, and the backyard beyond.

"Sophia." Rafael's voice echoes down to me.

I look up—he stands at the top of the stairs, hands on the railing, smiling in greeting. "Welcome."

I stare up at him.

"What, no greeting for your beloved husband?" He smirks as he says this. He snaps his fingers. "Bring her."

Hands nudge me toward the stairs, and I climb them, dread filling me with each step.

Dread and hate.

He hasn't changed much, despite the years. A few more lines on his face, a deeper sense of certainty regarding his place in the world. He's still absurdly handsome in a rakish, hawk-like, prima donna sort of way. His dark brown eyes are sociopathic and empty despite the gleaming, white-toothed smile he shows me—a shark's grin.

I stop a few feet away from him, back straight, holding his gaze without flinching, without showing any emotion.

"You look well, Sophia." He scans me. "As lovely as ever."

I hold my tongue. He'll get to the point eventually.

My silence annoys him, though. He's used to having an effect. Instilling terror.

I am the terror. I am the nightmare.

It seems he has forgotten.

I have not.

He regards me for a moment. "Surely you have something to say to me, Sophia. It has been many years, after all, and you are my wife."

My eyes burn as I stare at him, refusing to so much as blink.

He sighs. "It's like that, is it?" He's been speaking in English, I only now realize—flawless, unaccented English. He could be from Ohio.

"Your friends are guests of the Croatian government, by the way." He juts his chin at someone behind me; a small tablet device is thrust in front of my face, showing Sol, Scarlett, and Lorenzo surrounded by agents in the Zagreb airport. "I tipped off a business associate. I felt you and I would need time to become…reacquainted."

Fuck.

I show nothing. Certainly not the thread of panic that blossoms in my belly.

"I am well aware of your little group of outcasts. I am sure they will attempt to rescue you, and I have taken appropriate measures. Soon, you will all be my guests, and then the real fun will begin."

He watches me closely, looking for a reaction. I give him none.

"Well, the years certainly haven't softened you, have they?" His hands go into his pockets, and he stalks around me. "I was content to let sleeping dogs lie, as it were. But then, a would-be rival attempted to assassinate me. They failed, but they killed my girlfriend and our son."

I'm tempted to bait him with a statement of sympathy, but I can't bring myself to do it. No point.

A sigh, frustrated and long-suffering. "Cut to the chase, is it?" He leans his backside against the railing and crosses his arms over his chest. "Very well. You know what I want. Give me the identity and location of my son, and you and your friends will be allowed to live. No questions asked. It can all be over right this minute, Sophia. His name and his location."

I am no lady, but I'm still woman enough to find the way men hawk and spit disgusting. In this case, however, I'll make an exception. I hawk snot and saliva and spit it directly into his face.

Blinding light bursts behind my eyes with a vicious lance of pain—I'm knocked backward, unable to catch my balance, I hit my ass hard, biting my tongue. Agony throbs through my skull where Rafael's thug pistol whipped me.

A deafening blast concusses my eardrums—a massive revolver firing. A body thuds to the ground.

"No one lays a hand on her but me." Rafael's voice is a serpent in the grass, soft and slithering and deadly. "You understand me?"

"Yes sir," comes the answering chorus.

"Clean this mess up." His hands grasp me by the elbows, and he hauls me to my feet. "I apologize for that, Sophia. My men are quite loyal, you see. You should not provoke them."

I'm dizzy from the blow, my vision swimming, my head pounding. Blood trickles hot down my face and pools coppery in my mouth. I spit blood at his feet rather than at his face because I may as well space out the agony coming my way.

"Tough as ever, I see. A blow like that would have kept most men I know on the ground." Black spots swim across my vision, and nausea bubbles through me—I have a concussion for sure.

Rafael dabs at my face with a handkerchief. "Sophia, Sophia, Sophia. You can't just play nice? Tell me where he is. He'll live in the lap of luxury. He'll have everything he could ever want. Wealth, power, women. I suppose that last one isn't a selling point for you, though, is it?"

I allow him to dab the blood away because as much as I want to jerk away, it would serve no purpose. Spitting in his face was calculated—proving a point.

"Still won't speak, eh?" He steps backward and hands the bloody handkerchief to someone; he sighs. "I do not want to have to do unpleasant things to you, Sophia. Truly, I do not. Notice, none of your friends were harmed, no matter how many of my men you killed? I just want my son."

I speak for the first time. "You will not believe me, but I truly do not know. I made sure of it."

"Ah! She speaks!" He rubs his forehead with his fore-knuckle. "You are right; I do not believe you. What, you expect me to believe you dropped him off at an orphan-age? Or a fire station?" He shakes his head. "No, *cariño*, I do not believe you would do that. Not after what you went through for him."

I shrug. "Believe what you want, Rafael. It is the truth. I do not know his name or where he is. And if I did, I would not tell you. So do what you want to me. It's all been done before."

He nods. "Yes, yes. You're very tough, I know." He paces back and forth in front of me a few times. "Tell me something, *cariño*. That godawful mess you made at your father's estate. Did you enjoy it?"

I frown at him. "What?"

"Thirty-two people—nineteen men and thirteen

women. I wish I had a video recording of your rampage. It must have been incredible." He laughs, a merry little thing that's almost a giggle. "My god, the blood! So much blood. You even murdered the stablehands! The midwife!"

"But not you."

He smiles, shakes his head. "No, not me. I bet you wish, however."

"No, not really."

He frowns. "No?"

"It will be much more satisfying when I kill you this time around."

He sniffs a laugh. "You think so, eh? Well, I imagine you would be dreaming of that. I don't begrudge you the dream, but I must say I find it very unlikely, even for you."

"I'm going to rip your intestines out and strangle you with them, Rafael. Out of spite and out of principle that the world will be a better place without you in it. And then I will never kill again." I don't know what possesses me, then. "I have nightmares of that day. I was out of my mind. I see them in my sleep."

Rafael pierces me with that blank, sociopathic stare. "Do you? Hmm. I suppose I always thought you were like me."

"You know you're a sociopath?"

"Of course I know. There's nothing to be done about it, but it's good to know oneself." He turns away, thinking, and then back to me. "Sophia, do you know why I killed your father? Aside from the obvious."

"Aside from the obvious?"

"Are you a parrot, now?"

"The obvious being taking over his empire."

"Correct—aside from that."

I shake my head. "No, I have no idea. I never even considered there was another reason."

"Greed was a large part of it. Self-preservation was another. He was starting to see certain parts of me that he didn't like. The parts you always saw. He was going to have me killed."

"Then why marry me off to you, if he never intended to make you his heir?"

"He was going to wait until you sired a whelp, of course. Once he had a male heir to take his ill-gotten crown, I was going to end up at the bottom of a swamp." He shrugs. "So I struck first. But there was another reason that very nearly trumped all the others. Can you guess?"

I shake my head, making my vision swim and my brain throb. "No. I couldn't begin to guess."

"For you. Because of what he did to you. I killed all the men who raped you, you know. After I took power, I found out who they were, lined them up, and shot them, one by one, with my own hand. You were never going to marry me willingly—I knew that and so did he. But that? It was unnecessary. Barbaric. It ruined you. You went into that nasty little room one person and came out another. A broken, pathetic, miserable, shattered little eggshell of a person. If he had just locked you up until the wedding and drugged you into compliance, everything would have been different. We would never have had a real relationship, of course. I'm not capable of such things, for one. You would never have come around to caring for me, for another. But we could have had a business alliance, at least. I run the business and you run the dirty work. You're damned good at it. But no. Your father was a monster, and that's coming from *me*."

Jesus.

Maybe it's the concussion, but…that actually makes sense. And honestly, he's right. I saw him for who he was. I knew he was a sociopath, although, at sixteen or eighteen or twenty, I didn't have the understanding of what that meant. I just knew he wasn't right. But he was hot, and he seemed to like me insofar as he liked anyone. Had Papa not drugged me, I eventually would have seen the wisdom in working with him. I could have steered him away from trafficking people. I'd have had my boytoys, and he'd have had his little whores, and it'd have all been very *Narco*.

I look at him. "I almost wish that had happened, Rafael."

"I do wish it." He sighs. "You really won't tell me?"

I shrug. "I really don't know. I made sure I didn't so that when this happened, he would be safe from you."

"I won't hurt him, *cariño*. I want to give him all of this, one day."

I nod, knowing it's futile. "I know. That's exactly what I'm protecting him from."

He sighs sadly. "But you do know how to find him."

I don't answer. We both know it's true.

"I believe you, Sophia." he steps close, brushes at the gash on my temple, examines the blood on his thumb, and then licks his thumb—it's an absent-minded thing, not meant to scare me. Which makes it all the scarier. "Unfortunately, I'm going to have to make you talk. Or at least try."

"I won't tell you, Rafael. You're wasting your time."

"What about your friends? I can make another call and have them sent to me. Perhaps watching me carve pieces off them will change your mind."

I don't answer that either.

He shakes his head. "It is good to see you, *cariño*. Even under these circumstances." He flips a hand at me. "Take her to the barn and lock her in with Demon."

Fuck. What the hell does that mean?

I don't bother asking. I'll find out soon enough.

As his men haul me away, I can't help but worry about Sol, Scarlett, and Lorenzo.

Lorenzo most of all.

Because Rafael was right about another thing: I very well might break if I have to watch him torture them.

I hold onto my faith in their abilities. But even more than that, I have faith in Lash.

See, I know more about him than I've let on. Of all the Broken Arrows, he's the most dangerous.

The deadliest.

The secret?

He swore an oath, just like the others. But unlike them, his did not contain the prohibition against killing.

My employer's orders. I questioned it at the time.

Now?

I'm starting to understand.

Lash is going to have to save us all.

EPILOGUE

PART 2

Tatiana

"DRIVE AROUND THE BLOCK, PLEASE, GEORG."

"Yes, Ms. Juric."

I am not my father's daughter; I am my mother's daughter. That said, I was still half-raised by the man, despite my mother's best efforts, which means I'm always alert and aware, constantly scanning my surroundings, which is how I pick up the blacked-out Mercedes SUV that's been following us for the last several miles.

As Georg, my driver, makes a right-hand turn on Vukovara, I remain twisted in my seat, watching the G-Wagen as it slides out into traffic behind us, three cars back. It's a pimped-out ride, as the Americans would say, with oversized spinning chrome rims, thin tires, blacked-out windows, and after-market LED light bars.

I sigh. "Idiots."

"Problem, Ms. Juric?" Georg asks, glancing at me in the rear-view mirror.

"Yes," I snap, annoyed at this ridiculous delay to my tight schedule. "We have a tail. G-Wagen three cars back."

Georg's eyes flick away from mine, scanning our backtrail; his brow furrows as he spots them. He cuts aggressively across traffic and makes a sharp, tire-squealing left turn against the light, eliciting a chorus of honks. He guns the engine at the last second, and the powerful motor sends my BMW 8 series rocketing forward. Another left, weaving around slower-moving cars, and then a sharp, fishtailing right, and then a sudden tap of the brakes and stomach-churning slide puts us underground in a parking garage. Georg slows, then, winding down to the bottom of the garage, backing into a space in the farthest corner.

We sit in silence for ten minutes or so, waiting.

"I believe we are clear, Ms. Juric," Georg says.

"Very well. I have a meeting with Draga and Tomas…" I check my Bulova watch. "Ten minutes ago. Dammit."

I slide my phone out of my crocodile Birkin and ring Draga. She answers on the third ring. "Draga, yes, it's me. I've been delayed—my apologies."

"Not at all, Ms. Juric. Tomas and I have been review-ing the numbers. If you wish, we could have the meeting now. Your physical presence is not strictly necessary."

"Excellent—I have another meeting across town in an hour. Put Tomas on speaker, please."

"Yes, Ms. Juric…here we are." A pause and the rustle of papers as Draga gets situated. "Now. Our numbers this quarter have been excellent…"

I put the tail out of my mind and focus on Draga's and Tomas's reports, digging into the details of my company's latest quarterly reports.

I'm immensely proud of what I've built—I took a quarter-million Euro loan from my father when I was twenty, and over the last eight years, I've grown my busi-ness into ten million Euros per year, with year-on-year growth of twenty-seven percent. Not bad for a girl without a university degree. I did poach my father's second-favorite business advisor—Martin has been indispensable to the process, teaching me much of the fine details of running and growing a profitable business

When Tata first heard my pitch, he called it silly—the grasping of a bored little girl with too much time and not enough business sense.

My company buys top-shelf couture from around the world a season or two post-trend and resells it in pop-up boutiques, utilizing flash-sales strategies and aggressive pricing to move products, prioritizing stock movement over price tag; we utilize social media as the driver of our primary sales—most of my inner circle executives are social media, marketing gurus. We push heavily on IG, TikTok, and YouTube, resulting in a young clientele with lots of money and huge followings—our growth is as much due to social media word of mouth from our loyal followers as any traditional advertisements. Our pop-up boutiques last for seventy-two hours, with the specific location only revealed via our official socials posts at the last second— the lead-up to the reveal is a bread-crumb trail of hints and clues that eagle-eyed followers can decipher, share, and discuss.

We host clusters of pop-ups in a specific area of a specific city over the course of a month and then move to different cities and start all over again. This has developed a devoted cadre of fans who follow our zigzagging across Europe, following clues and competing to be among the first thousand clients who receive a bonus gift bag filled with collectible pop-up specific swag.

My mind is racing as we shift from numbers to the

details of our next pop-up campaign, back here in our hometown of Zagreb, where we began.

Georg glances at me. "Shall we head to your next meeting, Ms. Juric?"

I nod, covering the mouthpiece. "Yes, Georg, thank you. Just keep an eye out. Probably someone connected to Tata thinking they can use me to get to him."

Georg snorts. "You think they'd know better by now. Your father's methods of dealing with such antics are well known at this point, I should think."

"You would think, yet every year, there's at least one attempt. After Tata took care of the last one so publicly, I had imagined I'd get at least a few months off before the next one."

"Shall I call him, ma'am?"

I shake my head. "Not yet. Perhaps it was simply an opportunistic attempt."

"Perhaps, ma'am."

Georg exits the garage and sets us on a course back across town to my next meeting—a location-scouting endeavor with my advance team.

There's no sign of the tail, so I let myself put it out of my mind, trusting Georg to keep watch as I go over the specs and details of the location we're touring today.

It's an old church in Low Town that's been remodeled into different businesses multiple times over the years; the latest endeavor fell apart when Covid hit, and now it's been sitting empty. It's at the heart of an up-and-coming neighborhood, so a pop-up there now is ideal. We just have to hope it's in good enough shape that we can flip it without excessive overhead—that's part of my business model: we rent in the more expensive areas, but when we do a cluster in an area with lower real estate values, we buy a property, flip it, host the pop-up, and then lease it out, so we make money on the actual pop-up and then again on the property lease; it was tough to get that aspect off the ground, requiring me to put a ton of my capital back into purchasing real estate, which was a huge gamble. Tata advised against it, but it's paid off, as I now own several million euros worth of real estate throughout Europe.

Georg pulls the BMW to a stop in front of the prospective location. It's quiet, a mostly residential area with narrow, winding streets. The church is from the nineteenth century, red brick with twin spires at the front and lovely stained-glass windows that have somehow survived the last hundred-and-some years. There's a decent amount of parking in the area, and a vacant lot next to the church has been fenced off with a chain link, a weather-faded sign advertising that it's been for sale for a very long time.

Ana and Katya, my location-scouting team, are already here, walking around the exterior of the church with their tablets and headsets, styluses scribbling notes, and taking photos.

Georg, also my bodyguard, follows me at a precise distance, gaze restlessly roving the area.

Ana and Katya spot my approach and bustle toward me. "So, ladies. What do we think?" I ask, reaching for Ana's tablet. I scan her notes and photos, and then head for the entrance—the agent gave me the code for the lockbox, which I open and let us inside.

"It's prime, Tati," Ana says, taking her table back. "Our research indicates this neighborhood will see a boom over the next few years—the median age of the residents has gone down significantly over the last five years, and early investors are already seeing growth. I think we should snap it up while we can—the agent has offers in, but they're all low-ball. We can come in high and still turn a profit."

"Do you have any initial thoughts on what we'll do with the space?" I ask.

It's open, with exposed brick walls and newly re-done floors. The roof was redone in the latest remodel in 2019, along with the plumbing and electrical. It has a ton of natural light, and several back rooms as well as a size-able basement.

Katya answers my questions. "We were thinking a restaurant. There aren't many in this immediate area. We've been in preliminary talks with a potential restaurateur who might be interested in the space after we're done.

"It seems like it's in pretty good shape," I say, scan-ning the ceiling for water spots, checking the walls and flooring, testing light switches, and peeking into the back rooms and basement.

"We'll have Jakov do a thorough inspection before we put in an offer, but it looks great to us," Ana says.

"Excellent," I say. "Let's move on it. Pending a green light from Jakov, put in an offer ten percent over the high-est current bid, and see if you can nail down the restaura-teur. I'd like to have a lease in place the moment the pop-up is over."

We all exit together and I lock the key back in the lockbox. Georg is in the corner of my eye by the BMW, so I address him without looking.

"Well, we're ahead of schedule, Georg, so perhaps we'll have time to grab some lunch before my next meet-ing. Fancy anything in particular?"

I finish locking the box and give it a tug, and then spin the tumblers. Georg doesn't answer.

Ana and Katya are conspicuously silent—usually, they chatter my ear off in unison every moment I'm within ten feet of them.

"Georg? Did you hear—"

Ana's face is pale and shocked, her lips trembling. Katya looks as if she's about to puke.

"Girls? What's—?"

Georg is slumped over the hood of my car, blood sprayed across the white hood and streaming down, dripping onto the concrete.

There's no one in sight, however—no cars. No threatening male figures waiting to snatch me.

I step in front of Katya and Ana, pushing them together behind me. I reach into my purse and withdraw the little Sig Sauer Tata gave me for my last birthday and forced me to practice with at the range until he felt I was proficient.

I edge the three of us into the corner of the covered entry of the church and instruct the AI voice assistant of my cell phone to call my father. He answers on the first ring.

"Tati, darling. How are you?"

"Georg is dead, Tata."

"What? *How*?"

"I'm in Low Town scouting a location. I went in to look and when I came out he was dead. Someone shot him. I didn't hear anything. There was a car following us earlier, but Georg lost them."

"Stay where you are. I have someone in Low Town

right now. Send me a pin." He waits until he receives the pin I send him. "Stay on the line, darling. I'll be right back."

I keep the phone to my ear with my left hand and clutch the pistol with my right, finger outside the trigger guard as I was taught.

A few moments later, he comes back on the line. "Someone is on the way," he says. "He'll be there in a minute or two. Do you see anyone?"

"No. No one. Nothing. I didn't hear anything, Tata."

A low growl. "The bastards won't give up, will they?" He sighs. "Stay right where you are. My man is driving a black Range Rover. You know him—it's Filip."

My heart is pounding—I'm too scared to be upset, yet, but later I'll mourn. Georg has been my driver and bodyguard since I was in primary school.

A squeal of tires announces Filip's arrival—a black Range Rover screeches to a halt in the road; the driver's door flies open and Filip jogs toward us.

Filip is one of my favorites of Tata's men. He's young, handsome, and nice, plus he's well-groomed and doesn't smoke. He rounds the hood of the Rover and trots up the steps, reaching for my arm.

"I've got you, Ms. Juric. Come with me, please."

I tug my arm away. "Ana and Katya first, Filip."

"My orders are—"

"I don't give a damn!" I snap. "They're my employees and I will not leave without them."

Filip sighs. "Very well." He gestures toward the car. "Ladies—please."

Huddling together, my girls shuffle down the steps, trying to hide their eyes from the gruesome sight of Georg's body and the gallons of blood.

Filip glances back at me, an odd, sad look in his eyes. "I'm sorry, Ms. Juric."

"Sorry?"

I don't get anything else out—before I can utter another word, Filip draws his pistol from the shoulder holster and fires two shots—*BANG-BANG!* Ana and Katya topple forward, red holes blasted through the front of their skulls.

Shocked, I forget my own pistol for a second too long. Filip snatches it from my hand and then puts the hot round barrel of his against my temple. "Let's go, Tatiana. Now."

———◆———

Tears streaming down my face, I look at him, unmoving. "Filip? What…? I—I don't understand."

"Your father isn't the highest bidder anymore." Filip grabs my arm and shoves me down the steps. My three-inch heel catches on the top step and I go tumbling down, scraping my elbows and palms bloody. I lose both shoes in the process, as well as my purse. Filip grabs my phone and flings it into the vacant lot, and then hauls me to my feet, shoving me toward his car.

He yanks open the rear door. "Get in."

I climb in, looking back at Ana and Katya, face down on the sidewalk, their blood mingling with Georg's.

Filip's dark eyes find mine in the rearview mirror. "No funny shit, Tatiana. The money is for you alive, but it doesn't say anything about hurt. Get me, Princess?"

I nod, fighting to stuff my emotions down so I can find a way out of this. I'm barefoot, without my phone and gun, and now I have no clue who to trust. I thought Filip was loyal. Clearly, so did my father.

We take a long, circuitous route out of the city to the airport, where a guard opens a gate and lets us through to a restricted section, where the private jets are hangared. We pull into one of the smaller hangars, where the hulking, shadowy shapes of small jets and private prop planes stand in a row. The Rover's headlights flic on automatically in the gloom, illuminating a small folding table at which is a man wearing glasses tapping at a laptop. Beside the table, a man is handcuffed to a chair; his head is hanging, so I can't make out his face, but his hair is long and black, and I see a hint of a long beard.

"What's going on, Filip?" I ask. "Who are they?"

Filip twists in the seat. "Shut up. No questions, no talking."

"This isn't worth it, Filip. You know what Tata does to people who mess with me."

His face contorts into a rage-filled rictus. "Oh yes, I know. His precious princess. Well, *Tati*," he sneers my father's nickname for me, "what my new benefactor is paying me *does* make it worth it."

"Filip, please. This won't end well."

He grins, an ugly sneer. How did I miss the evil in him all this time? "Shut *up*, Tatiana. Remember what I said. The money is for you, alive. Which means I can do whatever I want to you as long as you're still breathing when I turn you over."

I clench my jaw shut—I believe him. When he sees that I'm shutting up, he nods and exits the SUV. Rounding the hood, he opens my door and yanks me out, shoving me toward the table.

"Wait here. Don't fucking move, you snobby bitch."

Filip wiggles his gun at me. "I'll shoot you in the knee if you so much as twitch wrong. Get me?"

I nod once.

He vanishes between the airplanes and returns with another folding chair, which he jerks open and sets down next to the bound man.

"Sit."

I sit, and Filip handcuffs my hands and feet to the legs of the chair; with a horrible grin, he rips open my blouse, baring my braless chest.

His grin widens into a greedy leer. "Better than I imagined, princess."

I lift my chin and glare at him. "Get a good look, Filip. Better enjoy it while you can."

"Thinking your father is coming to rescue you, eh?" He smirks. "Well, we have plans for that."

He tosses the gun onto the folding table; the man at the laptop stops typing, withdraws a pair of rubber gloves from his pocket and a disinfectant wipe from a package on the table, and thoroughly wipes down the weapon. When it's clean, he stands up and crouches in front of the man handcuffed to the chair beside me, who seems to be either unconscious or drugged, as he doesn't resist when Filip's companion presses the pistol into his hand, carefully ensuring his prints are all over the handle. He even ejects the magazine and makes sure his prints are on the slide and hammer as well.

That done, he goes back to his laptop and resumes typing.

A few minutes later, he looks up at Filip. "The package is ready to upload."

"Show me."

The be-spectacled man turns the laptop so Filip can see it and taps the spacebar to play the video. It shows a person, who I assume is the man beside me, shooting Georg, Ana, and Katya, and then shoving me into the Range Rover. If I hadn't experienced the incident myself, I would believe it's real—it's that good of a deepfake.

The man in the video is Roma, unless I'm mistaken. He's broad-shouldered, heavily muscled, and devastatingly beautiful.

Filip nods. "It's perfect, Ivan. Good work. Send it to Stjepan."

A moment later. "Done."

Filip grins at me. "No going back now, princess. Your father dearest thinks *he*," here Filip points at the man beside me, "has kidnapped you." Just then, his phone rings, and he answers it, pretending to be out of breath and upset. "I…I lost her, sir. He came out of nowhere, just bam-bam-bam. I don't know where he got a gun, sir. One second, he was under control, the next, he was gone. You sent me to get Tatiana, and…" he fakes a choked-up pause. "I'm sorry, sir. I let you down—" he listens. "Yes, sir, I understand. I'll find her. No, you don't need to worry, sir. Everyone—yes, sir. We're on it, sir."

He listens a bit longer and then hangs up, grinning at me. "There. That's bought us some time. Now we wait."

He crouches in front of me. "I'm really not supposed to—the new boss wants you for himself. But I figure I can have a little fun with you first. He won't know the difference, will he, whore?"

He fondles my breast with a rough hand and then viciously pinches my nipple, causing me to cry out; my cry of pain only makes him grin more.

"Filip!" Ivan barks. "Enough. Mercado was very clear—he wants her alive. No bullshit. You heard him."

"He won't know, Ivan. She's a loose little slut. Fucks anything that moves, as long he has enough money." He sneers at me, rage-filled. "Not so much as a glance my way, though. I'm just her precious Tata's henchman. She would never dare sully herself with the likes of me."

Oh, the irony. I would have. I liked him. I thought he was cute and kind. It was my father who categorically refused to let me date his men. That was the one no-no he never wavered on.

I don't bother saying anything though—I know well enough that it won't make a difference, now.

Fighting to remain calm, I breathe in slowly and evenly through my nose and exhale the same way through my mouth, ignoring my fear, panic, and humiliation.

Ivan leaves the table to confront Filip. "It's not worth it. We get millions when this is over, Filip. *Millions*. You can have anyone you want, then. Just not her. I know how you feel about her, brother, but she's not worth it. If you soil his prize, Mercado will cut you into tiny little pieces and feed you to his pet fish. So, keep your dick in your pants and your hands off of her, finish the op, get paid, and we can go hunt down some prime pussy. Okay? I know a guy, Filip." Ivan's voice drops to a murmur. "He works for the Syndicate—he can get us into a Syndicate brothel. That shit is *exclusive*, Filip. Like, only the highest rollers get in there. I'm talking the hottest bitches on the planet will be gagging on your cock in…" he looks at his watch. "Forty-eight hours. *If* you play your cards right."

Filip looks at me over his shoulder. "She needs to be taught a lesson."

"She will. Just not by you. You know what they say about Mercado, right? The shit he likes? I promise you, she'll get what's coming to her."

My blood runs cold at the implications.

Filip growls in frustration. "Fuck. No one will know, Ivan."

Ivan shoves Filip toward the exit. "*He* will. You *know* he will. And I know how you like to play, Filip. I've seen what's left of them when you're done."

Filip laughs—a dry, horrible little chuckle. "I wouldn't do that to her. I just want a little taste."

Ivan pulls a baggie of white powder from his back pocket. "I've got something else you can taste. Pure Colombian coke. We each get a whole fucking key of this shit if we pull this off, Filip."

They go outside, huddling together just outside the hangar. Ivan dips into the bag and snorts a hit, tips his head back, and then whoops loudly, handing the bag to Filip.

"Psst." A soft hiss gets my attention, and my head whips around; the man must've been playing possum. "Get ready."

I ever so gently rattle one handcuff. "For what? Unless you have a key?"

His eyes glint in the gloom, and his teeth flash white. "I do not need a key."

I hear rattling, a soft breath as he does something that makes him strain, and then I hear a crack of a joint dislocating. Seconds later, he's crouching behind me.

His voice is hot against my ear. "Do you have any bobby pins in your hair?"

"Yes, quite a few," I whisper.

My hair, black and quite long, is done up in an elaborate updo, courtesy of my glam squad.

I realize belatedly that the man spoke to me in English, whereas I'd been speaking Croatian with Filip.

"Do you know what they were saying?" I hiss as the man runs his fingers over my hair, finding a bobby pin and withdrawing it.

"Yes," he answers.

"Who is this Mercado?"

"A very, very, *very* bad man. I'll explain later. For now, we must go." His English is excellent if accented—Croatian is not his first language, nor is English.

My English is good but not as good as his, so I revert to Croatian—I'm too freaked out and confused to have the brain space to translate my thoughts on the fly right now.

"Can you understand me?"

He snorts. "I speak a dozen languages fluently, Tatiana Juric," he says in flawless if accented Croatian.

"How do we get out of here?" I ask. "There's only one exit."

"Think carefully. Did he leave the keys in the car or did he remove them?"

I close my eyes and focus. "I don't know. I didn't see him take them, but they could be in his pocket. It's a key fob. I don't know."

"Can't risk it, then."

This whole time, he's been quickly and quietly using the bobby pin to unlock my handcuffs. When the last one is unlocked, he grabs my wrist and tugs me off the chair and into the shadows deeper in the hangar. Since he seems to know what he's doing, and since he's a victim of this whole convoluted scheme as much as I am, I opt to go with him.

It's my best shot at the moment. He shoves me ahead of him, and we duck underneath a jet; he puts me behind the front wheel assembly.

"Wait here. If you are squeamish, do not watch."

"I'm not."

"Suit yourself."

I grab his wrist. "Wait—-who *are* you?"

He drops to a knee in front of me, and I can just barely make out his dark eyes and white teeth in the dim light of the hangar—it's past sunset now, the light of day fading.

"My name is Lash, Tatiana Juric."

"You know me?"

"I knew you when you were a gangly, beautiful, colt-ish teenage girl. I worked for your father."

"I don't recognize you."

He shrugs. "You wouldn't. You never knew I existed."

"But you know me."

"Yes, I do. Only from afar, but I know you."

"What's happening, Lash?"

"A very complicated bit of business, Lovely One." Somehow, he makes the endearment sound like a nick-name. "A double cross, among other things."

"My father is going to think you kidnapped me." I keep hold of his wrist—which is thick and dense with muscle.

"I know. I will keep you safe and return you to him. You have my solemn vow." He twists his hand so now he has my hand in his and kisses the back of my palm. "You will be safe as long as you are with me." "My father will be very angry. And so will this Mercado person." My heart pounds—not from fear, now, but something else. Something to do with this man, his touch, his kiss on my hand. "They'll kill you."

He kisses my hand again, making my skin tingle and tighten; his grin is a flash of white in the darkness. "They will try, and they will fail." He lets go of my hand, creeping backward into the shadows, melting out of sight. "Remain here, and remain silent."

"Okay."

"Tatiana?"

I frown. "Yes?"

Something soft and warm lands on my face and shoulder, smelling of male sweat and cologne. "To cover yourself. Filip will die first for his sins against you, and he will die screaming."

I shrug out of my blazer and then the ruined blouse, and shrug into the shirt. It's huge on me, hanging past my hips, the sleeves around my forearms, even though I get the impression that this Lash isn't much taller than me.

"Thank you," I whisper.

There's no answer.

I peer into the gloom; Filip and Ivan are now smoking cigarettes and passing a flask back and forth.

A patch of shadows shifts.

I can't make out what happens, but Filip's body contorts backward, and he screams as he's hauled into the shadows, kicking. Ivan pulls his gun and fires, the noise deafening and the muzzle flash blinding, but he curses floridly in Croatian.

A second later, there is another long, gurgling scream from Filip, one that trails off slowly.

"Filip?" Ivan calls, his voice shaky.

Silence.

I can just make out Ivan, turning in circles, gun extended, shifting this way and that.

A shadow passes between Ivan and the light from beyond the hangar.

I hear the crack of a bone snapping, and Ivan screams.

"Delete the video," Lash growls.

"I—I can't. I mean, I can delete it, but it won't stop Stjepan from seeing it. He already has. It's too late."

"Then it's too late for you." *BANG!*

Thud.

"You can come out," Lash says in a normal pitch.

I emerge from beneath the airplane and join Lash. Ivan is at his feet, staring sightlessly at the ceiling, a pool of blood spreading beneath his skull. "Now what?"

A phone chimes and Lash bends to retrieve the device from Ivan's pocket; he holds the phone over Ivan's face, and it unlocks.

"Dammit," Lash hisses. "Damn them to hell."

"What?"

"Your father has my friends. This is even more complicated than I thought. Mercado is a very crafty and duplicitous man." Lash pockets the phone. "Come. We must leave this place before their co-conspirators discover their deaths. We will make plans on the way."

He stops to rifle through Filip's pockets, coming up with the key fob for the Range Rover. I climb into the front passenger seat as Lash takes the wheel. The dome lights illuminate him.

He's even more absurdly, devilishly gorgeous in person than in the AI deepfake. His beard is long and shiny and braided to a point at his chest, with elegant, curving mustaches. His hair is bound back in a low ponytail, and his eyes are deep and dark and wise and kind. At least, they're kind as he regards me.

And my god, his body.

Massive, bulging, rounded shoulders, arms nearly the size of my thighs, a heavy, hard chest, and flat, rippling abs. He's scarred all over, as well, speaking of a life of violence.

For a moment, we merely stare at each other.

"You have truly blossomed into a beautiful woman, Tatiana. Given a thousand years, I could not a find the words in any of the languages I know to adequately capture your beauty," he says in English and then switches to Croatian. "You can trust me, Lovely One. I will not rest until you are safe once more."

He makes my pulse race. "I...I..." And, apparently, leaves me tongue-tied. "I trust you, Lash. Perhaps I shouldn't, but I do."

He takes my hand and kisses the back of it, his glittering black eyes never leaving mine. "Your faith in me is a priceless gift, Lovely One." Croatian again. Then back to English. " We must go. Time is short, especially for my friends."

He whips the SUV in a tight circle and nails the accelerator to the floor, and we're off into the purple light of a dusky Zagreb sunset.

And for some reason, I am not afraid, despite the dangerous, deadly game we're caught up in.

Lash will protect me.

ALSO BY

JASINDA WILDER

Visit me at my website: **www.jasindawilder.com**
Email me: **jasindawilder@gmail.com**

If you enjoyed this book, you can help others enjoy it as well by recommending it to friends and family, or by mentioning it in reading and discussion groups and online forums. You can also review it on the site from which you purchased it. But, whether you recommend it to anyone else or not, thank you *so much* for taking the time to read my book! Your support means the world to me!

My other titles:

Forbidden Fruit

Wild Ride: Biker Billionaire

Delilah's Diary

Big Girls Do It:

Big Girls Do It
Married
On Christmas
Pregnant
Rock Stars Do It
Big Love Abroad

The Falling Series:
Falling Into You
Falling Into Us
Falling Under
Falling Away
Falling for Colton
The Ever Trilogy:
Forever & Always
After Forever
Saving Forever

From the world of *Wounded*:
Wounded
Captured

From the world of *Stripped*:
Stripped
Trashed

From the world of *Alpha*:
Alpha
Beta
Omega
Harris: Alpha One Security Book 1
Thresh: Alpha One Security Book 2
Duke: Alpha One Security Book 3
Puck: Alpha One Security Book 4
Lear: Alpha One Security Book 5
Anselm: Alpha One Security Book 6
Sigma
Gamma

The Houri Legends:
Jack and Djinn
Djinn and Tonic

The Madame X Series:
Madame X
Exposed
Exiled

The Black Room (With Jade London)

The One Series
The Long Way Home
Where the Heart Is
There's No Place Like Home

Badd Brothers:
*Badd Motherf*cker*
Badd Ass
Badd to the Bone
Good Girl Gone Badd
Badd Luck
Badd Mojo
Big Badd Wolf
Badd Boy
Badd Kitty
Badd Business
Badd Medicine
Badd Daddy

Goode Girls:

For a Goode Time Call…

Not So Goode

Goode To Be Bad

A Real Goode Time

Goode Vibrations

Dad Bod Contracting:

Hammered

Drilled

Nailed

Screwed

Fifty States of Love:

Pregnant in Pennsylvania

Cowboy in Colorado

Married in Michigan

Christmas in Connecticut

Billionaire Baby Club:

Lizzy Goes Brains Over Braun

Autumn Rolls a Seven

Laurel's Bright Idea

Club Sin:

Rev

Kane

Chance

Silas

Saxon

Blood Heir

Blood Heir
Blood Bonds
Blood Reign
Blood Bonds

Standalone titles:

Yours
The Cabin
The Parent Trap
Wish Upon A Star
Big Hose

Non-Fiction titles:

You Can Do It
You Can Do It: Strength
You Can Do It: Fasting

Jack Wilder Titles:

The Missionary

JJ Wilder Titles:

Ark

To be informed of new releases, special offers, and other Jasinda news, sign up for Jasinda's email newsletter.